THE PATRIOT LIST

Bullseye smiled and tapped his finger on the desk by the guard's computer keyboard. "Eleventh floor. Pretty please."

"I'm not... I'm not afraid of you." The guard's hand closed around something in her desk drawer. "This is America."

"This is Osborn's America, sweet cakes. The rest of us are just living in it."

"*Osborn gives me pills to stop me wanting to eat people,*" Venom added. "*They work sometimes.*"

The guard pulled her hand from the drawer, clutching an X-26 military issue TASER.

Venom's distended jaws snapped over the woman's shoulders. There was a crunch of Kevlar, a gristly choking sound as Venom tried to swallow the guard while dangling upside down above her desk.

"Gross," said Bullseye, and slurped the dead woman's shake.

Banana. His favorite.

It was great being good.

ALSO AVAILABLE

MARVEL CRISIS PROTOCOL
Target: Kree by Stuart Moore

MARVEL HEROINES
Domino: Strays by Tristan Palmgren
Rogue: Untouched by Alisa Kwitney
Elsa Bloodstone: Bequest by Cath Lauria
Outlaw: Relentless by Tristan Palmgren

LEGENDS OF ASGARD
The Head of Mimir by Richard Lee Byers
The Sword of Surtur by C L Werner
The Serpent and the Dead by Anna Stephens

MARVEL UNTOLD
The Harrowing of Doom by David Annandale

XAVIER'S INSTITUTE
Liberty & Justice for All by Carrie Harris
First Team by Robbie MacNiven
Triptych by Jaleigh Johnson

MARVEL UNTOLD

THE DARK AVENGERS IN:

THE PATRIOT LIST

DAVID GUYMER

FOR MARVEL PUBLISHING

VP Production & Special Projects: Jeff Youngquist
Associate Editor, Special Projects: Caitlin O'Connell
Manager, Licensed Publishing: Jeremy West
VP, Licensed Publishing: Sven Larsen
SVP Print, Sales & Marketing: David Gabriel
Editor in Chief: C B Cebulski

Special Thanks to Tom Brevoort

First published by Aconyte Books in 2021
ISBN 978 1 83908 064 7
Ebook ISBN 978 1 83908 065 4

Cover art by Fabio Listrani

Distributed in North America by Simon & Schuster Inc, New York, USA
Printed in the United States of America
9 8 7 6 5 4 3 2 1

ACONYTE BOOKS

An imprint of Asmodee Entertainment Ltd

Mercury House, Shipstones Business Centre

North Gate, Nottingham NG7 7FN, UK

aconytebooks.com // twitter.com/aconytebooks

The world has been saved from alien invasion. The failed planetary defense organization, S.H.I.E.L.D. has been disbanded. Its leaders are disgraced and in hiding. The citizens of Earth have a new hero.

His name is Norman Osborn.

And he approves these Avengers.

PROLOGUE

Several dozen large TV screens bathed Norman Osborn's suite of subterranean offices in an inconstant glow. It was the nearest that Norman had come to bathing in ninety-six hours. He was in the same white collared shirt and dark green tie that he had been wearing on his flight into Andrews Air Force Base on Friday afternoon.

It was now Monday. The middle of the night.

Sleep was for less material men.

Dark rings of sweat conspired to occupy large swathes of his shirt, spreading outwards from several points of incursion at once. His tie had been pulled out around the neck and now lay over his chest as though something had crawled onto his shoulder and died. His media team were forever advising him to avoid being photographed wearing anything green. "Negative associations in the public subconscious," they said, but damned if you could get in front of the Joint Chiefs without a tie, and it was the only one his staff had been able to find aboard the Quinjet without notice.

Victoria had been fuming. "Green ties don't find their way into the H.A.M.M.E.R. director's wardrobe on their own." She had threatened to fire the entire staff. But Norman had bigger worries than what color he was seen wearing on page nine of the *Washington Post,* or the jobs of a few aides.

He had actual worries.

Real worries.

The Secretary of Defense had summoned him to the Pentagon to discuss the unrest that was currently spreading across the Middle East from East Africa. Not that any of the men and women around that table had given a damn about what was happening halfway around the world, beyond how it made them look at home.

It was almost enough to make a person laugh.

On the multiplexed screens that made up one wall of his office, the regional networks played out soundless images of protest and riots. Baghdad. Cairo. Dar es Salaam. Repeating over and over on an endless loop of rolling news. On one screen, the picture carrying the digital stamp of Kenya NMG alongside the scrolling Swahili banner text, showed masked men waving placards as they stormed a H.A.M.M.E.R. facility in Kisumu. Another, from Al Jazeera, had civilians fleeing through the streets of Sana'a, the Yemeni capital. Norman scribbled an urgent memo to himself to find out who commanded Sana'a station and see that they got a huge pay rise and a promotion.

When he was finished, he looked down at the deranged handwriting.

He could barely read it.

Tearing the top sheet from the memo pad, he scrunched it up and threw it away. In a day or two, perhaps. After the situation in the world had calmed down. There was no sense in making things worse.

As far as Norman had been briefed, the locals in these countries didn't seem to appreciate the S.H.I.E.L.D. outposts, situated in their territories since the Second World War, being unilaterally taken over by H.A.M.M.E.R. Nor did their governments approve, it seemed, of the manner in which a number of senior agents, liaison staff, and Nick Fury's protégés, had been replaced, extradited to the US, or mysteriously disappeared over international waters. Nor were they hugely enamored of the fact that Norman Osborn himself was an appointment of the president of the United States.

Where did they think Fury had come from exactly?

The sky?

Seething under the cold gray light of the screens, he fed the bitterness he felt at the world's ingratitude, goaded the anger. Did they have the slightest idea what he did for them, the threats he dealt with every day so that their children could sleep safely at night? Or did they know, but think that someone with a different-colored passport could do it better?

At the same time, half an eye on the news broadcasts, he studied the summary pages of the quarterly financial report, apprised himself of the latest updates from the R&D division, familiarized himself with the field reports from Ares' new spec-ops unit, skimmed the covert surveillance he had placed on his various children around the world, and drafted a press release on the "Restive Minority" in the Middle East to be ready for the Monday morning news. He popped a pill bottle without reading the label and took two with a glass of water.

Norman rarely needed more than a few hours' sleep a night. His mind had always been able to run in several directions at once. He didn't see why nobody else's could. It demonstrated a tragic inadequacy of will on their part.

Was it any wonder then, that lesser people should find the time to wash and eat and clothe themselves and–

He turned sharply in his chair.

Victoria Hand finished clearing her throat.

H.A.M.M.E.R.'s deputy director was a young woman with the stern, icy features common to such highly driven individuals. Her black hair was drawn tightly back into a long ponytail, a few red-dyed strands of loose fringe looping over the smart lenses of her glasses. She was wearing a lavender skirt suit with a Glock 18 holstered inside the jacket. She looked sharp at any time of day. Or night.

"What is it, Ms Hand?" he asked, in tight control of his demeanor in spite of his impulse to snap. "As you can probably see, I am the living definition of *very busy*."

"Sir, you've been working non-stop on this all weekend. You need to learn to delegate."

"I don't trust anyone else to do what needs to be done, or to do it right. I won't fail the way Stark and Fury failed. I won't give them that satisfaction." He gestured, idly, as though the vast wall of screens simply happened to be on in the background. "Are they ungrateful, do you think, Ms Hand? Or suffering from some kind of collective paramnesia? I remember the pictures from Tehran and Nairobi after my appointment. They were as happy to be saved from the Skrull invasion of Earth as any American citizen."

"What I think, sir, is that you need to rest. The world needs you. Your best you. It doesn't need…" she looked down at him, her business-like outer shell softened by her obvious concern for his wellbeing, "…this."

Norman pulled his eyes from the screen. He looked at her for a moment, his anger at the world subsiding. "You came for something, Ms Hand. What is it?"

Victoria sighed, seemingly reluctant now, having come this far, and handed him a piece of paper.

"A reporter called. For you. Asking for a comment on this."

Norman took it.

He read what was on it.

"Where did she get this?" he hissed, the mask he wore every day slipping just briefly, the Goblin of which he was still the master taking the moment of laxity to show its face through his.

"Where?" Norman repeated.

"She didn't say."

"Did you even ask?"

"She didn't talk to me," said Victoria, firmly. Deputy Hand was one of the few people in this building, in the country, that refused to be bullied by Norman Osborn. It was why Norman had hired her in the first place. "She telephoned H.A.M.M.E.R.'s media department."

"All right," said Norman, composing himself. "Fire them all."

"Sir?"

"The entire department. And gag them. Literally. Or legally. I don't care which. Is any of this in the public domain yet?"

"Not yet, sir. I told them that someone would get back to her with a comment."

"Good." Norman crumpled the memo in his fist. "Assemble the Avengers."

"Sir, do you really think that–"

"You wanted me to delegate, Ms Hand, so I am delegating. Send in the Avengers." Smoothing the dark green tie over his crumpled shirt, he sat back in his chair and returned his captive attention to the wall of screens, the manifest ingratitude of about four billion people for Norman Virgil Osborn on a twenty-four-hour loop. "They need to be reminded who the heroes are."

PART ONE

NEW YORK

CHAPTER ONE
Great Being Good

The *New York Bulletin* occupied the eleventh floor of a building on East 53rd.

Bullseye didn't read newspapers. Not since he'd discovered YouTube. But the *Bulletin* was one of those that even a native New Yorker would be amazed to learn still existed. Instead of the grisly crime sprees and costumed vigilantes that filled the breathless reportage of the *Bugle*, the *Bulletin* went in for the kind of serious local journalism that the internet was supposed to have killed off already and that nobody had ever read anyway. The *Daily Bugle*, meanwhile, had a glossy forty-six story skyscraper in Midtown Manhattan, while the *Bulletin* was here, sharing premises with a low-rent law firm, a couple of ESU spin-outs, and a lot of empty office space belonging to a Symkarian tax exile.

The *Bugle* probably didn't get midnight calls from Avengers with seriously ticked off bosses either.

Go figure.

The reception desk was in the ground floor lobby, black and chrome and big enough to stop a bus. During work hours there would have been a receptionist, pretty probably, with a light smile and breezy telephone manner. Bullseye would have preferred to be doing this during work hours, and not just for the probably pretty receptionist. Witnesses were inevitable, even at night, and a daytime visit was easier to explain.

And, not least, because he'd barely had a night off in weeks.

If he'd known that being an Avenger would be so much like *work*, he'd have told Osborn where he could stuff it, and seen out his tour with the Thunderbolts in peace.

The woman behind the desk looked up as he pushed his way through the doors and shrugged off the cold.

She was a little under average height, somewhere in her fifties, with gray hair in a tight bob and faded tattoos across her knuckles. She was wearing a black ballistic vest with the corporate logo of a private security firm emblazoned across the breast panel. There was something about her, in the way she sat, that put Bullseye instantly on alert. She was lounging back in a swivel chair, reading from a battered thriller novel in a plastic library sleeve, a single desk lamp and a couple of black and white security monitors the only sources of light. A large milkshake from the Turkish place across the street sat on the desk in a puffy Styrofoam cup.

What Bullseye saw was a skin-deep veneer of relaxation over a wire-taut core of aggressive watchfulness.

It said ex-military, and not especially happy about the *ex* part either.

Her eyes widened a little as Bullseye approached. She set down the book. "Hey, you're Hawkeye. I saw you on TV. That was some good work you guys did out in San Francisco."

Bullseye smirked at her.

Spending a weekend shooting at peaceful protestors and putting down west coast mutant kids had done it for him, too.

And who could have imagined it would be so popular with Joe Public as well? Osborn had spent a whole week almost happy. Even after having his backside handed to him by the X-Men on live TV. Bullseye had turned the thirty-second clip of him getting pasted by Cyclops into the screensaver on the giant display in the Avengers Tower briefing room.

The guard gestured enthusiastically to one of the visitor chairs. "What can I do for you, buddy?"

Bullseye remained standing. "I need you to let me through to the eleventh floor."

"The *Bulletin* offices?"

"One of their reporters has been a naughty girl. It seems she's gotten hold of something she shouldn't have."

The guard sucked in through her teeth and shook her head. "No one there right now."

"Yeah, that's probably best."

"I'm sorry." The woman spread her hands. "I can't let you up without the nod from my boss." She opened up a drawer and pulled out a pad of post-it notes. She started rooting around for a pen. "I can give you her cell."

Bullseye glanced up. He marked the CCTV cameras, two of them in the rear corners, their angles covering the entrance and intersecting at the security desk, and idly fantasized about stabbing the night guard through the eye with a milkshake straw or slicing her carotid artery with a bookmark. "Look. Your boss works for my boss. Everyone in this country with a gun and a badge is pretty much working for my boss. So just open the damned elevator."

"I don't wear a badge. And maybe your boss should have got himself a warrant."

Bullseye leant across the desk. His body armor, a flexible

composite of carbon steel and fiberglass painted in a deep shade of purple, creaked menacingly. "I'm an Avenger, you know."

"I know. I've seen you on TV."

She reached back into the desk drawer.

For a weapon, probably.

Bullseye *hoped* it was a weapon.

"Don't make me ask this guy to cut in." His gaze flicked upwards.

The woman followed his eyes.

"Hi."

Spider-Man, or the thing that a combination of powerful drugs and exceptional PR had somehow tricked a gullible planet into believing was Spider-Man, dangled from the lobby's high ceiling by a thread of glistening black slime. He looked more-or-less humanoid, an athletic physique wrapped in a black latex suit, but his upper body was dribbling like candlewax, running towards a head that was already looking too large and was too full of teeth by half. The smell, though, was something else altogether, and the thing that the TV cameras just couldn't catch. He stank like something that had been cut open and left to die in a sewer.

And Bullseye should know.

"He hates the mainstream media," said Bullseye.

"I hate them a lot."

"And he hates newspaper people most of all."

"I want to eat them."

Bullseye smiled indulgently and tapped his finger on the desk by the woman's computer keyboard. "Eleventh floor. Pretty please."

"I'm not… I'm not afraid of you." Her gaze was fixed upwards. Venom was annoying as hell, but he had a way of getting a person's attention. Her hand closed around something in her desk drawer. Bullseye saw the flex in her bicep and the stiffening of the tendons in her arms. Definitely ex-military. But Bullseye doubted she'd seen anything close to what she was asking for right now. "This is America."

"This is Osborn's America, sweet cakes. The rest of us are just living in it."

"*Osborn gives me pills to stop me wanting to eat people,*" Venom added. His jaw hung open, too wide, his neck stretching as though his head was weighted and his spine was made of warm plastic. Disgusting alien goo dribbled onto the expensive tiles and over the surface of the black and chrome desk. "*They work sometimes.*"

The guard pulled her hand from the drawer, clutching an X-26 military issue TASER.

Venom's distended jaws snapped over the woman's shoulders.

Her feet kicked as she was lifted off her chair and shaken. Electricity buzzed around Venom's many rows of teeth with a *tick-tick-tick* sound as the guard's TASER discharged inside his mouth. Black smoke billowed from Venom's nostrils as though he was some kind of long-necked Chinese dragon. There was a crunch of Kevlar, a gristly choking sound as Venom tried to swallow the woman while dangling upside down above her desk.

"Gross," said Bullseye, and slurped the dead woman's shake.

Banana. His favorite.

It was great being good.

CHAPTER TWO
Violent and Warlike

It was half past one o'clock in the morning, March, and Irkan's Kitchen on the corner of 53rd and 1st was full.

Ares, God of War, admired the oily pita that had been delivered to his side-counter table by a cowering peon in an apron. It filled a brawny fist.

He loved America.

Tearing into the wrap released spiced meat to dribble down his coarsely stubbled chin and to drip, like the blood of cowards, onto the plate from whence it came. Chewing stolidly, determined as any soldier, he stared through the giant, partially opaque '*K*' of *Irkan's* and the general condensation that covered his window.

Four lanes of traffic grumbled from right to left, headlights beaming into the bumper of the vehicle ahead. Pedestrians in heavy winter coats flocked the sidewalks. Right outside his window a vehicle of the local law enforcement had parked up on the curb. Two officers, a male and a female, sat inside eating the same bad Turkish food as Ares, the windshield steamed up in the cold. A pair of bikers loitered over the handlebars of their massive, ground-hogging machines and conversed in a language that Ares could have followed had he cared to but could not have named.

New York may not have been the capital of this land, but it was the truest inheritor to Athens and Rome. All roads led there, and drew all peoples to it.

The city that never slept.

That was what its people called it.

He approved of the chest-beating exceptionalism in those words. He admired it. The city that never sleeps. *The* city. It reminded him of Athens, of Sparta, of Macedon even, in its pomp, when Alexander had put his sword to half the known world. It was why he had chosen America as a home-in-exile for himself and his half-human son. Why he had remained to fight for it rather than simply leave and find another. It was why, even though Tony Stark was enjoying his own taste of exile, and the Super Hero Registration Act with which he had blackmailed Ares into joining his Mighty Avengers was dead, and even though his son had since left him to side with his enemies, he was still fighting for his city.

The city that never slept.

A metaphor, yes, for no city literally slept, but also true.

The city did not sleep, but in darkness its character changed, like the harpies of Orcus, at once beautiful and bestial to behold.

Ares was a giant amongst mortal men.

His neck was thick. His back was broad. His muscles strained against the sleeveless black vest he wore. He was bristled like a wild boar. And beyond any overt measure of stature there was simply *more* of him than there should have been. His fellow diners could sense what he was, even if they could not form their understanding into words, and none dared sit too close. Even so, he could feel the terror that every man and woman in that place had for him, and for each other. He could feel it through the glass from the pedestrians on the sidewalk, from the four lanes of traffic and beyond, across the concrete gulfs of the great metropolis where eight million turbulent souls dwelled in constant, unconscious fear of one another and hated themselves, in their enlightenment, for the knowledge that it was so.

It was contemptible.

Humanity was a violent and warlike species. It had flourished in the darkness, even as it feared the shadows it cast.

And in that paradox, there was Ares.

His sense of New York by night was that of standing in a still lake, surrounded by the reflection of eight million stars. Only each point of light was a human being, silently, often unwittingly, wishing harm upon one another.

Those two bikers, for instance…

They were planning some specific act of violence.

Ares felt it. He felt it and intended to do absolutely nothing to intervene. To do so would have been to cheat another of the honor. Perhaps the next Spider-Man, the next Daredevil or Punisher, would be made in New York this night?

He saluted the unsuspecting pair.

Where would anyone be, human or Olympian, without conflict to give them purpose, the foe against whom to define them?

He tore another bite off his pita and turned to his companion. In his towering arrogance, the mutant believed himself fearless, though even he sat with the buffer of an empty seat between himself and the God of War.

"Eat, Wolverine," he said, spraying half-chewed meat from his full mouth. “There is crap enough here to fill both our boots.”

Daken, as Wolverine was truly named, reclined in his corner chair. His arms spread across the cushioned back, legs folded under the table, as though supreme indifference was the virtue of kings, and an elixir that could be traced back to its wellspring and imbibed at need. In spite of his tattoos, smooth chin and tall mohawk, in his yellow uniform and mask he was instantly recognizable as Wolverine.

And no one seemed particularly interested.

Because this was New York. Home of the Avengers Tower. The Fantastic Four. The Taylor Foundation. Stephen Strange. Even in half-decent Mediterranean restaurants in East Midtown, at half past one in the morning, the presence of a renowned super hero was less comment-worthy than the Turkish Süper Lig soccer on the radio.

“I would sooner deep fry my middle claw and eat that,” said Daken, with a world-weary contempt that belied his apparent youth.

“An army marches on its stomach,” Ares declared.

Wolverine’s grin was a flash of smirking white. “Even if Norman had never told me, I’d know that you were the God of War. You paraphrase Napoleon Bonaparte like a champion.”

Ares scowled and returned his attention to his pita wrap and window view.

“Don’t be like that,” said Daken. “Give me some Sun Tzu, you Mediterranean stallion, and then finish me off with a bit of Churchill.”

Ares put his head in his hand.

As one whose very existence served to manipulate the basest instincts of those around him, he was not entirely unaware of the similar, albeit subtler, influence being worked on him whenever he was in Daken's presence. The only thing that he struggled to comprehend was how it functioned. He was a god, was he not? Not a villain like Bullseye, Moonstone, or Venom, none of whom could stand to be around the same table as Daken without tearing out somebody's eyes.

They were mighty, Osborn's Avengers, and greater, like for like, than their ousted counterparts.

Mac Gargan was a superior, if unreliable, Spider-Man. Karla Sofen had proven herself the equal in battle of the original Ms Marvel although she was, as the humans of this time and place would put it, a dangerous sociopath. Lester was both a better shot and a more dangerous hand-to-hand combatant than Clint Barton, with only the minor drawback that he was murderously insane. Daken, meanwhile, was unquestionably the more skillful and intelligent warrior than his father. If he only cared enough about anything but his own pleasures to put those skills to work, he would finally cut free of Logan's shadow.

And then there was the Sentry.

What was there to be said about the Sentry?

He was, quite possibly, the mightiest being that Ares had ever encountered. He was a god, even to the eyes of a god, the one hero Ares had stood beside and had no idea how to kill. There was no shame in admitting that the certainty that he would one day be forced to do so frightened him a little.

Zeus himself would tremble if forced to do battle with the Sentry.

Nevertheless, Ares knew himself to be a more than marked improvement on the Asgardian God of Thunder.

The one member of Osborn's Avengers that Ares could not, with confidence, call an upgrade on their predecessor was Osborn himself.

But there, events still had lessons even for the God of War: if Tony Stark, Nick Fury, and Steve Rogers had been more deserving, then Osborn would not be ruling from their former citadel now.

Drawing his hand from his face, he looked back at his companion. Daken had risen partway out of his chair and, for once, was actually looking across the street at their target.

Ares turned back to the window, just as a large black road-modified Stryker APC cut across the four lanes of traffic and screeched to a halt outside the front entrance of the *Bulletin* building. The rear hatch flew open and a five-man squad of private troops wearing tactical armor and toting assault rifles jumped out before advancing on the building. All five were inside, the doors to the building closing behind them, by the time the two startled police officers from the car outside Irkan's Kitchen were popping their doors and pulling on sidearms, the female talking urgently into the radio velcroed to her ballistic vest.

Daken, bored, checked the time on an elegant-looking cellphone.

"Less than ten minutes. I owe Karla fifty dollars."

Ares wiped his mouth on his bicep and got up out of his chair.

He picked up his axe where it had been resting against the side of the table. Nobody in the restaurant showed any more shock or interest in the weapon than they had in Wolverine.

Ares really did love America.

"Follow them."

CHAPTER THREE

Super Villain-Dense Environment

Bullseye whistled along to the elevator jingle as the car ascended. The lights, buried under the plastic buttons, blinked off the floors. *Five. Six. Seven.* Running ever further out of tune, he knelt to unpack and assemble his compound bow. It had fiberglass limbs, an aluminum riser bristling with scopes, cameras, stabilizers, and an automated quiver keyed to RFID tags in his gauntlets that allowed him to switch munition types with the flick of a toggle, and a brazen Oscorp logo around the grip.

One of Osborn's first acts as director of H.A.M.M.E.R., after eliminating everyone on Nick Fury's most-dialed list, of course, had been to tear up all those contracts that Stark Industries had enjoyed with the US military and the now-defunct S.H.I.E.L.D. and award them to Oscorp subsidiaries, coincidently making himself about half a trillion dollars richer than he'd been as leader of the Thunderbolts.

Bullseye's kind of hero.

He attached the bowstring and checked the tension.

The bow was fully collapsible, breaking down to the size of an aircraft carry-on bag, but still packing a draw weight of over two hundred pounds.

Eight. Nine. Ten.

At the eleventh floor the jingle cut out. The speakers emitted a satisfied *ping*, as though together they had scaled mountains, and the doors slid open.

Venom was already there, clinging to the ceiling on all fours, about half a yard ahead of the elevator door. The ceiling wasn't high, so his head, albeit upside down, was level with Bullseye's. It looked as though he'd been there some time. The puddle of drool underneath him was wide and deep.

"That's a neat trick you got there, Mac, but don't expect to make me jump."

Gargan's upside-down mouth lolled open, a tongue rolling out from it like a rope ladder and dangling an inch off the nondescript office carpet.

Bullseye brought up his bow. A little sleight of hand positioned a thirty-one-inch-long steel arrow with a high-explosive tip onto the string.

Mac Gargan had presumably had some kind of redeeming quality once. You needed something about you to survive this city as a PI long enough to get noticed. But, given how he'd allowed himself to be bribed into being transformed into the Scorpion, he'd probably never been all that bright. Since bonding with the Venom symbiote there was even less of the original man left inside that ever-shifting outer skin of alien hunger and neurotic rages. It was only a cocktail of dangerously off-label Oscorp medications, and a shared loathing of the hero whose identity they were trashing, that held it all together.

"Put those teeth where I can't see 'em, Mac, or look forward to six kilotons of Osborn's finest in your happy place."

Venom gave a demented grin, his mouth growing so wide that it split down the middle, drifting apart on a sea of tar to become two.

"I've got more mouths than you've got arrows," said Venom, his voice coming like slurry from both mouths at the same time.

Bullseye grimaced. "Damn it, Mac. Your pills are way off today."

"Wanna swap?"

"Nah. I've got a whole other set of problems."

Venom dropped from the ceiling, somehow shifting his orientation so that he was now facedown, and landed on the carpet on all fours.

"You're just so slooooooow."

Bullseye lowered his bow, easing the tension off the string. "Yeah, well, Osborn doesn't trust you on your own, so suck it up."

He stepped out of the elevator.

Bullseye had been inside a few newsrooms in his time. Usually, to kill journalists. Sometimes, like today, it was to destroy whatever the powerful and rich thought incriminating or embarrassing. Often, it was both. He'd also given his share of interviews to the press. He understood the power of media fascination as well as Osborn did.

And kind of like gas stations, they were the same everywhere.

The *Bulletin* offices conformed neatly to type.

Power display lights and monitors on standby mode described a maze of crisscrossing paths through the two dozen or so desks.

Bullseye took a moment to train his eyes to the gloom.

"What's this reporter woman's name?" said Venom.

"Greene, I think."

"Sounds tasty. Healthy. She got a desk here?"

"Nah, this is for the nobodies. She's got an office over the street."

"If we find her, can we eat her?"

Bullseye smirked. He couldn't think of a good reason why not. "If you've still got room in there."

Venom made a sound like a dog with an ice cream.

"This way," said Bullseye.

Leading with an array of tactical scopes and his arrow nocked, Bullseye zigzagged through the desks. Objects came and went. Framed photos of important people in famous places. Awards no one cared about. Old-fashioned telephones. Big computers with beige cases. Filing cabinets. Wire drawers full of clippings. All glinting under Bullseye's scopes and then fading as he passed them.

At a gloomy kitchenette palisaded with glass and smelling of coffee, he took a left, then another, instinctively doubling back on himself and tracking towards the front of the building. Passing a row of cheap laminate wood doors leading to a row of streetside offices, he silently mouthed the names on their frosted window panes until coming to the one that read '*S. Greene*'.

Bullseye put his ear to the glass and listened.

Nothing.

If there had been even one living soul on the floor then Venom would have smelled them, and eaten them, long before Bullseye became aware of them. But he hadn't become the world's most famous living assassin by trusting in other people's ability to not screw up.

Not Osborn's, and sure as hell not Gargan's.

He sidled up to the door, easing the arrow from the bowstring and hanging the stave over his shoulder as he tested the handle.

It wasn't locked.

He laughed quietly.

Chumps.

He went inside.

Greene's office was a neat freak's sanctum. Seriously, this was the room of a person with problems, and Bullseye had enough of those to know. Papers and stationery lived in neat stacks in desktop organizers. The chair had been pushed in under the desk when the last occupant had gone home for the night. The only clutter on the wall was some kind of professional accreditation from Empire State University, which surprised Bullseye.

His experience of the *Daily Bugle* was that any hack with a laptop could be a journalist.

The windows onto East 53rd rattled gently with the passing traffic. Even eleven stories up they were barred, an observation that'd earn the non-native a smug, "That's New York" and a wry shrug.

It was the cost of doing business in the most super villain-dense workplace on Earth.

Venom would've made short work of that particular security feature, but the number of eyes on the street had made brazening through the front desk the better option, and even with one security guard eaten he stood by his choices. Moonstone might have gone straight in through the roof with her intangibility, but Karla had her hands full with her own assignment. And the Sentry... well, it turned out Osborn was one of those people who preferred Manhattan without big glassy craters in it.

You think you know a guy...

Venom panted loudly as he surveyed the room. "*She's not here.*"

"Yeah, we knew that already."

Venom looked confused. "*We did? Why are we here then?*"

"Why do you even bother going to Osborn's briefings?"

"Vicki brings pizza." Venom drooled with remembered pleasure. *"The Sentry let me finish his pepperoni."*

The Sentry didn't eat. It freaked Bullseye out a little.

Sliding a thumbnail-sized flash drive with another shameless Oscorp logo on the case from the cuff of his gauntlet, he walked to the woman's computer.

"What's that for?"

"Didn't ask. Didn't care. Still don't, if I'm completely honest."

"What's this reporter have on Osborn anyway?"

Bullseye hesitated.

He still didn't know what some local hack could possibly have over the most powerful man on the planet. Osborn had a *literal* army of H.A.M.M.E.R. goons to make problems like this disappear, not to mention a chokehold on every city, state, and federal law enforcement and homeland security agency in the country. As far as Lester was concerned, this was a job for H.A.M.M.E.R.'s ridiculously over-resourced legal department. If Osborn was using the Avengers instead then he was either cracking a nut with a hammer or he was sending somebody a message.

Either way, it told him that there was something worth having on this computer. Bullseye wasn't the sort to care what rich guys did with their flash drives. He just killed people. Getting paid for it was kind of a bonus. But he couldn't deny a tickle of curiosity.

Venom put his hand on Lester's shoulder.

"Let me."

Bullseye closed his fist around the USB stick. "Don't think I'm letting those fingers anywhere near this drive."

"Don't need it. Don't trust Osborn." Venom hunched over the computer, a pair of eyes and a slobbering mouth squirming out from the inky flesh between his shoulder blades. He leered up

at Bullseye. "*I'm better than a USB.*" As he spoke, he extended his hands and spread his fingers, each one then splitting into more fingers and sprouting in turn into tendrils that whipped towards the computer's ports. They burrowed into the computer case, swarmed over the monitor, ensnaring the tower and its peripherals in a slimy black web of alien tissue.

The computer groaned, blinking, lurching into its startup sequence as the Venom symbiote squeezed its tiny buttons.

Bullseye watched, appalled but horribly fascinated. It wasn't two am yet and this was only the second most disgusting thing he'd seen today.

He loved it.

The monitor flickered on, immediately presenting a password demand before just as swiftly withdrawing it under Venom's hideous probing.

The operating system booted up.

Like the office, the desktop background was tidy and plain.

A truly sick mind.

"You really are good for something," said Bullseye.

Venom bared his teeth. "*What are we looking for?*"

"You think Norman tells me that? Maybe that's what the USB was for."

"*Maybe I can–*" A second, grisly set of features grew out of the back of Venom's head. Bullseye recoiled from the hideous face manifesting under his nose, snarling as if in disgust to mask his moment of shock. "*Fresh meat,*" Venom growled. "*Five, riding in the elevator, armed.*" He licked his lips. "*Heavily.*"

"This is what eating security guards gets you in Manhattan," said Bullseye, rattled by Venom's latest display of unsettling weirdness and hating himself for it.

The night guard's bodycam must have been beaming a live

feed to a mobile HQ roving around nearby. Private security in New York had upped their game in the years since Bullseye had first set up his stall in the city.

He turned to Venom. "You can take five guys."

Both of Venom's mouths grinned, but there was just enough humanity buried under all that mutational therapy and tarry alien skin to be suspicious. "*And leave you alone with the computer?*"

"It's your fault they're here, Gargan. Time to take one for the team."

"*Going through the front was your idea.*"

"Do Osborn's doctors really need to find out that they've got to up the dose on your meds again?"

Venom visibly shrank to a more human form. "*I can take five.*"

From a standing start, Venom leapt at the window, molding his body perfectly to its size and shape and punching through it like a river of sewage through a blockage at the outlet of a pipe. Broken glass and bits of mangled steel drizzled over East 53rd Street.

To the distant sounds of screaming from the sidewalk below, Bullseye pulled up the office chair and, tentatively, in case Venom had left any of himself on it, put his hand over the mouse.

"So then, Norman," he said, leaning forwards, ignoring the barks of automatic gunfire from further down the hall. "What's your dirty little secret?"

CHAPTER FOUR
Only Second-Degree Murder

Dr Karla Sofen, PsyD, PhD, aka Moonstone, kept an office on the top floor of Avengers Tower. She could fly, turn intangible, manipulate the limitless energy of her Kree gravity stone to do almost anything she wanted, but there was still no beating this view. The lights of the Empire State Building, Bank of America Tower, the Chrysler Building, and scores of smaller skyscrapers illuminated the city skyline like Christmas decorations brought out nine months early just for her. Of course, it wasn't technically *her* office any more than it was Norman's building (something of a tax loophole left from the previous tenant, apparently) but, possession being nine tenths of the law and so forth… As she saw it there were exactly seven people in the building with the authority to throw her out and they either didn't know (Victoria), didn't care (Norman), or were out trashing New York somewhere (pretty much everyone else).

Or they were sat across a glass conference table from her, illuminating an otherwise unlit room with their golden aura.

There weren't many things that frightened Karla.

In the unofficial world hierarchy of powers, she put herself unselfconsciously into the top thirty. Maybe top fifteen. She had been the leader of the Thunderbolts, and now she led the Avengers. Even in the Norman Osborn vanity project version of the team they were still humanity's headline super hero force. It wasn't the sort of gig that took on showboats or deadweights.

The short version: she could put up a fight against almost anything.

Then there was the Sentry.

He looked like the first thing most people would think of when asked to imagine a hero, which just went to show how deceptive appearances could be. Radiant as a sunrise. Flawless as a god in marble. His eyes were circular plates of gold, his long hair something woven from sunlight. And yes, he was good-looking, too. If there had been even just a little more fairness in the world then the Sentry would have been its most famous hero. Unfortunately for him, however, he photographed poorly. Pictures with him in frame tended to overexpose, even digitally, or returned an otherwise perfectly captured scene with a dazzling sunburst where the Sentry was supposed to have been. To sit near him, alone in that kind of presence, was to feel something of what the camera must feel. It was like standing over a fission reactor. Or on a S.W.O.R.D. platform in a decaying orbit, primed to self-destruct. It didn't go away. It didn't get better. He was the force of a million supernovas wrapped up in human form. You didn't *get used* to the Sentry.

Karla reached over the desk and took a sip of very strong black coffee.

The Sentry didn't need to sleep.

Karla did.

She set down the cup and scribbled a few last-minute observations into her notepad.

The Sentry watched her with blank, pensive, shining eyes.

"Do you know why Norman asked me to speak with you today?" she began.

"N- Norman says you can help me."

With all the might he possessed the stutter was quite disarming. Karla smiled reassuringly. Her "Dr Sofen" face. It had been a while since she'd been allowed to wear it, but you never forgot. The Sentry may have been functionally omnipotent, but he was also a socially awkward agoraphobic schizophrenic with a memory like Swiss cheese, and she was his doctor.

There was only one god here.

"Have you spoken with a therapist before?"

"Yes."

"Of course. Doctor…" She looked meaningfully over the squiggles and doodles that passed for notes on her pad.

"Worth," the Sentry supplied. "Cornelius Worth."

Karla tapped the butt of her pencil on her notepad. "Ah, yes. Of course. Dr Worth. Here it is." She knew Worth professionally. Psychiatrists were like super heroes, purely in the sense that they all knew each other. He was well regarded in his field, and a bit of a wet blanket. "But the reason, I think, that Norman asked *me* to see you rather than some generic H.A.M.M.E.R. shrink is that I've made understanding the particular stresses that people like us experience my specialty. I am, I think, much better qualified to understand the effect that powers, powers like yours and mine, can have on a person's mind."

Karla watched him, waiting to assess his response.

The Sentry, however, had become suddenly, totally, still.

Given that complete lack of movement, the subsequent

change in his aspect was difficult to explain. A coppery burnish eroded his golden halo, and the light in the room, of which he was still the solitary source, seemed to dim.

"*Your* power," he said, in a voice as cold-blooded as it was clear-spoken. "And *mine*." A crack appeared in his face. Karla realized that it was a smile. "Is that a joke?"

Karla retreated back into her chair, crossing her legs defensively, and accidentally kicked the underside of the table. Her coffee spilled.

She swore as it ran over the lip of the table to burn her lap.

When she looked up the Sentry was himself again, her office as well lit as it was supposed to be.

"Bob?"

The Sentry smiled warmly. "Yes, Karla?"

Warily, Karla got up and moved around the table to another chair. With half an eye on the Sentry, she picked up her coffee-stained notepad and brushed it off. As an afterthought, she rearranged some of her molecules to replace the wet pants with dry ones.

She cleared her throat again. "I'm sorry, Bob. Where were we?"

"I think it's all right to be a little nervous, Karla."

"Why should I be nervous?"

"Because it's been so long since you've been legally allowed to practice."

Karla gaped for a moment, too recently shaken to think what to say.

"CLOC volunteered to run a search on you when I told him about our appointment," said the Sentry. CLOC was the creepy AI housekeeper that haunted the corridors of the Watchtower, the not-at-all freaky custodian of the stronghold that had one day just appeared above the roof of Avengers Tower. The Sentry claimed to have built CLOC, but then the Sentry claimed a lot, from time to time, and Karla wouldn't have counted on the guy in front of her to work the dial on a toaster. "He said you spent time in prison and lost your license."

"Did he also tell you I devised the enhanced interrogation methods used by the CSA against superhuman combatants, and that I assisted Norman as a psychoanalyst with the Thunderbolts?"

"Actually, he did."

Karla blinked.

Good for CLOC.

"What did you do?" the Sentry asked.

"Didn't CLOC tell you?"

"It wasn't part of his search parameters, so no."

While she composed herself again, Karla decided the best answer was the honest one. Trust, after all, was an important first step in effective therapy. "I persuaded several of my patients to attempt suicide."

"Why?" he said, after a long time silent.

"I don't know. It was before I found my moonstone and gained my powers. In a way, I think it felt like having a super-power. I could destroy a life, or simply take one, just with my voice."

"How many is several?"

Karla shrugged. "They only gave me fourteen consecutive life sentences. So, let's say that many. It was only second-degree murder. You should have CLOC break a few more federal laws and get you Lester's rap sheet some time."

"Are you going to try something like that with me?"

Karla smiled. "Would you like me to?"

The Sentry looked strangely remorseful. "It wouldn't work."

"You'd be surprised how persuasive I can be."

And, for someone so appallingly powerful, the Sentry had a fragile mind. It was one of the reasons Norman had been so insistent on therapy.

"I'm not saying you couldn't talk me into trying," he said. "Just that it wouldn't work. I tried killing myself once."

Karla leant forwards, morbidly curious. "How?"

"I threw myself into the sun."

Karla slumped back. "That would normally do it."

"I thought I could kill the Void," the Sentry went on. "But I couldn't. He promised me he would come back, and he did." He leant forward, elbows to the table, hanging his head in his hands and pulling at his hair. The glass table threw churning reflections of his light. "And he did."

"Tell me about the Void."

The Sentry's voice hissed. "Director Osborn says there is no Void. He only exists in my head."

"What do you think?"

"I don't… I don't know anymore. Someone once told me I created the Void myself, in retaliation to a telepathic attack on my mind. I'm a little telepathic myself, I'm told."

"Uh-huh." Karla brandished her pencil like a wand. "What am I thinking right now?"

"I'm not… um… that kind of telepathic. I guess."

"Of course." She made some additions to her notes. "Perhaps you could tell me something about yourself. Something from your past?"

"Like what?"

"How did you get your powers? That's always a good ice-breaker."

"It was an accident in my college chemistry lab." He looked down. Definitely lying. "I… don't remember much about it."

Karla decided to let it go. There was always next time. "Tell me something else, then."

The Sentry looked hesitant, as though caught between what he wanted to do and what the part of him that still longed to be a hero told him he ought not do. In Karla's experience, it was a rare breed of hero where the super-ego won out over the selfish id.

"I mentored the Hulk," he said softly.

"The *Hulk* Hulk?"

"And I fought Galactus."

"Of course you did."

It seemed there was no stopping him now. "Reed Richards was best man at my wedding."

"OK."

"Captain America was there, too. Sue Storm was Lindy's maid of honor."

Karla set her pencil down before she gave herself RSI.

Lindy was the plain, perennially anxious mouse who could occasionally be spotted scurrying from place to place on the rare occasion that she decided to venture outside the Watchtower, and then only with the ever-vigilant CLOC as a chaperone. She was attractive enough, but compared to an Adonis like the Sentry, she just wasn't in the same league. Karla wasn't even sure they were playing the same ballgame. At her best guess, Lindy was at least ten years her husband's senior. But then, none of them really knew how old the Sentry was or if he actually aged at all. And Norman was currently dating his own son's ex and no one had batted an eye, so really, who were any of them to judge?

"But I made the world forget me," said the Sentry. "And I forgot, too. As the Void was a part of me it was the only way.

It was Reed's idea, I think. We lost the Watchtower and rented an apartment in Queens. I took drugs. I drank. I lived off social security. Lindy suffered. But we loved each other. No one remembers the Void anymore."

He looked up from his intense reflection in the glass tabletop and Karla gasped to see that his eyes had turned completely black. Light still radiated from him but it was intermittent and uneven, creating spaces for shadows that seemed to stretch outwards from him in all directions, creeping along the ceiling, the walls, stretching slowly but inexorably like taloned fingers across the table. Even the lights of Manhattan seemed to be shining from a galaxy away. Karla gripped the arms of her chair and drew herself up into the back, delving inside herself for the moonstone that was the source of all her powers. The Kree artefact had long ceased to exist as a physical object, her body having absorbed its energy into herself, but in times of danger, times like these, it was calming to have a physical focus from which to draw power.

Although if the Sentry even accidentally tried to kill her, she knew that there wasn't a lot she could expect to do about it. If the Sentry got it into his head to destroy the world, there wasn't a lot *anyone* could do about it.

"Do you want to know what I wonder, Dr Sofen?"

With a chill, Karla realized that the Sentry never called her *Dr Sofen*. He always referred to her as *Karla*.

"Yes, Bob," she said. "I would love to know what you are thinking right now."

"I wonder… If I could do *that* to an entire world. If I could make seven billion people forget their greatest hero then what else might I be capable of doing? What if all of this is another delusion I have subjected humanity to because Robert still longs to be a hero?" The darkness wearing the Sentry's face laughed bitterly. "Can you imagine a world like that, Dr Sofen, one in which you and I are Avengers?" The laugh died. His expression set hard. "I used to have a dog called Norman. It is almost too obvious."

"This is real, Bob."

The Sentry leant forwards, his golden costume shimmering as though the room was on fire, and Karla retreated further into her chair. "I could stop believing in you so easily, doctor. So easily. A thought from me and you would cease to exist. Is that not the mark of a delusion?"

"That's enough now, Bob," she said. "Bob?"

The Sentry's lips drew back into a soul-deadening grin.

Karla felt her heart hammering in her chest, her gaze sucked into his black hole eyes. "Void?"

"Norman says there is no Void."

"Norman says a lot of crap sometimes."

The shadows continued to stretch across the table. They reached the edge. Karla drew up her knees and climbed up into her seat.

Witheringly, the Sentry parroted her therapist's non-answer back at her. "What do you think, Dr Sofen?"

Karla answered hoarsely, not daring to pull her eyes away. "The Void exists."

The Sentry grinned and sat back. The shadows withdrew to him. "Stay out of this head, Dr Sofen. Next time Norman asks you to poke at what is in here, you tell him to come and do it himself." Then he blinked, his eyes dazzlingly golden, the light shining back into the room. His expression grew concerned. "Karla? Are… are you all right?"

"I…"

Stiffly, almost calmly, Karla gathered up her things from the table.

She even managed to smile.

"I think that's enough for today."

CHAPTER FIVE

Impressed

Daken stepped onto the sidewalk outside of Irkan's Kitchen and breathed deeply of East 53rd. It was the perfectly flawed complement to the burnt asphalt and tire rubber smell coming from the armored truck's hard stop outside the *Bulletin*. Like sushi and a bone-dry Koshu wine. He looked up towards the eleventh floor of the building. His mind as sharp as his senses, he broke the scene apart as he been trained to do as a young samurai in Tōhoku, Japan, interrogated it piece by piece.

Five heavily armed private security guards, practically soldiers, were already inside the building and riding the elevator up to the eleventh floor. Two more in tactical body armor and military assault rifles made seven in total. One was sat behind the wheel of the truck. The other was on the sidewalk, standing guard over the doors. The two cops who had been enjoying a harmless takeout lunch at Irkan's, or providing Osborn with an additional layer of surveillance, Daken could not be certain either way, were making a bee-line across the road. The two lanes of traffic still trying to honk and growl their way around the obstructing truck only added to the confusion. The pedestrians, however, a smarter breed generally than their motorist cousins, were rapidly clearing the area.

All except two.

One was a stocky man in a tan-colored padded leather vest, exposing sun-worn skin and muscular arms, with a motorcycle helmet over his head. The other was dressed in what appeared to be traditional Arab dress: a heavy dishdasha robe, a ghutrah headscarf that entirely concealed his face, and a shadowy bisht over-cloak that seemed to snap with a life of its own after the passing cars.

They trailed the two cops.

Who were they? What were they doing here?

Was it the same thing Daken was here for?

He flashed a casual killer's breezy smile.

What *was* he here for?

A second after he had stepped out of the restaurant, Ares ducked through the doorway and joined him on the sidewalk.

"You know, I could watch you squeezing in and out of doorways all day. If ever you can't face the subway back to the Bronx and need a place in Avengers Tower to crash..." He shrugged. "My door is always open."

Ares ignored him completely. Or pretended to. Daken could smell the Olympian's discomfort in his presence, the pheromones produced by his secondary mutation subtly enhancing Ares' pre-existing dislike of him. Daken had no particular end game in mind. Beyond potentially annoying somebody, somewhere down the road. Life, for Daken, was just one spinning plate after another. Sometimes they fell and broke. Sometimes they didn't. It was all the same to Daken.

None of them were his plates.

"This is no ordinary private security." Ares glowered across the street, muscles taut, huge tendons standing up like ridges from his neck. "Even for this city."

"Must be the Symkarian on the ninth and tenth," said Daken. "Some habits die hard."

"These men are soldiers. I feel how they chafe to be surrounded by civilian targets."

"I'm more interested in those two." Daken gestured to the two men crossing the road after the cops.

"Good!" Ares gave him a clap across the shoulder that almost propelled him into the path of a red SUV doing ten miles per hour. "You are not wholly the arrogant barbarian that Osborn thinks you to be."

Daken reached behind his head and massaged the bruise out of his back. "Back atcha, big guy."

Ares spent a moment taking it all in, much as Daken just had. It took the God of War a little longer, but who knew what thoughts moved behind those unfathomably hard eyes? He was fundamentally beyond human, or even mutant, comprehension. There was a firmness to his expression that belied the Olympian's depth, but the abiding impression one took was not of cruelty. They simply *were,* to the most callous and extraordinary degree. It was a face that would watch the world burn, provided that it did so through him and on his terms. And when it did, Daken hoped to be there.

"Osborn has claimed this building and its contents," said Ares. "These soldiers will pay for their trespass."

"Venom and Bullseye can handle five guys," said Daken. "If they can't then they don't deserve to be Avengers."

Ares looked down on him with the full weight and

condemnation of a god. "None of you deserve to be Avengers, but Osborn has chosen you for the role. He has given you this chance to prove yourself worthy of the honor."

Daken's fake grin became a real snarl. "Because I love making Director Osborn happy."

"Then gain us entrance to the building," said Ares, as impervious to sarcasm as he was to physical harm. "Aid Lester and Gargan and return Osborn his prize. I will see to these two. Whoever they are, they will face the God of War."

"One question."

Ares turned, just as he had been about to step out into the traffic.

"I know that Moonstone commands the Avengers whenever Osborn misplaces the keys to the Iron Patriot suit, but who put you in charge?"

Ares grunted. "I am the son of Zeus and Hera. I commanded armies at Troy."

He turned his massive back.

Daken watched him go. "Yeah," he murmured. "But on whose side?"

Ares did not hear him, however, because the Olympian was already halfway across East 53rd and still going, separated from Daken now by the noise of two slow-moving lanes of cars and ground zero to half a block of slowly panicking pedestrians. It was also just then that the guard on the *Bulletin*'s door noticed him coming.

"Freeze!" The mercenary swung his assault rifle around, and then, "Hell, Antoni," presumably talking via an open radio link to his companion in the truck. "It's Ares and Wolverine."

The cops turned, looking appropriately relieved at having a potential shootout taken off their books. The two strangers who had been following the cops looked around as well. The muscular guy in the tan jacket and bike helmet went straight for the weapon at his hip.

Daken's claws slashed from their sheaths of flesh, twelve inches of ultra-hard bone, one either side of his clenched fists and a third curving up from the wrist. He crouched, ready either to sprint across the road or dive for any of the ready sources of civilian cover depending on the nature of the weapon that emerged. When the stranger pulled a golden shamshir sword from its sheath, Daken smirked. It was possible to tell a human from a superhuman by the way a person walked. It was bearing. It was presence. It was confidence at the nucleic acid level. This guy was human.

Compared to two mercenary soldiers packing body armor and assault rifles, Middle Ages over there wasn't bringing much to this party.

Or so Daken thought.

Still twenty yards ahead of Ares, the swordsman turned his draw into a pivot and a downstroke, screaming in a language that sounded something like Farsi.

The curved sword flashed, a beam of light blasting from its body in the split-second that it spent horizontal, crossing the two empty lanes of road in the fraction of a fraction of a second less time than it took for it to reach Daken's eyes and hit Ares with the force of a souped-up watercannon to the chest. The Olympian slammed into the side of the yellow cab that had been attempting to crawl behind him. The vehicle's body steel, safety-tested so rigorously to grant its occupants an extra percentage point or two's chance of survival in the event of a collision, crumpled like aluminum underfoot. The car hit another, both scraping and howling across the road and onto the sidewalk and into the windows of Irkan's Kitchen, which promptly exploded into the street.

Daken raised an eyebrow.

Now he really was impressed.

The swordsman swore in accented English, his words lost under the aggressively atonal wail of car- and intruder-alarm systems, as he surveyed the unintended collateral damage. His robed companion appeared to remonstrate with him, urging him to strike again, until, with a grinding of steel and a shifting of wreckage, Ares threw off the two mangled halves of the taxicab and rolled out the crick in his neck. He pointed across the street to the human swordsman, somehow fashioning a universal gesture that said *my turn* more succinctly than mere words.

Confronted by the God of War, the mortal did the one sane thing still available to him.

He ran.

The robed stranger glared balefully after his fleeing companion. Daken could see no face through the ghutrah, just a pair of glowing red eyes, but he could *feel* the hate in the look. He turned to Daken and appeared to nod as though in recognition, or in challenge. Shaking a mummy-like gray claw-hand from his sleeve, he swept through a complicated sequence of magical-looking gestures and, despite the fact that Daken's eyes were on him the entire time, appeared to fade into the exhaust smoke and concrete dust as though he had been a trick of the eyes all along.

Daken scowled. "I hate teleporters."

At least he had a good idea of where the stranger was going.

He looked up.

The eleventh floor.

Just two mercenary soldiers packing body armor and assault rifles, two city cops, and a few hundred witnesses to get through first.

He clenched his fists and started walking towards the building.

He just *loved* making Osborn happy.

CHAPTER SIX
Too Many Bad Things

At the end of a thirty-yard scramble across the front of the *Bulletin* building, Mac Gargan webbed the steel cladding either side of the window frame, threw himself back out over the street for maximum force before launching himself at the glass. He smashed through and hit another wall.

This one was of gunfire.

Five soldiers in padded black armor and bug-lensed helmets sheltered behind desks in a staggered firing line facing his entry point, shredding office furniture and interior walls with high-caliber bullets as though they were papier mache. Their aim was good, unpanicked, the baleful green beams of tracking lasers spraying the walls moments before hails of automatic fire ripped them apart.

They'd been waiting for him.

Gargan's inward dive slammed to a halt against fifty rounds per second. He hit the ground in a storm of powdered MDF and plasterboard, green targeting lasers bouncing wildly off each other and strobing through the dust. He writhed on the floor like a man drowning in oil while the alien symbiote thickened into a bullet-resistant carapace and spat out the bullets that had already punched through.

Hell, that hurt.

No, it doesn't, said the Venom symbiote, the echo of a psionic growl in his head.

Yeah, he thought, his own inner voice. It actually didn't.

Get up and start killing, loser. I'm hungry.

Gargan sprang onto all fours and pushed off the ground.

His body twisted around its central humanoid mass, adopting new shapes and changing them again a dozen times before reaching the near wall and sticking to it. He didn't stay there long, using it instead as a springboard to launch himself clear across the soldiers' heads and onto the ceiling. Bullets gave chase, a spray separating and spreading as they hared after a fast-moving target. The soldiers were good though, falling back and spreading out, keeping their distance and renewing their encirclement.

Gargan threw a web and swung around a thick structural column that a few seconds of gunfire had stripped to bare concrete, buying the symbiote a second or two to regenerate their injuries. Plastic foam fell from the pulverized ceiling tiles like snow as he emerged from around the column and dropped behind a filing cabinet. Bullets banged into the side of it with a sound like a manic compulsive trying to grate an iron bar.

He licked his lips and growled, the vibrations running through the metal cabinet and into his spine in uncanny sympathy with the symbiote's psychic urging to stop cowering and feed. He hardly needed convincing.

It was why Venom had chosen him.

It got a host with fewer qualms about indulging its various unsavory appetites, and *he* got a bewildering array of alien powers and the strength to do whatever he wanted with them, to whomever he wanted to do it to.

Until Osborn, and his doctors, and his drugs.

Kill them all. Then kill Osborn.

Gargan gritted his teeth and shook his head. Before the pills, he'd rarely had the willpower to deny the symbiote. He didn't like denying it now. Letting it do what it wanted was easier.

Kill Osborn.

"This isn't the time for–"

He checked that thought.

A premonition of pain and fire, a spider-sense of sorts, squirmed through the psychic ganglia that tethered his brain to Venom's weirder extrasensory perceptions. He whirled away from the filing cabinet and leapt, just as a rocket-propelled grenade tore it to shreds. An expanding fireball lifted Gargan up and flung him into the wall, knocking yet another hole through the front of the *Bulletin* building and kicking him out over East 53rd Street.

The siren wail of alarms drifted up from street level, the rattle of gunfire and the screams of onlookers. Daken and Ares were having their own fun.

So long as they leave the bodies for us.

Trailing vaporous clouds of symbiote matter, Gargan launched sticky bundles of webbing that splattered securely to the outside wall. He threw them sparingly. Venom's webs were extensions of the symbiote's body. They weren't infinite, and the RPG blast had already left his inky black skin looking scrappy, his own flesh showing through in patches and coming out in goose bumps in the March cold.

He was practically indestructible. But the symbiote could be hurt by fire.

Someone had come prepared.

The webs yanked taut. He pulled back with a roar, muscles straining and swelling, launching himself back towards the building and in no mood to fuss too hard over windows. He crashed through steel and concrete like a missile and into the unused offices of the Symkarian exile on the tenth floor.

He rolled through rubble, traveling several yards over factory-fresh carpet covered with a clear plastic sheet before coming to a halt beside an empty cubicle. He panted while the symbiote regenerated.

After this we're going to kill Osborn.

"I'm not going back to Thunderbolt Mountain," he said aloud. "Or the Raft."

Thunderbolt Mountain wasn't so bad. At least you got to be you. Or me… Whatever.

Gargan shook his head to clear it of the extra voices.

He couldn't remember what it was like to be lonely in his own head. He reminded himself that he'd chosen this. He'd chosen it all.

"Shut up, I–"

He looked up, various senses squirming for his attention.

The ceiling exploded.

A torrent of bullets tore through it and Gargan roared in pain as they hammered into the wounded symbiote. Their targeting devices were definitely allowing them to track his movements through the walls. That was some rare and expensive hardware they were packing.

Gargan made a mental note to strip them before he ate them.

It wasn't as if Osborn paid him.

He launched himself at the ceiling, erupting through the weakened floor of the eleventh like a kraken attacking from beneath the ice.

The angles of fire coming in through what had been the ceiling gave him a general idea of where his attackers were and, faster than a human could react to him, he carpet-sprayed the area with webs.

One hit a soldier fully on the armored vest. The man flew back through desks and ruined furniture before being webbed messily to a partition wall. Another web caught a soldier's gun, yanking it out of his hands and leaving it dangling just out of reach. A third caught a glancing strike as he ducked, and then struggled, caught fast, his shoulder indelibly stuck to the underside of the desk he had been sheltering behind.

Gargan landed. The floor creaked under his monstrous weight, and he leapt again just as it fell from under him, coming down this time on top of a large office printer that another soldier had been using as cover. It died like a car in a crusher. The soldier swung his gun around. Gargan smacked it aside on the back of his hand. A third arm burst wetly from his chest, took the armored man by the neck and lifted him bodily off the ground. Without intending to do it, or even being conscious of having done it, he had grown to twice human size. His distended maw gaped, wider than a man was broad, black saliva dripping from his teeth.

He tried to remember that thing he had mentally resolved to do.

Oh yeah.

Strip them before eating them.

Hell with that!

His neck snapped forward, jaws crashing shut–

–over nothing.

Gargan drew back, flexing his inexplicably empty fist.

He snarled, re-absorbing the third arm into his body, and looked up.

A shadow bloomed out of the bullet-riddled gloom by the elevator doors, deposited the wounded soldier, and in a rippling of the ambient darkness, turned back. The shadow met his eyes. Two slashes of red in a mummy-like wrap of absolute black. Gargan felt a chill go through him like a knife. Through Venom's memories, Gargan knew the sensation of absolute cold against his skin. This was that, but taken further. It went through meat and through bone and into a soul that Gargan had done too many bad things to want revealed to the world. Venom bared his teeth with frustrated hunger, rejecting the fear and, as a psionic side-effect of so doing, denying it to Gargan as well, projecting the full gamut of alien hatreds, avarice, and aggression onto his host's brain in its place.

With a roar, he launched himself across the room.

The shadow rose up to meet him, neither floating nor flying, but *drawn,* as though the space between him and Venom, his destination point, had been commanded to close and it had obeyed. A curved black sword appeared in skeletally thin gray hands, dark robes rippling out like a cape that then frayed into shadow. Laughter rattled out of him. Like breath forced out of a dead man's chest.

Gargan swung a giant-sized fist, bellowing in surprise as it met no resistance whatsoever before sprawling across the floor and gouging out concrete and carpet with his knuckles.

The shadow cackled all around him. Its voice was a corpse's whisper, accented by dead languages. "Try again, Spider-Man."

The goading pushed Venom into a frenzy.

He grew upwards from the ankles, sucking his prone body up

after himself and dumping the recycled mass into the creation of two wrecking ball fists. He launched himself with a berserk howl, tendrils bursting from his upper body, growing barbs and teeth and whipping towards his enemy. The shadow swordsman flowed effortlessly out of reach, freely altering his size, shape, and position in space as though all of these could be commanded with an expression of will. In a swirl of tenebrous dark, the shadow retaliated. Venom turned his furious onslaught into an equally frenzied defense, weaving acrobatically, and elastically, around the free-flowing black sword, pitting alien ESP itself against the shadow-man's eerie powers, and busting a gut for the right to a tie.

The black sword cleaved through a clutch of tendrils, and Gargan shrieked.

Pain – sudden, debilitating, total – went through him like a blunt saw. Venom and Gargan screamed together as one, the psionic connections between their two minds catching fire and blazing with the other's agony. In that moment the symbiote came close to rejecting him outright, and he it. The only reason they did not was that their loathing for the one who had done this to them was greater.

"The kiss of the Black Blade is an exquisite torture, is it not?" The shadow had no scent. No warmth emanated from his body. No breath drifted from the slit in his headdress. There was no emotion, neither kindness nor malice, in his words. "Even after I surrendered the last vestiges of my own soul and left behind my flesh, I could not relinquish this weapon. No. But I have taught it to crave that which I can no longer give it." With a flourish, he inverted the sword and lifted it high. An execution stroke. "The evils of a human soul."

Venom's remaining tendrils were shriveling back, recoiling

from the Black Blade's cut like worms from bright sunlight, melting back into a central body that was no longer growing but shrinking, man-sized and wailing like a child at the cloaked shadow's sandaled feet.

He could do nothing to defend himself.

"Go to whatever hell deserves you knowing that it was the Black Raazer who sends you there."

A scream rang out from the direction of the elevator.

Raazer turned with an enraged hiss.

Gargan exerted enough command over his own body to look up.

The mercenary that Raazer had earlier rescued from Venom's jaws stood before the now-open doors. His face was pale. He had surprisingly little to say. Daken's claws emerged from the ceramic panels of his protective vest.

"Damn," said Daken, his yellow uniform soiled with the bloody scent of at least fifteen different people. "That elevator is slow."

The shadow drifted back, lowering his sword into a guard to caution against both the newly arrived Daken and the injured Venom. "Your claws cannot touch me, Wolverine, and I can cut in ways that even you will not quickly heal from."

He carved the air with a hand gesture, and the soldier in Daken's arms vanished. Daken stumbled, betraying just how much he had been leaning on the dying man as a crutch. Another set of brisk gestures followed. The rest of the mercenaries, freed from Venom's webs when Raazer's Black Blade had struck the parent organism, and in the process of picking up themselves and their weapons, turned to smoke and disappeared. "But the fate of minions does not concern me. This battlefield has already been won. The world cries out against tyranny and my brotherhood has answered: the end of the Iron Patriot's dark reign is nigh."

His cloak fluttered, fading into the ambient gloom, then his gray hands, his glowing red eyes. Last to vanish was his voice, a scratch like twigs on a window pane as he left them with his parting words.

And then he was gone.

Gargan looked mutely at Daken. Daken looked at Gargan.

For a minute they knelt on ruined carpet or slouched against the bloody side of an elevator door in a silence that even a mutual hatred for one another could not fill with words.

"Good work, team," said Bullseye, appearing from a bullet-mauled corridor with a computer under one arm and, for some reason, Sarah Greene's framed degree certificate under the other. "Seriously. Good hustle tonight. Six out of ten. Way to show nobody the Avengers are no pushovers."

Gargan glared at him for almost as long as he and Daken had been glaring at each other.

With a sigh, Daken shook his head and drew a small cellphone from his pocket.

"Nice girl's phone," said Bullseye. "Couldn't you get it in pink?"

Ignoring him, Daken waited for the number he had just pushed to dial. Snubbing the speakerphone, he held the handset to his ear. "Hello, Ms Hand. We have it." He glanced at Bullseye as the person at the other end of the call spoke. "About ten minutes. Tell Karla I'll be stopping at an ATM on the way back. She'll understand." Another pause. "Well, whenever she's free, then." He ended the call and returned the device to his pocket. "The deputy director seemed very anxious to debrief us. I can't for the life of me imagine why. And she would very much appreciate it if we could find our way back to Avengers Tower without destroying too much more of New York." He flashed a smile as fake as his uniform. "Who wants to tell Ares?"

"Where is he?" said Gargan.

"Oh, about halfway towards Queensboro Bridge, I expect. Just follow the line of burning cars."

Now can we kill Osborn? Venom growled in his thoughts.

"Yeah…" Gargan sighed, to no one in particular. Perhaps to everyone. He wasn't sure. "I guess it'll have to be me, won't it?"

CHAPTER SEVEN
No Respite, No Quarter

"Citizens of New York!" Ares bellowed, ignoring the impotent flash of headlights and the blasting of horns as he strode against the flow of traffic down Sutton Place South. Apartment blocks rose high on his left. The dark gulf of the East River was to his right. His axe, made for him under the most extreme duress by the god Hephaestus, was a pleasing and almighty weight in his right hand, flashing in the lights of the swerving traffic, promising only destruction and war. "You have to the count of ten to begone from my path."

A white sedan rushed towards him, its horn blaring a continuing note of challenge.

Ares strode on.

"One!"

There was a tire shriek and a gust of scorched brake pads and rubber as the vehicle spun out of Ares' lane, its horn becoming a receding whine as it careened on past.

"Two!"

There was no courage on this world. No conviction to do

what was needed regardless of its cost. This, thought Ares, as cars continued to roar by on either side of him, was why Earth still needed the God of War. Its people should have seen through Osborn and his Avengers long ago. They had, in fact, but they did not wish to see and so pretended that they had not. They wanted to be protected. They wanted to feel safe.

The world had changed and it needed Norman Osborn.

It lacked the backbone to stand without him.

"Three!"

He had pursued the swordsman on foot from the corner of 53rd and 1st and the man was still fleeing. He was running north on the sidewalk, aiming perhaps to cut across the residential district and lose Ares in the busier neighborhoods of Queensboro Bridge and the Upper East Side. The helmeted warrior barreled through the handful of pedestrians still out at that hour. Looking fearfully over his shoulder, he blundered into a tired-looking woman who appeared to be returning home from a long shift in the city. He scrambled back onto his feet, another look over the shoulder, but not so fearful yet as to fail to check that the woman was unharmed before racing on.

He was a hundred yards ahead and stretching his lead.

Ares lengthened his stride. He was tireless. He could maintain this pursuit until he ran his quarry into the Arctic Sea or the man's heart burst from exhaustion or terror, but he was not the quickest, and if the swordsman made it as far as Lennox Hill, even making it onto the subway, then Ares could lose him. He cursed himself for not going to his own bike rather than pursue the human on foot, but the surprise attack had demanded a response.

The human warrior had struck the God of War.

Honor demanded that he pay for that slight in blood.

"Four!"

A small silver hatchback hurtled towards him, its driver, inattentive or willfully slow, slamming the brake at the last second to send her car screeching towards Ares. He stopped the vehicle under his foot, causing it to brake like a skateboard by pressing down on its hood and driving the front bumper into the asphalt. The fascia wept sparks, its rear bumper lifting briefly off the ground before slamming back down with a crash that shattered the rear windshield and both rear passenger windows. The car's two occupants, both of them female and dressed as though for a night in Midtown, stared up in horror through the splintered teeth of their windshield.

Ares looked down.

His patience was wearing thin.

"I commanded you to begone." He squatted down onto his haunches. "So." He slid the fingers of his left hand under the hatchback's front bumper. "Begone." The front doors fell open, the car's occupants both tumbling out onto the road as, with a grunt, Ares pushed off through his thighs and gave the car a shove. The vehicle spun over the lanes of traffic, traveling just over a hundred yards before it crashed onto the sidewalk on its roof and bulldozed through the front pavilion of a smart riverside apartment.

Ares beat his hand clean against his vest, watching with immense satisfaction as the wounded came stumbling out of the dust of the damaged building front. Cars careened to avoid dazed pedestrians and debris, piling into one another and crashing over the opposite curb.

"Ten," said Ares, and started off after his quarry again. "The Avengers thank you for your cooperation."

A stricken pickup lay in his way. The driver in its high cab was unconscious, blood matting his scalp and smearing the side window where it rested. Ares put his foot against the driver's side door and shunted the truck violently aside, whereupon it slammed into the back of another. The swordsman from outside Irkan's was crawling out of the rubble that the building had spewed onto the sidewalk, pulling off the motorcycle helmet he was still wearing in order to cough up dust. The face beneath it was dark-skinned, with a short, neat beard and wavy black hair at shoulder length.

Bullseye would have labelled Ares' throw a miss and laughed that he could have done better. Ares respected his comrade's fearlessness and perfection. But he had never intended to hit the man.

He would do that with his own hands.

Preferably after learning who he fought for and why.

Only then would he grant his adversary the mercy of ending this.

Still coughing, the swordsman got his hands under his chest and pushed himself up off the sidewalk. He took in the destruction around him, the wrecked apartment front, the mangled hatchback, the wounded stumbling from the sidewalk and into the road, and his expression hardened.

"Of all of you, I had hoped you at least might be sympathetic." He spoke in English, unaware, it seemed, of the All-tongue of the Olympians. "But I see now why you fight for the Iron Patriot." He brought his sword up into a ready stance, before unleashing another blast of white-golden light across the street. Ares tore the hood off a yellow cab and swung it up like a shield, intercepting the light blast in an explosion of rainbow motes and streamers of indivisible colors. The impact force staggered him into the body of the cab, and he gave a roaring laugh, rejoicing in the mighty ringing in his left hand.

"If you fail in your first attempt to lay low a god, then you should be sure to have a better ploy in reserve before trying again."

The swordsman ran at him with a yell, firing off a flurry of short blasts from his sword. The pummeling bent Ares back over the cab roof, the final blow driven like a fist across his jaw, twisting his head around and leaving him with visions of stars. The warrior leapt, his sword a golden extension to the arc of his descent. Ares rolled along the body of the car.

The sword noisily sheared the vehicle in two.

"What kind of champion endangers so many lives to capture one man?" the swordsman yelled.

"The kind that captures his man," said Ares. "The kind your people begged for."

"Not *my* people."

The warrior drew his sword out of the steel guts of the cab and sent it flashing along a rising diagonal towards Ares' neck. The blow carved a slit through Ares' vest, the sight of godsblood encouraging the human into a whirlwind of thrusts, slices, and wild lunges. Every blow was a kill-stroke with the weight of intent behind it, carving Ares' impromptu shield to steel ribbons. The man pitted his skills against a god. He could end this quickly or he could die in the valorous attempt. Ares threw the first blow of his own. It would have knocked in a concrete wall and the human yielded to it rather than attempt to parry his strength, bending away from the Olympian war-axe and immediately countering: a predictable reversion of back foot to front, defense to attack, weakness to strength.

Ares recognized the form.

He knew every martial art ever devised or practiced, and this one was hardly common. Not in this hemisphere of the world.

Ares decided that he had learnt enough.

Now he was ready to end this.

His axe smashed into the road as the human threw himself desperately aside, breaking deep enough to rupture a water main. Pressurized water erupted from the ground in a frothing geyser. Up and down the block, lights began to wink out. The screaming spread with the darkness. Ares ignored it. The swordsman moved to wipe sodden hair from his face, but Ares allowed for no respite, no quarter, his axe moving with such blistering fury that for a matter of seconds even the water from the ruptured main stopped fountaining, cut down at the trunk and unable to replenish itself faster than Ares could carve it apart. The human warrior was an able swordsman, but Ares' skills surpassed those of any mortal fighter on Earth. The human brought every ounce of skill to bear in avoiding Ares' blows, until the Olympian gave him no other choice but to counter his strength head on.

Ares' axe struck the mortal's block with an uppercut so powerful that the ground beneath their boots cracked and the water gushing from the main vaporized to a blasted mist. His blow broke through the block. The sword vibrated but would not break, and Ares' strength instead smacked the warrior and his crossed blade like a baseball with a bat.

The human left a man-sized hole in the third story of the apartment building opposite.

Ares laughed, then squelched across the flooded street towards the damaged structure.

Humans were fragile. After such injury as Ares had just done to him, this one was now most certainly dead. Honor was satisfied. Glory was claimed. But Osborn would undoubtedly appreciate a body.

He approached the magnetically barred entrance gate at a

determined walk and did not stop. The steel gate bent around him and then came off its hinges, the breadth of Ares' shoulders pulling great hunks of masonry away from the walls.

The elegantly nondescript foyer on the other side was lit by emergency lighting and deserted of people, although muffled screams carried through the walls. The experience of Skrull invasion was recent in the city's memory. The building's residents would now be cowering in their apartments or in converted shelters in the underground parking lot.

If they had simply done that when Ares had told them to, as opposed to after he had started throwing cars, then it would have gone better for them.

He had a choice of elevator or stairs.

He took the stairs, climbing stolidly to the third floor whereupon he emerged onto a landing that was similarly plain to its counterpart on the ground floor, but for one apartment with a gaping hole in the wall and a mound of rubble in the communal hallway. Ares moved towards it. A cool breeze blew through the hole, disturbing the light pall of dust. A corresponding hole in the building's outer wall about thirty feet on made for a tunnel through which Ares could make out the dark band of the East River and the lights of Roosevelt Island. There was no body amongst the debris. Scuffed footprints headed towards the back of the building.

Ares was impressed.

Perhaps there was something more than human to this adversary after all.

Despite his earlier reservations when Osborn had ordered him and Daken to stake out the *Bulletin* offices and watch others at work, he was starting to enjoy himself. He had not been given the freedom of battle like this since Osborn's invasion of the

X-Men's sovereign island of Utopia. And this fight was all the more satisfying for the fact that Ares was winning it.

Footprints and the occasional blood smear led to an open door onto a fire escape. The metal platform overlooked an alley that, with the power out, was completely unlit, the buildings themselves too proud to allow the adjoining neighborhoods to share their light. It smelled of unemptied trash. The human warrior lay in a heap on the first flight of steps, clinging to consciousness like a gladiator, his grip on his sword secondary only by comparison. His biker's leathers had been ripped open, revealing a brilliant, sleeveless, undercoat of gold, turquoise, and emerald threads.

"Surrender," said Ares. "You have fought honorably and well. Osborn may be lenient if you come in willingly and answer the questions he will no doubt have for you."

The man looked up at him, along the plane of the metal stairs, dark eyes watery with anger. "There is a H.A.M.M.E.R. outpost in my country. I have witnessed their kindness with my own eyes."

"Then stop resisting and die. Or fight harder and win. The choice is yours."

"Do you not wonder why we fight at all?"

Ares shrugged. "No. But I rejoice that someone does." He stepped out onto the fire escape, the metal platform groaning under his greater-than-human weight, and bent forwards to pry the human's sword from his feebly protesting grip.

He held the weapon in his left hand, and through the power of his touch he *knew it*.

Here was an edge that could cut through any armor and open the flesh of a god, a blade that could withstand the blow of one of Hephaestus' axes without shattering. His understanding did not extend to who had made it, or when, or to what good or evil end, only the perfect manner in which these things manifested in the weapon's function.

He gave the blade a trial whirl, frowning as he sensed a resistance in spite of the eager hum that the super-sharp edge dealt to the air as it moved.

"No one may wield that sword while I live," said the mortal. "And no one who would willingly follow the Iron Patriot or turn S.H.I.E.L.D.'s peacekeeping armies into an occupying force to subjugate half the world, could ever be deemed worthy of holding it."

"I am the God of War," said Ares, gripping the weapon tightly and glaring down at the vanquished mortal who thought to judge him. "I am the master of all weapons."

"No!" The human lifted just enough of his upper body from the stairs for Ares to push him back down under his boot.

Ares let go of his axe.

It dropped to the metal platform with a clang.

Mortal warriors had a tendency to grow attached to their weapons, cherishing them, passing them down as heirlooms and investing them with the properties of relics. A precious few warranted such esteem, but the majority were just things, instruments for the administration of death, and there were enough of those in the world to be cavalier in their treatment.

Even a weapon of Olympus could be readily replaced.

Hephaestus could always be compelled to fashion him another.

With his right hand free he took the human's sword two-handed. Immediately, he sensed its protest. It shuddered like an unbroken horse in his grip as though attempting to break away. He gritted his teeth, grip tightening until rock would crack and steel deform. The sword, however, continued to defy him. He growled, bending every ounce of his godly will towards its subjugation. Still, it resisted him.

"Stop!" he heard the mortal yell. "Release it, Ares, please. I will surrender!"

Ares roared in agony, as though the weapon in his grip were being melted down and the golden metal running down his forearms. He let out a howl of defiance, refusing to admit defeat to a sword.

Even as it exploded in his hands.

The blue lights of first responder vehicles twinkled through the blacked-out neighborhood like a single candle captured in a piece of stained glass. The plaintive wail of sirens drifted across the moonscape stillness of the rubble, challenged only, and occasionally, by the airhorns and loudhailers of the patrol boats on the East River, and by the faintly tragic *whup-whup-whup* sound of search and rescue helicopters. None of them, as yet, were hovering quite low enough to notice the rubble of the collapsed apartment building shifting, the ground rising, an eighty-ton slab of unbroken concrete sliding to one side in a cataract of dislodged debris as Ares reared up out of the demolished building and roared.

His vest had been incinerated off his back in the explosion, but he was otherwise unharmed. It would take more than a mystic blast and being buried under an apartment block to stop the God of War. In the time he had spent buried, the sword slash he had taken across the chest and his bloody lip had already healed.

It was his pride that still suffered.

The sounds of his rage and his shame rebounded back to him,

redoubled, from the Gothically vigilant tower buildings that bordered the devastated apartment.

"*Get away, did he?*"

Venom was crouching on a heap of masonry wreckage, what the gangrel beast appeared to assume was a safe distance away, almost invisible in the darkness except for where flickering blue lights caught his shiny, extraterrestrial skin at exactly the right angle. There was no way of knowing how long he had been there.

But Venom was not a patient creature.

"For now," said Ares. "Did you witness any mortals fleeing this place?"

"*Some.*" Venom licked his lips. "*But no guys with swords. He's probably buried here with everyone else.*" He gave a growling sigh. "*Such a waste.*"

"He is alive."

Ares knew it. If the man had survived Ares, then he had survived this.

"What of the objective?" he said.

"*Bullseye took the woman's computer and set fire to the building, which seemed to make him very happy. He and Daken are taking it back now. Vicki ordered us all back to Avengers Tower without making too much of a scene…*" The alien monster looked over the wreckage, silver eyes unblinking, enormously amused, it seemed, by the hundred-foot diameter wasteland centered on Ares' ground zero. "*So there's that.*"

"Ms Hand is an accountant," said Ares, treating the word with the disgust it was due. "She is a politician." The deputy director reminded him somewhat of Zeus, his father. Such awesome power in her hands, such craven unwillingness to see it used. "Nor do I desire or need Osborn's approval." Powdered rock and concrete ran from his shoulders like grains of sand as he heaved himself up out of the rubble and onto his feet. His axe came free next, gray dust drizzling from its enormous blade. Venom wisely withdrew himself to an even safer distance. “He has no hold over me.”

His grip on his weapon grew tighter until it shook.

He commended his foe on his trickery, but he swore then that he would *break* that man over his knee and see his sword bent to his will or sundered outright by his hand. And if it cost him the Earth, and Olympus, and the esteem of men and gods, to do it then he would still not let that stop him.

He had been made to look like a fool.

And honor demanded retribution.

CHAPTER EIGHT
Small Boys in Capes

Karla's usual routine, after going up against something as powerful as the Sentry, was to drink three bottles of wine, take a hot shower, and then fall into bed. She was barely halfway into bottle number two when her door buzzed and she opened it to find Victoria Hand, an armed escort of H.A.M.M.E.R. agents in purple combat armor, and orders to an emergency debrief to which she was technically already late. She threw the deputy director a weary salute, downing as much of the bottle as she could before Victoria was able to pull it out of her hand. With just a little exertion of her moonstone powers, she changed out of the comfortable dressing gown and slippers that she'd retired in and into the ridiculously revealing outfit that Carol Danvers had left for her as Ms Marvel.

Thanks, Danvers, she thought, as Deputy Hand and her soldiers frog-marched her to the nearest elevator. *Positive female role model, my ass.*

The Avengers briefing room was in the upper stories of the main building, not far from where Dr Sofen kept her "office". Large windows, numerous flatscreens, and suspended holographics lent the space an airy feel, and a lightness that was not at all welcome at that time of the morning or on sleep-sore eyes. After Bullseye's gag with the Cyclops footage, the screensavers on the large monitors had been password-protected, the consoles reduced to sleekly reflective surfaces, the holo-projectors casting out unseparated mists of dewy white light. Inside that ring of black screens and ghost projections, like a space bug under a H.A.M.M.E.R. exobiology team's lens, was an oval-shaped table.

Touchscreen interfaces had been incorporated into the metallic edge trim, but most of the table's smarter features had been locked on account of the fact that most of its current users were, developmentally at least, small boys in capes.

Everyone else was already here.

Going clockwise around the table from the entrance, the first person sitting there was Venom. The symbiote skin had peeled back from Gargan's head to look like a run-of-the-mill black spider-suit, revealing a gaunt, hangdog face with strung-out eyes and massively dilated pupils. Bullseye was sitting beside him, slouched back in his chair with drooping eyelids but with a smug grin on his face as though he had just killed somebody's grandmother. He reeked of smoke. Karla wasn't sure why, but, by the severe frown on Victoria's face as the deputy director entered behind her and caught his eye, she had a feeling she was about to find out.

The size of the active Avenger roster increased or decreased regularly as new members joined and others died, got kicked out, or left. *Noh-Varr, you poor sap*. Only an alien, she thought, dropped in clueless from deepest, darkest Hala, could have lived alongside this group for months before realizing that maybe, just maybe, they weren't quite the heroes that Norman Osborn had sold them as.

There were sixteen chairs around the briefing table currently, and with plenty of wasted air between Bullseye and the next hero along.

Daken was looking improbably well groomed and sleek, as always, eased into his chair's cushioned back with one ankle crossed over the opposite thigh and a tiny, steaming cup of espresso coffee on the table beside him. Moving swiftly on, because considering Daken was like spending time staring into the eyes of an inexplicably beautiful snake, the next around was Ares. He was wearing a black crew-necked T-shirt that appeared to have been picked up at a gas station where the clothing lines just didn't go beyond XXL. The cotton stretched towards transparency over the Olympian's enormously muscled arms and chest.

Around from the God of War, coming back towards Karla, was the Sentry.

He spoke to no one, looked at no one, existing inside his own shimmering halo as though the last few hours had not occurred, or had occurred to someone else. Which might actually have been somewhere close to the truth. He gave Karla a nervous smile as she and her escort approached the table, while she ignored him as coolly as she could after one and a half bottles of white wine, and took the seat beside Bullseye.

He leered at her from behind his Hawkeye mask.

There was a reason that she couldn't remember the last time she'd seen seven am from this angle: there was some seriously *Through the Looking Glass* energy going on right here.

While Karla got herself seated and her H.A.M.M.E.R. escort took up discreet positions around the room, Victoria circled the table distributing plastic folders. No one who got one bothered to look at it. The closest anyone came was Daken, whose empty smile wavered just for a moment as the deputy director walked by and knocked his espresso. But then, Victoria was the only one here who had ever bought into Norman's "hardcore team for hardcore problems" and "for the greater good of the American people" spiel.

It would be sweet if it wasn't so sad. She didn't even have the excuse of being from outer space.

"I'd prefer a breakfast," said Karla, as her folder slapped the table beside her.

"The caterers start at eight fifteen," Victoria replied, without missing a step.

"We're in the middle of Manhattan." Karla pointed at the Sentry. "And he can fly at the speed of light. He could be back here with bagels before Norman even gets here."

Bullseye idly raised a hand. "I'll take a bagel." Beside him, Venom looked positively ill, and Bullseye turned his raised hand to pat him companionably on the back. "It was that second security guy, Mac. Always stop at one. Especially on top of pizza."

Venom slumped over the table with his face in his hands and groaned.

"That's enough," said Victoria, coming to the end of her circuit and pausing to draw a strand of red-dyed hair behind her glasses. "None of this is funny. The director is ready to see heads roll. I'm sure you all know why."

"Actually, I don't," said Karla.

"We're here," said Daken, with an aesthete's weary sigh, "because Lester screwed up."

Bullseye leant angrily over the table, stabbing an accusing

finger towards Daken. "It was ET here who tripped the alarm, and I don't particularly remember anyone telling me that that building had such heavy-duty security." He turned towards Ares. "I don't seem to recall wrecking an apartment block and killing the power to half of the East Side either. Good work, by the way. I heard you killed a house with a car."

Ares didn't answer.

He looked like Vesuvius, just before it exploded.

Daken smiled at Karla. "I've got your fifty, by the way."

Victoria crossed her arms and looked from one to the other. "Are you telling me that the two of you placed *a bet* on whether or not Hawkeye would fail in neutralizing what Director Osborn has classified as a critical national security threat?"

"Of course not," said Karla. "That would be unprofessional and absurd. Not to mention unpatriotic."

Daken stifled a laugh.

"We bet on *how long* it would take him to fail."

"And it wasn't just the two of us." Sipping casually on his espresso, Daken gestured with his head towards the agents guarding the briefing room. "They look so innocent, don't they, in those helmets? But they have names and everything, you know."

Before Victoria could go any further into that, Karla asked, "So, what is this national security thing I'm only hearing about now?"

"*Ask Lester,*" Venom drawled, lifting his face from his hands. "*He's the only one who saw what was on the computer.*"

The look on Bullseye's visible face was pure innocence. "And you think I'd look? After I gave Normie my solemn word?" He waved a hand dismissively. "But I suppose I might have glanced across something. Purely by accident, of course. Maybe if you'd just let me use the USB rather than showing off, I wouldn't have had to."

"Speak," Mount Ares grumbled. "I, too, would know what this night's work was for."

Bullseye shrugged, as though thinking about it. Daken, Gargan, perhaps even Karla, too, if it had been her, might have been tempted to sit on whatever classified material they'd recovered to use later for their own purposes. But Bullseye was just the kind of performative egotist who'd happily fritter away a hypothetical future advantage for five minutes as the center of attention now. He was, to put it mildly, a showoff. "It was just some security footage from Avengers Tower."

"What was on it?" Karla asked.

Another shrug from Bullseye. "There must've been thousands of hours. I have a life."

"All this action for, what, a day or two of video?" said Daken.

"There is a lot of heedless talk that passes in this building," said Ares.

Daken grinned, set down his espresso cup, and leant towards the Olympian. "Go on, Ares. Quote Pathé. I can tell you want to."

The God of War ground his teeth, pointedly avoiding looking at their Wolverine, and went on. "We have many enemies. None are mighty enough to challenge us, but we are exposed, we have a public face and a known position. We can be undermined or embarrassed, and there is much that is discussed here that we might consider trivial but which Hydra, or Fury's loyalists, or even the X-Men would find valuable."

"If you're talking about blackmail, just say blackmail," said Daken.

"I am talking about blackmail," said Ares.

"Blackmail on whom?" said Daken.

"Who wants it back so bad?" said Bullseye.

"*Osborn,*" Venom hissed, his forehead still resting on the table.

"Hundred bucks says it's a sex tape," said Karla.

Bullseye cackled.

Victoria, who had been following the conversation with the stunned expression of a substitute teacher for a remedial class, suddenly blanched. "This is wildly inappropriate speculation."

"Well, I find Norman's hair wildly inappropriate," said Bullseye. "Let the *Bulletin* print that. Oh yeah, someone burnt their offices down." He crossed his arms behind his head and reclined his chair back. "You're welcome."

"Is a little professionalism too much to ask for, Hawkeye?" said Victoria.

"Says the woman who still hasn't produced my bagel."

"I'm the second highest ranking military officer in the world. I'm not the maid."

"Speaking of things which aren't here..." Daken made a theatrical check of the time on his phone's display. "It's seven fifteen. Norman does know that being fashionably late has always been a joke, right?"

Victoria turned from Bullseye, her face shifting hue from frustration to exasperation. "God dammit, Wolverine. You'd actually interrupt a lecture on data security by showing off an unsecured personal device? How many times have you been reminded that you can't bring a phone in here?"

"I don't want to be a pedant, but I think what you mean to say is *may not*. Cannot expresses inability. May not implies the absence of permission."

Victoria's hand went straight for the concealed-carry holster in her suit jacket. For a woman in her position, Karla imagined, it paid to skip the handful of steps between polite first warning and deadly force. "Set the device on the table, face down, and slide it towards me."

Daken stared at her for an uncomfortable span of time, his smile fixed on his face.

He set the phone down on the table.

He slid it towards Victoria Hand.

Karla silently applauded Daken's restraint. Not murdering the deputy director and her entourage out of hand counted as real progress on his part.

Victoria leant forward to pick up the phone, but before she was able to, the metal bunker-style doors behind her irised open. She turned to look over her shoulder.

Norman Osborn, the Iron Patriot, strode in.

His armor gleamed in the standby lights from the projectors: red, white, and blue in lustrous silvery tones. The color scheme had been scientifically designed and rigorously focus-grouped to suppress the pre-frontal cortex and promote uncritical adoration and, to the surprise of absolutely no one in possession of a psychology textbook, it worked.

The world loved Norman Osborn.

Or, at least, the parts of it that mattered did.

The helmet was retracted into the gorget, presenting Osborn's head like a five-carat diamond on a platinum band. His skin was the peculiar perma-brown of the mid-Atlantic hyper-rich set, his expression one of engraved contempt.

His eyes, though, were what separated him from the billionaire crowd. They were like windows of strengthened glass, the kind of window that Karla knew well, the kind where the person on the other side could scream and rave and beat on the glass until their hands bled and never be heard by the honest, hard-working, mentally sound citizens of the world outside. His face gave no outward sign of it, but Karla wondered if she really could be the only one who saw the madman howling on the other side of the glass.

Nickel-titanium boots clumping on the hard floor, Norman walked up to the briefing table. The H.A.M.M.E.R. agents stiffened to attention and Victoria, pocketing Daken's phone, threw a sharp salute.

Karla decided that, yes, sadly, she was the only one who saw it.

"Director Osborn, sir," said Victoria.

"Thank you for herding these cats for me, Victoria," he said, his voice gruff like a smoker's, although Karla had never seen him indulge in that particular bad habit. Addressing the table from its head, he turned to his Avengers, arms spread like a crag-faced patriarch welcoming his fractious brood to his home. "Like you, I've been up all night. Drafting a statement laying out H.A.M.M.E.R.'s position on the Middle East situation, amongst other things." He smiled at them, his whole face softening, and gave a laugh that could have been made for late night TV news. "Now, I love free publicity as much as anyone. You all know that. So, I'm sure everyone here can imagine how *thrilled* I was at being able to shelve that draft and instead sit back, like every other person on this wretched planet, and watch the Avengers trash my city live on CNN. I've just come off the phone with the president. The president, ladies and gentlemen. You'll excuse me for being late, but would you believe he had a lot to say? I've not even been taking Mayor Jameson's calls."

Venom gave a limp snarl at the mention of New York's mayor.

"My only regret is that those same viewers won't get the chance to see the footage that Victoria seized from Harlem International Security about an hour ago." Here, Osborn laughed again, bright enough for the cameras, but warm as a March morning at one thousand feet, and leant over the table. The near-field communication in his gauntlets woke the touchscreen controls which, in turn, activated the holo-projectors. An image ghosted into life above the table. At first it looked like nothing, a darkfield with occasional ropes of silver running through it, but then Karla noticed the ripple of peristalsis and grimaced. She was looking at Venom from the inside, as captured by a security guard's body-cam. "Is there something you want to say, Spider-Man? Before I carry on?"

Venom gave his head a vigorous shake.

"Because I'm the one who pulled you out of that padded cell in the Raft and put you on my team in the first place," Norman went on. "I feel a great sense of personal responsibility for your medical wellbeing."

"I'm all right, sir. These pills you've got me on really help. I hardly want to eat anyone at all."

"That's good, Mac. I'm pleased to hear that. It sounds as though only a slight tweak in dosage is needed."

Norman gestured for a pair of H.A.M.M.E.R. agents, who closed in on Venom's chair from behind. Gargan sensed their approach before they were within six feet of him and began to turn, but not before the two agents had tasered him in the back. The Oscorp weapons were far from the standard non-lethal police issue, and Venom's raw scream made Karla wince as he slumped face forward onto the tabletop.

He was already unconscious, electricity crawling up his spine. Steam curled off his back.

"Take him to the basement lab and tell Doctor Fiennes to triple the dose." Two more agents approached the stunned hero as the original duo holstered their weapons. Bullseye shifted his lean body in his chair to make room as the four men between them hauled Venom out of his seat and dragged him towards the door. "And be sure he wakes up in no doubt about getting any more second chances."

Karla found herself reminded again of her session with the Sentry.

Norman didn't care about his star Avenger's mental stability any more than he did about the volatile cocktail of experimental drugs he was pumping into Mac Gargan. To him, they were all just interchangeable villains in heroes' masks. Knowing Osborn as she did, he probably already had a new Spider-Man in mind, in case Gargan needed to be cut loose at short notice. Norman was a compulsive list-maker. It was a common coping mechanism in patients who struggled to settle on decisions or control their thoughts. Karla had taught the technique in her own practice. Before she had started killing off her patients. Somewhere in Osborn's office, there would be lists of Wolverines, of Hawkeyes, and of Ms Marvels. Karla was not without a little vanity, and wasn't incurious as to who Osborn had in line to replace her if she failed him. She hoped they'd be names that would do her justice.

Not that she intended to give Norman the excuse, of course.

She'd become rather fond of New York.

And, to her surprise, she'd found that she rather liked being treated like a hero as well.

The only two Avengers who were, arguably, protected from summary replacement were the two whose identities he did not effectively own.

But if Ares, or even the Sentry himself, thought that Norman would not find a way, then they vastly underestimated his ruthlessness.

Why else did he have Karla digging into the Sentry's life?

"You need to stop doom scrolling this whole Middle East thing," said Lester. "It's making you cranky."

"Don't even get me started on you, Hawkeye," said Osborn.

"I did what you pay me to do," Bullseye snarled back. "What I've always done for you. I got your job done. Maybe if you were as good at getting the right intelligence as I am at killing people then we'd have gone in better prepared for the level of security. And for whatever that *thing* was that had Mac over the ropes before I got there."

Daken coughed.

Bullseye brazened out the correction and said nothing.

Contrary to what either of them might protest, they both still wanted to impress the boss in their own way. They knew who signed their checks. And who had the power to see them in chains, in straightjackets, or in a hole in the Mojave, if he was not duly impressed.

Victoria cleared her throat. "If you would care to look inside your folders, you'll see the information we have been able to pull together on this Black Raazer."

Karla drew her folder towards her.

It was a crisp, glossy black with the H.A.M.M.E.R. logo offset to the corner and TOP SECRET emblazoned across the cover. She sighed at the pretentiousness, *of course it's top secret,* unlooped the string-tie, and emptied out its contents.

There was a lot.

For all the latter-day failings that had led to its dissolution and replacement, S.H.I.E.L.D. had always been consistently good at keeping records. There were intelligence dossiers. Transcripts from mission debriefs. Incident reports from altercations between S.H.I.E.L.D. forces and suspected terrorist actors across the Middle East and North America. A few came with surveillance images captured by spy drone or satellite, or even body-cam stills similar to the one that had so viscerally rendered Venom's duodenum. Most had almost nothing to show, a hint of an outline, a humanoid swirl, but had been included in the file out of typical S.H.I.E.L.D. completeness. A few were clear enough to make her shudder. There was a potency of evil that had survived the capture to film, and even the subsequent scanning of old physical files to digital storage. It reminded her of those few precious photos that existed of the Sentry. The same effect, but opposite. And if that wasn't an unnerving thought then she did not know what was.

She wondered what issue he had with H.A.M.M.E.R. A guy like that should probably *be* one of Osborn's Avengers.

"His real name is Razer," said Victoria.

"Inventive pseudonym," said Daken.

"At least he's got one," Bullseye countered.

"Daken isn't my real name. It means something in Japanese, you moron."

"Raazer was a sorcerer from ancient Persia," Victoria continued, firmly ignoring them both, glaring at Karla and Sentry over her glasses. "His exact age isn't on file, but my predecessors presumed him to be immortal."

Bullseye leant back to address Osborn. "You've been holding out on us. When do we get a sorcerer?"

"Master magicians aren't as easy to come by as assassins," Osborn replied.

The sneer fell from Bullseye's face as the implied threat sank in.

"I didn't get to see him fight for myself, but from what he did to Venom..." Daken paused himself before nodding graciously towards Victoria. "Excuse me. *Spider-Man.* He is rather high-powered. How is it I've never heard of him before now?"

"We don't know," said Victoria. "Whatever his personal agenda, he doesn't seem to take much of an interest in world events. The last report of him in the file is from the first Gulf War. He was part of an Iraqi super hero team called Desert Sword. Nothing major since. At least, not on S.H.I.E.L.D.'s radar."

Karla prodded at her files to spread them out. "Then what's brought him out of his hermitage now? We were talking before about Hydra, the X-Men. And sure. Yeah. I see why they'd want whatever we've got for no better reason than it's ours. But what's on this stolen footage that's any interest at all to a guy who's not shown his face to the world in, what, twenty years?"

Osborn didn't answer.

Ares, too, had his files spread out on the table in front of him. He was hunched over the documents, lips moving soundlessly, a blunted, bloody fingernail tracing the text from English to Arabic to something that looked similar to Arabic but different, Farsi maybe, and back to English. "The sorcerer is Persian," he grunted.

"Keep up, big man," said Daken.

"The swordsman I fought was also Persian. Or Persian-trained. I recognized a form of varzesh-e pahlavani in his fighting style. It, too, is ancient, uncommon in this country, but still widely practiced in that region."

"All right, I'll bite," said Bullseye. "Where's Persia?"

Daken stifled a smirk. "Could you be any more American?"

"Yeah, I always forget that you're half…" Bullseye wafted his hand airily as he trailed off.

Daken leant forward dangerously. His claws quietly unsheathed from his wrist and he leant them lightly on the table. "Half what?"

"You know…" Bullseye flashed a grin. "Canadian."

"Enough of this baiting," Osborn snapped. "This isn't a locker room, or a frat house. Persia was an ancient empire. More or less where Iran is today."

"Is that enough for us to assume that Raazer's colleague is an Iranian national?" Victoria asked Ares.

"No. But it is likely he hails from somewhere within the reaches of their old empire, or was perhaps trained by Iranian forces."

Bullseye tutted. "Does this country even have borders? This is why I voted for the other guy."

"Thank you, Ares." Victoria jotted something down with a stylus on an electronic pad. "This could be useful. Anything to narrow down the algorithms."

"You are certain then that he was not slain in his attempt to destroy me?" said Ares.

"H.A.M.M.E.R. has taken full control of the search and rescue operation on national security grounds," said Osborn. "They've found no one matching your description yet. We are working under the assumption that he somehow survived and has evaded capture."

"Probably the same way that Raazer got himself and the guards out of the building," said Daken.

"Might these soldiers also be in league with the Persians?" said Ares.

"We looked into it, but it doesn't seem so," said Victoria. "They're just a top-end local private military company that a nervous Symkarian billionaire hired on behalf of his building to protect his investment."

Ares nodded. "Both combatants appeared keen on preventing civilian casualties when we fought."

"Until knocking out a city block to put you down and escape," Karla pointed out.

"Yes," said Ares. "Until then. Though I do not believe it was the means he would have chosen."

"Fortunately for everyone, most of the building's residents had already fled to their underground shelters," said Victoria.

"Well," said Bullseye, lounging back into his chair. He cracked his knuckles. "At least we got the computer."

Osborn snarled and thumped the table.

Karla startled at his loss of self-control. Even the Sentry appeared to notice. Servomechanisms whirred as Osborn withdrew his fist from the table. The polish was only slightly scuffed.

The Hulk had sat at that table.

"I tell myself that I deliberately hired imbeciles. I can't now remember why, but it's the only explanation that makes sense to me. Yes, you got the computer. But not the original file. Or the group that stole it from the backup servers in the first place. They're still out there. Who knows how many copies of the footage they've made, or where they intend to distribute it next? So far, the Black Raazer and Ares' swordsman are our only two leads. Somehow, they knew where this footage would be at the same time I did. Perhaps even before. I need to know how."

"H.A.M.M.E.R. is working on it as a priority, sir," said Victoria. "As are the NSA, CIA, and their sister agencies across the Five Eyes alliance. We still have witnesses to interview, satellite data to look at, and forensics to complete on the two sites and on the journalist's computer. If these two show up anywhere on Earth, then we'll know about it."

"And what about the reporter woman?" said Bullseye. "Where's she?"

"Rikers," said Osborn. "Fortunately for us, there are still a few principled journalists working in this country. She called my office for a quote rather than simply running the piece. I had my media department invite her in for an interview and detained her. I'll let her out in a week or two, once this business is locked down. Believe it or not there are still a few Americans out there who believe the First Amendment applies to journalists and some of them even sit on the Supreme Court. Those sorts of people might balk at the indefinite detention of a New York reporter alongside super-power terrorists and war criminals. But we've had telepaths working her over for the last few hours and we're confident in her story that she received the footage on a CD through the mail."

"Does this have anything to do with the protests against you and H.A.M.M.E.R. in the Middle East?" said Karla.

"You follow the news. I'm actually impressed."

Karla shrugged. It wasn't hard to look like class president when this was her class.

"Raazer did seem to have something against you personally, Norman," said Daken, appearing to take some relish from that fact. "I can't personally imagine why, but it takes all sorts."

"As of right now the Iranian lead is pure coincidence. But the timing is a PR disaster. We need a very visible win right now, and the president agrees." Osborn manipulated the touchscreen controls and the glistening footage of Venom's digestive tract disappeared, replaced by a large 2D map of the United States with a digital pin at the foot of Lake Michigan. "Fortunately for us, a pro-Utopia mutant rights group is planning to march on Chicago city hall at noon to protest the expulsion of mutants from American soil. We're going to be there to make sure it doesn't stay peaceful."

Karla, Daken, and Bullseye all groaned.

"We've been working all night," said Bullseye.

"Plus, you know, it's Chicago," said Karla. "I'd rather be sent back to Thunderbolt Mountain."

"Would this be a good thing for us to do, do you think?" asked the Sentry, his voice faint, but drawing attention to it like a new star in an empty sky. "Is this the work of heroes?"

"Yes, Bob," said Osborn, handling the Sentry with a gentleness he did not always demonstrate towards the other members of his team. "This would be a very good thing for us to do."

The Sentry looked relieved. "That's good. I... I was worried."

"Looking strong on the mutant issue always plays well with the American people, so that's what we'll all be doing while Deputy Hand and the full intelligence machinery of our great nation find our missing fugitives." Osborn looked pointedly at Victoria. "I expect you to have something for me by the time I get back."

Victoria saluted. "Count on it, sir."

"I don't see why we can't just send in the Sentry," Bullseye complained. "He can sort out the mutant problem in Chicago and the rest of us can finally get our bagels."

"We don't nuke our own citizens, Hawkeye."

"Even Chicago?" Karla asked, innocently.

Osborn smiled.

This was the real Norman. The man the TV cameras never got to see.

"Not as a first resort, Ms Marvel." He turned back to Bullseye. "Though I applaud your commitment to confronting this global menace head on."

"Well, you can count me out of it," said Bullseye. "I'm not going."

"Oh, you're going."

Bullseye gestured towards the H.A.M.M.E.R. agents stationed around the room. "Even the goon squad gets two days off a week."

He leant towards Norman. His voice lowered. "What if my aim should slip, Normie? What if I were to accidentally shoot a police commissioner or the mayor or something? You know, someone important. What then? How d'you think that'd *look*?"

Osborn pinched the bridge of his nose and closed his eyes.

His voice, when it came, was low and dangerous.

"Fine. You can share a bench with Gargan on this one. If that's really where you want to be." His eyes opened, his demeanor once again quietly under control. "The rest of you I want suited up and with me on the Quinjet in thirty minutes. That includes you this time, Ms Marvel. And you, Sentry."

He smiled beneficently, as though there wasn't a resentful bone in his body.

"Let's show the people their tax dollars at work."

CHAPTER NINE
The One Man

The Sentry's boots touched lightly down on the Avengers' roof. There was a crunch of concrete, golden veins spreading out through the grain and glowing. The wind off the Atlantic blustered through his cloak and made a halo from his hair. The perfect likeness of a hero. He felt the wind as a physical sensation against his face, but the cold could not touch him, nor the uncertain threat of the thousand-foot drop at his back. The sun was still rising through the outstretched fingers of New York, gleaming off steel and glass and shimmering over his costume. He felt it go through him.

He did not feel the cold, and so he had no need for warmth either.

Fifty yards behind him, the lip of the roof projected an angled carrier-style runway over Manhattan. The sleek profile of a Quinjet sat ready for take-off, jets howling as it was made ready for flight. Ignoring the awed stares of ground crew in high-vis jackets and ear-mufflers, the Sentry walked past them. He had time.

The Watchtower erupted from the utilitarian concrete of Stark Tower like a tooth that had turned rotten in the gum. It reminded him variously of the crown of an alien queen, a dead bird, a benevolent spider, a shadow closing around the sun. The Sentry did not remember creating it, but he knew that he had: he had been told that he had done so, and something about that knowledge felt right. The golden orb pincered in its highest turrets throbbed like a pulsar. For the briefest of moments, while its ambience was at its fullest, the Sentry felt himself centered. As if a torch had been shone on his psyche and, for the split-second that the light was on him, like the answer to a quantum riddle, had found one complete person and a coherent set of memories inside. But the sense was fleeting, and worse for having been there at all once it was past.

Norman had promised to help, and he had done so much for him already. Moonstone, too. Far more than Tony Stark, who had made similar promises for years and delivered only half as much. And if the director could do no more than reverse what Colonel Fury had done to destroy every link back to his past, then it would be more than the Sentry could repay.

Given the opportunity again, the Sentry would probably kill Nicholas Fury.

There would be nothing that anybody could do to stop him.

The thought pleased him.

He wondered if that made him a bad person.

He would ask Lindy about it when he saw her. And maybe Karla, too, since Norman had asked him to be frank with her.

It would be a long flight to Chicago, crawling along at the Quinjet's top speed.

As he approached the base of the Watchtower, where the semi-sentient liquescent metal interfaced with the structure and internal wiring of the Avengers building, the doors to the turbovator opened for him.

CLOC floated out on silent anti-gravity motors to greet him. It was a golden metallic sphere bristling with dendritic cabling, and with a large red iris in one hemisphere. Its name was an acronym for Centrally Located Organic Computer.

<<*Welcome home, Sentry.*>> Its synthesized voice called to mind the text-to-speech software of another era, but then CLOC was very old. How old, the Sentry was not sure. He remembered most of those years, but there were gaps, and not all the memories were properly arranged in his head. <<*I understand you are flying to Chicago today. Would you like me to find the latest weather forecast for northern Illinois?*>>

"No thank you, CLOC."

Without waiting for a reply, he stepped into the turbovator. The doors hissed shut to still his fluttering cape and, like a car in a mag-lev, he was launched upwards.

The walls of the turbovator were harder than steel and completely transparent. Avengers Tower was already above all but the highest buildings in New York, and even their rooftops crawled away as he sped upwards, the horizon retreating around the radius of the Earth in miles as he rapidly gained altitude in feet.

Knowing where he wanted to go, as somehow the Watchtower always knew, the doors opened onto his quarters.

He stepped into a studio apartment.

There was a bed, unmade, an old-fashioned cathode-ray TV set playing commercials. Food cartons littered the arms of an upholstered couch that sagged with old age and neglect. The Watchtower could fashion anything from nothing. Like the Sentry, *exactly* like the Sentry, its powers were unknowable and limitless. Why Lindy chose then to live in what was effectively a recreation of their old apartment in Queens and eat junk out of cardboard containers baffled him. Sometimes, he got the impression that she had been happier caring for a mentally ill drug addict than she was as the wife of Earth's mightiest Avenger. That made no sense to him, but he needed so little by way of food or comfort himself that he indulged her wishes. The curtains lazed, half-drawn. The apartment faced away from the dawn. For late nights and slow mornings.

The Sentry radiated the gloom with his presence, but for a few persistent shadows at the corners of his perception.

"Lindy?"

There was no reply.

He looked around the empty room.

There were memories here, even if they were not all properly stored in his mind. He had been the world's favorite hero. Its most terrible monster. An alcoholic. An addict. A bum. He had tried to kill his wife in this room. He'd become an Avenger. Thrown it all away. Until Norman had offered him his hand.

Robert Reynolds suffered from an illness. He was sick, just like Norman Osborn had been, and illnesses could be treated.

Lindy would help him through it as they had helped each other through everything else. They loved each other. That was what mattered. Everything his gaze touched vibrated with her presence.

"I know you are here, Lindy. I can feel your aura."

He watched, listening.

Still, the old room gave no answers.

His eyes flashed with a sudden anger, the room growing perversely blacker as the corner shadows took root and blossomed there, nourished by the light.

"WHY ARE YOU HIDING FROM ME?"

The curtains stirred under the force of his shout, and he felt an immediate, overwhelming guilt at having lost his temper.

"Sorry, Lindy. I'm sorry. That wasn't me, it was…" He trailed off. "I'm sorry."

He noticed the frumpish way in which the curtains settled, but something kept him from simply walking over and pulling them aside.

A half-light returned to the room as his own gloom deepened.

He lingered in two minds by the turbovator.

"Norman is taking me on a mission. We are going to help some people." He watched the curtain hopefully, but his wife did not emerge. "I will be back tomorrow. We can…" He trailed off again, trying to think back to what they had done together, before the Sentry and the Void had become all that he could remember. "We can… eat, or… or something."

Again, he waited.

Again, nothing.

Crestfallen and confused, he returned to the turbovator. Only as its doors closed on his old life did he remember that there had been an important question he had wanted to ask Lindy about the rightness of killing his enemies.

Never mind.

There was always Norman and Karla.

They would help.

As the turbovator returned him to the roof, CLOC having mysteriously vanished as it was wont to do when unneeded, the Sentry felt better.

A new man.

The perfect likeness of a hero.

He was a good person: Norman Osborn told him so.

•••

At a spoken command, the helmet unfurled from the Iron Patriot armor and closed over Norman Osborn's head. The nickel-titanium alloy sealed out the fierce wind and the howl of the Quinjet, its pilot cycling up the lift jets for launch, and replaced it with a head-up display.

"Get me Deputy Director Hand," he told his armor.

Victoria's head and shoulders appeared in a subscreen in the upper left corner of his HUD. She was in some kind of control room, surrounded by technicians operating computers, brusquely cutting off an agent mid-sentence to take Norman's call.

"Director Osborn, sir. Have a pleasant flight."

"Thank you, Ms Hand, I'm sure I will. I want you to lock the building down while I'm out of town. I don't want to hear about any more breaches when I get back."

"Yes, sir."

"And I meant what I said in the debrief. I'll be back in a few hours and the first thing I'm going to ask for is a progress report. I'm going to want to see some progress in that report."

"We're chasing down some leads now, sir."

"Good. And open the Patriot List for me. I want a replacement Spider-Man located and ready to go, just in case Gargan continues to resist treatment."

"And Hawkeye?"

Osborn chuckled. "No. A little insubordination is already factored into his asking price. He's as good as they come for what I need, but keep his status under review."

"Count on it, sir."

He cut the call without a signoff, just as the Quinjet engines howled, blasting smoke and heat against the Iron Patriot's expressionless visor, and propelled the aircraft off the side of the building and into the sky. The Quinjet was capable of vertical take-off and landing, but it was less fuel-consumptive to use the runway. Another Norman Osborn improvement to the flash-bang-whiz Tony Stark way of doing things. Stark had had some reasonable ideas, Osborn didn't deny, some minor practical successes. But he lacked Osborn's creative genius. The Iron Patriot, assembled from seized parts and partial schematics was, to any reasonable view, a far superior iteration of the #25 design that Osborn had been left with.

The helmet's HUD filtered out the smoke and particulates, returning a clear isometric view almost before his eyes had noticed the impediment at all. Brackets fluoresced over Moonstone and the Sentry, their cloaks tearing around them in the Quinjet's jet wash. Osborn had not yet worked out how to prevent the armor's systems from tagging Karla as hostile. It would be there in the menu options somewhere, he was sure, but he had not quite got around to finding it yet.

"Ready to go?"

Moonstone scowled. "I'd be feeling more ready if I were riding on the plane with Daken and Ares and the in-flight breakfast. I'm *literally* freezing my butt off up here."

Osborn laughed as a blast from his boot repulsors hurled him into the sky, short controlling bursts from the attitude jets in his gauntlets stabilizing his flight path as he rocketed after the Quinjet. The tags in his HUD showed Moonstone and Sentry matching his course and speed and sliding into a three-pronged arrowhead formation with the Iron Patriot coasting ahead of the Quinjet and the two Avengers flanking.

"Seeing a problem and acting is a fine thing, Ms Marvel," he said, his armor projecting his voice over the scream of Mach 2.1. "We are more in the *being seen to be acting* business."

•••

The CANSA F-IX was a deltawing stealth transport with muffled VTOL jets and reactive camouflage paneling rendering it effectively invisible to ground-based detection. It was the workhorse of Hydra's commando legions, capable of inserting a small squad of elite agents quickly and covertly into the most heavily defended installations.

This one was stolen.

Its current commander had named it *Leviatano*.

The operative, codenamed Val, hung onto the ceiling handgrip, monitoring the thermal registers and flight telemetry as they spiked across the cockpit's gel-based forward screen. The Quinjet was boosting out, Iron Patriot and his Avengers flying as escort. Decrypting the Quinjet's communications would have taken decades, but the radio intercepts from the ground control stations that bristled the rooftop told her that the entire Avengers team, with the anticipated exception of Venom, of course, were outbound for Great Lakes Naval Station in Chicago.

So far, so good.

"Put us down," she instructed her pilot.

"Putting us down," he answered, his voice muffled by an oxygen mask and helmet.

The *Leviatano* broke out of its holding pattern and descended vertically towards the short runway on the roof of Avengers Tower that the Quinjet had left vacant.

Take-off and landing were two of the most energy-intensive maneuvers an aircraft would perform. There was a brief window of opportunity in which the energy and noise from the take-off of the much larger Quinjet would obscure the CANSA's approach.

The best camouflage technology in the world could only do so much.

Keeping a hold of the ceiling grip, Val turned towards the small aircraft's passenger compartment. Nineteen soldiers clung one-handed to their own grip holds. Their midnight-purple body armor was complete with H.A.M.M.E.R. patches and insignia looted from the Mogadishu base during the riots. They carried hybrid assault rifles on shoulder straps, bulky but powerful weapons capable of single-shot as well as semi- and fully automatic fire, and of toggling between physical hard rounds, directed energy blasts, and electrical tranquilizer rounds. Oscorp at its best. The armor was heavily padded, although its principal purpose was intimidation rather than wearer protection. It would slow a low-caliber bullet or stop a knife, and the refractive nanolayer bonded to the exterior weave might sap enough power from an energy attack for the wearer to squeeze off one last shot. Val was under no illusions about the survivability it would confer against the Iron Patriot or Ms Marvel. Never mind the Sentry.

Val pulled her own helmet on over her head with a *twist-lock* action and a hiss of magnetizing seals.

The rear doors opened with the CANSA still six feet off the runway. The ground crew reacted with astonishment to the hatch filled with armed soldiers opening up in thin air above them.

Val watched through the green-tinted, flash-proof lenses of her helmet, responding to their amazement with a well-placed tranq-bolt to the neck of the ranking crewman. The man flopped to the ground with a hundred thousand volts dancing through his peripheral nervous system. The rest of her team picked off the remainder of the crew, leaping out of the aircraft as they fired. Val exited last, just as *Leviatano* itself crunched onto its landing gear, her operatives already setting about pillaging the unconscious bodies of the ground crew for access cards and IDs. The stolen war gear would pass cursory inspection, but to get inside the building would require proper and current codes, and to penetrate as far as they hoped would require additional passes, all of which would need to be obtained en route.

She turned her head, forewarned by a gut premonition and a shiver down her back, as the uncertain profile of the Black Raazer appeared out of the imperfect blur of *Leviatano*'s camouflage.

Glowing red eyes, buried in a dark hood, took in the bodies on the runway. "Hashim and Sirocco are so determined to avoid deaths. I tell them it is unavoidable. Men must die if the regime we despise is to fall. I agreed to follow you because you do not share their squeamishness. You could be…" Raazer had no face that Val had ever seen, but she could hear the sneer in his words, "the One Man."

"That time has not come yet."

"But it will."

"It will," Val agreed. After the destruction on East 53rd the night before, unplanned but not entirely unwelcomed when weighed against the greater good, it had arguably come already. Another reason that Hashim was not here for this. He would need a few days to cool off after the unexpectedly heavy casualty count that his battle with Ares had brought. "For now, stay with the plane and wait on my signal."

"I can get you inside."

"Save your strength. Six hours ago, you fought Spider-Man and Wolverine and won. Remember why I brought you and not the others."

The shade bowed his head and hissed, "Lest the Sentry return."

"Are you still certain you can nullify him?"

"I have been anticipating the challenge since first you summoned me."

Val hoped that the sorcerer would be forced to wait a little longer yet. His presence was for insurance purposes only, or she would have stood him down along with Hashim after his earlier, excellent work. Val could have dropped the material she had on Osborn onto YouTube and had a billion views and a congressional hearing by now. By handing it to a genuine news outlet instead, giving Osborn advance notice of what was out there, she had forced his hand.

Her own agents, meanwhile, and the security firm whose services she had obtained through a Symkarian alias, had ensured a very public and bloody disaster. Norman Osborn was no Nick Fury. He was not a spy. He was a businessman. A showman in armor. Fury had never cared whether or not the world hated him, and large parts of it always had, but Osborn craved its validation and loathed that it would not give it. He would want to retaliate immediately, and publicly. He would want to parade his mightiest heroes on the evening news until no one was talking about New York anymore.

But Val, like Fury, was a spy.

She took nothing for granted.

Raazer, as much as her soul cried in his presence, stayed.

She turned away, the ancient sorcerer already fading into the hazy profile of the camouflaged plane, and moved towards the door that would take them off the roof.

One of her operatives had already swiped the electronic lock with a keycard lifted from the jacket lanyard of one of the ground crew. The door opened. A guard stepped out to challenge their passphrases. Confronted by an agent in a H.A.M.M.E.R. uniform, he hesitated, for the crucial half-second before experiencing a hundred thousand volts and unconsciousness.

The operative stepped over him, followed by the rest of the insertion squad and finally by Val herself.

Inside, they divided their stolen IDs between them and split into teams.

Osborn had proven remarkably resilient to popular outrages over his abuse of power. If he was to be brought down, then it would have to come from the men who had raised him so high in the first place. It would have to come from above.

And if Osborn's political paymasters had enjoyed the morning's debacle, then they were going to love what was coming next.

CHAPTER TEN
Always a Disappointment

Mac Gargan had learned that it was better not to struggle. He'd been strapped down in Dr Fiennes' chair too many times since Osborn had pulled him out of the Raft with warm words and giant promises.

The chair looked like an open coffin, burnished gunmetal and heavy rivets, bristling with cables, diagnostic equipment, and restraints. It was an iron maiden, which someone with more curiosity than morals – and Gargan knew a few of those – had removed the lid from so that they could better watch what happened to the person inside. Dr Judith Fiennes, Osborn's head of research, would always smile as she strapped him in. The chair was made of the same metamaterial that the Kree built their warships out of. The Sentry and Ares working together, she had once wistfully explained, wouldn't have been able to break free if she were ever to get one of them in her chair.

The thick leather restraints around his ankles, thighs, wrists, chest, and neck were presumably for his doctors' peace of mind. Physical restraint, on its own, would do almost nothing to hold down Venom.

That was done, however, by the powerful sound system that had been rigged up directly over the chair.

The symbiote was resistant to almost all forms of physical damage, but it was vulnerable to heat and it could be hurt by sound. Whenever the symbiote so much as twitched, waves of ultra-low-frequency sound blasted from the speaker systems to force it back down his throat into its lair in the pit of his stomach. The experience was a hideously painful one. It was like throwing up acid, only backwards.

A masked and lab-coated research assistant approached the chair.

Gargan shivered, naked, in the cold chair. The symbiote was always warm. He never felt warm anymore without it.

The student produced a syringe and Gargan jerked against his restraints as the symbiote attempted to lunge out from his mouth. A punishing sonic blast drove the symbiote back down. The deep bass note ran through his body, vibrating the soft parts pressed up against his bones as though an invisible force was crushing him to death against the chair. Worse even than the sensation of his organs getting mushed inside of him was the presence of Venom, in all its mad, violently frustrated hunger, being pushed into an ever smaller, ever more malignant ball in the center of his belly.

Mac Gargan had learned that it was better not to struggle.

But Venom never learned.

Gargan ground his teeth, closed his eyes, and whimpered as the symbiote gave up the fight for another minute. The supervising researcher shut down the sonic restraint. Gargan's body relaxed in pain. A single tear trickled down his cheek.

Kill Norman Osborn, the symbiote slurred in his mind.

"There's nothing to be afraid of," the senior scientist told his student. He was a Black man with an East Coast accent, and a face that was otherwise anonymous for the facemask, hair net, Perspex goggles, and high-buckled lab coat that covered it. Like every boss that Gargan had ever had, he said this from the back door while his student dealt with the big bad alien super villain in the torture chair. "He can't hurt you."

Can't I?

Venom attempted another lunge only to be driven down by another pummeling of sound.

The scientist chuckled. "See?"

Gargan was glad that Dr Fiennes herself rarely administered his treatment in person anymore.

She made Lester look like a bunny rabbit.

Gargan had vague recollections of being a private detective before he'd thrown it all away to become the Scorpion. He kind of remembered how to find skeletons. After a few sessions under the proverbial knife, he'd decided to do his due diligence on Dr Fiennes.

From what little there was that existed, he'd figured out that she'd been a mid-ranking scientist who'd defected to A.I.M. during Fury's tenure. Osborn's directorship, a thorough re-writing of S.H.I.E.L.D.'s ethical code, and an unlimited faucet of DARPA cash had, apparently, tempted her back over to the good guys. Osborn had put her in charge of Venom's treatment program, as well as something called "Project Sentry", and held her under even closer surveillance than his Avengers.

Venom couldn't have ripped off her head and eaten it if he'd wanted to. That was probably why Gargan seldom saw her these days. She was a busy woman. But every so often, in his worst dreams, he'd come around from a tasering, strapped down in the chair, to see Judith Fiennes snapping on latex gloves and smiling.

The student warily circled around the chair, checking the IV lines and consulting the blinking machines hooked up to Gargan's vitals.

He briefly considered screaming. But he'd learned that it was better not to do that either.

It was hardly the sort of ward that H.A.M.M.E.R. agents popped into unannounced to pick up an aspirin. Not unless they'd been deeply negligent in the forms they'd signed.

Remind you of any sucker you know?

This was a room built specially for him.

That was the kind of personal touch that made Osborn so awful to work for. He went that extra mile. There was one chair. One restraint system, tailored exactly to Venom's dual physiology. Hardware and control systems for the sonic emitters filled the chrome-fronted cabinets on the walls. There was no other equipment. Only a large freezer and a few boxes of latex gloves on a bench by the security door. Gargan wondered if Daken had a room like this one, if Osborn had a specially made dungeon for Moonstone or Ares. Probably not.

Gargan was special.

He bit down on a scream as the symbiote attempted to sneak a tentacle through his gut wall and crush the student's windpipe like a plastic bag, resulting in both of them being flattened into the chair under a blast of sound.

The scientist at the back of the room read off a checklist that he had on a clipboard. "Serum 8-B, check?"

"8-B," the student read off the side of the plastic vial he was carrying. "Yeah." He proceeded to tap the air bubble to the head of the syringe and squirted it out. Gargan sobbed helplessly, the symbiote raging in silence from someplace behind his eyes, while the student slotted the syringe into the IV cannula.

His thumb hovered over the plunger.

The scientist looked up from his checklist. "What are you waiting for?"

"He's… he's crying."

A smile creased the older guy's face around his protective gear. "Yeah."

"But it's *Venom*."

"It's always a disappointment, son. Go on and put it in him."

Gargan tensed himself for the real pain.

The security door buzzed, a red light blinking from the intercom. The research assistant looked up, taking his thumb off the plunger and leaving the syringe to dangle from its nest of plastic lines.

Gargan breathed out in relief.

The scientist, who was already by the door, turned to the panel and consulted with a scratchy voice on the other side of the intercom. It was impossible to read his expression behind his mask and goggles, but whatever was said finished with him punching a lengthy code into the panel and the door opening.

A pair of H.A.M.M.E.R. agents walked in.

They had their helmets on, visors engaged, assault rifles in their arms. One of the agents, an officer from the collar pins and shoulder insignia, conferred with the lead scientist while the other bustled his confused-looking student from the lab. Before leaving, he took the syringe from the cannula and put it on the side. He shut the door behind them.

Gargan wondered if this was going to be it.

Had Osborn finally decided to just put him down?

Unable to stop it, Venom made one last-ditch spasm at ripping out of his restraints before howling back into its lair.

They're not here to kill us.

Osborn's doctors were just as capable of administering a lethal injection as a H.A.M.M.E.R. firing squad was of delivering a kill shot. And if Osborn really was going to give that order, then he'd want to keep it neat. Why kill a man in a hail of bullets when you could do it with an IV drip and a signature on a form?

And it would take a lot of bullets to finish off Mac Gargan.

"Are you the one I spoke to?" the scientist asked the remaining agent. "Was it you who told me to be in work today?"

The agent nodded.

"Then the rest of the money…?"

Damn, thought Gargan. That didn't sound promising.

"You will find it in a rucksack on your apartment balcony. Just like the last time." The agent was female, with a honeyed accent that Gargan couldn't place. French, maybe, or Italian. Or Spanish. It was hard to remember that he used to be good at this sort of thing. "Two million dollars waiting for you when you get home. After which I suggest you disappear."

The scientist shuddered as he fished a key from his lab coat pocket and moved to the large chest freezer. It was padlocked. "You don't have to worry about that. I was here under Director Fury. And Director Hill. I should be the one paying *you* to get me out of here." He unlocked the freezer unit, jimmied the frozen lid, and then lifted it up in a wheeze of deep-chilled gas.

Frosted metal storage racks filled the freezer, each one labelled with letters and numbers on flaking magnetic tape coded by color.

"Give me serum 17-G," said the agent.

The scientist paused while pulling a pair of unwieldy insulated gloves over the thin latex pair he was already wearing. "Are you sure?"

"Yes."

"But–"

"Now please, Dr Phillips. You are not the only one with travel plans."

The scientist straightened. "Look. If you'd told me that you were interested in Dr Fiennes' experimental serum, then I'd never–"

The agent held out her hand.

Dr Phillips' sudden attack of duty disappeared like the gas from the freezer.

"You have already taken far too much money to be having second thoughts now, Dr Phillips. Director Osborn is deeply paranoid. All it would take from me is one anonymous phone call…'

She pulled off her helmet.

The woman underneath was olive-skinned and dark-haired, with a stripe of white through her fringe. Gargan felt that he ought to recognize her. Silently, he raged at the symbiote that had brought him all of this, and could not relinquish its psionic grip on him even now to think of anything but how badly he wanted to eat her. There was something noble, regal even, about the way her lip curled as she studied him. The look in her eye would have cowed popes. Dr Phillips mumbled something that even Venom's alien senses couldn't pick up, and fumbled with the storage racks.

One came up on its rails with a metallic clatter. It was filled with hard plastic boxes. He shook the thick over-glove off his right hand, depositing it to the lab bench, and then pulled out the box labeled 17. Pulling off the other glove with his armpit, he set the box on the benchtop and opened it.

He withdrew a frozen syringe.

The contents were still liquid, a custardy yellow color.

Ripping the sterile wrap from the needle, he shuffled towards Gargan's chair, too nervous by now to observe the proper procedures before jabbing the needle into Gargan's cannula IV and squirting it in.

Gargan grimaced, tensed.

It would take a moment for the injection to displace the saline in the tubes and reach his veins. An air embolism was pretty low on his list of worries right then, too.

As Dr Phillips shuffled away, the woman leant over him, cupping his head in her hand, and looked into his eyes. She was close enough for him to taste her breath. For once, Venom was sufficiently subdued to not try to bite her face right off. Lowering her lips to his ear, the serum already halfway to the end of the tube, she used what was left of this moment to explain to him exactly what was about to happen to him.

And why.

Kill Norman Osborn, the symbiote screamed, before serum 17-G hit Gargan's arm, and then they screamed together, nothing crossing the psionic connections between them but pain.

CHAPTER ELEVEN
Better Safe Than Sorry

Bullseye leant back in the boss' big leather-upholstered chair with his feet up on the briefing table. A large soda balanced precariously on the armrest, ice cubes clunking against one another like tiny icebergs as he fidgeted about in the seat. The blinds over the massive windows were down. The flicker-glow of the vast flatscreen TV at the far end of the table illuminated the darkened room like an old-fashioned theatre. Bullseye's lips moved silently to the images on the screen. TV was his guilty pleasure, but he preferred to watch it with the sound turned down. Screenwriters were lame in general, and Bullseye's own invented dialogue was better.

Picking up an ice cube with the suction of his straw, he aimed his improvised pea shooter lazily down the table, and then blew.

The ice cube flew eighteen feet and struck the up-channel control on the TV remote before skitting off along the table and onto the floor.

Bullseye, he thought, with a bored smile, as the channel flicked seamlessly over to C-SPAN.

They were covering the Chicago riots.

Rolling footage showed demonstrators in jeans and T-shirts, teenagers mostly, fleeing through the streets. Look close enough over the heads of the terrified crowds, and you could just about make out the white plume of Ares' helmet. The God of War had blocked the protestors' route to the courthouse with an upturned school bus. He was standing on it. It appeared to be on fire. Bullseye dunked his straw back into the soda and took a slurp. Damn, but he had a sudden craving for nachos. In another shot, Moonstone defended the steps of the Harold Washington Library from being stormed by mutant protestors. Or violently blocked a few hundred frantic kids from getting off a street that had Ares in it. Depending on your point of view. In a split-screen, Norman spoke soundlessly to camera. The banner text said, "Iron Patriot condemns mutant terror." The Sentry was behind him, looking heroic as only the Sentry could, blue cloak fluttering out like Old Glory, while his golden aura, as if by happy accident rather than cynical calculation, lent a bright, early morning halo to Norman's star-spangled armor.

"What a jerk," he muttered.

Someone behind him noisily cleared their throat.

Bullseye leant back in his chair, far enough to make the tilting hinges creak, and looked back, upside down, over the headrest.

Two stockily built H.A.M.M.E.R. agents in full body armor and helmets, bulky assault rifles held crossed over their chests, stood guard at the door. Supposedly, they were there for his protection, but in reality they were there to stop Bullseye wandering off and getting into trouble. None of them – except Ares perhaps, Bullseye wasn't sure what his deal was – were exactly free agents these days. It was Avengers Tower, Thunderbolt Mountain, or the Raft, and, given the options, being the hero really wasn't so bad. To Norman's credit, he had to know that two minimum-wage goons weren't going to keep Bullseye from doing whatever Bullseye wanted to do. That was why there were ten more in the corridor and an electronic bracelet around his ankle.

Like almost everything Norman did, it was for show, and Bullseye played along.

It was either that or admit to himself that he wasn't ever going to try to escape. He wasn't scared, not really, not even of the Sentry, but there was nowhere on Earth he could go where Norman couldn't get to him and he knew it.

"Don't worry about hurting his feelings," he said, turning slightly to smile towards the camera that Norman had broadcasting a continuous live feed to his office computer, and throwing it a wave. "He *is* a jerk." Straightening his chair again, he sucked up another ice cube and launched it towards the remote control.

The channel flicked back.

Bullseye fidgeted into his chair back and sighed at the TV.

"Oh, Ross. When are you gonna grow a sack and stab that girl in the eye?"

Bullseye wasn't against a little hard work. It depended on the work. He could watch Ares do his thing all week. But Bullseye wasn't one for rules of engagement and policing protests. If Norman wasn't even going to let him kill any of them, or do it with proper style, then he might as well have kept the real Hawkeye on his payroll.

He stirred the straw around his cup, then raised the half-empty soda up over his head.

"I'm out of ice over here."

"So?" said one of the guards, his thick, black-eye purple body armor making him unwisely brave.

"So, my soda's gonna get warm."

From the corridor outside, through the briefing room's mammoth security doors, he heard what sounded like the *ping* of the elevator. New guards coming on shift. It was probably too much to hope that the burgers he'd ordered out on Norman's tab hadn't been intercepted at the front desk. He laughed to himself at the thought of Norman discovering the unexpected $39.95 spend on his credit card bill come the end of the month.

Slowly, like a leaky tap, the laughter dried up.

God, he needed a life.

The boredom must have shown on his face, because the two visored guards turned to one another and shared a look.

Inside the building, above a certain level, the secret identity of Osborn's Avengers was the most open of open secrets. Victoria was the only member of Norman's inner circle who diligently referred to everyone by their codenames and even remotely tried to keep it all under wraps. Norman himself, Bullseye sometimes thought, didn't seem to care less. As if he was teasing the world with the truth, wanting them to know it, and daring them to care. If Clint Barton ever stepped out of line with the help, then a S.H.I.E.L.D. agent would've happily told him to get lost. But nobody was going to try that with Bullseye. Not if they didn't want to be carrying pieces of themselves home in a cardboard box when they clocked off.

"I'll go to the machine," said the one on the right.

He lowered his rifle, holding it one-handed while he swiped his ID card. The access control went *bleep*, and shunted out a keypad for him to punch in a code. He did. The door irised open, and then ground shut behind him as he stepped through.

The guard on the left backed right up to the wall and raised his gun, aiming at the back of Bullseye's chair.

Bullseye could almost close his eyes and be right back in Thunderbolt Mountain.

Happy days.

From the corridor outside, he heard an electrical *snap,* like a shorting fuse, and then a thump that sounded like nothing but a heavily armored body hitting the floor.

Leftie swung his aim towards the door and backed towards the briefing table. "Ted?" he called out. "Ted?"

Bullseye crossed his arms behind the back of his head and leant back, returning his attention to the TV and chewing on his cardboard straw like a hick on a corn stem.

Ted? Seriously?

There was another *bleep* sound and the doors started to iris open again, shuddering along as though reluctant about going through the rigmarole all over again so soon. In the reflection in the TV's corner trim, Bullseye watched as a quartet of H.A.M.M.E.R. agents entered the briefing room, leading with their assault rifles as though responding to a disturbance and dispatched to secure the room.

Leftie lowered his gun.

"What's–" he managed to open with, before one of the newcomers tranqed him.

The guard dropped his rifle with a clatter, grunting behind his visor as arcs of electricity crawled over his ceramic breastplate, easing him through a jerk and a spasm towards the floor. A second agent prodded him with his toe. He didn't move.

"Find the cameras," ordered a third. "Re-route the live feeds, and–" He stopped as Bullseye swiveled around in his chair. "H-Hawkeye. Sir." The others all pulled up short. One of them made a shaky salute as though he wasn't sure whether he was meant to or not. They looked tense, inasmuch as you could through that much armor. But Bullseye always knew when someone was sweating. "We didn't … we weren't expecting …"

Bullseye raised his eyebrow, biting down on his straw to tilt the far end upwards.

"We were just …" the agent began, then yanked up his weapon. "Ahh, dammit."

Four military-grade assault rifles swung towards Bullseye, who grinned.

Finally.

Some entertainment.

He spat out the straw, propelling it towards the leader's throat with perfect aim, and with just the right amount of directed force to punch through the flexible under-armor between helmet and gorget and go straight through his esophagus and trachea. The agent folded to the ground, choking, pawing at the innocuous little cardboard pipe sticking out of his neck.

At the exact same time, the other three opened fire.

Kicking off with one foot, he spun the chair around.

The armored frame, hidden beneath the plush upholstery and expensive memory foam padding, took the brunt of the kinetic impacts, while embedded energy dampeners, essentially high-tech shock-absorbers, soaked up and flared off the electrical charge.

Bullseye's grin widened, his cheeks aching with the charge radiating off Norman's chair. The director was a paranoid fool, and Bullseye loved him for it.

With the agents still unloading tranquilizer bolts into the back of the chair, Bullseye was already pushing out of the seat and rolling across the table. Three quarters of the way down, he scooped up the TV remote and, in one smooth motion, flipped it over and slapped it into his open palm. Four AA batteries popped out. He fanned them between his fingers, like a stage magician performing a card trick, and launched them back across the room.

There were two *thunks*, barely audible over the electrical hail of gunfire, two cries, and two agents crumpled with AA-sized eye-holes in their visors.

One left.

The remaining agent swore, operating a ratchet mechanism down the side of his gun stock to switch from tranquilizer to solid shot, and then toggling to fully automatic.

Bullseye brandished the remote control. "Oh, you'd better believe I wanna play."

The agent screamed as he backed away towards the still-open door, hosing Bullseye and everything within a yard to either side. Bullseye laughed as gunfire ricocheted off the briefing table and chewed up the chairs, batting bullets out of the air with the remote control until the agent was out the door and fleeing down the corridor.

He lifted the mangled nub of plastic and frowned back towards the TV, disappointed, but not entirely surprised, that nobody in the show had been bloodily murdered yet.

Man, TV sucked.

With a heavy sigh, he tossed the useless remote aside and went back to his seat. It was entirely unscathed, albeit a little warm from the amount of electrical charge it had taken in. Reaching under the seat, he unpacked his compound bow from its carry-case, the work of a moment when he put his mind to it, and wrapped his fingers around the Oscorp logo on the grip. Bow in hand, he marched out into the corridor.

A dozen H.A.M.M.E.R. agents lay stunned in the hallway. A couple more were crouched by the open door of the elevator, seemingly taking the pulse of one of them.

It was possible, likely even, that the insurgent agent had already escaped by the service stairs, perhaps even heading up rather than the more obvious down for an aerial extraction from the roof.

He stuck his tongue between his front teeth and sucked in a breath.

What was it that Victoria had been harping on about just that morning?

Oh yeah.

He nocked an armor-piercing arrow to his bowstring from the automatic quiver on the riser and took aim at the furthest of the still-conscious figures.

Better safe than sorry.

CHAPTER TWELVE
The Irritating Thing About Plans

Val and her colleague rode the elevator upward from the medical research wards to the roof. It was a total journey of about three minutes, provided that nobody called for the elevator on the way. Her weapon rested with its muzzle against the floor, her helmet hanging from a toothed clasp on her hip. Putting it back on would have meant trapping the rancid offal stench of Venom against her face, and she was already resigned to the necessity of showering for a month. Her fellow agent, codenamed Corm, a mountain of gently rattling armor in their rising car, shifted restlessly from foot to foot. His trigger finger played anxiously, his armor making a *tack-tack-tack* sound around the inside rim of his weapon's trigger guard.

"Stop it." Her voice was breezy and casual, but with authority bred into both syllables. "You are going to make me nervous."

The agent mumbled an apology, let a big breath out, and took a firmer grip on his rifle.

Val went back to watching their upward progress on the control panel, listening to the reports through her earpiece as they came in.

Red, Blue, and Green teams all reported successful infiltration. All were safely back aboard the *Leviatano* and waiting on the others' return.

As she listened in on the chatter, watching the indicator lights blink on the elevator control panel one by one, she tapped a finger against the armor panels of her breastplate. Underneath the plate was a necklace. It had been a gift to a great-aunt from Il Duce. No one in what was left of her family ever spoke much about that. One of the diamonds in the pendant chain was removable, which had always suggested to Val that she was not the first spy in her family and had redeemed her great-aunt somewhat in her esteem. In its place was a micro-USB that had spent fifteen productive minutes plugged into Victoria Hand's laptop while the deputy director had been occupied coordinating the manhunt for Hashim and Val and Corm had paid their visit to "Spider-Man".

It was all about this.

Everything else was about waving enough false flags to keep the Osborn bull from stopping long enough to realize it.

After a while, she frowned.

"What is it?" Corm asked.

"Yellow team," said Val. "They have not checked in."

"The briefing room?"

She turned her head aside, covering her ear with her hand to catch what was being said more clearly. Her frown deepened.

"Sir?"

"Hawkeye is here."

"Here in the building?"

"And on the rampage. Yellow team is down."

Val had learned through various former S.H.I.E.L.D. colleagues and government contacts that the Avengers were not who they were pretending to be. Spider-Man's true identity had come to her by chance, leaked by an asset in the medical staff, but the rest of the team remained unknowns. She could only assume that they were as bad or worse than Venom.

"The Avengers are supposed to be out of state."

Val swore in florid Russian. She was fluent in two dozen languages, and did not think of any one of them as being her *first*, but Russian had always been her default preference for swearing. She looked up at the car's ceiling. The elevator was thirty to forty seconds from the roof and the safety of the *Leviatano*. With Hawkeye running amok, it was only a matter of time, and perhaps less time than the thirty to forty seconds that she needed, before someone picked up a telephone and had the building locked down.

She thought fast.

There was a decision to make, and all of her options were bad.

Reaching out, she punched the button for the nearest floor.

The brushed aluminum doors slid quietly open onto the seventy-eighth floor.

Agent Corm turned his visored face towards her.

"That is the irritating thing about plans." She brought her rifle to her shoulder, off-hand to the foregrip, eye lowered to the scope, and moved ahead of him. "The other side always has their own. We take the long way from here."

Sweeping out of the elevator, she emerged onto a vast open-plan gallery, a glass-enclosed piazza of potted trees and stucco fountains, dappled light falling in through angled panes forty feet high. The central reservation was bordered by ten or more stories of balconies, mezzanines, and executive office windows, promenades crisscrossing through the sculpted bowers of the trees. It was interior design elevated to the form of arch political statement. It was grandiose, majestic… and entirely pointless.

If architecture could be read like the words in a newspaper obituary, then it would have said, "Tony Stark" in bold italics. It surprised her that Norman Osborn had not yet turned it into something utilitarian and functional and was unexpectedly glad that he had not.

There was more than a little of the grandiose, majestic, and pointless in Val, too.

Lifting her aim, she swept it across the garden walkways and balconies. There were only about a billion potential angles to cover.

It slowly dawned on her that she had made a mistake.

A whimper echoed through the vaulting hall.

She lowered her rifle, Corm cutting in behind her to cover the upper levels.

Val cursed again. It was eleven am. Coffee break for those keeping office hours. She had not spotted them all before because they were trying so hard to be quiet and still, but now she was looking in the right places she saw them. Hundreds of desk agents and backroom staff cowered under food carts and picnic tables. A handful of H.A.M.M.E.R. security agents, riddled with arrows, were strewn over the piazza or thrown over tables. Another bobbed face-down in a fountain. One, not far from the elevator, had been pinned to a tree and slumped forward over the arrow piercing his heart.

"Hawkeye," Corm murmured.

He was nervous again now.

Val didn't blame him. She had made a *really* terrible mistake.

She was ready to order him back and take their chances with the next forty seconds in the elevator when Corm said something that sounded like "*Hrrk*". Turning, she found him trying to tilt his head and roll his eyes towards the arrow sticking out of his neck. He slumped into the wall, trailing a blood smear as he slid down it to the floor.

Val whirled, instinctively tracking the arrow's trajectory, and bringing her rifle's scope back into line with her eye. The archer appeared in her sights. He was crouched behind a mezzanine railing in the partial cover of an overflowing plant pot, his bow drawn, every detail crisp under the enhanced magnification of her scope.

The winged half-mask that obscured the top half of his face made no effort at hiding the sneer on his lips, nor the pitiless pleasure in his eyes.

His lips made words.

Val read them through her sights.

"Hello, beautiful."

As Bullseye's father used to tell him, before he'd broken both his legs and burned him alive, he was psychotic, but he wasn't stupid. He'd known that if there were more insurgents at large in the building that they could have made it anywhere by now. He couldn't be everywhere at once, and even he couldn't just go room by room killing everyone, but he *did* know his building, and he knew how to game his chances. He'd known, for example, that the seventy-seventh to eighty-ninth floors were a shooting gallery. He could've picked any one and had a veritable buffet of available targets.

His father would've been so proud of him right now.

If not for the leg-breaking and the burning.

Obviously.

Loosing his arrow, he sent it deliberately into the wall next to the woman's eye, forcing her to duck back and spray her own return fire wide. Medium-gauge bullets rattled off the safety rail, turning the hanging basket beside him into a soggy explosion of ceramic pieces and soil, while Bullseye cackled, vaulting over the rail and into a swan dive. He dropped three stories, snapping through sculpted branches, somersaulting twice and hitting the ground in a shower of leaves and a roll. Office drones screamed as they scattered from the tables they'd been cowering under. His roll carried him back to his feet. The woman struggled with her gun for a moment, still processing the abrupt shift in their positions. With a grin, Bullseye threw away his bow. It was a straitjacket. He'd always hated it. He wanted to smell this woman's hair as he slit her throat.

He wanted to get… creative.

Breaking into a sprint, Bullseye took the staircase from the floor of the seventy-seventh up to the elevator on the seventy-eighth. The woman was already charging down to meet him, swinging her rifle stock like a club.

Bullseye blocked it on his archery guard, then threw a jab towards her face. Her trailing elbow whipped up to meet his ulna bone, and turned his fist over her shoulder. She pivoted like a gymnast, lifted her back leg, and slammed a heel kick into his sternum. He wheezed out a laugh as he stumbled back down the stairs, thankful for the armor, as she spun again, a roundhouse kick delivered towards the side of his head. He bent athletically and let it pass across his chest. She followed up with the rifle stock. He turned his body side-on towards it, narrowing her target, slid his arm down the inside of the stock and pushed it wide, just as she squeezed the trigger down.

The noise of the magazine unloading into the floor was immense, point-blank fire kicking up shrapnel from the parquet tiles like a bored kid at the beach. The woman let go of the rifle and threw a knife-hand punch at Bullseye's throat. He blocked it on his forearm. Their arms tangled. She drove a knee into his groin. He braced his shin against her leg. She snarled at him across the X of their locked arms. Her face was white with dust, just about obscuring the white stripe that ran through her black hair.

Bullseye hissed through gritted teeth, "I'm gonna ask Norman if I can keep you."

"I've known little boys like you. Always waiting on Daddy's permission."

He bared his teeth in sudden rage, followed almost immediately thereafter by a strangled yelp as she pulled him into a Judo breakfall. The woman landed on the smooth tiles, using the impact shock to weaken his grip and throw him over her shoulder, sending him into a far more painful and inelegant sprawl over the stairs.

The agent stood over him, chest heaving, covering him with a Beretta M9 sidearm in a steady two-handed grip.

"Did anyone ever tell you that you fight like a g–"

The nine-millimeter bullet smacked into his forehead before he had the chance to finish. The back of his head snapped back into the step it was pressed against while the rest of his body jerked in shock. His arms flailed over the stairs.

And then he lay still.

The woman gasped and dropped the pistol to her side.

Bullseye coughed, unable to contain his laughter any longer. He relished the mortified disbelief on the woman's face as he lifted his head off the stairs and flicked the little bit of blood from his eyebrow. "Adamantium skeleton," he said, drawing a pocket knife from his belt. "How about you?"

CHAPTER THIRTEEN
Dangers and Possibilities

Val put ten rounds in Hawkeye's chest before making the decision to run, pushing through the panicked crowds of H.A.M.M.E.R. civilian staff. Turning as she ran, she squeezed off two short bursts from her Beretta. The shots winged a woman in a gray suit and tie, ripping her jacket sleeve and throwing her into a food-tray dolly, and sent her intended target skidding into the cover of a taco cart. She hissed in frustration as she ejected the magazine and slammed in another. He was hurt, she was certain, moving slower, laughing less. He might have adamantium over his bones but it was flesh and blood that wrapped them, and he healed no faster than any other human.

She could still make it to the roof.

A flight of stairs led up to a promenade-style mezzanine fronted by restaurants. It had a solid banister that effectively obscured it from the view of the floor. She fled towards it, sliding the last few yards along the ground before rolling into the cover of the banister and scrambling to the next floor on hands and knees.

At the top, she sank back against the rail and gave herself a moment to breathe.

She could still make it.

Rising and turning, she glanced over the top of the barrier, only to jerk back down as a plastic fork buried itself in the opaque glass.

Hawkeye's mockery screamed up at her from the crowd.

Val resisted the urge to call in Raazer. It was not the need to enable her own escape that tempted her, but the burning desire to kill *that* guy.

Firing a short, unsighted, burst over the top of the rail, heedless of the screams from below, she kept low and hurried in the direction of the elevator shaft. Her conscience was mainly for cosmetic purposes, an accessory that she held onto to complement the right garment or occasion. She assuaged it with the knowledge that there were no truly innocent bystanders here. She did not relish the collateral harm the way Raazer appeared to, but in their own small and insignificant ways, these people were all complicit in Norman Osborn's reign.

Tucked away behind an upmarket burger restaurant, terrified faces peering out at her from its windows, she found the plain, beige-colored door she had been searching for.

Showing it no mercy, she barged through, ripping the deadbolt from the strike plate and bursting onto a service stairwell.

The Beretta went up. It went down.

The staircase was empty.

Kicking the busted door shut behind her, enough to fool a passing inspection, she sprinted up the stairs. The breath rasped in and out of her mouth. Her thighs burned. Her borrowed armor clattered loudly enough to bring all of H.A.M.M.E.R. down on her head. Breaking into Norman Osborn's house and tangling with his Avengers was never going to be straightforward, but if she had realized that she would run into Hawkeye and be forced to shoot her way out then she would have pulled Hashim out of bed, called in Sirocco and Majid from their business in Africa, and gone in with all her guns blazing. It would have been easy to blame herself for the oversight, but the world was not that neat. It was what she did to rectify it that mattered.

Four flights up and blowing hard, she shouldered through a second door.

The service stairs ran all the way to the eighty-ninth, stopping only one floor below the penthouse levels occupied by senior H.A.M.M.E.R. staffers like Director Osborn and Deputy Hand, and by the living quarters and training facilities of the Avengers. But exiting directly onto the eighty-ninth felt obvious, and she was already exhausted from her fight with Hawkeye and escape. Better to switch stairs here and find another way to the roof.

The doors emerged onto another promenade. The safety barrier tracked a graceful curve, spilling cherry blossom and willow fronds over a steel handrail. The tinkling of fountains echoed from the piazza below, smoothing out the cries of the wounded. The projecting signs of the various store fronts carried the logos of banks. There was a travel agent, a couple of hair salons. Stark Tower was like an international airport or a hospital. A person could live their whole life inside without ever stepping into New York.

Some did.

At the sound of a mechanical hum from the promenade ahead, she pulled into the front portico of a bank, drawing the Beretta to her chest.

It was coming closer. She could hear voices, too, one patiently electronic, the other belonging to a woman and frightened. It sounded as though she was arguing, but in that dispirited way a person might argue with a faded photograph or a gravestone, a foil that never argues back but never concedes a point either.

Val retreated further into the cover of the portico.

It was still possible that she could double back, but she did not know where to, and she was painfully aware of the fact that Hawkeye was still somewhere at large. With a grunt she pushed herself out of the bank's doorway, not having to work nearly as hard as she would have liked to accentuate her exhausted stumble. She lowered her pistol, smearing the glaze of parquet finish and sweat across her face with a rub of her elbow. Neither of the voices coming towards her sounded like Hawkeye, and to anybody else's eyes she would be just another wounded H.A.M.M.E.R. employee fleeing the shoot-out on the seventy-seventh.

A levitating golden orb floated out of the artificial garden ahead of her. It trailed flexible cabling like the stingers of an android jellyfish, a large central eye turning the surrounding foliage and immediate floorspace into a puddle of sickly, devilish red.

<<*There is an active shooter in progress, Mrs Reynolds. I am interfacing with my subsidiaries in the Watchtower and summoning a turbovator to this location.*>>

Tony Stark had once described the paranormal levels of control that the Watchtower managed to exert over the rest of the building. The punchline had been that it was the reason the city had let him have it so cheap.

"A haircut, CLOC," came the other voice. "That's all I wanted. A haircut and a coffee without *him* having to know about it."

<<*I am sorry, Mrs Reynolds. I predict a 92.3 percent likelihood that the building will not be under attack at this time tomorrow.*>>

"Can't you see how he's changed since coming back here?"

<<*I am sorry, Mrs Reynolds, but my programming does not permit me to speculate on Mr Reynolds' psychiatric condition.*>>

"He says he worries for me, CLOC. But it's… frightening. *He's* coming back, I know it. The Void."

<<*Perhaps I could play you some soothing music.*>>

The other speaker came into view behind the robot.

She was a woman, mid to late forties, sandy-haired, in a pink tank top and patterned sweatpants as though on her way to the gym. As though ready to run. Dark rings around her eyes showed through her heavy makeup, telling of sleepless nights and long, anxious days.

Val pulled up short.

The dangers and possibilities introduced by this moment drew up their positions in her mind. She knew this woman. They had never met, but she *knew* her, from a thousand magazine covers and online gossip columns.

It was Lindy Lee-Reynolds.

The Sentry's wife.

"My God," said Lindy, staring at Val. "Are you hurt?"

<<*Please do not approach her, Mrs Reynolds.*>>

"Can't you see she's hurt?"

CLOC buzzed aggressively, tendrils rising like the hackles on a cat and twitching. <<*Facial recognition algorithms return zero matches for this individual amongst listed employees. Furthermore, the Beretta M9 is a non-standard issue sidearm for H.A.M.M.E.R. agents. I calculate a 95.6 percent probability that this individual is an intruder. Please wait while I apprise building security and contact Mr Rey–*>>

Val shot the thing in its central orb before it could finish.

She held the trigger down, bullets sparking off its metal shell until it dropped to the ground with a hollow *clang*, a heap of tentacles draped over its brutalized golden core.

Lindy gasped, hand to mouth, looking down at the mauled machine. Then she did something that Val had not thought a person could still do.

She surprised her.

"I tried to kill CLOC once," Lindy said. "It doesn't stay dead. The Watchtower will send another, and then it'll call for my husband."

"I'm not staying," said Val, already moving around the downed robot and its charge and making for the next staircase.

Not content with having done it once, Lindy went and surprised her again. She grabbed Val's arm as she passed. "Take me with you."

Val could only stare back. "What?"

"Please." She looked Val fully, pleadingly, in the eyes. "Before he comes back."

"Your husband?"

"The Void."

"Who's the Void?"

"Please," Lindy said again.

"You have no idea where I'm going. Or even who I am."

"I don't care. I just… Please." She let go of Val's arm. "I can summon a turbovator. I can get you anywhere in the building that you want to go. Just… take me away from here." She looked as though the effort of not crying was going to break her.

Val was sure she was going to regret this.

"All right," she said, putting her arm around the woman's shoulder and leading her away from the murdered robot. "Call us a turbovator and get us to the roof. And I'll protect you from the Void."

Bullseye pressed down on the seeping gut wound. Red blood and dark bile oozed up between his fingers. He figured that was probably bad. Grimacing through the pain, he peered around behind the thick trunk of a pot-grown willow, watching as the Sentry's girl ran off in the intruder's arms. He'd been giving serious thought to just killing them both, because after the day off he'd had, he was pretty sure he'd earned it, but this was *so* much better.

The Sentry's tragic little princess getting herself voluntarily kidnapped rather than going back to her tower.

It was priceless. Almost as good as cutting her open and hanging her from the balcony for her husband to find, plus he didn't even have to get up.

He couldn't wait to tell everyone.

Sliding the knife back into its hidden pocket, he picked himself up and limped towards the nearest elevator.

He was, after all, in a quite extraordinary amount of pain.

But he was happy.

The turbovator doors slid open, spilling Lindy and Val onto the roof. The wind whipped at them, as though the Watchtower had activated one last defense protocol to push them back into the turbovator until CLOC could reassume control and prevent their escape.

The CANSA's engines howled from the landing strip. The pilot had been holding them idle, ready for a quick take-off, but with the last agent now returning, fire blasted from the horizontal VTOL jets.

Three operatives waited at the foot of the ramp with their weapons up, jet wash flickering across the tinted panes of their visors. Two fell back into the aircraft. The third hurried out onto the roof to intercept her, drawing Lindy's other arm over his shoulder without asking questions, and guided them both up the ramp and into the aircraft.

Leaving Lindy in the other agent's care, she banged on the ceiling and yelled to the cockpit. "Hawkeye is on the way and there is every chance that the Sentry is going to be alerted very soon. Get us out of here now."

"Roger that," the pilot called back.

If there was one threat she could have made to encourage haste, it was the threat of the Sentry.

The ramp drew up, even as the aircraft lurched into vertical take-off.

Val grabbed at a ceiling hand-grip to keep from pitching right out the open hatch before the plane stabilized itself and the doors *clanged* shut.

Relieving herself of the breath she had been holding, she turned back inside. Lindy was fetched up in the aisle, sitting back against an empty row of passenger seats. She was panting, close to hyperventilating. Val didn't know if it was stress or just relief. Just in that moment, she allowed herself to feel a little bit in awe of Lindy Lee-Reynolds.

The courage it must take: to break free of a man as powerful as the Sentry.

The Black Raazer stepped out of the shadows that the loss of Yellow team had left above the vacant seating, making Val start and crouch by the woman's side. A desiccated claw-finger reached towards her face, but stopped short of touching it, as though repelled by the human warmth of her skin. The red gleam of his eyes made her think of CLOC, but the sorcerer gave off no light that could reach beyond the boundaries of his hood.

"You have taken *his wife*."

"I know. I need you to cast another spell, to mask her aura as you have the rest of us."

"It is different. We are as shadows to him. There is no spell in creation that will keep him from finding her in the end. And us with her."

Val had first encountered the sorcerer on a mission in the Zagros Mountains. He had been living alone in an abandoned Zoroastrian temple, somewhere along the border between Turkey and Iraq. He had helped her locate the Hydra cell she had been tracking, and, in return, she had failed to file the report that would have allowed her superiors to keep tabs on him. She had known that someone with his skillset and complete lack of soul would be an asset to her one day.

This was the nearest Val had heard him come to real emotion.

Real fear.

Lindy mumbled desperately, grabbing at the sorcerer's robes and getting a handful of moldering finery. As though pity could be wrung from dead men's eyes.

"Please," she kept saying, repeating herself over and over with the power of prayer. "Please, please ..."

"We are not leaving her behind," said Val.

"I thought you were strong. Perhaps you are too emotional to lead this fight."

The CANSA hit turbulence as it boosted out over Long Island Sound and hit the Atlantic, heading east. It buffeted Val against her hand-grip, and she felt her already worn patience fray. "You are two and a half thousand years old and spent the entire twentieth century bound to the Black Sword of Baghdad, so just this once I am going to let that comment slide."

She felt the invisible grin.

Raazer had probably, in another life, been a man who thrived on conflict, in whatever form it took and from whatever source it came. He was on her side, arguably her most powerful ally, but she felt only gladness that he was technically dead.

"I apologize, *khala*. You are our leader. But I am not wrong."

Val shrugged. She was tired. The strain of thinking up words and having her lips make them was becoming more effort than she wanted to spare. "I understand if you cannot do it, Raazer. Even Stephen Strange failed in the end when he tried to trick the Sentry."

Raazer was silent for a long while.

For a two millennia-old wraith, he was a deeply uncomplicated man.

"I did not say I could not do it," Raazer hissed. Turning his vacant hood aside, he lowered his gaze towards the terrified woman on the aisle floor and made a succession of arcane passes above her chest. "I said that it would not hold for long."

CHAPTER FOURTEEN

The Power of One Million Exploding Suns

"Yes, Mr President." Osborn cut out his boot repulsors and slammed home with the full, concrete-splitting force of his displeasure. "No, Mr President." With a dangerous, nuclear hum, the Iron Patriot straightened, killing the palm repulsors, and surveyed the roof through the winking, dancing, mocking brackets of the HUD.

Air accident investigators in ruffling windbreakers were taping off areas, doing their best to work around the gouges that the Sentry had already pulled out of the concrete in his mad search for his wife. Forensic teams in purple Oscorp-branded overcoats drew oil samples from the landing strips, took measurements, dusted the door panels for prints, performed preliminary analyses with portable chromatography sets and field spectrometers and swore in the articulate way that only scientists could whenever another flickering tremor from the Watchtower set their instruments awry.

An entire H.A.M.M.E.R. battalion, complete with armored and anti-aircraft support, watched over the work. A missile tank was parked at the eastern corner. Two men sat at the controls in an elevated cupola, as though in charge of the most aggressively up-modified tractor in the United States. A technical support officer in smart goggles did something complicated with an enormous radar array "borrowed" from H.A.M.M.E.R.'s sister organization, S.W.O.R.D. Intended for monitoring near-Earth space for alien vessels, it probed the Manhattan skyline for a cloaked aircraft.

The words horse, stable door, and bolted, came immediately to Norman's mind.

He closed his eyes with a tired growl.

The caller ID on his HUD glowed through the backs of his eyelids.

The voice of the one man in the world with the power to drag Norman Osborn over the coals gnawed on his ear.

"We're still looking into what happened, Mr President."

It was hard to imagine that his morning had started out so well. The mutant rights march through Chicago had turned violent with only the slenderest of provocations. The Chicago mayor and the Illinois state governor had both gone on live TV to praise the Iron Patriot and his Avengers for the protection of their streets from mutant lawlessness. Only a few of the East Coast networks were still talking about Ares' rampage through Midtown, and the security footage that Bullseye had retrieved from the *Bulletin* had yet to resurface anywhere else. Norman allowed himself the hope that it had, in fact, been the only copy still out there.

It was lunch time on Eastern Standard Time.

His good morning was old news.

With an impatient yawn, he opened his eyes, stretching his mouth and working some of the tension from his face.

Floating in the HUD, next to the communication display, a diary reminder to breathe mindfully for two minutes before breakfast pulsed with Zen-like persistence. He'd muted the note six times already. He muted it again. Almost immediately, the next item on his therapist's list of activities popped up to occupy the vacant space. Write down one positive thing that has happened to you so far today, it read.

He snorted, eye-rolling that one from the HUD outright.

He hated therapy. He preferred the drugs. But regular appointments with a government psychiatrist that wasn't Moonstone had been Victoria Hand's one condition on taking the deputy's job.

"Yes, Mr President, I remember the Barton incident. And the Spider-Man incident. Actually, Mr President, now you mention it I do remember the time that Fury broke into the Tower. I also remember the time that you walked into the Oval Office to find the colonel sitting in your chair with his feet up on the Resolute Desk and drinking your scotch. I don't tell you how to lead the free world, and I'd appreciate it if you didn't tell me how to go about protecting it from criminals like Fury."

A threat detection alarm bleeped in the HUD's upper left corner.

Osborn turned and looked up.

There was a *whoosh* of incoming air, and then an effortlessly controlled impact as a partially transparent Moonstone touched down on the roof beside him, her red cape settling slowly over her shoulders as though still eager to fly.

They had been flying over Indiana, escorting the Quinjet at cruising speed, when the alert from CLOC had come in. Osborn had still been digesting the alert, screaming at Ms Hand for her uncharacteristic negligence in allowing intruders into the Tower and being talked out of having Lester shot, when the Sentry had simply vanished. There had been a twinkling, then a thunderclap, like a hundred sonic booms compressed into a single shock wave that had almost thrown the Quinjet into a spiral, and the Sentry had simply been gone, a golden contrail disappearing over the eastern horizon.

Osborn had read every file on the Sentry that existed, several that technically did not exist at all, and a few that his predecessor had actively sought to bury or destroy.

He knew the Sentry was fast.

It was the *acceleration* that had shocked him.

Osborn had no idea just how fast the #25 armor could go, beyond the theoretical tolerance limits that had been noted in the technical schematics, but he'd pushed it well past Mach 8 and still come nowhere close to keeping up with the Sentry.

The Quinjet was a good half an hour behind. It was probably approaching Pittsburgh about now.

Only Moonstone, in her intangible form, had the speed to match him.

And even then, not quite.

He turned to her. "Satellite and building surveillance captured the Sentry entering the Watchtower. We know he's in there. We can *feel* that he's in there. I need you to find him, tell him we're doing everything humanly possible to find her and get her back, and for the love of all that's good, if he really feels the need to destroy something, try to get him to contain it in the Watchtower."

Moonstone gave a laugh as the shift from intangibility to tangibility rinsed through her, hardening her outline, deepening the colors of her costume and picking out the highlights in her hair. "Anything else you want me to do while I'm at it? You want me to poke Thanos in the eye? Fly around the Baxter Building a few times shouting nerd?"

Norman snarled, the Patriot Armor amplifying the menace of his voice. "Believe it or not, Karla, you're not the only one here who would rather not fight a round with the Sentry. But you are the only adult on my team. I'm not asking you to fight him. I'm ordering you to talk him down. You're his therapist, for God's sake."

With a parting scowl, Moonstone shimmered back to full intangibility and rocketed off on a wide arc towards the roof of the Watchtower.

Norman watched her go. "I'm sorry about that, Mr President. Staff. You know how it is. Thank you for holding..."

"Robert Reynolds is the most powerful being on this Earth," Norman told her.

This had been before. About a month ago.

Before his live TV humbling by Cyclops' X-Men. Before the cabal he'd built to control his neat little world had collapsed under the weight of its own animosity and mistrust. But then, as Moonstone saw it, if your plan was to equitably partition the Earth between the likes of Doom, Loki, and the Hood, your plan had some holes in it. He'd not yet rediscovered his sartorial preference for green, and had welcomed her to his office in a dark purple suit with a silver tie. His hands alternated between fiddling with his gold cufflinks and sipping an expensive-looking brandy from an expensive-looking crystal glass.

He was even smiling.

"Possibly the most powerful being in the entire universe," he went on. "The jury is still out on that one. Why do you think I fought so hard to get another of Stark's leftovers on my team?"

Moonstone shrugged.

Norman took a sip of the brandy, winced as though it had gone bad, and offered up the glass. "Can I get you a glass, Karla?"

"No, thank you, sir. Brandy makes you look old."

Norman laughed indulgently at that. "The Sentry is my nuclear option. He's what keeps the world, the universe, in its place. Because *we* have *him*. But you know the paradox about nuclear weapons, Karla?" He held up his glass and smiled, the knowing smile of the richest, most powerful man who had ever walked the Earth. "They're only doing what you got the damned things for if you never have to use them. The Sentry's doing everything I need from him by sitting on his couch up there in the Watchtower. Do you understand what I'm trying to get at, Karla?"

She shrugged again.

Norman sighed and set down his glass. "Do you know what happened, Karla? The last time the Sentry really let himself loose?" A smile crept across his face. If it was a joke, he didn't deign to share it. "I don't either. Apparently, Reed Richards and Stephen Strange conspired with the Sentry after the event to make sure that we would all forget. But Stark and Fury were concerned enough about what had almost happened to write some of it down, and those files are in my possession now. If I told you it took the combined strength of the Avengers, the Fantastic Four, the Inhumans, the X-Men, an Atlantean legion led by Namor himself, as well as an entire S.H.I.E.L.D. division with Helicarrier backup just to slow him down, what would you say?"

Moonstone whistled. "I'd say… damn, I guess. Really?"

"Really." He picked up his drink again, swirled the brandy against the inside of the glass. "In the end it was one woman who took him down. One woman who was able to get inside his head and rein him in. To run with the nuclear analogy a little further, Karla, my ultimate weapon needs a kill switch. That's what I want you to do for me."

"Why me?"

"Telepaths as powerful as Ms Frost don't advertise in the Yellow Pages. But why you, specifically? Because you're an absolute monster of a human being, a gifted psychiatrist, but one with demonstrably poor morals and no ethics. Bullseye just kills people for a living, Karla. You're what he might have amounted to if he had an IQ of one hundred and sixty-five and bothered to put himself through med school."

"Comparing me to Bullseye? You know how to flatter a woman."

"Remind me never to introduce you to my ex-wives, Karla." He set down the glass and leant across the table. His voice dropped to a hiss. "Get inside his head, Karla. Do what you're best at, and make me my damned kill switch."

Moonstone felt something that was almost close to empathy for one of her patients.

Robert genuinely believed that Norman wanted to help him, but Norman had never cared about helping anyone. He didn't even want the Sentry. Not really. He just wanted a Sentry-shaped stick that he could hold over the world.

And now here she was.

The only adult on Norman's team.

A hero.

Moonstone put the thought aside. A woman didn't get to do the things she'd done and call themselves a hero afterwards. But then what, when you got right into it, was wearing someone else's mask and roleplaying the thing you'd always most despised but cognitive behavioral therapy by another name? Spend all of your time doing good, pretending to *be* good, then what did that make you?

Not a hero. She knew that much.

And yet, here she was.

Maintaining a wary distance between herself and the Watchtower, she flew a wide circle around the tower's grasping limbs, searching its uniformly dark, unreflective windows for any sign of the Sentry. Its dark, herringbone arms spread out as though to draw her towards them whichever way she flew. The Watchtower always made her think of an inkblot drawing. What a person saw in its architecture depended on their own personality. To Moonstone it looked like a hanged man. A burnt tree. An undead giant reaching out with crooked talons to pluck her from the sky.

Moonstone was no hero.

As a trained psychiatrist, she knew when she was being played, and Norman was playing her. She knew that. Cynicism was an armor that weighed nothing at all. But a part of her had felt a thrill of pride when Norman Osborn had called her an adult. As though, for the first time in her life, someone had seen her for exactly what she was and been proud all the same.

"Damn it," she muttered to herself. If she'd been one of her own patients then she would have diagnosed herself with father hunger or paternal transference. And then she'd have kept it to herself to extort a few dozen extra sessions at two hundred dollars an hour. "Damn it."

She could almost feel herself fidgeting under her skin. The discomfort was similar to having just walked through a spider's web in the dark. Was she really so broken that Norman Osborn looked like a desirable father figure to her subconscious? One who'd try to get her killed for a sympathy bump in his poll numbers and then run away with her fiancé, like he had with his own son, Harry? To say nothing of the twins he'd bundled off to France. She didn't even know what was up with that. "Damn it, I need some deep therapy of my own."

The structure of the Watchtower was completely black, spitefully resistant to illumination in spite of the stunted, infant sun that it grasped in its own tenebrous claws. She didn't know what it was made of. She had no idea what would happen if she were to attempt to pass through it whilst intangible.

She wasn't sure she wanted to be the one to find out.

A window would do fine.

Moonstone was no hero.

She swooped over its pincer-like upper limbs and back around.

All the islands of New York were spread out before her. The Atlantic was a dark sheet, tinged with red under the late winter sun. The wind tugged at her cloak, fighting to free her hair from her mask. She began to descend again, diving into the shadow that, at that time of the early afternoon, fell between the north and south towers of the Avengers' building, when a swell of golden light burst through an upper-story window. It threw out broken glass and the semi-solid, semi-organic *something* that comprised the Watchtower and ejected it over the Avengers' rooftop. A terrible, grieving scream made the entire, conjoined superstructure groan in sympathy.

The Watchtower's perpetually burning beacon flickered. Dark veins crept through the orb's golden surface. As though it was about to crack.

"Damn it," she said, again, whipping herself into a delta roll and looping into a climb towards the Watchtower.

She punched through the broken window, arms at full stretch, the frame's jagged edges biting opportunistically at her cape as it ruffled out behind her. Inside, she braked with such suddenness that her cape gusted ahead to swallow her like a parachute.

The Sentry hovered before her in all his radiant terror. Energy boiled off him as light and heat, a bright young sun throwing off its corona in a sudden, once-in-a-generation rage. Moonstone exerted a little more of her power towards restoring her blistering skin. She felt like a sunscreen commercial; the one where the model gets her face lit up under a UV light to expose the hidden damage to her otherwise flawless skin.

She swore that if she came away from this with a melanoma then she would wring Robert's brain so tight that water would come out.

"*WHERE. IS. SHE?*"

The cry of the Sentry was less a shout than the direct manifestation of the voice of God, words with the power to bend physics simply by their being. To create light from the formlessness, and the emptiness. And to raise a vault to separate the waters of the ocean from the waters of Heaven. Moonstone felt the air shiver, as though the molecules around her were excited to obey but had not yet been told what to do or what they were to become. The floor groaned under the gravitational singularity of the Sentry's power.

He was so stupefyingly bright. His presence burnt a halo into her eyes, a black ring of a man that, paradoxically, in spite of his awful brilliance, she could not wholly see at all.

She felt like a moth, sent willingly out by another moth to fling herself at the sun.

"We'll find her," she shouted, both hands raised up against the glare. "All of H.A.M.M.E.R. is looking for her. Every agency in the world is going to be looking for her."

She gasped in pain, as though a hot iron had been drawn from her skin, as the Sentry pulled his gaze from her and cast it instead about the room. Moonstone couldn't tell what manner of space it might have been. The Sentry had turned it upside down. The walls trembled under his refocused attention. As though the ceiling was about to cave in, the Watchtower collapse, and the world explode.

Don't destroy the world, she thought. *Not with me right here.*

"WHY CAN I NOT SENSE HER?" the Sentry screamed, the golden light of pure rage blasting from his eyes, his mouth, his fingertips, like the first ignition stage of a rocket. "I SHOULD BE ABLE TO FEEL HER AURA. BUT THERE IS NOTHING!"

"I don't know," Moonstone shouted back. "I don't know enough about how your power works, but then neither do you. I'm sure there's an explanation. Maybe Norman already has an explanation. So let's just head downstairs now. You and me. We'll let Norman and his people come in here and do what they need to do. They'll find Lindy."

The Sentry threw his head back and howled.

He was Norman Osborn's nuclear deterrent, and he was about to detonate in the silo.

Moonstone was not without some ability of her own when it came to manipulating energy, but even she only sensed the attack coming the split-second before it hit her. She was fast enough herself to see the golden blur of the Sentry coming at her, raised her arm to block it, then cried out in pain as the Sentry somehow went *through* her and hammered his elbow in between her shoulder blades from behind.

She had never been hit that hard in her life.

It was like being punched in the back by an asteroid.

The blow threw her clear across the room, through the wall,

through the next wall, and skidding halfway down a corridor with her own little avalanche of rubble. She groaned, movement spawning pins and needles everywhere that was currently still in contact with her spinal column, and propped herself up on her elbows.

The Sentry stepped through the hole in the wall.

Pain, in the visceral form of light, hit her in the eyes and savaged her forebrain via the optic nerves. She screamed and turned away, burying her face in her armpit.

"Maybe we can't find Lindy because Lindy was never here." The Sentry's voice was noticeably deeper than it had been before. "I remember her!" he screamed back at himself. He clenched his fists and the light spasmed. Veins bulged from his forehead. "After everything that's been done to you, everything you've done to yourself, how can you be sure anymore what you remember?" The Sentry's hands fell out of their fists. He put his face in his hands and screamed through his fingers. "I remember it. I remember meeting her in college. Our first date. I remember proposing to her at my secret spot on the river. We had our wedding reception at Richard's place. I…" His voice trailed off into a gritty sneer. "There is no Lindy and there never was. How could there be? Who would love a weakling and a coward like you? You can't even acknowledge that I'm in here with you, and you're *nothing* without me." The Sentry whirled away from where Moonstone cowered on the floor, throwing a punch at the shadow of something only he could really see, and sending his fist through the wall. "I love her!" He chuckled at himself. "Are you sure?"

To her horror, Moonstone realized that Robert was arguing with himself.

The Sentry was arguing with the Void.

She wasn't sure that the Robert personality had any involvement here.

"Lindy was unhappy," she said, speaking as gently as she could, the way one would approach an unexploded bomb. "She had no friends. Mac and Lester treated her like the butt of a joke. She was a little bit afraid of you, we all are, but she was *real*, Bob. Everything you remember, everything that you just said about your wedding, and college, it happened. And she *did* love you."

"SHE'S LYING TO YOU, SENTRY!"

The Sentry, or perhaps it was the Void, snarled and threw up a blazing hand.

Moonstone rolled onto her back and brought her fists up over her face, just as a blast of golden energy leapt from Robert's fingertips and battered through her defenses with the power of one million exploding suns.

The floor she had been lying on was obliterated, the paranatural material nebulized into a searing plasma.

The Watchtower disappeared.

The world ended.

There was only fire.

When it ended, Moonstone found herself drifting in a pall of superheated gases, her vision bleached, her skin burnt to a black crisp and clad in a few wispy scraps of costume and the smoke of an annihilated building. The cries of Norman's investigators reached for her like the despair of a ghost through the smoke.

She should have been dead.

It had worked. She cursed Norman and his monolithic arrogance, but he'd been right. The Sentry was essentially omnipotent, but his god-like powers teetered over a fragile ego. Stricken by helplessness over his missing wife, distracted by the antipathy between his two dominant personalities, his full might had simply not been there for him to call upon.

It hurt to smile, but she felt she owed herself one.

It had worked. She'd made Norman his kill switch, and she'd used it, too.

Who even needed Emma Frost anyway?

Wincing as she repaired the monstrous damage done to her body, using her powers to weave the cooling plasma and smoke-borne debris into an intact costume, she lowered herself to the broken lip of a ledge, which was all that remained of the corridor she had been lying in.

She sat down by the Sentry.

He looked smaller. At least four inches and a hundred pounds smaller. His long hair had become tawny and knotted. Even the immaculate golden uniform had faded, swelling and rumpling between glances as though it had always been a worn yellow sweater and corduroy pants, hanging loosely off a painfully underweight frame.

He was not the Sentry anymore. Or the Void.

Moonstone was afraid she'd broken him.

"Was Lindy really that unhappy, Karla?" Robert asked her. "I thought… I only wanted…"

And then the most powerful being on Earth, perhaps the universe, folded to the ground and cried.

CHAPTER FIFTEEN

Why Don't We Play a Little Game?

The Secret Service agent switched on the camera. For a few seconds, the wide-angle fish-eye lens was filled by her face while she satisfied herself with the angle and setup. Then she dropped out of shot. The camera covered a plainly furnished office, currently vacant and easily repurposed as an interrogation room. It looked down from an elevated vantage in one corner. In the middle of the shot was a metal table with three chairs, two with their backs to the camera and one facing towards it. The agent returned to frame and took one of the two seats. Beside her was a male agent in a dark suit. On the other side of the table, Bullseye lounged over the back of his chair with one leg crossed over his lap. He was wearing his Hawkeye costume and mask. His midriff was bound up in bandages. He smiled for the camera.

"Commencing USSS interview of Lester, surname not on file, aka Hawkeye; Special Agent Garcia and Special Agent Barry interviewing."

Bullseye's eyes lingered a moment longer on the camera. "You know, I feel kind of uncomfortable being questioned like this without handcuffs. It's like I'm naked or something."

"You're a witness here, not a suspect. Anything that you saw or heard that morning might help us locate Mrs Reynolds-Lee."

"Why isn't Vicki asking these questions?" Another flick of the eyes to the camera. Another ghost of a grin. "I bet she'd have the cuffs out by now."

"The president has concerns."

"Oh yeah?"

"The Secret Service doesn't comment on operational matters."

"Should I have a lawyer?"

"That's really not what this is about."

"I want one. His name's Murdock. You can find him, right? Being the government and all."

The two agents shared a look.

The female agent leant forward and opened up a folder. "So, I'll start…"

The interviewee sat with his hands wrapped around his stomach. He was dressed in a backless medical gown with an Oscorp logo on the breast pocket. He was shivering, restless, rocking backwards and forwards in his chair.

"Mr Gargan," said one of the interviewing agents, tapping gently on the table. "Mr Gargan, are you all right?"

"*M-mmm,*" Venom mumbled.

"There's no need to be nervous," said one.

"You're not in any trouble," added the other.

"*My stomach. Wanna be sick. But it won't come up.*"

"Have a drink of water." The lead agent filled a glass from a pitcher at the edge of the table. She pushed the glass towards Venom.

The interviewee looked at it as though uncertain what it was for.

He licked his lips…

The agent studied the case folder, spending half a minute flipping through the pages. "According to the official body count provided for us by Oscorp investigators, you killed seventeen H.A.M.M.E.R. employees yesterday."

Bullseye looked down into his lap and grinned. "That's your first mistake." He looked back up. "Well, second mistake. I just noticed that tie."

"What mistake would that be?"

"Trusting Oscorp."

"Are you saying that's not what happened?"

Bullseye flicked his hand, as though waving off a mosquito. "I killed sixteen H.A.M.M.E.R. employees. The woman got the seventeenth…"

"So, Mr Gargan, if you're ready now, the entry logs for Dr Fiennes' lab show that access was granted to two individuals additional to your usual treatment team. Can you tell me who they were?"

Venom muttered something inaudible.

"What was that, Mr Gargan?"

Another meaningless grunt.

"We need to know what you remember, Mr Gargan."

"What happened to Dr Phillips?" The other agent took over. His partner sat back. "Is he dead? Or did he leave the lab with them?"

Venom looked up, as though confused by these people, and dribbled.

"Do you understand the questions we're asking you, Mr Gargan?"

"*Don't... remember...*" He shivered. Black sweat budded from his brow and trickled down his face. "*Don't... feel.*"

"We've left a message with Dr Fiennes, Mr Gargan. Just try to hold it together for a little longer. Do you think you can do that for us?"

"*Cramps. So hungry.*"

"Your doctor will get back to us as soon as she can. We can't just get you an antacid."

"Who knows what effect it would have on your symbiote's physiology?" the other agent added.

"*My skin hurts.*"

"Have another try of the water, Mr Gargan..."

"Let me just get the sequence of events straight in my head, Hawkeye." The agent closed the case folder in front of her. "You had this woman in your sights, but instead of taking the shot, you decided instead to engage her in hand-to-hand combat."

"Yeah, that's right."

"Why?"

Bullseye shrugged. "I thought Norman would want one taken alive. You know." He gestured back and forth across the table, indicating the three of them. "To question. Or whatever." He glanced up. His eyes grinned towards the camera. "I don't pretend to understand what goes on under the shiny helmet. Above my paygrade, am I right?"

"Did she say anything? A name? Or a place?"

"Who she works for?" her partner chipped in.

"What she wants?"

Bullseye pursed his lips, then shook his head. "Nah, we didn't talk much. It was a whirlwind romance."

"Could you describe her?"

Another shrug. "Hot."

The female agent sat back, tossing her notepad and pencil to the table with a frustrated sigh. "Is that really the best you can do?"

"Really hot."

"No recognizable features?"

Bullseye gave a leery whistle. "I'd say."

The two agents shared a look. The camera caught the female agent's clenched jaw.

Her partner quietly took over.

"And then she got away," he said. "How did that happen?"

Bullseye spread his hands, displaying his bandaged midriff. "A bullet to the gut'll slow you down. Try ten."

"Forgive me, sir, but you're Hawkeye."

"No kidding."

"What I mean is: you're an Avenger. You still couldn't catch her?"

"You implying I'm lying?" He gestured to himself. "Are you saying this face ain't honest?"

"You could have taken the kill shot as she fled."

"There were a lot of civilians in that hall."

"Do I need to remind you that you killed seventeen H.A.M.M.E.R. agents?"

"Sixteen. And five bad guys."

"And you couldn't take the shot?"

A slow smile spread across Bullseye's face. "Why don't we play a little game right now? Just the three of us. I disarm you both, and shoot you in the stomach, and then you both get to chase me. Does that sound like fun … ?"

"Mr Gargan? Mr Gargan?"

Venom didn't move. He sat back in his chair, head lolling. A tarry black ooze trickled from the corners of his mouth. It formed into a twitching layer over his chin, like a rancid beard or the beginnings of a mask.

"He's catatonic. We need to get his doctor in here now."

One of the agents got up and walked around the table. She squatted down by Venom's side and gently rocked him by the shoulder. A thin tendril of black sputum flexed out from Gargan's mouth and, right at the very edge of shot, whipped around her wrist. She didn't even notice it, and the camera caught nothing more, as the male agent put his face into the lens. "Pausing USSS interview of Mac Gargan, aka Spider-Man …"

"So then you pursued her," said the agent.

"Like I said."

"And you witnessed Mrs Reynolds-Lee's kidnap."

"Yeah." He brushed an imaginary tear off his cheek, the lizard smile never leaving his face. "If I'd only got there thirty seconds quicker. Poor Bob. The guy's broken up. I heard that he wouldn't even go to sleep unless Karla held his hand and left the bathroom light on." He looked around as though there might have been eavesdroppers in the room. "None of this is getting back to him, is it?"

"Not unless it could help us find Mrs Reynolds-Lee."

"Sure." Bullseye threw up his hands and grinned. "It's not like we're talking about a guy with super-hearing or anything."

"I understand that the Sentry is still asleep."

"Yeah, well, all right then." Bullseye leant conspiratorially across the table. "I've heard they've been having problems."

"What kind of problems?"

"You want me to act it out for you?"

"Are you implying that Mrs Reynolds-Lee could have conspired with her captor?"

"Your words, not mine."

"Then what are you saying, Hawkeye?"

"Just that she could've put up more of a fight. That's all."

"You're talking about a civilian. Against an elite combat operative."

"She'd just beaten you down," the female agent, Garcia, cut in with obvious satisfaction.

Bullseye jabbed a finger at her. "I'm the real victim here. I'm the one who got shot. I'm just telling you what I saw. She had CLOC with her. She could've run. That's all I'm–"

A bang on the wall caused the camera to shake, distortion lines wobbling through the picture's horizontal. When they passed, there was a dent in the wall, the paneling bulging into the room.

Special Agent Garcia put her finger to her earpiece. "Agents Simpson and Jaskowlska aren't answering." She got out of her chair and walked to the door, turning to address her colleague. "Pause the interview. I'll check in on Spider-Man."

The male agent got up and turned to the camera.

"Pausing USSS interview with Lester, surname unknown, aka Hawkeye…"

CHAPTER SIXTEEN
Square Pegs in Round Holes

The interview footage paused, a flickering Oscorp logo wandering over the grayed-out screen.

It was at moments like these that Norman Osborn wondered not only why he persevered with the likes of Lester and Gargan, but why he had ever hired them in the first place. Might it not be novel, he occasionally wondered, to employ an actual hero to do a hero's work? Perhaps it would not feel so much like forcing square pegs into round holes, and cause him fewer headaches and broken fingernails in the process. In his experience though, genuine heroes brought more problems to the table than they ever actually solved. They were the global defense equivalent of a Broadway prima donna: everything had to be done right, and it had to be done their way. You couldn't just buy them off with a million dollars a month, amnesty, and an upgrade in their accommodations from a prison cell in Coyote Springs, Colorado, to a ninety-second floor Manhattan penthouse.

He'd offered Danvers the team leadership role, after all, and she'd thrown it, and the tattered remnants of her military career along with it, back in his face.

Moonstone. Bullseye. Venom.

Daken. Sentry. Ares.

His Sinister Six.

He made as though to laugh, then let it out as a cough, glancing around to make sure no one had seen. No one had, so it had probably been nothing. The pressure of the last few days was getting on top of him, that was all. He hadn't slept enough. Hadn't found the spare hours to speak with his therapist. He was just tired, that was it, too much screen time stressing his eyes and his mind. He was imagining things.

He probably hadn't even been about to laugh at all.

Rubbing his eyes with gauntleted fingers, he turned from the screens.

The two he had been watching belonged to a bank of a hundred, suspended from the ceiling as a single unit by a massive trunk of armored cabling. Each screen carried mute surveillance footage, either from somewhere in Avengers Tower, or from strategic vantage points along Park Avenue, Lexington, and Madison, delivered live by secure cable through to the suite of fortified bunkers that comprised H.A.M.M.E.R. command and control.

The operations hub, deep under the Tower's basement, was abuzz.

Controllers in civilian clothing sat hunched over computers, elbow to elbow, daylight-starved faces ranked up like an odditorium display of severed heads underlit by the pixelated glow of monitors. A murmur of low conversation filled the air, the occasional legible snippet of intelligence jargon rising above the clack and chatter of mouse-clicks, keyboards, and their human operators. It offended the nose. Most of the operatives currently on duty had not left their stations since the early hours of the morning. Osborn doubted any of them had brought a change of shirt.

Moonstone, Ares, and Daken made a good show of looking busy.

Deputy Hand entered through one of the security annexes, her arrival heralded by a nervous hubbub from the civilian staff. She dutifully held out her arms as a H.A.M.M.E.R. agent waved her over with a scanner wand.

In light of the heightened alert status, Hand had changed into H.A.M.M.E.R. fatigues and combat armor. The plates looked dark, almost black, in the bunker's muted lighting, while the padded shoulders made her appear abnormally broad, her bare head markedly small relative to her armored body. A Kree energy rifle, part of the armory that Captain Marvel, Noh-Varr, had obligingly left behind before going AWOL, and powerful enough to punch a hole in a Dreadnought, hung by its shoulder strap.

The scanner wand bleeped and whined as it traced over her. After a few passes, the agent nodded and stepped aside. Deputy Hand took up the rifle and nodded back. Norman watched, noting the spread of intense work that followed her as she navigated the bustle of work stations and armed guards to approach the monitor bank.

A pair of Secret Service agents, assigned to Norman Osborn's protection at the nagging demand of the president, eyed her with exaggerated coolness. They stood with hands on hips, casually sweeping back the jackets of their dark suits to expose sweat-ringed white shirts as well as the ready grips of the SIG-Saur P229s holstered at their hips. What the president expected of them that Norman Osborn as the Iron Patriot could not do far more effectively for himself was beyond him. He indulged himself with a small smile. But then, the proletariat were hardly renowned for promoting geniuses to high office, were they?

The agents blended into the background as Victoria stepped up onto the dais and, with a characteristic absence of flourish, presented him with an envelope.

Osborn took it from her in one of his star-spangled gauntlets. He raised an eyebrow. "Ms Hand?"

"It is my letter of resignation, sir."

"I didn't hire you for your dramatic flair, Ms Hand."

"No, sir." She drew her hand back to her rifle and stood to attention. "You hired me because you needed someone who could manage your affairs. This happened on my watch. I take full responsibility for the consequences."

Norman took the envelope. It occurred to him that Victoria was the closest thing he had on his payroll to a real hero. The Avengers wouldn't have known responsibility for what it was if it came to them on an ICBM. He opened the letter, read it, and then, the micro-joints in the #25 gauntlets allowing him a tremendous degree of manual freedom, tore it into tiny pieces to scatter over the floor. "Are you done being melodramatic?"

Victoria's attentive stance loosened slightly. "Um. Sir?"

"Get back to what I'm paying you for before I fire you."

There was a brief smile, quickly mastered, and then a smart salute. "Yes, sir." Turning away, she took a seat at the table that had been installed to allow a reduced staff to monitor the screens. It was necessarily small, given the amount of hardware, personnel and, lately, guards, that needed to be packed into a compact subterranean space. She unslung her rifle and set it down, picking up one of the communal tablets from the stack. Then she nudged her glasses off the bridge of her nose, her biometrics unlocking the device and linking the operating system to her cloud.

Moonstone, Ares, and Daken glanced up as she joined them.

They had all 'volunteered' to assist with the search, but of the three of them only Ares actually appeared to be doing so.

The Olympian had built himself a small fort of intelligence dossiers, surrounding himself with battlemented walls originating from spy agencies all over the world. One piece of paper at a time, he picked them up and glared at them, not reading them so much as presenting an ultimatum. Most H.A.M.M.E.R. agents, once they worked their way above the line fodder, were polyglot. Norman himself spoke fluent French and conversational Symkarian. He employed a translation department with a staff of two hundred and licensed an AI linguistics program to himself from an Oscorp subsidiary, but none of them could do the work as quickly or as cogently as an Olympian gifted with the All-tongue. Ares was the God of War, after all, and war, in the information age, went far beyond the trenches or the battlefield.

Every minute or so, a junior aide would lay another manila brick on top of his fort's walls, and he would glare at them until they, too, departed.

The same aide never came back twice. Norman had no idea he employed so many.

Moonstone, on the other hand, was nodding off over her fifth cup of coffee, apparently unaware she had been reading the same page for so long that her tablet had gone to sleep. Daken, in turn, had returned to browsing his personal cell since the entertainment from the USSS interviews had been curtailed. It shouldn't have been possible for him to get service down there, but Daken was one of those rare individuals who could pick up a bar of signal even in an underground bunker. Norman wouldn't have been surprised to discover that the Patriot Armor itself was a walking Wi-Fi hotspot: he still hadn't quite found the time to get around to a thorough line-by-line debugging.

Daken smiled and issued the fakest laugh Norman had heard that wasn't directed at one of the president's jokes.

"What's so amusing?" said Victoria, in the tones of a teacher asking a delinquent in the back row if there was something he wished to share.

Daken turned the cell around in his hand so that everyone surrounding the small table could see the screen. It was showing the Avengers' official social media feed. "I didn't know that it was Captain Germany's birthday." It shouldn't have been possible for Daken's smile to get any wider than it already was, for his teeth to somehow get *whiter*, but they did. The wretch smiled like a wolf raised to imitate men. "We sent him a cake emoji." He turned his phone around and lounged back into his chair. "That's nice of us."

One of the intruders' more childish acts, but the one that made sure this was a news story that would run and run, had been to hack the Avengers' and H.A.M.M.E.R.'s various social media accounts. He might have dismissed it as an irritating prank, a stunt pulled off by bored students in MIT, Carnegie, or Singapore hoping to get themselves noticed by USCYBERCOM or be offered a job at the NSA, were it not for the tremendous amount of preparation, the danger, that went into physically uploading malware into Avengers Tower's computers. Not to mention the file taken from Deputy Hand's computer. A computer nerd playing for kicks in his college dorm wouldn't have cared about that file.

Norman had all the fingers he needed on one hand to list off the people in the world who knew about the file. One was the man he worked for. Two were in the room now. One of those two was him.

For all its operational insignificance, the social media hack was arguably the most annoying. It was certainly the one that was agitating his employer. He scowled. The best minds in the world, the most expensive lawyers, and he still hadn't even managed to wrest back control of their account. Never mind tracking down and eliminating the perpetrators. He ground his teeth. There'd be no civilized midnight rendition to some CIA black site in a South American dictatorship for these guys. No. They'd made Norman Osborn the butt of a hundred late night talk show jokes. They'd made him an embarrassment to the president. He fully intended to humiliate them in turn. He would publicly grind them under his boot heel. Just as soon as he found them.

And if he had to crack the world open to get at them, then he would.

"My birthday is in July, by the way," Moonstone murmured, setting down her tablet and wrapping both hands around her coffee. "Since we're caring now. The tenth. But my mom always used to make me share it with Independence Day. So she wouldn't have to cook twice." A muttered curse disappeared into her beverage, and she smiled over the cup at Norman. "To this day, I associate stars and stripes with disappointment."

"You mortals and your whining." Ares set down the file he had been reading and turned his scowl towards Moonstone. His expression was a complicated blurring of wrath and rough affection that Norman had only witnessed once or twice, usually towards his truant half-Olympian son, but also, occasionally, for a particularly challenging foe. He appeared to have developed a reluctant admiration for his fellow Avenger following her takedown of the Sentry. "My father spared no opportunity to denounce me as the most hateful of all the gods, spurning me even when I returned wounded from battle with the Achaeans. Humans know nothing of hatred or neglect."

They both looked at Daken.

He bared his teeth.

"It's not a competition."

"Before we leave orbit of the subject …" Norman growled. He doubted even the example of the Olympians could have inspired worse than his own father. Fortunately, most of his life before the development of the Goblin formula was something of a blur, as though he had spent those years with only half his brain awake.

He was better now.

Much better.

"Sir." Victoria manipulated her tablet's touchscreen with brisk finger strokes, and then swiveled the display towards Norman. He didn't bother to strain his eyes or neck any further to look at the tablet, trusting Victoria to give him the precis. "I'm not sure whether any of this amounts to something, but it's definitely more than nothing. The intruders were meticulous and careful, but they unavoidably left trace physical evidence behind. Not to mention four bodies in the briefing room and one in the canteen, as well as a trove of equipment for the labs to pick over."

Daken chuckled, pocketing his cell. "I wonder if Lester would have killed them if he'd realized he was being so helpful."

"*Hawkeye,*" said Victoria, with a pointed look towards Norman's Secret Service detail, "provided us with some significant intelligence breakthroughs in this regard, yes."

Daken shook his head wryly.

The USSS agents were surveilling the room with an air of studied detachment and professional disinterest in whatever they might overhear. Norman was sure they were as diligent in their responsibilities as Victoria was in hers. But would they be so circumspect if it was the president himself asking them for information?

"Code names only, Wolverine," he said. "Even here."

Victoria nodded her gratitude and went on. "All of the recovered bodies have been identified as former members of S.H.I.E.L.D., all of them serving abroad when the transfer to H.A.M.M.E.R. took place."

"A lot of agents went missing at that time," Norman mused. "A lot of very expensive equipment, too."

"We have some intelligence from Five Eyes that at least two of the five fell in with Timothy Dugan's Howling Commandos PMC."

"Who are they?" said Moonstone, not looking as though she remotely cared.

"A mercenary company with registered offices in London, Canberra, and Johannesburg, and a well-known front company for disaffected former S.H.I.E.L.D. agents and Nick Fury loyalists."

"If you know this, then why have they not already been crushed in battle?" Ares grumbled.

Norman sighed. "Because if a few hundred angry young men want to empty the pockets of despots around the world so that Nick Fury can rain on my parade, then nobody much cares. Did you know it costs over one hundred dollars a day to incarcerate an American citizen on US soil?"

"And," said Victoria, "they do seem more interested in fighting old wars against Hydra and their affiliates, as well as the mercenary activity that pays their bills, rather than prosecuting any new vendetta with us or H.A.M.M.E.R."

"Until now," said Ares.

"Actually, there's no evidence for that. And even for the two agents that we know *were* Howling Commandos, we have pretty good evidence from the South Africans that they parted ways with Dugan months ago." She reached for her tablet and pulled up some crime scene photos from the briefing room. "Now, the armor they were wearing was standard kit, nothing distinctive about it at all. It could have been what I had on last week and we'd have no way to know about it. The weapons, on the other hand…" Manipulating the touchscreen with the deftness of a concert pianist, hours of daily practice showing its value, she expanded one of the photos to blow up the image of an OS-11 quad-mode assault rifle. "H.A.M.M.E.R. bases outside of the United States tend to be situated in pretty volatile parts of the world." She shrugged. "It's in the nature of the global peacekeeping work that H.A.M.M.E.R. does. Suffice it to say that the last thing any of us wants to see is Oscorp-branded weaponry finding its way into the hands of the sorts of terrorists and warlords we're supposed to be opposing."

"Not without paying for them anyway," said Daken.

Victoria glared across the table.

She believed in H.A.M.M.E.R.'s mission. She believed in Norman Osborn. Fury, in her long-held opinion, had been allowed to grow old and soft in post with no one around or above him with the ruthlessness to make the change. Excising him from the organization he had helped to found had been an act of triage needed to save it. Norman Osborn was the hero the world demanded, even if they didn't know it. His Avengers were the hardcore team that would finally break through decades of intractable problems and apologize for collateral damage or consequences later. And, very much in spite of the fact that the likes of A.I.M. and Hydra were still out there, that there were still monomaniacal despots and solo super villains intent on taking over or destroying the world, she had never once wavered in her conviction.

But that was no reason to give Daken, or anyone else, the ammunition they needed to go pushing her buttons. Daken was eminently replaceable. They all were.

Except, that was, for Victoria Hand.

Norman had come to depend on her.

Perhaps too much.

"What Deputy Hand is *trying* to say," he added, "is that I took deliberate steps to make it almost impossible to obscure the origins of my weapons. It would be a lot more complicated than just filing away a serial number. They're microchipped, and isotope-tagged. I helped to develop the procedures myself. The identity of each individual weapon is ingrained, literally atomically, into the body of every gun my factories produce."

"And these…" Victoria nodded, dismissing her earlier tabs and calling up a satellite map on her tablet centered over the Horn of Africa. She pinched her fingers to zoom in. "These five OS-11s were all manufactured in Oscorp's plant in Ethiopia. Whoever was behind this put some effort into scrambling the microchips. Clearly, they knew what they were looking for and what they were doing, and if we had been left holding just one weapon, we would probably not have been able to pull any useful data from it. However…" She smiled thinly. "Thanks to Hawkeye's efforts, we have recovered enough geolocation data to be ninety-nine percent certain that all of the weaponry was shipped from Ethiopia to the H.A.M.M.E.R. base in Mogadishu, Somalia, where it remained until last week."

"This is one of the bases that fell in the rioting." Ares made a tight fist, veins popping along his brawny forearm. It was clear what the God of War felt H.A.M.M.E.R.'s response to popular discontent in the region should have been.

Norman did not disagree. "That's correct. And I'm not sure it helps us much either. Anyone could have looted the base under the cover of the riots. The perpetrators might even have orchestrated them as a cover for just that purpose."

He liked that idea, now it occurred to him. It meant that the people of the world were gullible, suggestible fools, pawns in a deep game, rather than simply refusing of their own considered volition to march to Norman Osborn's drum.

"It doesn't. At least on its own." Victoria glanced towards Ares. "But thanks to you, we may have a tentative ID on our Manhattan swordsman."

The Olympian sat forward.

At the same time, as though drawn in by whatever sub-psychic aggression was being generated by the God of War, Daken and Moonstone became similarly attentive and alert.

"Show me," said Ares.

Victoria called up a black and white photograph of a young, Arab male, beside what appeared to be a busy city center road. It was slightly blurred, as though captured by something passing overhead at high speed.

Ares made a low growl. He nodded. "Yes. This is the mortal champion who faced me and lives."

"His name is Navid Hashim, also known as the Arabian Knight, a Palestinian national currently in the employ of the Saudi royal family."

Norman ground his teeth in irritation. How much of the annoyance he felt was his own, arising from the never-ending slights perpetrated against him by the nations of the world, and how much was coming to him from Ares, he did not know.

The God of War, so far as Norman was aware, did not seem to exert his belligerent influence at will. But nor had DEVCOMM, DARPA, or Oscorp scientists yet figured out any effective means of keeping it out. He pinched the bridge of his nose, the grip of armored gauntlets biting hard into the skin, and closed his eyes, as though to do what provable science could not and reject the god's influence through willpower alone.

He started to giggle at the madness of it, before taking a deep breath, as his therapist had taught him, and exhaling it.

I'm Norman Osborn, he thought, sternly. No one else.

"Is Hashim an active Saudi agent?" he asked, eyes still closed.

"The last we checked," said Victoria. "The Saudis are no freer with the identity of their assets than we are. His last appearance on our radar was about a year ago. He was loaned out to MI-13 to help foil an attack on London."

Norman turned to yell at an operator. Any operator. "Find me someone in Washington who can get me the Saudi ambassador on the phone. I want to know what they know about this guy. Tell them I have no reservations at all about ordering the Sentry to wipe Riyadh from the face of the Earth and blaming it on Iranian WMDs."

The senior agent of his Secret Service detail looked his way, as though in surprise.

"You heard," Norman snarled.

"And while we hope the Saudi king will fall for your bluff," Victoria said loudly, "we do have a little more on the Arabian Knight. It turns out that the alias, although not Hashim himself, was also a member of the Iraqi super-team, Desert Sword."

"The same as the Black Raazer," said Daken.

"Good, Ms Hand," said Norman. "Very good."

Victoria absorbed the praise as stoically as she would have

taken criticism. She tapped her finger on the tablet image. "This was captured by a British UAV that was passing over the city of Bosaso about six hours ago."

"Forgive me, Ms Hand, that I don't know where that is."

Victoria grinned. "Somalia, sir."

Ares' fist hit the table. "Give me a Quinjet and one day. I will drag the Arabian Knight from his country by the ankles and lay him across the Avengers' table like a goat for slaughter and sacrifice."

"We will discuss the specifics later, Ares," said Norman. "Though I applaud your commitment to law and order. We still don't know who is behind this, what they plan on doing next, or why. And I don't know, but I'm assuming Somalia is a big country."

"About the size of Alaska, sir," said Victoria. "But as to what they might want, I do have a theory."

"Go on, Ms Hand."

"Well, sir, with all the information they have had access to, they could have done real damage to our interests. They could have set us back months. Instead, they've done this." She gestured dismissively towards Daken. "Made a few jokes at our expense on social media. It's as if they're actively trying to avoid doing collateral harm to the organization. The staff records they accessed, the material they took from my computer, even the footage they put in the hands of the *Bulletin* if it were to have gotten out: I don't think this is an attack on H.A.M.M.E.R. at all. Or the United States. I think this is an attack on you."

"I don't think I understand the distinction you're making, Ms Hand."

"Sir, I–"

"I *am* H.A.M.M.E.R. Do you hear me? Without me, there

is no organization. I hold direct control of the Initiative, the Thunderbolts, as well as the Avengers. I have the FBI, the ATF, the CBP. I have the National Guard in my pocket. Do you know how many legislators my money has put in office? International law is whatever *I* say it is. An attack on me is a declaration of war against the United States of America, and believe me, Ms Hand, that America will retaliate with the fire and the fury of overwhelming and entirely non-commensurate force." He realized that he was shouting. The entire bunker had fallen silent, but for the whir of computer fans. Guards, technicians, and even Secret Service had stopped what they were doing and were watching him. Moonstone was wearing an unkind and knowing smile, as though Norman had forgotten to get dressed and had come to the bunker in his underwear. If Daken's smirk grew any larger it would start to challenge the ability of his face to regenerate. Ares was nodding approvingly.

Somehow that was worse.

He panted as he calmed himself down.

"Sir…" Victoria's expression was one of real concern, but this was something she would not take further with the rest of the Avengers team in attendance.

That would come later.

"What was in the *Bulletin* leak?" Moonstone asked, sensing the moment of maximum suggestibility and probing at it like the outstandingly amoral psychiatrist she was. If Norman had not been so irritated, he might have been impressed.

"Nothing consequential," Victoria snapped.

"And the files from your laptop?"

"A list," Norman answered for her.

"Sir…" Victoria warned.

Norman felt the thump of blood through his head. Why not

let Karla know? Let them all know! Let them know who was in charge of their lives, and deaths, and see how unimportant and eminently replaceable they all were. But before he could shape the first word of an explanation, a movement from within the pool of IT agents gave him pause. A young woman, a plainclothes special agent if he remembered his introductions, was pushing towards the guards on the door. At the same time, Norman became aware of the small Secret Service cordon tightening around himself and the Avengers. The lead agent was speaking urgently into his headset. The others had already drawn their sidearms.

"Talk to me."

"Shots fired," the agent replied, one finger pressed to his ear. "Agents down." He turned to Norman. "Spider-Man has killed his interviewers and broken through security on that wing."

"Spider-Man…"

With a snarl, Norman turned back to the monitor bank.

One of the interview room cameras was still paused, but the one in Lester's room had been switched back on. Bullseye was sitting in his chair with his legs crossed over the table. He was whistling. A male agent was slumped in the opposite chair. His back was to the camera, but he was self-evidently dead, apparently garroted with the coiled wire from his own earpiece.

A bloody handprint smeared the other side of the small window in the door.

Though outwardly wholly composed, Norman felt the white heat of rage welling up inside him. Was it not enough that he had a world to keep safe, and in line? Did he really need to police superhuman threats in his own house? And with the president's own people so close? He could hear the voice of a maniac shrieking behind his ears. It took every ounce of self-control he possessed, and years of experience, to keep himself from screaming that voice aloud like a kettle approaching the boil.

He was collected. He was calm.

He was Norman Osborn.

Who else would he be?

"Ms Hand," he said, his voice entirely reasonable and calm. "Make whatever diplomatic preparations you need to commit to a full-scale operation in Somalian territory. Ms Marvel, Ares, Wolverine: come with me."

Daken breathed new life into his smile. It was the genuine article. The facsimile held nothing to it. "Can we kill him this time?"

At a muttered command, Norman's helmet spun out and enclosed his head. Sealed inside its nickel-titanium dome, unheard by anyone but himself, he finally let loose the scream that had been building inside his head.

"Yes, Wolverine." The gravelly intonations of the Patriot Armor obscured the hysteria that had crept into his voice. "You have my absolute authority to terminate Spider-Man once and for all."

CHAPTER SEVENTEEN
The Heyday of His Madness

The Iron Patriot tore through the bowels of Avengers Tower at two hundred miles per hour.

Doors came free of their hinges, windows exploded, clerks and secretaries dived for their offices amidst a storm of flying papers: every piece of debris that was not rivetted in concrete was picked up and funneled into the glittering vortex that tapered behind the Iron Patriot's wake. At a right-angle bend he banged into the wall. Repulsor burns from boots and gauntlets raked along the precast concrete, like the claws of a rabid animal sensing freedom, as he scrambled into the turn and boosted away down the corridor.

Kill Spider-Man, he thought. *Ha-ha-ha-ha-ha.* Icons danced across the 3D building schematic in his HUD, adjusting to his suit's abrupt changes in direction and speed. He'd flown at eight times the speed of sound. This should have been easy. It was nothing. He could do it with his eyes closed. Kill Spider-Man. He cursed under his breath as he scraped a few hundred feet along the ceiling, scraping up sparks and bringing integrity alarms from his helmet. He blink-selected a comms icon from the HUD menu.

"Is Spider-Man still on the fortieth?"

"Yes, sir," Victoria replied. "H.A.M.M.E.R. agents and Secret Service are engaged, but I was going to pull them back."

"No. Order them to hold their ground, and send in reinforcements."

"I have someone from the White House on the other line. The president wants an explanation as to how Mac Gargan managed to eat three of his people."

"I want Spider-Man to stay exactly where he is."

"Venom will tear those agents apart."

Venom, he reminded himself. *Right.*

"I'll be there in ten seconds."

A steel door blocked his way to an elevator shaft at the end of the corridor. A short blast from his palm repulsors turned it to slurry, and he scorched through the glowing red curtain of metal like a stone into a molten pool. Another repulsor burn, this time over a wide spread, arrested his forward momentum, while a fierce blast from his boot jets fired him upwards, clattering and corkscrewing up the elevator shaft. His HUD ticked off the floors, from the minus numerals of the bunker levels and blurring rapidly towards the fortieth.

Almost there.

He looked up.

The ceiling was far closer than it ought to have been. And it was descending. Fast.

The elevator was coming down.

He considered calling Victoria again, to check if anyone important was aboard, but then dismissed the thought at once. There was no time to make the call, or to go around. "I need to kill

Spider-Man." Pushing more power into his boot repulsors and to his forward shields, he boosted towards the descending elevator, punching through its floor like a finger through legal paper and out the other side. He passed through it far too quickly to see for himself whether or not it had been occupied. Weeping sparks, opened up like a metal flower, it shuddered to a halt between floors. Norman gave it no further mind.

"About your outburst in the control room, sir..."

"I know what you're going to say, Ms Hand. It won't happen again."

"Have you been performing the exercises that your therapist set for you?"

"I've not missed a single appointment, Ms Hand."

"That's not what I asked. Remember what the doctor said, sir. CBT is a talking therapy, but it's also a *doing* therapy."

Norman made an ugly face. He hated the therapy. He hated putting himself and his mind under another's power. He hated how that could make him look. For a man of his position, mood-stabilizing drugs were far more acceptable.

The fortieth floor flashed up on his HUD.

He could already hear the muffled patter of gunfire through the steel walls of the shaft.

"We'll talk about it later, Ms Hand. I'm a little busy at this exact moment."

Cutting the power to his boot repulsors, he reduced his ascent velocity with a braking burn from his shoulder jets and a little assistance from gravity. Then he thrust out his hands and slagged the elevator door.

"Respectfully, sir. You're always busy. This is the promise you made when you hired me. If you break it then I walk."

Norman muttered under his breath.

"I'm sorry, sir, I didn't catch that."

"I said I'll do the damned exercises."

A pause. "The world needs you, sir. It needs Norman Osborn. It doesn't need the Goblin."

"The Goblin isn't coming back, Ms Hand. You have my personal guarantee on that. Now, if you'll just hold the line a moment, I'm going to deal with Spider-Man once and for all." He wanted to howl with laughter, but he still knew better than to do it with Victoria on the line. He would just take a double dose to make up for the reminder he missed while in Chicago. A burst of angled thrust pushed him through the dribbling door hatch and onto the scene of a battle.

No, *battle* implied some kind of fair contest.

This was a massacre.

The elevators opened onto an auditorium that, like Tony Stark before him, he'd used for corporate functions, and for the occasional press event where the news was so spectacularly bad that only the most expensive of rugs could cover it. It had been designed and decorated to resemble a ballroom in the Regency style, elements of Greco-Roman amphitheater thrown in for good measure, but somehow the combination worked.

A pair of twinned staircases made mirroring passes towards the function floor from the doors. They were strewn with bodies, most of them slain while pushing up towards the elevator. Marble-effect pilasters projected from the walls, dinged by bullets, singed by plasma, while reproduction artworks and tapestries hung askew from their fixtures in tatters. Massive cathedral-style windows overlooked Manhattan. They were two bulletproof inches of laminated glass, frosted white from hundreds of ballistic impacts fired from the inside out. A heavy machine gun set up to enfilade the gallery listed on a tripod mount. The H.A.M.M.E.R.

agents who had crewed it were both dead. Their armor had been peeled open, exposed innards glistening with dark, alien slime.

Executive boxes and balconies, the directional tint of one-way glass making their gazes callous, looked down on the concluding act to the slaughter below.

A handful of soldiers were still fighting. A few dozen H.A.M.M.E.R. operatives and a couple of Secret Service agents took shelter in the orchestra pit, screaming as they unloaded their assault rifles and sidearms into the monster above them.

Venom.

There was no mistaking the creature for who he really was now.

He had swollen to over eighteen feet tall, hunched like a Neanderthal, oily ropes of sinew and ridges of bone-like substance contributing to a grossly over-muscled physique. His face was elongated, his jaw distended, his tongue dragging along the floor as he bounded hungrily towards the orchestra pit. Frantic bursts of fire thudded into his symbiote skin and drowned like bugs in tar. The Secret Service wasn't equipped for this kind of threat at all. It would take more firepower than even a H.A.M.M.E.R. platoon routinely carried to bring Venom down.

He roared like a maddened gorilla as he leapt into the pit.

A swipe of his hand sent agents flying. Tentacles erupted from a hundred places all over his body, snatching up H.A.M.M.E.R. soldiers by the dozen and crushing them in their armor, his carapace devouring their return fire while he swept up a Secret Service agent in his jaws and noisily swallowed her without bothering to chew.

"Damn it," Norman muttered.

"Sir?"

"Our missing doctor. He must have injected Gargan with Serum 17-G while he had him in for treatment."

A most uncharacteristic expletive scratched through the suit comm.

Gargan's treatment program had begun life as a crude batrachotoxin restraint, specifically developed by the Commission for Superhuman Activities during his tour with the Thunderbolts. The program had later been spun out and subcontracted to Oscorp labs, refining it to the extent that Gargan could appear and function just enough like an actual human being to pass as Spider-Man without sacrificing too much of the symbiote's killer instinct and power. It was always a balancing act. The symbiote evolved and resisted. Chemotherapy invariably missed that sweet spot, leaving him either uselessly passive or a hyper-violent liability. As had been the case on the *Bulletin* raid.

That was nothing compared to this.

Serum 17-G was one of the many allowances that Norman had made to keep Dr Fiennes' "intellectual curiosity" in check after the former A.I.M. defector had been brought back in-house to oversee the program. She had been curious to learn whether the reverse treatment could also be applied, if the agency of the symbiote over the host could be strengthened as well as repressed, if Gargan's human qualities like self-interest and guilt could be chemically attenuated without entirely squandering his capacity to follow basic orders.

Of course, it had failed horribly.

Initial tests with laboratory samples had left a dozen junior research staff dead and cost Oscorp millions, but the results had been promising enough for him to allow Dr Fiennes to continue on a more limited scale. Norman had had no idea that she had been keeping a vial of the formula on site all this time. And if she had been working on it here, then it was inevitable that others would have learned of its existence, too. Scientists were terrible at keeping secrets. Almost congenitally bad. It was unfortunate that they were so necessary.

Just as soon as this crisis was put down, Norman Osborn and his head of research were going to have a very long, and very frank, conversation.

Routing his voice through the Patriot Armor's exterior loudhailers, Norman shouted a challenge and boosted himself over the guardrail on a burst of thrust. On the floor, Venom lowered the screaming agent he had been all set to stuff into his mouth and turned. He watched Norman come in with the cold, rapacious hunger of deep space and licked his black lips.

"What's the ETA on Daken and Ares?" Norman asked on his private comm.

"Five to ten minutes, sir. They were forced to call a replacement elevator."

Norman grunted. The elevator he'd broken through probably hadn't been occupied then. That was a bit of good news. "Have Moonstone redirected outside. I want her to set a perimeter. And contact Hancock Air National Guard for a squadron of helicopter gunships to back her up. Under no circumstances is Gargan to be allowed to escape. Is that clear, Ms Hand? I'll not have this turn into another PR debacle that ends with the president watching Karla and me battling Venom over the Upper East Side on CNN."

"Shall I wake the Sentry?"

"No!" He took a breath. "No. Robert is too unstable right now. Let him rest." Extending both hands towards Venom, he spread both lots of fingers wide and routed all auxiliary power to his palm repulsors. "I'll take care of this myself."

A flurry of white-hot repulsor beams lanced from his palm emitters towards the orchestra pit.

Venom slobbered with unintelligent laughter and launched clear, moments before the beams struck. Norman tracked him, throwing out repulsor-fire, but Venom somehow managed to scramble ahead of every attack. It appeared that Gargan's spider-sense had been enhanced along with his predatory instincts. No doubt Norman could expect to find the rest of his alien abilities similarly bolstered as well.

Dr Fiennes could look forward to some definite words.

The Venom symbiote crunched into the walkway, crumpling the handrail under his mass, and then threw himself back over the gallery floor. Norman saw him too late to react. The symbiote was just too fast. Venom's fist impacted his helmet like an anvil swung by a giant ape. He flew back from the blow, alarms ringing in his head, attitude thrusters burning, and crunched into the window. The bulletproof glass splintered under him like ice but didn't shatter. Warnings stuttered across his HUD: micro-fractures detected in several armor panels, shield strength down five percent across the board. He couldn't silence them quickly enough. Before he could try to move, a glob of black webbing splatted across his visor. Everything went dark except for the glowing holo-display of the HUD and its myriad alarms. He brought his hands to his face, partially on instinct, partially with the considered intention of burning the symbiote matter away with a repulsor blast, only to be yanked face-first out of the window and smashed with appalling strength to the floor.

He groaned. The fluid-filled shock absorbers and padding in his suit could only take so much of a beating before transferring some of it through to him.

Guided solely by sensors, he fired his boot repulsors, skidding along the broken floor like a firework let off in the shop and rammed Venom's chest. His thrust lifted them both back into the air, locked together, pummeling one another, as they careened wildly from wall to wall to wall. Still blind, buffered from the full fury of the engagement by the padding of the Patriot Armor, Norman tracked the damage through the warning chimes and shield profiles of his HUD. The Goblin serum that he had developed as a younger man had made him stronger, more agile, accelerated his ability to heal, as well as increasing his already genius-level intellect and creativity to beyond any conventionally achievable human limit. Of course, there had been a few minor drawbacks, too. But even he, in the heyday of his former madness, would never have attempted to tackle a creature like Venom alone. Stark's armor, however, had offered him more. As the Iron Patriot, he could hit harder, and take more punishment, than the Green Goblin ever could. He could go toe to toe with almost anything. Of all his Avengers, with the obvious exception of the Sentry, only Ares was stronger than him now.

And finally, he could kill Spider-Man

With an outraged snarl, he sent a sonic attack through his loudhailer that was nowhere near as finely tuned as the one operating in Dr. Fiennes' lab, but which was enough to shock the Venom symbiote into loosening its grip. A low-energy repulsor blast to his own helmet burnt the webbing from his visor. His vision cleared just in time to see the fist flying towards his face. His open palm came up to block the blow and caught it. The Patriot Armor's motive systems howled their protest as their strength competed with Venom's to slowly, arduously, twist the symbiote's arm out to one side. With Venom's body open, he countered with a short jab, delivering the kinetic impact of a runaway train to the symbiote's gut. The alien wheezed, vomiting up corrosive phlegm over Norman's visor and partially obscuring his vision again. While he was distracted by that, Venom's captured wrist melted around the Patriot Armor's grip until all of a sudden it was *his* grasp around the Patriot Armor's arm and he was hurling him towards the ground.

Norman crashed through one half of the stairs.

The entire installation came away. Wood frame, gold foil, steel rebar, and marble-effect laminate all came collapsing down on top of him. The armor responded automatically by activating lamps. Halogen brightness dazzled back at him from the fabulously expensive mass of rubble. He tried to shift it. The Patriot Armor could lift upwards of seventy tons, under laboratory conditions at least, but there wasn't the space under the rubble to apply its full strength.

Gargan had become even more powerful than he could have imagined.

Dr Fiennes would be thrilled.

She'd be less thrilled when her pink slip came through. Or when Bullseye threw her out of Avengers Tower. Provided he didn't just let Venom eat her. There would be a wonderfully circular kind of justice in that.

Victoria's voice echoed dully through the HUD to interrupt his revenge fantasies.

Under the circumstances, she sounded jarringly calm.

"I didn't want to raise this in front of the others, sir, but it might be advisable if you were to refrain from terminating Mac Gargan. We still don't know who has the list, and that could compromise our recruitment of a replacement Spider-Man."

"I'll… try… to bear that… in mind," Norman growled in reply, silently adding *while I kill him* as he pushed back against the rubble.

"Sir? Is there a problem?"

"I'm... perfectly... fine... Ms Hand."

Venom's fist descended like a jackhammer, unerringly seeking out Norman's chest through the intervening rubble and pounding the Patriot Armor into the floor. Norman coughed blood, through the HUD and against the physical visor screen. Pain spotted his vision.

But at least the rubble was cleared.

"I've had... about as much of this... as I'm going to take... Gargan."

The unibeam emitter, the star-shaped blazon in the center of his breastplate, delivered a volcanic eruption of directed force into Venom's chest. The symbiote shrieked as it bled off dead cellular matter in a noxious steam. For a brief moment, Gargan himself was left partially exposed. He tottered like a lopsided doll, bits of naked human flesh shivering and vulnerable and patched together with symbiotic skin. He looked invitingly defenseless, but already the symbiote was healing, reliquefying and reincorporating its vaporized constituents to sheathe Gargan in flesh once more. And the Patriot Armor's unibeam was drained. It would take time to build up the power for another shot like that.

He raised a hand as though to ward off a blow.

Venom smacked it aside before he could fire off a repulsor beam. Then he stepped on Norman's shoulder, pinning the arm to the ground, and hunched over him. A deep sigh rumbled up from the symbiote's cavernous chest, rousing his prehensile tongue to roll out of his mouth and wrap itself three times around the Patriot Armor's neck and squeeze. The alien hoisted him out of his litter of debris and into the air.

"*Kill Norman Osborn.*"

Norman kicked desperately, suspended six feet off the ground, Venom's tongue slowly crushing the armor around his neck. His eyes rolled up towards the ceiling, looking for some way out.

And he smiled at what he saw there.

Daken flung himself from the balustrade with a whoop, landing astride Venom's swollen neck and plunging both sets of claws into the monster's head. The alien roared, throwing his head back like a rodeo bull, while Daken twisted his claws in, clamped his thighs, and laughed. Norman tried to keep his grip on Venom's tongue, but it was like holding onto a lubricated rope or a length of intestine. It squished under his grip and slid through his fingers, centrifugal forces throwing him clear, and into a block of rubble on his back.

He looked up with a groan, just as Venom succeeded in throwing Daken off his shoulders and into the reinforced glass plates of the window. The head that Daken had thought impaled submerged into his chest, while another emerged from his shoulder. It split in half around a gaping mouth, and disgorged another tongue.

Ignoring the mutant, Venom returned his attention to Norman.

Filled with enough anger to power the Patriot Armor, refusing to be beaten by Spider-Man *again,* Norman stood. He raised a hand to defend himself, knowing it wasn't enough.

Suddenly, Ares was there.

The God of War threw a haymaker that almost wrenched Venom's newly made head right off his shoulders and sent the rest of him smashing through the wall. The alien struggled to right himself, but Ares, entirely unhurried, already had his ankle. Venom splattered the cavity wall space with black webbing, suckering himself to the wall, but rather than prevent Ares from pulling him out he merely ensured that a ton of wall came out with him. It came down on top of him as the Olympian dragged him up. Wrestling with disjointed limbs and endlessly sprouting tentacles, Ares got one hugely muscled arm around the symbiote's throat. He drew a sound like crushed gristle from Venom's neck, patiently choking the frenzied alien to his knees.

"Thank you, Ares." Norman's voice was croaky and hoarse. He turned his sore neck, and winced, reaching up to test the buckled gorget rings of his armor. The Patriot suit was going to be in the shop for a week. "You, too, Wolverine. That couldn't have been better timed." Standing up to his full height, he looked down on the struggling alien symbiote. Such strength Gargan had in him. What a waste. "Would one of you please stop him from wriggling."

Daken punched his claws into Venom's chest.

The symbiote howled, shuddered, and shrank a little into Ares' neck-lock. His attempts at writhing loose became feebler.

"Sir," came Victoria's almost forgotten voice through his HUD. "We have an update from the ground in Somalia that you'll want to hear."

"I'll call you back, Ms Hand."

He cut the link, then looked up at Gargan and made a fist.

The Patriot Armor whirred.

"I'm told that it's not in my best interests to kill you, Spider-Man. I intend on making this as unfortunate for you as it is for me."

How much force would it take, he wondered, to beat a serum-enhanced super-Venom into unconsciousness? Somewhere over the last minute and a half he had come to the decision that he would let Dr Fiennes off with one more warning. He had been something of a scientist himself, after all, and the empiricist in him wanted someone around who could appreciate the fascinating real-world data he was about to provide.

He glanced at Daken and Ares.

His helmet, star-spangled metal, was expressionless.

"Hold him still. Who knows how long this is going to take?"

PART TWO

BOSASO

CHAPTER EIGHTEEN

Famous Faces

The yellow and blue cab deposited Daken and the others at the side of the road. It pulled a U-turn back into traffic, wheels spinning on the loose sand as its driver raced back, northbound, to his next fare at Bender Qassim Airport.

Daken watched it disappear into the busy haze of dust cars and container trucks bound for the seaport. Of exhaust fumes. Of heat. Of sand. There was no curb to speak of. The sidewalk was a verge of raked sand either side of a congested but unmarked road. Whitewashed buildings with colorful rooftops lined the road on both sides. Wild date and fever trees offered stultifying oases of shade that bustled with street traders. Stores and cafés competed for what was left of the sidewalk, like ships tangled together after a heavy storm, a riot of flags, awnings, multilingual signage, teenagers wearing flip-flops and sandwich boards, through which seasoned locals expertly wove.

Daken sniffed, testing the roadside's savor like a master sommelier sampling a fierce scotch whisky. Its main body and aroma came from the road, baked metal, melting rubber, diesel, but with a distinct secondary bouquet of frying rice, decaying seaweed, and sand.

He took another sniff.

"That'll never not be disgusting."

Bullseye sweated like a ham in foil under the African sun. He was dressed in a Yankees jersey and shorts. The *bullseye* brand on his forehead shimmered with pooled sweat. How he ever managed to pass through any airport security, anywhere in the world, was a mystery to Daken. Bullseye's aroma was a blending of genetics, diet, and questionable lifestyle choices that came together in Daken's nose as a perfume that was entirely distinct to him. Daken could have tracked him through a packed baseball stadium with his eyes closed.

"Arabian Knight was here," he said.

He looked left, then squinted right. The sun glimmered and danced off car roofs and windows. The scent was clear enough that, in his mind, it was almost conceivable that he might see the swish of Hashim's coat as he disappeared into the crowd. But of course, he saw nothing of the kind. The scent was a day old, traipsed over, and over again, by countless strangers.

Moonstone took a step back from the road, holding up the surveillance photo of Hashim that Victoria had provided. If she had really wanted to be certain that this was the right spot then she could have surveilled it from above, as the spy drone that had taken the photo would have, but the rationale for sending the three of them was that they could act incognito. Victoria had offered to lead the mission herself, while Robert had pleaded with Osborn for permission to join it, but the deputy director of H.A.M.M.E.R. and the Sentry were two of the most famous faces in the world. The Somalis had cable TV. As heinous a shock to the system as that might be for some. Ares, on the other hand, had demanded, rather than begged, and once Osborn had refused on the same grounds it had looked, for a delightful couple of minutes, as though the two might come to blows. Before Victoria had spoiled it with an agreeable compromise and an appeal to the Olympian's honor.

And as for Venom...

Daken smiled to himself, enjoying the sensation of heat against his face. It reminded him of his dojo in Tōhoku. There was little about his childhood that he had not later been taught to hate, but it had been home at a time when he had not known what a home was. And it had been warm.

Gargan could consider himself lucky if Osborn ever let him out of his cell again. Never mind the country.

Moonstone lowered the photograph. She was wearing a red, white, and blue hijab and designer sunglasses that glinted in the sun. Unlike Lester, she had actually managed to make herself look semi-inconspicuous. "This is definitely the spot where the picture of Hashim was taken." She stuffed the photograph into the side pocket of the duffle backpack she had over one shoulder, and turned to Daken. "Any trace of Lindy?"

Daken shook his head.

Lindy's likeness had been distributed amongst the local cops and H.A.M.M.E.R. stations, but Norman had sent his Avengers after Arabian Knight. He couldn't have cared less about Lindy.

Bullseye scratched the heat itch on his arm. It was ninety degrees, even in March, and humid, in spite of the desert landscape, with the closeness of the sea. "I'd murder a cold beer. We should've got the cab to leave us at the hotel."

"Norman didn't book us a hotel," said Moonstone. "Think of it as an incentive."

"Who'd have thought you'd turn into Norman's golden girl?"

For a moment, Daken thought Karla was going to push Bullseye into the path of the giant articulated container truck that was cannoning down the road in their direction.

The vehicle rumbled past with a wheeze of hot, diesel-scented air.

The moment went with it.

Daken couldn't help but be disappointed.

Both of his fellow Avengers were hot. They were both tired. Bullseye was on so much pain and anti-psychotic medication he could pollute the nearest river just by showering. They had both spent a day and a night cooped up in a sealed cabin with Daken and his mood-altering pheromones. Osborn had refused them the use of a Quinjet, or even a private charter, wanting to draw as little attention to their arrival in the country as possible while they had the advantage, and had sent them coach.

If ever one of them was going to snap and give Osborn his migraine for the day by murdering the other on a public street, then it should have been now.

"Let's split up." Daken's smile was as brilliant as the whitewash on the houses. Even his sweat was chic. Jewels of perspiration picked out his features like diamonds on a gold watch. "Someone here will have seen him."

"There's got to be five hundred people on this sidewalk, and that's just those in spitting range," said Bullseye. "It's not like our guy's got blue skin or horns or anything."

"He's a six and a half foot tall Palestinian with a golden sword," said Daken. "He should stick out a little."

"All right," Moonstone breathed out. "We'll ask around." She turned to Bullseye. "Try not to kill anyone. We're on holiday."

Bullseye made a face. "Self-control isn't my thing."

They broke up.

Bullseye went left. Daken right. Moonstone stepped up to the road with a view to darting between the rumbling line of trucks.

"Oh, by the way." Daken grinned over his shoulder. The others paused. "This is a Sharia country, Lester. You can't get a beer here." Laughing, he allowed the roar of the HGVs and the bustle of the street market to drown out Bullseye's vociferous cursing.

His pale face and Mohawk attracted some attention from the crowds. Bosaso was a busy port, but not a hugely cosmopolitan one. Most of the trade that passed through was bound across the Gulf of Aden, to Yemen and Oman, and to the neighboring nations of the Red Sea and the Persian Gulf. He smiled easily as he strolled through, as aloof as a prince and with the same divine right to wander wherever he pleased, idly fingering bolts of brightly colored fabrics, smelling spices in baskets, lingering over carts frying up bowls of vegetables and fish.

He was in no hurry.

He had accepted the invitation to join Norman Osborn's Avengers to spite his father. There had been no other reason, and he had never needed a better one. He hated Karla, loathed Lester, scorned Gargan, pitied the Sentry, admired Ares just a sneaking bit, and if there was one man he despised almost as much as he did his father then it was Norman Osborn. That little *almost*, though, made all the difference. It made the whole tired charade worthwhile, even if it meant doing as he was told and swallowing the hokum that periodically issued from the director's mouth. Because however onerous and demeaning he found playing with others, he knew that Wolverine and his Avenger buddies were hiding out in a lockup or a basement somewhere, watching it all play out on TV and hating it just a significant fraction more.

And so Daken did the work, and took his sweet time doing it.

He approached a food cart at which a woman in a headscarf was serving Persian cuisine. Fava beans sizzled with chilies in a shallow pan. Hummus, falafel, and pita breads filled metal trays. Daken sniffed the spiced aroma. Hashim had been here, to this very stall, lured perhaps by a taste of his home country before continuing with his business. Whatever his business might be.

The vendor was standoffish at first, wary of the foreigner at her cart, but after he ordered a sambusa and a sweet, cream-filled basbousa in endearingly halting Arabic she warmed to him noticeably. In reality, he spoke the language as well as she did, but in his experience nothing charmed a local like a tourist trying his best. At times like this, when he only had a minute or two to work on a person, it was useful to give his pheromones the extra help. Give him a month and he could wrap a sworn enemy around his finger, but a single pass was enough to nudge a stranger into a more receptive mood, or to trigger someone already disposed towards aggression into outright violence. Like in Chicago. It helped that he was a good-looking, well-tailored man, with a charm that he could turn on and off like hot water.

"The Palestinian?" she said, in answer to his inquiry, wreathing her now-smiling features in a great *hiss* of steam as she stirred her pan of beans. "Yes, he was here. Hashim, you say? He never gave his name, but if he's a foreigner then he'll be staying in one of the hotels on the beach." While Daken slowly ate his sambusa, a crisp pastry stuffed with spiced vegetables, she served another customer and, under the subtle urging of his pheromones, thought a little more. "Now I think on it, I believe I saw him earlier today." She nodded, as though consulting with herself. "Yes. I saw him getting into a limousine."

"A limousine? Is that unusual?"

Another nod. Then a shake. "There's been a few running

through Bosaso this last day or so. Heading west." She jerked her head backwards. "On Mareero Road, along the coast. I don't know where they're going. Nothing out that way but desert until you get to Bacaad."

Daken thanked her by buying two more basbousa and paying in American dollars. Karla and Lester could both do with having their days brightened with a little sweet, Iranian-inspired goodness.

He bit into his own as he drifted back into the crowd.

He was in no hurry.

CHAPTER NINETEEN
A Slightly Better World

The limousine pulled up at the end of the dusty driveway. Navid Hashim got out. Coming after a two-hour air-conditioned drive out from Bosaso, the desert heat enveloped him like a sauna towel. He leant back in over the passenger seat and pulled out the briefcase that was handcuffed to his wrist. Its contents weighed less than the case itself: two dozen plastic envelopes, each one containing a few sheets of legal paper. Drawing his ponytail over his shoulder with one hand, he shut the limo door with his knee. Immediately, the driver pulled away, hauling his vehicle's extended bulk around the turning point, and then roaring back towards the highway trailing a cloud of dust.

He hesitated a moment, then proceeded up the driveway to the barrier checkpoint.

The guards waved him through.

He was expected.

The colonial Italian-style villa sat amidst the dunes, overlooking the seething blue waters of the Gulf of Aden. Its walls were crisp and white, climbing orange and passion fruit vine scrambling between Tuscan windows with turtle-shell green shutters. A sand-pitted wall encircled the grounds, well patrolled by soldiers in dusty fatigues and sunglasses. It looked like something from the *One Thousand and One Nights*.

Or worse.

Like a drug lord's desert stronghold from a Hollywood action movie.

A few of the soldiers were former S.H.I.E.L.D., but the Contessa had deep pockets and, as Hashim was beginning to discover, few scruples, and most of the fighters he saw here were mercenaries and local militia. Those men and women of S.H.I.E.L.D. who had believed in something had gone with Dugan and Fury. Those who wanted to get paid and get even had thrown in with the Contessa.

Hashim had not thought he had believed in anything. He had seen where the wrong conviction could lead otherwise good people.

But then New York had happened.

There hadn't been a quiet moment since his escape that he hadn't spent wondering how many innocents had lost their lives during his battle with Ares. It was probably considerably more than the tally being circulated by the Americans, given that H.A.M.M.E.R. had taken over the search and rescue and were the ones supplying the figures. When he closed his eyes, he saw the faces of those he had passed as he ran. He recalled the young woman that he had knocked over on the sidewalk and paused to help back up. Was she injured? Dead? If he had simply run, rather than help her, and got further away, would she have escaped unharmed? Was there something more he could have said or done to prevent Ares from picking up his sword?

The guilt, he thought, he could have handled.

But the Contessa had seemed so… pleased.

He and Raazer had gone in to protect the *New York Bulletin* reporters, but the building had been emptied except for security, and he was left with the feeling that Valentina's intention had always been to provoke a bloodbath. He felt angry, used, but with so much blood staining his soul now he could see no other way out but forward.

Hashim shuddered as the other recurring memory suddenly hit him.

He had fought the God of War.

Inside the walls was a garden. It was not large, the demands of nurturing a green oasis in the middle of the desert prohibiting anything grander, but against the arid backdrop it was quite beautiful nonetheless. Juniper, tamarind and cape chestnut trees lined the winding path to the villa and filled the late afternoon air with their scent. Soldiers lounged in the shade of the trees with assault rifles in their laps, or sat on the steps of armored trucks with air conditioning and BBC Arabic spilling out through the open doors.

Hashim passed through their bored stares, trying to pretend the mercenaries did not trouble him, and approached the villa.

The flags of Somalia and Puntland hung limply over a stone-terraced portico.

Expelling his self-pity on a shake of the head, he stepped up to the porch and pushed through the front door.

A Somali man in a butler's uniform met him in the vestibule.

Hashim self-consciously kicked sand off his boots rather than traipse it over the immaculate mosaic floor tiles.

"As-salaam alaikum," he said, with a small bow.

"Wa alaikum as-salaam," the butler returned.

"I am here for Anisah Majid. She is expecting me."

The butler nodded and, without indicating whether or not Hashim was supposed to follow him, turned and exited the vestibule by the rear door.

Hashim shrugged and followed.

The vestibule led to a Roman peristyle, a colonnaded path encircling a magnificent grove of lemon and orange trees. Locals in servant liveries, instantly recognizable to anyone who had ever passed through an international hotel, worked under the shade. A stage had already been assembled at one end, and electricians were busy hooking up a microphone and setting up lighting. Others were laying out tables and chairs, setting out name cards, preparing a buffet table, and even, to Hashim's mild distaste, stocking a bar.

The plan had been for the Contessa to host the evening in person, but the capture of Mrs Reynolds-Lee had necessitated a change in plans. Undoubtedly, the Contessa's guests would view her absence as a cause for concern. They might even suspect betrayal, hence the scrambling of an eleventh-hour private jet from Sheik Saad airport for Hashim. Ensuring that both of the Contessa's senior lieutenants were present would reassure her guests as to her good faith when they arrived.

He looked over the preparations as the butler took him the long way around the peristyle.

Is this who they were now?

Kidnappers of women?

Consorts of criminals and terrorists?

When the world's villains became heroes, were its heroes forced to become villains in order to stand apart?

The Contessa had promised him a bloodless revolution, but the Iron Patriot had the power of an absolute monarch over the mightiest military regime ever created on Earth. He would not relinquish it peacefully, not even if he was given no other way out but death. Hashim did not know why this had been less obvious when the Contessa had first approached him. It had been simpler then. The evil of Osborn's Avengers had been clear to all who cared to see, while the Contessa's *rightness* had been equally plain. Back then, the only sin he had been guilty of committing was to imagine a better world.

His footsteps and the butler's echoed off the floor tiles, mingling with the gurgle and splash of what sounded like running water.

A sense of coolness radiated off the stones, subtler and more pleasing than the drying blast of the limousine's air conditioning. Monkeys rustled playfully through the fruit trees as he passed. Wild birds twittered and squabbled amongst themselves, uncaring for Hashim, or for the men and women working below them. Engraved columns and swirling mosaics, sheltered from sun, wind, sand, and time by the villa's thick walls, sought to lull him with their spectacle.

Hashim had known houses of greater opulence in Riyadh and Medina, and even during his short assignment with the Contessa in London. But the place he would always think of as *home* was the tin-roofed shack he had shared with his parents and siblings in Gaza, and the sight of such casual decadence never failed to rouse him to anger. It was the same anger that had fueled him as a young man. And yes, now he considered it, that familiar rage against the world's injustices had been an influence in his decision to reform Desert Sword and pledge himself to the Contessa as well.

S.H.I.E.L.D. had not been perfect. They had not brought peace and fairness to those parts of the world that needed them most. But the will had been there. Too many children under

H.A.M.M.E.R. were growing up in camps, as he had, displaced by the proliferation of wars. Too many young men were being given good reason to be angry and every opportunity to make the mistakes that he had been fortunate enough to escape.

He did not demand a perfect world. He just wanted a slightly better world.

The world as it had been.

At the rear of the peristyle there was an open doorway leading out onto a garden path. It ran flush against the side wall of the main structure, all the way to the sandy beach about five hundred yards away. A speedboat, a wooden dinghy, and a couple of jet skis bobbed against a private jetty. The speedboat was armed. There was also a machine gun set up in a pill box on the shoreline. The Gulf of Aden was a busy port, and several navies patrolled it, including H.A.M.M.E.R.'s, but Somali pirates did still occasionally venture in off the Indian Ocean when the payoff was big enough.

The splashing sound that Hashim had been hearing through the house was coming not from the sea, which was far enough away to be just a murmur of lapping waves and scraping sand, but from a swimming pool that had been excavated from the desert sand and beautifully tiled.

"Ma'a al salama," said the butler, averting his eyes from the pool with a slight bow, and then withdrew to the house, leaving Hashim on the path alone.

He turned and walked on, parallel to the pool, as Obax Majid, the mutant better known as Lightbright, completed her length and slung her arm over the tiles. She gasped, tugging the pair of swimming goggles she was wearing off her face and turned towards Hashim.

She was Somali, with dark skin and long hair worn in locs. Her eyes were the gauzy white of thin cloud on a sunny day, the lack of iris or pupil making it difficult to know what she was looking at or what she was really thinking. Her mutation granted her super strength and heightened physical endurance, flight, and the ability to conjure energy beams from her hands. She had been trained in hand-to-hand combat by Silver Sable. Her body emitted a gentle light that was at once soothing and distracting.

After less than a second under her gaze, Hashim was already feeling uncomfortable.

Ducking her head back underwater, she rinsed her face, blowing water from her nose and mouth as she resurfaced, and then wiped her face on her bicep. "You must be Navid Hashim." She pulled herself out of the pool, not bothering with the towel that had been laid for her across a deck chair, merely drawing wet dreadlocks from her chest and over her shoulder. Her footprints were already drying out in the sun.

Lightbright offered her hand.

She was wearing only a yellow swimsuit, but there was an intensity to her that was almost leonine. It was confidence. It was power. It was ruthlessness. It presented an authority that could be in no way altered or diminished by the clothing used to dress it, and that Hashim was welcome to avert his eyes if modesty should so compel him, but he could look forward to being held in the same contempt as the butler and the other servants if he did.

He hesitated only a moment before accepting her handshake.

Her grip was fiercely strong, not at all damp, and slightly warmer than his own.

"It is good to finally meet in person."

"Thank you. You have a beautiful home."

Lightbright's expression soured and she relinquished his

hand. "It is the Contessa's. Paid for by the ravaging of my country. When our common aims are met, I plan on bulldozing it into the sea."

Angry young women. Angry young men.

This was the company that Hashim had always kept, that he understood, and around which he felt strangely comfortable.

And perhaps that was the real reason he had aligned himself to Valentina's cause.

So he would not have to be angry alone.

As though approving of his terseness, Lightbright nodded towards the briefcase manacled to his wrist.

"It is all there?"

"Printouts of all the files taken during the Avengers Tower heist."

"And the originals?"

"Wiped, the drives destroyed."

"Good. They will have less value to their potential buyers otherwise."

"We are really doing this?"

Lightbright raised an eyebrow. With nothing in her eyes, it was impossible to tell whether she empathized with his doubts or not. "That was always the goal."

Hashim knew that. Perhaps it was the same as eating chicken without having to wring the neck yourself. It was supposed to be the Contessa here.

"I heard what you did in New York," she said.

Again, the face of the American woman flashed before Hashim's eyes. The look of shock in that moment before he had run into her.

"It was … bloodier than I had prepared myself for."

Lightbright smiled sourly. "It got Osborn out of the city, so in that regard it was just bloody enough. We fight for freedom, Hashim, for the overthrow of a tyrant. Either the goal is worth its cost or it is not. If it is not, then you should have told the Contessa *no* when she came to you."

Hashim wondered if he should have.

But the price always looked fairer before it came due.

"I will assign you guards for tonight," said Lightbright, and Hashim had the distinct impression that they were meant less for his own protection and more for her own peace of mind with regards to the safety of the files. "I have prepared a room for you in the villa where you will stay until you are needed in the atrium."

"Is there anything I can do to help prepare?"

Lightbright looked him up and down. She gave him a humorless smile. "You can change into something more formal."

CHAPTER TWENTY

Director Sofen

The soldier shone his flashlight through the cab's passenger side window. The innocent face of a criminal psychiatrist smiled back into the light. A large German Shepherd barked frenziedly at her passenger door, although not, apparently, with any unusual degree of intent or malice, as the flashlight slid away into the evening and the soldiers moved on to harass the next vehicle in line. The cab driver mumbled something to Daken, who was with him in the front, and to which he gave a disinterested smile and a nod. Moonstone, on the other hand, was the quintessence of an American abroad, and proud of it, and couldn't even feign half-hearted interest.

"The armed checkpoint up ahead has him nervous," Daken translated, summarizing quite ruthlessly, too, as the driver was still babbling away.

"Yeah." Bullseye leant halfway out of his open window. Like a dog locked for too long in a hot car. "I think we all got that."

A long line of idling cars snaked ahead of them. Most of them, if not all, were considerably beefier and more expensive-looking vehicles than the sand-pitted city cab they'd ridden out of Bosaso in hope. In the time they'd spent on the desert road the sun had set on them. It was sinking over the Bari desert, turning the sky above its dunes a dusky rose. The powerful floodlights on the house's serious-looking perimeter walls kept the stars from coming out. In place of them were the lights from around the Gulf of Aden, the twinkling jewels of moving ships, and of the small Yemeni towns glittering across the water.

Moonstone leant her arm over the front passenger seat, eliciting a creak of imitation leather and a stale whiff of cheap tobacco, and a complaint from Daken, and tried to get a view of the checkpoint ahead.

She wasn't sure what she'd been expecting to find out here in the middle of nowhere. A bunker, perhaps. Or an old fortress. Like the Alamo. Whatever she'd been imagining for the Arabian Knight's desert hideout, she was pretty sure that it hadn't been this. It looked like some billionaire eccentric's private party.

As she watched, or tried to, the soldiers manning the checkpoint stepped off the driveway and raised the barrier. The big black Land Rover at the head of the line growled forwards, the soldiers stepping back into the road to stop the next vehicle in line as the barrier came back down. Moonstone swore under her breath. She'd been hoping to catch a glimpse of the passengers as they got out, but the vehicles were parking up in the privacy of the compound's walls. The row of cars crunched forwards. Under some literal prodding from Daken, and under duress, their driver did the same.

"Arabian Knight is inside." Daken's nose was raised slightly, turned to the in-flowing air from the dashboard fans. "I can smell him quite clearly here."

Bullseye made a face. "It's like he's *in* you right now."

Daken turned his head very slowly around. Bullseye grinned at him.

"It's kinda kinky."

Daken looked forward with a sigh.

Leaving them to their bickering, because everyone had their own way of coping with being cooped up in a hot car and surrounded by Somali soldiers, she frowned towards the guard post ahead. She counted about ten soldiers and the one large dog, but there were more men on the walls that she couldn't see, hidden behind the floodlights, and undoubtedly more still in the house itself. Not to mention Arabian Knight himself and an unknown number of superhuman-class combatants from the super-team, Desert Sword. She also didn't know who, or what, was waiting outside with her in their cars. Moonstone wasn't invincible. Bullets could hurt her while she was tangible. But she could handle a few dozen regular guys with guns. Daken and Bullseye were just backup. There were just one too many unknowns for her tastes, and if a fight were to break out here on the driveway, however brief, it'd give Arabian Knight and his comrades ample time to escape before she could get to him.

She pressed her head to the ceiling, tempted to go just a *little* intangible for a better view of the checkpoint over the larger intervening cars.

Lester may have suffered from too much of a compulsive personality for him to secure any kind of long-term advantage from the footage he'd briefly had in his possession at the *New York Bulletin*. But Moonstone had plans. She had ambitions of her own that didn't necessarily revolve around being Norman Osborn's first choice lackey forever.

Director Sofen had a nice ring to it.

She'd been a public figure, as a team leader with the

Thunderbolts. She was known. And a world that had accepted Norman Osborn as its protector-in-chief could be made to take Karla Sofen into their hearts. She'd even indulge it with a little of the same Captain America cosplay. If that was what it took. She was just waiting for that *something*. That leverage. That angle. Whatever Desert Sword had, it was important enough to take, and important enough for Norman Osborn and Victoria Hand to want back.

If it wasn't also a good enough reason to postpone the slaughter of the help, then Moonstone didn't know what was.

"Is the woman from Avengers Tower inside, too?" Bullseye asked. There was an eager look in his eye.

"I wasn't in the building at the time. I wasn't in the same state." Daken shrugged. "I'm good, but I'm not that good."

"And Raazer?" asked Moonstone, remembering the single photograph of the sorcerer in his S.H.I.E.L.D. file, like incarnate evil captured to film and somehow wholly transferred to digital. If there was one person that she didn't want to fight without the Sentry and Ares, and yes, even the Iron Patriot, right beside her then it was the Black Raazer.

"His scent was dust and sand and death." Daken shook his head, gesturing to the desert all around them.

Moonstone understood.

"What's going on in there?" Bullseye muttered, leaning out the opposite side window without caring a damn for being conspicuous. "It's as though they've just punched the Avengers in the face and then invited all their friends over."

"We have to get in there and find out," Moonstone murmured.

"We can't just roll up in our taxi and ask to be let through," said Daken.

Moonstone frowned. "Can't we?"

"We know where Arabian Knight's hiding," said Bullseye. "I say we call in the Sentry to flatten this place and we can all go home."

"Having the Sentry destroy it is your solution to everything," said Daken, wearily.

"I've not found the problem it won't fix yet."

"We *could* just ask to be let in," said Moonstone, thinking the idea through even as she spoke it aloud. "Desert Sword don't know who we are."

"They know who we are," said Daken.

"They knew who Venom was," Moonstone corrected. "Victoria's convinced that was down to loose talk amongst the medical research staff."

"Well, if the overpromoted accountant is sure…"

"When Raazer spoke to you, he called you Wolverine, correct?"

Daken nodded reluctantly. "Correct."

She turned to Lester. "And the agent you fought in Avengers Tower: did she refer to you as Bullseye or as Hawkeye?"

"Hawkeye. I guess."

Before either of the two men could debate the point further, her regular tourist's outfit rippled, her moonstone's power of control over her surface molecules transforming it into a skin-tight silver costume that extended all the way down her legs to her ankles. The stars-and-stripes hijab that she had created for herself to cover her blonde hair shed its color, hardening into a crystal mask that covered her eyes. Even her expression changed. Her smile became a little tighter, her eyes a little harder. Even Norman might have needed to look twice to be certain she was the same woman. She saw the driver's huge eyes staring at her through the rearview mirror as she stretched out across the back seat. Luxuriating. As though the red, black and gold of Ms Marvel had been as much a restraint as a disguise.

The driver blurted something that brought Daken out in a smile. He didn't feel it important enough to translate and Moonstone didn't ask.

She didn't want to imagine the kind of thing that'd make Daken smile, and she'd been a prison psychiatrist in another life. "Can you imagine three characters less out of place at a shady gathering of international criminals and terrorists than Moonstone, Daken and Bullseye?"

"What about this guy?" Bullseye gestured his head towards the driver in the seat in front of him. "He looks as guilty as hell."

"Yeah..." Moonstone sighed. "Can either of you two handle a manual clutch without looking like an idiot?"

Daken raised his hand.

With a nod, Moonstone turned back to the passenger side window and her partial view of the checkpoint, as a grinning Bullseye unplugged his seatbelt and tightened it into a garotte around his fist.

Moonstone was allowed to be a monster. Moonstone was allowed to be OK with it. But for some reason she didn't want to watch.

As though there was a little bit of Ms Marvel still in there.

Deeper than her Kree power could dig out of her so easily.

CHAPTER TWENTY-ONE

Big in Japan

"I'm underdressed."

They'd only just passed out of the vestibule and into the atrium, and Bullseye was already complaining.

He also wasn't wrong.

About a hundred people in black tie and dinner gowns mingled under the elegant, sweet-scented canopy of citrus trees. Tables had been laid out and prepared with table settings, but as far as Moonstone could tell these were being largely ignored. For that small mercy, she was grateful. Nothing would have made her, Bullseye, and Daken, once he was done parking the cab, stick out like being the only three people standing in a room filled with men and women sitting around tables in evening wear. Instead, they congregated in discrete little groups of between five and eight around the buffet table and the bar.

Karla recalled the research conferences and summer schools she'd attended as a grad student. The American Psychiatric Association mixers where everyone had "mixed" in their own little groups with the people they already knew, getting slowly drunker, and occasionally getting drunk enough to propel one of their number in the direction of the plenary speaker to impress him or her with the erudite question they'd spent the evening formulating.

This was a different crowd, but the social dynamics of *us* and *them* were uncannily similar.

Everyone's attention was on the unaccompanied microphone on the stage.

The effect of it was electric. There was almost enough energy in the crowd for her to reach out and shape.

"I could kill a waiter or something…"

"Uh-huh," said Moonstone, not really paying attention.

A few individuals, like Moonstone, were in costume. Courtesy of her time on the CSA extraordinary rendition program, and as a profiler for Osborn's Thunderbolts, she even had a few names to go with the menagerie of outfits.

"Talk about Z-list," she muttered under her breath.

As though to physically distance herself from any hint of an association, she withdrew to a corner table. It was round, draped with a pristine white cloth, and with seating for twelve. The lemon tree that spread its canopy overhead rustled and shimmered. Its leaves looked and sounded like hand-rolled shapes of metal foil in the lighting from the stage. A column carved into the likeness of the Roman pantheon peeked from beneath the foliage. The way gods did. Moonstone smiled sourly. She supposed you had to regularly see a member of the Roman pantheon eating takeout pizza to see the funny side.

"I should have just come as I was," she said to herself.

Better that than be recognized in public with these people.

None of the middle-grade henchmen on show were exactly

Avengers class. They were regional players, at best. Big in Japan, presumably. A few minutes ago, she'd been daydreaming about ousting Norman Osborn as director of H.A.M.M.E.R. A public figure, she'd thought. Team leader with the Thunderbolts. Known. Well, if she ever planned on tossing the Ms Marvel persona out the window then the last thing her actual reputation needed was to be seen with this lot.

Leaning across the table, she picked up one of the folded seating cards. It was more functional than the kind you'd see at a wedding, just a name written in plain font. She read it aloud. It meant nothing to her. She wasn't sure whether that surprised her or not. Even she couldn't know everybody. She unfolded it, turned it over, hoping to find some hint of the name's affiliation like the cards at the APA dinners. *Dr K. Sofen, UCLA*. But there was nothing. No clue at all. Apart from the name, it was just a blank piece of bent card.

She flicked away the card in disgust, and then hailed a passing waiter.

He was carrying tall glasses of bubbling white wine on a silver tray.

"Give me a glass of that champagne," she said.

"It's Franciacorta," he replied with an aggrieved sigh and a mild Italian accent.

"Whatever," she said, and took two.

She sipped at one and shooed the waiter with her eyes. The fizz was so powerful it almost broke into her frown. Holding the glass in front of her face, almost like an ancillary to her own mask, she studied the ten or eleven costumed villains who mingled across the separate groups. But there was not much help to be had there either. They were mercenary types. Born henchmen. Not moral, or intelligent, enough for an agenda of their own. They were the sort who'd work for anyone who'd meet their price, and generally no one good. Separate from the groups they appeared to work for, those individuals did occasionally cross companies, passing on their way to the buffet or the bar to trade in-jokes and pleasantries. There was a camaraderie amongst the super villains-for-hire circuit. They had more in common with one another than with those who hired them, or those whose deaths their money bought. Even supposed arch-rivals insulted one another by their real names, rather than that of their costumed personas, when they fought.

And that, Moonstone thought, with unexpected nostalgia, was real closeness.

The costumed henchmen spoke to one another using the lingua franca of the mercenary circuit, English, but elsewhere, Moonstone would swear to hearing twenty different languages being spoken at the same time.

She wished Ares was here.

Staying casual, she turned her back on the atrium crowd and looked up into the branches of the lemon tree, as though one of the brightly colored birds had just caught her fancy. While drawing her hair back from her wine glass, she tapped on the communicator bud in her ear canal. "Daken," she subvocalized, the vibrations of the words through her facial bones enough to trigger the receiver in her ear. "I could use you in here."

"The soldiers are holding all of the drivers outside," came the buzzing response.

Moonstone tapped out her irritation with the wine glass on her lip. She bet that Norman never had to deal with this crap. He rarely led a mission himself anymore. Not unless there was going to be a camera somewhere. "Are you telling me you can't get away?"

"I'm telling you that I can't get away without disposing of three guards and twenty witnesses."

"Do I need to send Bullseye outside?"

A sigh. "Give me five minutes."

Daken cut her off before Moonstone had the chance to do it herself.

Seething over Wolverine's pettiness for a second or two, she took a deep breath and composed herself. She took another sip of the wine. Daken was much easier to deal with over the phone. When she spoke with him in person, she felt such a compelling urge to punch him in the face, or to drag him with her into a closet, that she could never be entirely sure afterwards what she had said. She worried sometimes that it was her, but the effect he had on Mac, Lester, and Ares was broadly similar.

Some people were just annoying.

"Do you know how to work one of these?"

Moonstone turned.

Bullseye was standing behind the next chair around with a bowtie dangling off his finger. She pursed her lips and looked him up and down. He was wearing a tuxedo. She hadn't actually noticed him leave, but if her time in charge of the Thunderbolts had taught her anything, it was to not get caught up on every trifling detail.

"You've got blood on it," she said.

Bullseye looked at it. "Oh yeah."

She took the tie off him and stuffed it into the breast pocket of his jacket. Then she undid the collar button of his white shirt and patted down his jacket. "It looks better this way. You don't want to be mistaken for a waiter."

Bullseye grinned down at her.

Moonstone grimaced. "Don't make me drop you over the

Indian Ocean from forty thousand feet." Her hands, still on his chest, and about twenty times stronger than his entire upper body, pushed him firmly away. "Because I absolutely will." Without bothering to care what his reaction might be, she turned back to the crowd filling the atrium.

A small knot of activity drew her eye.

An African woman in a bright yellow floor-length dress had entered from one of the side passages, and was crossing to the stage. A number of guests moved to intercept her as soon as she appeared, demanding to know the whereabouts of someone called Valentina, but no sooner did they approach her than they were stumbling to get out of her way, confused and ashamed at having so crassly attempted to impede her, and melting back into the crowd. The woman went through them like sunlight through fog. Her long dress, Moonstone noted with professional approval, had a slit leg to facilitate hand-to-hand combat. The complicated strapping that supported the outfit around the open back and thighs was just perfect for the concealment of a small handgun or a knife. Her hair draped the dress' shoulders in dreadlocks that fell as far down as her waist. Her eyes were swirling, luminous voids of white.

Moonstone took another gulp of wine. "Obax Majid."

"You know her?" said Bullseye.

"She was an anti-registration terrorist during the Civil War. Before getting her butt handed to her by Iron Man and landing herself a cell in a CSA prison. I read all the files."

"Someone let her out?"

"It must have happened before Norman's time."

Norman was better than that.

He never let anybody out.

"Was she with Desert Sword?" said Lester.

She shrugged. "It didn't exist then. The question never came up. But if they turn over their membership half as fast as the Avengers, then I'd say the odds are pretty fair."

"Is she dangerous?"

Moonstone watched as Lightbright took to the stage and crossed to the microphone. With the hard, inscrutable smile of an angel, she surveyed her audience. Moonstone felt a shiver of perfect serenity wash over her. She wanted to sit down, smile, take out a pen and draw love hearts on the backs of the seating cards whilst absorbing every word that the woman had to say. Even diluted a hundred-fold by the crowd, Lightbright's mutant power was irresistible.

The audience fell silent.

Even the waiters became quiet and stopped their service to watch the stage.

"Yes." Moonstone ground out the word with a fantastic effort of will. "She's dangerous."

"Good."

Moonstone glanced up.

She supposed it took more than a casual brush of a mutant's energy to pacify *him*.

"Is she the one you fought in the Tower?"

Bullseye looked briefly irritated at the question, and didn't answer.

Moonstone took it as a no.

Lester was an exemplary murderer and a first-rate bully. But the day Bullseye went straight-up toe to toe with a superhuman opponent like Lightbright was the day that Norman finally got the pleasure of peeling him off the sidewalk and sending his body to the *Daily Bugle* for their front page. And deep down, he knew it. Moonstone had always suspected it was why he acted the way he did. It was classic little man syndrome. Why else would a killer with such a stellar body count continue to pick on ordinary guys and under-powered saps like Daredevil?

She turned back to the stage.

When her earbud trilled, she almost jumped.

Without pulling her eyes from Majid, she took the incoming call.

It would just be Daken, calling back.

When Victoria's voice buzzed through instead, she frowned, confused.

"Report..."

But of course.

Norman and the rest of the Avengers were on standby at Al Anad airbase in Yemen, waiting on Karla's call.

Clearing her throat and taking a long slug of wine, as though a mutant's power could be overcome with some ridiculously expensive Italian white, Moonstone hid her moving lips with the wine glass and answered. "Hawkeye and myself are inside the house. Wolverine is in the grounds. No sign of the Arabian Knight so far, or any other known members of Desert Sword, but..." She glanced again at the stage and fought the desire to stop protesting and hang up. "But Obax Majid has just come in and it looks as though she's the one in charge." Pulling her eyes away, she cast them once more over the atrium. "I count eleven superhumans in addition to her. Enough to be a challenge if I had to fight them all at the same time." Once again, not blasting her way in through the front door had proved itself to be the smartest course of action.

"You've done well. We're coming in. Sit tight and wait for backup..."

Karla let the voice in her ear drift away from her.

She turned back to the stage.

Lightbright was speaking.

"Norman Osborn." The mutant enunciated every syllable as though it mattered. "Norman Osborn." This time she spat it. Nods and murmurs spread through her audience. "None of us are here tonight because we are friends, but because of Norman Osborn, for as long as we are here together, we are allies." Her face remained beatific, as capable of expression as a statue, but her voice grew cold. "You have traveled far, to my country, because your own strongholds are no longer safe. They feel the grip of a tyrant." She gave a smile. The light eddied around her eyes. "But now you are in my country. And I have fought foreign rule all my life."

Bullseye gave a sigh that Moonstone was sure had to be audible from the other side of the house. "Can I just shoot her already?"

"Why?"

"I don't know. There's just something about her that makes me want to."

"Well, live with it. We're going to get what we came for."

He looked sullen. "Girl scout."

Moonstone hissed under her breath as she turned back to the stage. "Go outside."

"Why?"

"I don't know. Just go. Help Daken or something."

Bullseye sneered, but departed without further complaint.

Meanwhile, Lightbright had finished her introduction and, under her tacit direction, waiters began moving amongst the audience distributing paper scrolls. Karla took one. She pulled off the ribbon and unrolled it. It looked like a menu at a New York restaurant trying to appear authentically East African, with about thirty items on offer and no prices. She read down the list.

Hydra defectors working for H.A.M.M.E.R. Criminals granted new identities and pardons in exchange for terms of service under Norman Osborn.

This was what Arabian Knight and Desert Sword had stolen from Avengers Tower.

It was a *Who's Who* of everyone and anyone whose identity could compromise Osborn, and themselves, if it were to become known. Karla didn't think she'd ever stopped to appreciate just how broad a church Norman was leading until she was halfway through that list. As a blueprint for world peace, it was certainly innovative. What were Hydra, A.I.M. and all the rest of them for if H.A.M.M.E.R. covertly espoused most of the same goals. No doubt, they were the groups making up Lightbright's audience now. Hydra. A.I.M. Roxxon. The Maggia families. Everyone who'd lost members and was hemorrhaging money to Osborn's regime. Perhaps even a few kleptocratic governments who were finding their activities squeezed out by the vastly better organized and equipped H.A.M.M.E.R.

Desert Sword were auctioning the files off *for money*.

Moonstone actually felt a little dirty. She had taken the Thunderbolts gig for the money, of course, but she expected better of other people. For no reason that she could put satisfactorily into words, she liked to believe that there were better people than her out there.

She felt her faith in humanity shaken.

At the bottom of the list, she paused.

She read the final item again.

The Patriot List.

Reaching up to her earbud, she quietly cut Victoria off.

A shiver passed through her as she read the explanatory text below the sub-title.

The full list of every candidate for Norman Osborn's Dark Avengers, it said, complete with how to contact them and the necessary blackmail to use against them.

Norman Osborn. So predictably pedantic. She had always known. She had *known* that a list like this had to exist somewhere and now she was close enough to it that she could almost feel the crinkle of paper between her fingers.

An elegant-looking woman in a yellow-trimmed suit stepped up to the stage and took the microphone from Majid. "We will begin with lot number one," she said, as Lightbright stepped down. Moonstone tracked her for a while, but soon lost sight of her amongst the citrus blooms and statues, and the sheer mass of people. "The identities of all Power Broker Inc. agents currently employed by Oscorp subsidiaries in North Africa. We will open the bidding at ten million dollars."

It looked as though someone was cleaning house.

But it was worse than that.

They were cleaning *her* house.

This wasn't about the money at all. Majid, or whoever she was representing, was making a play for the top job. For *her* job. By leaking these files, they could make an awful lot of money, yes, but they could also remove the elements of H.A.M.M.E.R. most loyal to Osborn and thus the most resistant to a change in regime without ever dirtying their own hands. By outsourcing the work to the most interested parties it could be done overnight. The names on these lists could be filling obituaries by tomorrow, and there were far too many to put into protection or reassign in time.

And whoever held the Patriot List could own the Avengers.

That was what this was all about. She knew it. Someone else fancied themselves director of H.A.M.M.E.R. All they needed to do was get rid of Norman Osborn. Karla didn't carry a phone, or a watch, but by her estimate she had thirty minutes before Norman arrived with the cavalry. Thirty minutes in which to get her hands on those files herself or, at the very least, to make sure that Norman started running out of backup Ms Marvels.

And anyway, how was it going to look if she couldn't handle a bunch of also-rans without help?

She tapped the earbud again. "Daken. About those soldiers you needed disposing of." She smiled glassily. "Bullseye's on his way out to you now."

CHAPTER TWENTY-TWO

Worth the Ticket Price

The last soldier in the roped off parking lot jerked, folding into a pleasingly neat heap in the flowerbed beside the gravel driveway. Bullseye tugged the throwing knife from the mercenary's earhole and wiped it clean on the dead guy's desert khaki. While he was down, he removed the man's sunglasses – sunglasses at night, how cool was that guy? – and hooked them over his own ears. He turned to Daken who was just finishing off the drivers, which, given who they drove for, was harder work than it sounded, and Bullseye had arguably drawn the longer straw with the soldiers.

"How do I look?"

"Like a grinning idiot in sunglasses."

Bullseye shrugged.

Keeping the glasses on regardless, he raided the corpse for his sidearm. A Makarov PM 9mm. Classic. He ejected the twelve-round magazine, checked the load was full, which it was, and slotted it back into the rack with a reassuringly hefty *click*. Further rummaging yielded three spare magazines.

Forty-eight dead soldiers, all neatly lined up in a row.

"Karla wants us to find Arabian Knight and get the files before the action starts."

"Why?" said Daken.

"Do you care?"

"Not really, no."

"Which way, then?"

The mutant drew a tissue from a pocket and wiped blood from his nostrils. He sniffed, then pointed towards a garden path that led into the darkness around the side of the villa. "That way."

Bullseye tucked in behind as Daken loped towards the side path. It wended unhurriedly around delicate topiary and prickly bushes that flourished in the darkness between the side of the house and the perimeter wall and which smelled faintly of New Yorker cocktails. After a hundred yards, the path became a terrace, and the side wall a corner. Daken dropped silently into a bush and effectively disappeared. Showoff. With a wiry flexibility and beanpole physique, Bullseye drew his pistol to his chest and slid behind a narrow kumquat trunk.

A rock garden ran another hundred yards or so towards the beach. A small jetty broke up the waves, extending into the water with a handful of boats. Nearer to the house, soldiers toting bulletproof vests and AK-47s patrolled around a stone verandah and a swimming pool. Bullseye counted six. Two more manning a machine gun on the beach.

Bullseye glanced sideways.

With sunglasses, he could barely see Daken at all.

But he looked good.

You want to see showing off?

Swinging out of hiding, he raised the Makarov PM and fired…

One. Two. Three. Four. Five. Six.

The soldiers patrolling the verandah fell down like dominoes, one after the other, the last to go splashing face down into the pool. He bobbed on his chest in a darkening cloud, buoyed by the padding of his tactical vest. Without pausing to appreciate his own artistry, Bullseye swung his aim towards the beachfront guard post on the jetty. With a smirk that made the impossible shot look effortless, he squeezed off two more rounds. There was a delay of about a second in which the two machine-gunners were, technically, still alive, after which both men gave a savage jerk and slid behind their gun nest's waist-high fascine.

I'll give you showing off.

"Yeah. I'm actually *that* good."

"Not exactly subtle or quiet though," said Daken, appearing with tigerish soundlessness and grace from the foliage at Bullseye's side. "But pretty good." Without waiting to check that the coast was clear, knowing better than Bullseye could that it was, the mutant took the steps up the verandah, and tore the lock out of the back door.

Karla heard the break-in behind her corner table. She coughed loudly to cover what she assumed to be the sound of Daken and Bullseye coming in through the back, feigning a sore throat, which conveniently, and quite believably, involved her draining a second glass of fizzing Franciacorta. She glanced quickly around the crowded atrium, but no one else appeared to have noticed the noise. A bidding war had broken out between four or five criminal factions for the identities of ex-Maggia convicts blackmailed into working as bag-men between Osborn and the Hood. It was currently going once at fifteen million dollars, and the competition was keeping things heated. Ordinarily, that would have been worth the ticket price on its own, but she was too distracted to enjoy the show.

How long was it since her last contact with Daken? Ten minutes? Norman and the rest of the help would be halfway across the Gulf by now. She didn't wear a watch, didn't carry a cell: the burdens of the figure-tight costume.

She sighed. The struggle was real.

Setting the second empty wine glass down on the table with the first, she turned from the auction stage and saw two armed silhouettes passing behind the screen of orange leaves, walking around the peristyle towards the broken back entrance. They didn't seem to be in any hurry, yet, but Karla could hear them attempting to radio someone who clearly wasn't answering.

She couldn't just walk out of the atrium to intercept them without someone noticing, but in doing so she might just be able to distract the soldiers for a moment or two. Karla was exceptionally good at distracting soldiers.

She turned back to the atrium and started.

Lightbright was standing in front of her, flanked by a pair of smartly suited and discreetly armed bodyguards. She glowed, an effect that had little to do with, but was powerfully amplified by, the dazzling yellow dress she wore. Karla felt her desire to leave ebb and her reasons for doing so become increasingly intangible. In such close proximity to that warm, soothing light, they seemed laughably unimportant. This, Karla told herself, holding onto lucidity with an ice-water grip, is why normal people hate mutants. The X-Men and their allies and their constant bleating for more rights had done as much to keep Osborn in power as the Skrull had ever done to put him there in the first place.

Lightbright, shorn of any expression in her pearly eyes, gave her an empty smile.

"Going somewhere, Moonstone?"

Bullseye saw the two mercenaries coming at about the same time that the two mercenaries saw him. They came around the corner from the direction of the front entrance with Kalashnikovs slung low in their arms. They didn't look predisposed towards shooting anyone, but Bullseye saw the moment that changed by the looks on their faces, clocking the mutant with the foot-high Mohawk and the blood-splattered claws standing in the broken door.

Bullseye swung round the Makarov PM.

"No."

Daken pushed his way in front, as if that would ever stop Bullseye from shooting, intercepting the first mercenary with a punch in the chest. His claws slid through Kevlar like a good knife through human muscle while the mutant's superior strength lifted him clear off his feet. The guy was already on his way backwards under the impetus when Daken ripped his claws back and kicked him on his way. The second soldier opened up with his AK, his fire effectively silenced by the body falling across his gun's muzzle at the exact moment that he pulled the trigger. Daken covered the distance in a single bound, the remaining mercenary managing to roll off his very dead comrade, losing the rifle in the process but pulling a knife. Daken glided around his desperate slashes, smiling all the while, as though dancing with a partner he was looking forward to killing later if they didn't dance well enough to make him look good.

Ducking under a last, reckless lunge, Daken sidestepped around the flailing soldier and punched his claws through the guy's wrist. A split-second howl of pain burst from the guy's lips on finding his favorite hand pinned to the stone wall, ending when Daken slit his throat. Arterial spray decorated the mutant's tattooed face.

Points for style.

"Good thing I didn't shoot 'em," said Bullseye. "That was really quiet."

Daken wrenched his claws out of the stonework. The unsupported body slumped to the ground. Bullseye wondered how a person could smile so much, under that amount of blood, and express so little. The tattoos showed more feeling. "No one heard," Daken said, stepping back over the body and turning towards Bullseye. "Come on."

With Daken going first, they ran along the corridor towards the larger main building at the back of the atrium. The auction continued to their left. There wasn't even a wall between them, just a few sweet-smelling plants and some statuary. The voyeuristic thrill of murdering two guys so close to so many pulled a smile across Bullseye's gaunt cheeks and made his heart thump with excitement. It was moments like this that made working for Osborn worthwhile. He ran on after Daken. The woman's voice from the stage called out thirty-five million dollars. A New York Italian accent in the audience met the bid. Bullseye gave a rueful shake of his head as he ran. If he'd known he could have made that much money on his night off then Desert Sword wouldn't have needed to break into Avengers Tower. He'd have stolen the files and sold them on to Don Karnelli himself.

At a doorway in the right-hand wall, Daken accelerated into a near-soundless charge.

They'd passed other doors on their way, but this one stood out due to the armed guard either side. Daken punched his claws through the throat of the nearest, while Bullseye took out the farthest, a perfect throw of the Makarov PM cracking his temple.

Both guys dropped either side of the doorway at exactly the same time.

Scooping the pistol off the floor, Bullseye smiled approvingly as he checked it over. They didn't make guns like this anymore. No one did weaponry you could pistol whip a guy with from fifteen yards away and still expect to shoot afterwards, not like the old Soviet Union.

"In here?" he asked, bringing Daken out in a wince with his careless volume, and gestured with his head towards the door.

The mutant nodded.

"Good. I want to be able to say I got the guy who beat Ares."

"He didn't beat Ares. He just ran away."

Lester grinned, feeling the muscles involved pulling on the bullseye symbol on his forehead. "Killjoy."

Daken tried the door.

Lightbright and her two guards stood between Moonstone and the rest of the atrium. "Going somewhere?" the mutant asked again.

"Bathroom?"

Karla wished she could have come up with something better but the mutant's lambency was making it difficult to care enough about lying well.

Lightbright looked over the empty wine glasses on the table, as though surveying all of Karla's dirty laundry. "You seem nervous."

"High stakes."

Lightbright met her false smile with an impassive wall. "And yet you have not bid once."

"My ticket hasn't come up."

The mutant took a step ahead of her guards, her cold, fog-bank eyes suddenly filled with menace. "I know you, Dr Karla Sofen. *Moonstone*. You were the leader of the Thunderbolts when I was a fugitive from the CSA." The darkening of her expression foreshadowed the hardening of her voice. "You worked for Osborn."

Karla made her shrug nonchalant. "Even Norman was working for Iron Man then."

"I don't see you on TV anymore," Lightbright went on. "Why is that? You used to be everywhere."

"Younger model?"

"I once visited the sweatshop in Burao, where children as young as five were put to work making Moonstone action figures for the American market. I burned it to the ground. And killed its American managers."

Karla backed slowly towards the table while she tried to figure out in her own mind what this shakedown was all about. Was it because she was suspected of still working for Osborn, or was it because she'd used to work for Stark? Wouldn't *that* be some delicious irony. Either way, she didn't see this encounter ending politely, and her backup couldn't have been more than ten minutes away.

Was she the leader of the Avengers, or wasn't she?

With her hands spread across the table behind her, she stopped retreating and met the mutant's smoke-bright eyes. "You see, Obax – and yes, I've read your CSA file, I know who you are, too – the thing about child labor in poorer countries, when it comes down to it, is that nobody really gives a crap."

Perched on the edge of the table, she punched out with an open hand, a brilliant yellow blast of moonstone power sending

Lightbright flying across the atrium. She crashed through the statue of Mars behind her, which was satisfying on many levels, knocked down several tuxedoed attendees, before crashing finally into the main stage.

Her two guards drew sidearms.

Point-blank, they opened fire.

Daken found the door locked.

Before he had even raised his claws to smash it open, several things happened at once. Twenty soldiers in desert khakis and ballistic vests came charging down the corridor from both directions. A blast of unearthly energy that looked suspiciously like Moonstone's flashed like the light source of a chiaroscuro film through the screen of leaves, and then a lot of people started shooting one another at the same time.

Daken took it apart in his head, took it one piece at a time, pulling Bullseye in close as the onslaught of fire shredded the shoji-thin walls of orange leaves between himself and the bulk of the shooters in the atrium.

He felt no great affection for his fellow Avenger, but his adamantium-laced skeleton made for an effective human shield.

Bullseye cursed him with blood-flecked grunts and staring eyes as bullets riddled his back and mowed through the soldiers who had been approaching on their left and right. As the initial flurry naturally thinned itself out, Daken rolled the furious assassin off him and dumped him to the floor.

"I'm... gonna... kill you," Bullseye gasped. "You won't even... see it... coming."

"Thanks," said Daken.

And then the next thing happened.

The door unlocked itself.

It opened out into the corridor, six foot four inches and a hundred and eighty pounds of Arabian Knight standing framed by the whitewashed wood. He was dark-skinned, long black hair tied back in a ponytail and with a short beard neatly trimmed. He was wearing a sleeveless, richly colored jacket with a padlocked briefcase chained to his wrist.

After a week-long manhunt, they had him: the man who had blown up Midtown East and bested Ares.

"Hello, tall, dark and handsome," Daken smiled, and pushed his way in.

CHAPTER TWENTY-THREE

Something That Happens to Other People

Bullets zipped through the air like popcorn stuffed too tightly into a microwave. They pulped leaves, chewed up wood, drilled through walls. Plasma bolts and exotic particle rays lent the atrium a syrupy tone, turning the air brown with the caramelized sugars of plant sap and burnt flesh. Most of the early combatants were already dead, their bodies strewn over the atrium around the stage, but the mercenaries pouring in from the front, back, and adjoining rooms made up for the losses and were contributing more than their share in order to keep the gunfight hot. The surviving attendees and their entourages had withdrawn to cover, firing in all directions from behind friezes of Olympus and overturned tables, with the exception of a handful of super-powered thugs still going determinedly at it, hand-to-hand, in the middle of a ten-way shooting match.

Moonstone could admire their dedication even as she bemoaned their intelligence.

Lightbright's bodyguards dropped the lightweight SMGs

they'd been carrying and drew batons. Had she not turned herself intangible the moment she'd thrown an energy blast into Lightbright, then the guns would have riddled her most impressively. Instead, the bullet spray had mown down the squad of mercenaries running around behind her and dinged the armored exosuit of Hydra's East Africa commander with a ricochet, effectively igniting this particular powder keg.

Hindsight was such a pain.

Snapping their truncheons to their full length, the guards simultaneously thumbed the activation studs to send electrical current flowing through the weapons' shafts. They slid smoothly into complementary stances, the guard to her left with his baton held out and low, the one to her right high and back. Moonstone had never committed the effort to improve her fighting skills. Ares had offered to train her, many times, but there were things she would rather do with her weekends than get sweaty and have her face punched repeatedly by the God of War. She was strong and fast enough that it rarely came up as an issue.

These two had clearly put in the hours that she hadn't.

With a scream, both men leapt, springing apart to come at her from left and right, high and low, at the same time.

She caught the wrist of the man on her left before he was aware of the fact she'd moved. He dropped his baton and folded to his knees with a scream. Moonstone crushing all eight bones in his wrist had something to do with it. At the same time, she willed herself fully intangible, the physical bond of her hand on the man's limp wrist dragging him after her into the same anti-gravitational phase. The second fighter's baton went through her. It went through his less fortunate comrade, too.

As far as their molecules were concerned, the rest of the universe was something that happened to other people.

The fighter swung around, off-balance, and Moonstone returned herself to the proper phase. She swung the crippled guard overarm and through the table.

It was not, she thought, without a shred of sympathy, his day at all.

The second fighter recovered, whipping a roundhouse kick at head height over the wrecked table. Karla blocked it casually on a finger. The guard struggled against her. "You're just embarrassing yourselves." She backhanded him to the floor and he skidded, unconscious, across the shooting gallery.

She turned her back for a moment, and the broken remnants of the auction stage exploded into splinters.

The force of it hurled her back from the smashed table and onto her side, showering her and the last few combatants still close by with sawdust. Lightbright emerged from the haze, hovering three feet off the ground and wreathed in a blistering corona of white light. Her eyes, glassy before, now blazed like caged stars. Wrathful energies gauntleted her clenched fists and her dreadlocks shimmered in their light like iron chains.

"Spoiled, arrogant, little girl. You think that because you get away with it in Osborn's America you can get away with it here. You have never been so wrong."

Moonstone drew on her own power source, but the will to use it just wasn't there.

Bathed in Majid's brilliance, every rationale she had for being there looked thin enough for her to see right through.

Taking command of the Thunderbolts.

Becoming an Avenger.

Trying so hard to please a man she mocked and loathed.

Genuinely trying to fix the Sentry.

She wanted to be a hero. A real one, rather than pretend. But it was too late for her and she knew it. It had become too late the day she'd looked in the mirror and realized exactly what she was. The day that she had gone upstairs and drowned her mother in her own bath, burning down the entire apartment afterwards, so that she would never have to go through the same realization that Karla already had.

That she was a monster.

She could never be a hero. Taking Osborn's job as director would be thin consolation. Her shoulders sagged.

She fought for *nothing*.

No one would even miss her when she was gone.

She didn't even raise her fists to defend herself as Lightbright's fist cracked her jaw.

Hashim's eyes widened in alarm. He ducked back into his suite, pulling the door shut behind him and slamming it into Daken's shoulder. The door broke in half over Daken's body. His muscles were denser than an ordinary human being's, his bones were harder, his skin repairing the cuts and traumas it suffered more quickly. A *lot* more quickly, but it still hurt, and the pain made him angry. Shrugging off the blunt force of fifty pounds of solid Italian oak, he bared his teeth in a growl and charged through the remains of the door.

The room inside was luxurious. A four-poster bed dominated the floorspace, silk curtains stirring under the sultry touch of the Gulf of Aden coming through the open windows. Priceless carpets adorned with Arabic geometries covered the dressed stone of the floor. Cut flowers, desert blooms picked from the garden outside, filled vases on every shelf, stand, and table.

Arabian Knight drew his golden shamshir one-handed as he stumbled back from the door. Daken followed him in, deflecting the first clumsy stroke that Hashim sent his way. Bone claws scraped and snarled across mystic metal as Hashim withdrew his sword and back-pedaled onto an exquisite Persian rug, swinging a roundhouse with his metal briefcase. Daken's claws snicked through the chain, centrifugal force sending the briefcase flying off the man's wrist and well wide of Daken's head. It struck the wall and broke open in a cataract of fluttering papers.

The files.

Daken made to call out for Bullseye when he heard the distinctive *pap-pap-pap* report of the assassin's pistol. Bigger guns returned his fire. With his heightened mutant senses, Daken heard every one of the two thousand bullets chewing into the thick stone wall behind him, and sighed. He had no idea what Bullseye was using for cover, but he had stopped screaming threats after Daken and appeared to have started enjoying himself.

Daken turned back to Arabian Knight.

It looked as though he was going to have to do everything here himself.

Hashim, it seemed, had come to a similar conclusion, with the rather sad difference that Daken was going to win and Arabian Knight was about to lose and lose hard.

Whipping his shamshir up high, Hashim hollered a war cry in his native Arabic, and ran at Daken with his ponytail flailing out behind. Daken crossed his claws, blocked, then exerted his substantially greater strength to hurl the man off towards the bed. Hashim skipped back along the carpet, whirling his sword in filigreed patterns, switching from hand to hand like a shamshir dancer at a wedding. The intent was to impress, to dazzle, to confound an inexperienced or less skilled opponent into following the sword instead of the man.

The Arabian Knight was accomplished, but Daken was nowhere near inexperienced or less skilled. He was three times Hashim's age, at least, and the only fighter he had ever rated more highly than himself was the God of War.

And even that, he would admit only to himself.

Without any kind of a tell, and impressing Daken a little, Hashim broke from his routine and lunged.

Daken arched back. He was stronger, faster, more agile: to put it bluntly he was just better, and the heavy-edged shamshir tore into the Persian rug. Daken slashed for Hashim's chest with his claws. Arabian Knight brought his sword up in time to knock them aside on the flat edge and strike for Daken's jaw with the pommel piece.

Daken whirled away, spinning like a cross between a child's top and a scythed chariot.

Arabian Knight turned after him with a yell, his sword shredding the silk curtain of the four-poster bed, carving through the mattress, the wooden frame, and finally into the stone beneath. The golden blade was more than sharp enough to cleave through the tiles, but not so sharp that it did not pull a little on its way out of the stone. Waiting for the split-second advantage and taking it with both hands, Daken swung back and punched his claws into Hashim's side. Something immediately felt not quite right, but Arabian Knight screamed as he should have and went crashing through the torn curtain, ripping it from its rail and rolling himself into a silk bundle along the floor on the opposite side of the ruined bed.

He lay still.

Daken stretched out his back. He cracked his knuckles.

There was no need to hurry.

Navid Hashim was dead.

With a groan, clutching at his side, Arabian Knight staggered woozily upright. He brushed tattered silk from his arms, and brought his sword back to guard.

Daken glared at him through the hacked remnants of the four-poster bed, torn curtains stirring in the warm breeze of the Gulf. The floor trembled as someone very strong hit something very hard. Bullseye's gunfight with Desert Sword's mercenary army remained a constant background scream.

Arabian Knight panted.

Daken assessed his injuries and his state of exhaustion, feeling the painful *pinch* as his own small cuts closed and his bruises faded. There was, he concluded, for the dozenth time, absolutely nothing special about this man.

His ongoing failure to die was becoming less amusing by the second.

"My clothing is woven from the invulnerable thread of my predecessor's magic carpet," Hashim replied, out of breath. "It is impervious to all harm."

"So that's how you survived Ares. He'll be so pleased to know that it is you, and not him."

"Why do you fight with these Avengers?" Hashim hissed suddenly, dropping his sword a fraction.

"They pay incredibly well."

"But you're a mutant. Osborn persecutes your kind. He fights you in the streets of your own cities. Promotes laws to keep you from having children. Encourages your fellow Americans to fear you."

Daken smirked.

Norman didn't persecute *all* his kind, only those he didn't care about: i.e., all the mutants that were not called Daken.

"I'm not American."

Arabian Knight shook his head in despair.

"What about you?" Daken asked him. "You seem to care a lot about the American people and my mutant rights. How are you with the deaths of a hundred New Yorkers while evading lawful arrest?" Hashim's shoulders sagged as though his sword's weight had suddenly become too much for him. Daken pushed the knife in deeper and twisted it. "Or with setting Venom loose in Avengers Tower?"

Hashim looked genuinely injured and surprised by that part. There was little guile in that face. "I didn't know anything about that. What happened?"

"He only murdered half a Secret Service detail and fifty-odd H.A.M.M.E.R. soldiers, before Ares and I took him down."

"I'm… sorry."

"This is all a roundabout way of saying that I've fought bigger and stronger than you and walked away. You're only human. Ask me one time what happened to Frank Castle when he tried to take me on instead of running away. Surrender. Let me have the files. And I'll tell you about all the pieces I cut him into on our flight back to the United States."

"Take them," Hashim breathed, as though the words were a relief to be rid of, lowering his sword completely and backing away from the bed. "I will not add the deaths of those they name to the burden already on my conscience. And the Contessa does not need these criminals' money. Take them. *Please.*"

Daken turned to glance at the broken briefcase where it lay, strewn with papers and bits of doorframe, by the cracked wall. The moment his head was turned, he caught movement in the corner of his eye as Arabian Knight spun on his heel and broke into a run. Daken readied himself, but Hashim wasn't running at him. He flung himself at the nearest window, crashing through the half-open shutters, and landing with a painful-sounding *crunch* in the rock garden on the other side.

"Son of a ..."

Torn between the man and the files, Daken snarled.

Never follow the sword.

Always follow the man.

And he wasn't going to be the one to explain to Ares how Arabian Knight had escaped them for a second time. "Bullseye!" he called back. "Grab the files for Karla. I've got the Knight."

CHAPTER TWENTY-FOUR

Thirty Minutes

Moonstone stumbled back across the atrium, not even raising her hands to defend herself. Lightbright followed through with jabs to cheek, chin, gut. Karla stumbled, doubled over, as Lightbright raised a fist to land a drop punch to the top of her head. She mustered the energy to move herself out of the way and threw a punch of her own at Lightbright's midriff. The other woman blocked it with contemptuous ease, then headbutted her full in the face. She staggered away, the taste of blood in her mouth. Lightbright wiped the red spots from her forehead.

"Pathetic. You hit like a therapist."

Exploiting that slit in the side of her long yellow dress, Lightbright delivered a butterfly kick that sent Karla reeling back into a stone column.

She realized that she had been literally beaten from one side of the atrium to the other.

That pricked at her pride.

Lightbright sent a straight punch towards the middle of Karla's face, her intention to crack the back of her head against the column she was slumped against. Karla was angered enough to force aside a little of the mutant's calming influence and turn herself intangible. Lightbright's fist crunched into the stone and bloodied her knuckles. She gave a bark of pain and Karla pushed her back, a furious schoolyard shove, to which Lightbright replied with a white-gold blast of energy that obliterated the pillar and sent Moonstone tumbling through the debris.

She lay on her back, seeing twinkling stars in the vaporized stone in the air above her, fighting for the strength of will to get back up and fight. The energy of the Kree gravity stone that powered her abilities was effectively bottomless, but it was useless if she could not make herself use it.

Lightbright was as fast as Moonstone.

She was as strong as Moonstone.

She could fly, she could wield energy, and she could actually fight.

But it was her soul-withering glow that was killing Karla.

Bullseye's bullet-hail laugh reached her through the smoke and din. She searched for the source of it, recalling the limited effect that Lightbright's aura had had on him, but for the first time in her life found herself disappointed by her failure to see him nearby.

Lightbright put a foot on her chest and pressed her back down to the floor.

Karla surrendered to it.

"You think you know anger?" said Lightbright. "Try living with the consequences of your people's actions, as I must. Then you will know a little of what I feel every day. *Then* you will know anger. Osborn is a charlatan and a monster. You see him every day. You know this. And yet you support him. One day soon, his mask will crack, and the world will drown in blood, but it will be parts of it like this that go first, as they always do." She looked disparagingly down at Moonstone, through the smoke and embers of her revolution. "Perhaps, in your privilege and power, you think that his breakdown will not affect you. Perhaps you think that you will ride it to a greater position of your own. I promise you…" She spread the fingers of her hand over Karla and her palm blazed with light. Her eyes shone, and Karla saw in them the same loathing that she had feared to see in her mother's, disgust for the monster that Karla was and the emptiness she carried in place of a soul. "You will not."

Moonstone looked up, but she wasn't looking at Lightbright. She was looking at the gigantic object hovering five thousand feet above her head. Dimly, she made out the heavy-bladed *whup-whup-whup* of a helicopter's rotors.

Despite it all, she smiled up at the mutant standing over her.

Their thirty minutes was up.

Ares stood looking down, the scuffed toes of his boots sticking out over the edge of the Helicarrier's primary flight deck. Cold brushes of scrappy cloud moved across his massive forearms, the axe in his fist damp with their dew. Thirty soldiers of his elite second-generation spec-ops unit, the Shades, waited behind him, backdropped by the sleek, rain-wet outlines of F/A-18 Super Hornets painted purple and parked in staggered ranks on the runway. They were the best in H.A.M.M.E.R. That made them the best in the world. They had been equipped as befit their status as elite soldiers and further prospered under the harsh tutelage of the God of War.

Their loyalty was to him and him alone.

No mortal or god could lay claim otherwise.

The soldiers were kitted out in bulky HALO armor. Thick

rubberized masks covered their faces. Their hands were gloved, their feet booted. The puffy outer layers of their war gear comprised a rugged harness for the oxygen tanks, insulation, pull-release parafoil, and of course, the weapons, that they would require to conduct a high altitude drop followed by a surgical military strike.

Ares was wearing a pair of torn jeans and a vest with no sleeves.

"There are no civilians," he said, his voice pitched to the same bone-jarring growl as the Helicarrier's four gigantic rotors. "There is no Geneva Convention. No Universal Declaration of Human Rights. The only rules in war are my rules, and unless I and I alone command otherwise then every man, woman, child, and beast currently alive below is to be slain."

"ARES, SIR!" the soldiers roared.

Colonel Li, the human commander of the Shades, joined Ares at the edge.

Although Osborn commanded a more US-centric organization than his predecessor, H.A.M.M.E.R. still drew its membership from all nationalities of the world. Bo Li had been a major in the People's Liberation Army, before being recruited by H.A.M.M.E.R. to its Fujian base and coming ultimately to Ares' notice for her heartless efficiency. Often, an agent could see out their full tour in their country or region of origin without ever serving abroad or mixing with other nationalities. This was true of all units but the Shades. Ares welcomed all peoples. Many did not even share a common language. His command of the All-tongue enabled a unique alliance of the world's most ruthless soldiers to operate as one.

"Deputy Hand said that she wanted prisoners, sir," she said, her voice deeply muffled by her need for breathing equipment and mask.

Ares looked down. "Then she should have journeyed to Olympus, and petitioned my father to send Norman Osborn the other God of War."

He stepped off the ledge.

Aiolos, God of the Winds, struck at him at once with a succession of mighty blows, and Ares laughed in the Anemoi's face as gravity pulled him down.

The clouds thinned.

Looking directly down, he could see the target area as a small square between his boots. It was a villa in the classical style that he knew well. It was burning. This was also a sight that he knew very well. The square grew larger. With precision aim and perfect timing, without the need for instruments of any kind, Ares was going to hit it right in the center. He could already make out the crackle and snap of gunfire, lighting up the villa's outline like the approach lights of a runway. Without yet being able to hear the sounds of it over Aiolos' whistling past his ears, he could *feel* the intensity of the conflict below.

It was a two-hundred-and-ten-gun salute to him.

It shouted his name with praise.

Without consciously doing so, he took the vibrations into himself and returned them, subtly changed. At his silent bidding, gangsters and mercenaries were driven wild by bloodlust, abandoning their cover to bludgeon one another with rifle stocks in the open. Ant-like fighters swarmed over the atrium to do battle.

The better for Ares and his Shades to slay them all.

He was the mailed fist of Olympus.

The ground rose and offered up its jaw.

He hit it like an asteroid.

The ground reared, as though to defy him, before the violence of his impact blasted it aside in chunks. Shattered tile and lumps of bedrock shredded burnt trees, toppled stone columns, obliterated faux ancient walls. Men and women were thrown to the ground, most never to rise again.

With a grunt, Ares rose from the twenty-foot-wide crater he had punched into the middle of what had formerly been the villa's atrium and lifted his axe.

He saw Moonstone.

She was spread out on the ground, lying in a dead-body curl over a boulder-sized lump of rubble where Ares' arrival had inadvertently hurled her. Whoever had beaten her before that had beaten her hard. An African woman that Ares did not know stood a few feet from Moonstone's body in a wounded hunch. Flying debris had cut her. Her yellow dress was torn. Stumbling, she raised a hand as though to warn him back.

"Back." A ferocious brightness emanated from the woman's outstretched hand, growing in intensity until its light filled his eyes and its warmth encompassed him.

For a moment he was feasting in the halls of Olympus, carousing with his father and mother and half-brother, before the centuries of animosity and warmongering had robbed them all of their joy.

He was cradling his newborn in his bear-like arms, promising the half-mortal child a human life.

"Back, I tell you," the woman hissed, investing each word with oracular weight as the light grew fiercer still. "Take your soldiers and go home. There will be no more fighting here."

Ares grunted.

He blinked away a tear.

And then he punched her with the back of his fist so hard that she ploughed a furrow fifty yards long through the tiled ruin of the atrium, undermining the north wing of the villa and bringing what was left of it piling down on top of her.

With a ruffling of advanced plastic wings, the first of the Shades began to arrive.

The paratroopers guided their descent to the perfection that Ares demanded, every last man and woman coming down within the square of the atrium before detaching parafoils and mercilessly gunning down demoralized combatants and wounded alike. Colonel Li came into a skipping landing, shrugging off her parafoil and bringing up her rifle, and glancing towards Ares.

"Sir?"

Ares rubbed his damp eyes, then pushed one nostril shut on the inside of his thumb and blasted out a wad of snot. "I am the God of War," he muttered, in the direction of the rubble. "There is nothing in me but wrath." He shook his head to clear it of the mutant's influence and gestured vaguely over the battlefield, grudgingly including the unconscious Moonstone in his summation of the work still to be done.

"Clean this up, colonel."

CHAPTER TWENTY-FIVE

Close Enough to Hear Them Curse

Arabian Knight pounded the wooden boards of the private jetty, throwing himself headlong into the speedboat moored at the far end of it. Keeping his head below the gunwales, he rolled in the bottom and gunned the engine, rising only to strike through the mooring chain with his sword. Daken snarled through his teeth and sprinted to make up the distance. The uneven ground of the rock garden turned under his feet. He skidded, fighting to keep his balance, but the stones almost seemed to be racing him, rolling of their own accord to the sea and an escape from the concussive wrath that Ares was now bringing to bear upon the villa.

There was a sharp crack from behind him, then a flare of pain between his shoulders.

He grunted and ran on, blood in his mouth, as soldiers called out. Broken by Ares and his Shades, they poured into the garden through the rear exits like ants from a nest flooded with boiling water. Automatic fire buzzed across the beach. A few more shots punched wetly into Daken's back. He stumbled onto the jetty, just as the speedboat growled, water jetting out from under its outboard engine, and leapt ahead of the jetty towards the Gulf of Aden.

Daken looked quickly around. In addition to the now-departed speedboat there was a wooden rowing dinghy and a pair of jet skis.

Grimacing as his healing factor pushed half a dozen bullets out of his back and pulled the small wounds closed, he leapt into the saddle of one of the jet skis.

It wobbled under him, almost capsizing, but he expertly adjusted his balance and held on tight, ducking his head to the steering bars as bullets whizzed over his shoulders.

He could recover from almost any injury, up to and including the loss of an entire limb, but it hurt the way it would hurt anyone, and the pain made it harder to think clearly.

As thoroughly as he could in just one glance, he checked over the controls.

It looked straightforward enough.

A lanyard dangled from the ignition. The other end was meant to be attached to the pilot's wrist so that, if they fell overboard, the engine would automatically cut out. Daken left it hanging loose and punched the big green START button.

The engine roared.

Daken applied throttle using the lever on the right handle, delivering a burst of thrust that threw him back into the saddle, the machine bouncing from wave crest to wave crest like an animal that had not seen water in days.

Holding on tight, near-blinded by spray, he shook his head to clear it and looked back over his shoulder.

After fifteen minutes of Moonstone and five seconds of Ares, the villa was in ruins and on fire. There was a parallel there, Daken was reasonably sure, for Norman Osborn's muscular approach to his peacekeeping role: the Bari desert was going to get peace tomorrow whether it wanted it or not. It was neither better nor worse than his father's way, but it did involve less handwringing before and after.

In the brief moment that he watched, a squadron of F/A-18s dispatched from Norman's Helicarrier began comprehensively carpet bombing the outbuildings, gardens, and roads.

Daken turned his face away as a Super Hornet powered in low, almost overhead, the roar of its engine jets followed a second later by a firestorm that consumed the jetty, both boats, the machine gun nest, the pursuing soldiers and most of the beach.

The men did not even have time to scream.

Water sucked back into the vortex created by the five-hundred-pound bomb. Daken felt it drag on his engine, threatening to pull his jet ski back. He squeezed the throttle lever down fully and roared ahead of the expanding fireball, streaking out into open sea.

Fat-bellied container ships winked in the middle distance. Daken counted hundreds. They were a string of soft lights, threaded onto a few safe lanes through the Gulf of Aden by PMC patrol boats and a handful of corvettes flying the ensigns of the region's navies. One of those armed vessels would be sailing in Daken's direction to investigate the explosions soon enough, once they had figured out amongst themselves whose responsibility it was. Unless Norman had already twisted enough arms in the State Department and amongst the East African and Gulf military's top players. Even then, eventually someone would have to come and look, in the same way that *eventually* one of those F/A-18s was bound to be dispatched to investigate the two boats racing away from the villa by sea.

But eventually didn't concern Daken.

For the time being it was just him and Hashim: the way he liked it.

The Arabian Knight and his speedboat were a few hundred yards ahead, speeding towards the Yemen coast, which was an undulating gray outline in the crescent moonlight, but Daken's lighter machine was pulling the distance closer every second.

He leant forward, willing himself faster.

This, for Daken, was what being an Avenger was for.

His mutant power enabled him to manipulate others, but he sought no friendships and abhorred the company of others with the exception of the most fleeting and immoral kinds. He didn't need Norman's money, or his penthouse. People like Daken always landed on their feet. He would have found someone to leech off and some way to get by. But bestriding the Earth like the heir apparent to a god-king, with the license to indulge in whatever sadistic whim he pleased, simply by virtue of who he was, of who he worked for: that was power undreamt of, and freedom that no amount of money alone could ever buy.

Arabian Knight turned in the pilot's seat of his boat.

He shouted something that the roar of two engines drowned into the Gulf of Aden between them. Daken ignored it and continued to close.

The golden sword flashed in the night.

Daken turned his steering bars and dragged his jet ski to the right as searing light carved a channel through the water right across his left. The superhot beam raised a cliff wall of steam that, even though he had evaded the attack itself, blasted across him and his jet ski. Daken snarled, his skin cooking faster than it could heal. The motor gurgled as it sucked in boiling water in place of air. With blistering fingers, Daken held the throttle lever tight, instinct pulling the steering bars back to the left as a second burning flash seared across his eyes.

As Daken burst through the second wall of steam and his retinas regenerated from the blinding burst, he realized that the attempt at blasting him out of the sea had cost Hashim his lead. He was close enough for Daken to hear him curse, and he laughed to hear his impotent rage.

The speedboat was twenty yards ahead, sixteen feet long and open-topped, painted blue and white and with a faded S.H.I.E.L.D. design on the prow. Arabian Knight took his hands off the controls to fire another blast. The beam flashed across Daken's shoulder, cooking the water around him into an erupting geyser as he steered his jet ski alongside Hashim's boat at speed.

Bringing his right foot up onto the saddle cushion, Daken threw himself the last few yards between himself and the speeding boat.

With the lanyard still attached to the ignition, the jet ski raced on without him, unmanned, while Daken crashed bodily onto the boat's deck. His arrival rocked the boat, throwing Hashim hard into the gunwale and giving Daken time to find his footing.

They recovered at the same time.

Arabian Knight's sword described a golden arc. Blocking with one hand rather than give ground, because there was no ground to give, Daken followed in with a left hook. Arabian Knight turned his body side-on to the blow and Daken's claws punched three holes in his bisht over-robes. The warrior attempted to recover his stance, but the narrow boat left no room for deft footwork or delicate swordsmanship. Daken blocked, parried, bled the Arabian Knight one cut at a time. Spray leapt over the gunwales as the out-of-control speedboat veered across the paths of the incoming waves, soaking Arabian Knight's long hair and beard, and turning his expression into a briny grimace of frustration. He was exhausted, running out of the adrenaline to keep going, while Daken was as fresh as he had been when he, Moonstone, and Bullseye had pulled up earlier that evening in a cab.

"Are you ready to surrender now?"

Arabian Knight shook his sodden head wearily. "Why did you even follow me? I gave you the files."

"Do you think I could care less about Osborn's secrets? If you had them with you now, I would throw them overboard to weigh down your dead body and tell Osborn you got away. I would have been able to sit back and watch as he tore the world apart trying to find the rock you were hiding under and get them back. As it is…" Daken shrugged. It genuinely made little difference to him. "I may as well bring you back alive. It pays to pick up points where you can."

Hashim bared his teeth, struggling all the way forward to the bowsprit while Daken stalked unhurriedly after. There was, after all, really nowhere he could go. "I would not surrender to Ares," he said. "And he, at least, had some notion of honor. Why should I surrender to you?"

Daken shook his head. "If you can't think of a good enough reason on your own, then I'm not going to stand here and try to convince you. I don't mind doing it the harder way."

He raised his fist, claws glinting in the seawater and moonlight.

Arabian Knight had his sword between them but was too tired to lift it to defend himself.

Daken expected him to break then, in the final moment before the end, and beg to be allowed to surrender. He was disappointed that the man did not.

The careening speedboat rocked suddenly in the water, as though an aircraft had just buzzed them, and Daken looked up, expecting to see one of the H.A.M.M.E.R. Super Hornets, or possibly a Yemeni fighter come to investigate, but the sky was empty. He frowned, lowering his claws, and turned back to Arabian Knight, staring over the taller man's shoulder in shock as a deltawing aircraft of unfamiliar design dropped its camouflage directly ahead of the speedboat's path. It had a profile like a snake: low, unobtrusive, and deadly, painted a faded green and with underwing hardpoints bristling with weaponry.

A pair of Gatling-style rotary cannons spun up.

They were spitting out shells before Daken could do anything more useful than curse.

The sheer volume of fire overwhelmed his healing factor, each shell powerful enough to punch through his toughened skeleton. The guns ripped through him, two hundred times a second, every successive shot sending him stumbling the length of the boat whilst collectively holding him upright for the one that followed microseconds afterwards. They hit so fast they could not be seen. But for the puffs of blood they made as they erupted from his back, it might have looked as though he were being punched repeatedly by an invisible assailant whilst being held up by the scruff of the neck.

His heel hooked the stern of the boat and he tipped over, arms flailing for a purchase but catching only more bullets, crashing into the freezing sea.

Over the deadening rush of water flooding into his ears, he was aware of the Gatling guns cutting out, soldiers piling out of the aircraft's rear doors and dragging Arabian Knight aboard. The switch of the aircraft's engines to vertical lift pummeled the water and pushed Daken down.

His skeleton was super-hard, his musculature unnaturally dense.

He did not float.

Reaching helplessly for the aircraft as it re-camouflaged and turned away, Daken went down.

CHAPTER TWENTY-SIX

What Success Looks Like

Victoria Hand had volunteered to command the Helicarrier through the graveyard shift. With the operations winding down, there was not a lot left to do and, watching the intermittently refreshing screens, listening to the peaceful murmur of the bridge crew at work, fielding the occasional anxious call from a diplomat in a more agreeable time zone, it was as close to what actual rest felt like as she could remember. Sipping instant coffee from the machine on the lookout deck, bathing her face in the fragrant cloud rising from the plastic cup, she focused her eyes on the mission updates as they scrolled on her private screen.

Every objective secured, suspect killed or captured, vehicle impounded, or structure destroyed, appeared as a triumphant line of text.

Daken had been fished out of the sea. His healing factor was more than capable of dealing with the trauma of being shredded by a gunship and then drowned, but the doctors wanted him under observation until the worst of his injuries had healed. Karla was in bed. From the look of her, as the H.A.M.M.E.R.

retrieval team had pulled her out of the medevac helicopter on a stretcher, she had earned it. Ares did not have dedicated medics on his team. The possibility of medical intervention, as he often told them, would only encourage them to get hurt.

Injuries were par for the course, and she had difficulty sympathizing with criminals. They could take it. As far as Victoria was concerned, this was what success looked like.

All of their primary objectives had been achieved. Lester and Ares had returned with the missing personnel files, and H.A.M.M.E.R. forces had taken several prisoners for interrogation, although not nearly as many as Victoria had been expecting. Better, it had all been neatly put to bed without the all-seeing eye of blanket CCTV coverage, twenty-four-hour cable news, and the presence of reliable witnesses that always complicated a cleanup. It was an unfortunate concern for the modern military that the way a mission looked in hindsight was as much a qualifier for success as the objectives met. Sometimes, H.A.M.M.E.R.'s work was ugly. Peace was messy, far messier than war, but it was worth it.

She had to believe that it was worth it.

If she didn't...

She blinked quickly, afraid that she might be about to nod off at her station, and took a sip of her coffee. Where was a nuisance call from the African Union representative in Washington when she needed one? In the small hours of the night, when her mind was tired and the world was quiet, it was too easy to ask questions that her morality found difficult to answer. But the world was safer now. Colonel Fury was on the run, topping Most Wanted lists in two hundred countries. Tony Stark was on trial in absentia for crimes against humanity in the Hague.

Her motives were pure.

She was doing what needed to be done to make the world a safer place.

Around her, a skeleton crew worked at the navigation, radar, and communications desks in near silence. The forward wall of the lookout deck was a colossal rank of armored windows, overlooking the quietude of the Gulf of Aden with just the occasional twinkle of a patrol helicopter to break the stillness. The aft wall, behind the desks, and the command chair, and its softly lit screens, comprised a huge map of the Earth and Moon. The landmasses of the former and settled areas of the latter were outlined in lights. H.A.M.M.E.R. stations, national capitals, and orbital facilities were each picked out with different colors. Large analogue clocks partitioned the Earth into time zones.

It was 4:30AM, East Africa Time.

Which made it about 8:30PM in New York.

Victoria wondered which time zone her body was currently working in.

Director Osborn was the hardest-working man on the planet, but however many hours he put into the job, Victoria put in more, curbing his excesses in the planning stages and sweeping up the debris afterwards. She did not resent it. It was necessary work. But a part of her missed being able to punch out after an eight-hour day in the S.H.I.E.L.D. accountancy department under Director Fury and having the freedom of New York in which to unwind. She sighed, rubbing coffee steam into her eyes, seduced for a moment by the hypnotic purr of the radar desk, the steady thrum of the rotors holding their flying fortress at anchor over the Horn of Africa, and the dubious comfort of the bridge commander's chair.

She remembered her first day as Osborn's deputy.

Director Osborn had labeled the Helicarrier as Fury's white

elephant and had ordered the scrappage of the entire fleet. He had intended to reinvest the eye-watering sums that it cost to keep a global battlegroup operational on modernizing the newly appellated "H.A.M.M.E.R." with more soldiers, better equipment, and smarter IT into a peacekeeping force fit for the twenty-first century. He had subsequently changed his mind and reversed the order. She thought she understood why. The Helicarrier was a potent symbol of force. It may have carried less destructive potential than, say, the Sentry, but it was about a thousand times more visible in the sky, which, arguably, made for a vastly superior deterrent.

Sitting back in her chair, she drummed her fingers on the padded armrests.

Had she known back then, when Osborn had first invited her up to Avengers Tower, what she knew now, then she might have subjected the director's volte-face on the Helicarriers to greater scrutiny.

More and more, she found herself thinking back on it.

Had the contradictory orders come from two different Norman Osborns? Had he been as unstable then, at the very beginning, as he was starting to become now? He was finding it difficult to keep to his appointments, he was missing his medications. It was not deliberate, she knew that, he wanted to be well, but the demands of the job made it harder. Had she simply been too ambitious and naïve to see it back then? She did not want to believe that she had consciously gone to work for a monster.

She shook her head.

That was 4.30AM talking.

Draining her cup, watching the screens for a while longer until the lines of text became blurry, she pushed herself up from the command chair and stretched.

Lieutenant-Colonel Martha Brown was walking idly around the central workstation.

Unlike Maria Hill, and the other deputy directors before her, Victoria did not have a military rank. A lot of the senior military staff who had served previously under Fury resented her promotion, she knew, particularly with Osborn coming to the post from a civilian background himself, but Brown, at least, had started from a position of respect and given Victoria the opportunity to lose it. She did not think that she had yet.

"I'm taking a walk," she said. "The bridge is yours until I get back."

"Yes, sir."

"If the president calls again for the director, let me know. I'll take it wherever I am."

"Yes, sir."

Victoria exited the bridge. The heavy steel doors whooshed shut behind her. The solitary guard on duty saluted as she walked on past.

Director Osborn had practically turned into a recluse since their departure from the US. He had been pointedly avoiding taking any calls, and had been coming up with ever more elaborate and unlikely excuses for avoiding his administrative duties during the flight. Victoria worried about him. Worrying about Norman Osborn was, arguably, half her job, but she had not seen him sink as low as this since the incident in Colorado where the Molecule Man had taken him captive and scrambled his brain. The pressures of his job were immense. Victoria knew that better than anyone. The security of Earth rested on his decisions, his actions, his alone. Victoria knew what a harsh inquisitor a person's own conscience could be. But this went beyond the usual stresses. The difficulties with Venom, and the ongoing political fallout, seemed to have pushed him towards some kind of invisible edge. He had become aggressive, reactive, and far too laissez faire about the image management issues that a figure with his kind of baggage needed to be engaged with.

At the far end of the dorsal corridor, the doors to the briefing room slid open.

She walked inside.

It was considerably more cramped than its terrestrial counterpart in Avengers Tower, containing one moderately sized table with a dozen chairs and space to skirt around. A single screen, about the size of the TV in the apartment Victoria had not seen in six months, was bolted to the aft bulkhead at the far end of the table.

The Sentry, tireless, timeless, was already there.

He sat in one of the metal chairs with his back to the door, and did not look up as Victoria walked to a chair of her own on the opposite side of the table. With his super-hearing he could have heard her approach from the moment she started off down the corridor. He could have overheard her conversation with Lieutenant-Colonel Brown. If he had wanted to. If his powers were anywhere close to reliable in his current state.

Ignoring her, he chewed on his fingernails, watching the interrogation play out on the small screen.

"Who're you working for?" came Lester's dry, petulant voice from somewhere off camera.

The mutant terrorist, Obax Majid, Lightbright, stared glassily through the screen. She was handcuffed to a chair that was bolted in turn to the deck. She had two black eyes. Her hair was torn. Her lips were broken. A middle tooth was glaringly absent. Victoria had seen her as the retrieval teams had clerked her in for detention. The injuries weren't from her battle with Moonstone and Ares.

The RNAi suppression of her powers, a therapy developed in the old days of the CSA before being ruled unethical by the UN and banned, had left her eyes listless and pale.

She gave no answer.

Lester punched her in the mouth.

Her head snapped back, but she otherwise gave no response.

The Sentry murmured something under his breath.

His eyes urged Lester to go harder, while the muscles of his neck and face simultaneously strained to make them look away.

"Is your face tired of this yet? Because my fist can keep this up all day."

"Has she said anything yet?" Victoria asked.

"No." Still the Sentry did not look up. "I've been watching all night. The only time she's spoken was to confirm her name. And to call Norman some." He cocked his head slightly while he worked loose a bit of thumbnail that had become caught between his perfect teeth.

If Victoria had ever allowed herself to think about it, then the Sentry would terrify her. He was a walking, thinking, emotionally unstable weapon of mass destruction who could vaporize her and whatever continent she happened to be standing on at the time with as much effort and forethought as she would put into flicking a fly off her eye. Karla had turned getting herself beaten by the Sentry into a kind of currency amongst the H.A.M.M.E.R. personnel on the Helicarrier but, even on his worst days, the Sentry was powerful enough to dismiss the entire Avengers team as an afterthought.

So she didn't let herself think about it.

"She's said nothing about where her accomplices are keeping Lindy." The Sentry put his head in his hands. "I don't think she knows."

"What makes you say that?"

He looked up then, his faintly golden eyes glistening and wet.

Victoria had read his file, of course. On top of the power to destroy them all, the Sentry was ever so slightly psychic.

"Whatever she does or doesn't know, she'll talk eventually." Victoria looked up at the screen. Lester was going at it and, true to his threat, by virtue of his adamantium-laced bones he was pulling no punches.

The Sentry had the luxury of feeling awful about it.

But peace was ugly.

It was messy.

If it was easy then cold-blooded murderers like Bullseye wouldn't get to live free on a government paycheck just so the world could go on turning.

"Be patient. If Lester can't get anything then Ares is due to take a pass at her in the morning."

The Sentry nodded.

For a moment, she feared that she was going to have to talk him out of heading downstairs to the interrogation room and taking over the mutant's questioning himself. He could kill her out of hand, easily. Bound or unbound, it wouldn't matter. But an interrogation had nothing to do with raw power and, thankfully, he was lucid enough at the moment to realize that and did not suggest it.

He didn't have the skills, or the stomach.

Lester had it.

Ares, Daken, Gargan, Karla, Osborn: they all had it.

The doors behind them opened.

Victoria turned, expecting to have to dismiss a curious guard or a cleaner, and was surprised when Director Osborn walked in.

He was dressed in a sharp, shamrock-green suit and tie with

a purple shirt and silver cufflinks. Despite, going solely on the information provided by the noises emanating from his door and the motion sensors set up outside his room, apparently being hard at work until well past midnight, he did not look in the least bit tired. He appeared fresh, alert, full of vibrant energy and – dare she think it – manic intensity.

"Sir, shouldn't you be in bed?"

"Shouldn't you be on the bridge?" the director returned, with a smile that he probably intended to be casual but which came altogether too sharply and with far too much teeth and made Victoria want to cringe.

"She hasn't said anything yet," said the Sentry, already turning back to the screen and his fingernails.

He wasn't afraid of Norman Osborn.

He was one of the few people in the world who could afford not to be.

Osborn looked up at the screen, his smile immediately twisting and inverting to become a sneer of such undisguised loathing that Victoria found herself taking a further step around the briefing table to put another chair between herself and the man behind it.

"I'm going to have to go down there and sort this out myself, aren't I? Tale of my damned life. Yes, I'd love to stop aliens from taking over the world, Mr Osborn, sir. I understand that you're terrifically busy, being the director of the Thunderbolts and all, but I'm just too pathetic a human specimen to lift this gun out of my pocket. Could you please do it for me? Honestly, if there was one thing that Lester could manage to do right, then you'd think it would be beating up a foreign national while she was spaced out on illegal drugs and tied to a chair, wouldn't you? But no, he can't even get that straight without me standing over his shoulder? And what's Ares doing right now? Chiseling his abs? He should be doing this."

"He's the God of War, sir," said Victoria. "I can't tell him what to do."

"You just need the right tone of voice, Ms Hand. It's all about attitude."

"Did you send him to the insurgent compound with orders to kill everyone, sir?"

In the blink of an eye, Osborn's sneer became a dazzling smile. In his expensive suit, in the company of his mightiest Avenger, it could have been the one he wore for the cover of *Time* magazine's *TIME 100* issue. "I rarely have to tell Ares to do anything, Ms Hand. We have that kind of special relationship where I know he knows what I want."

"We needed prisoners, sir. We're fortunate that Lightbright is tough enough to take a punch from Ares. What if she won't talk?"

"Oh, she'll talk. If Ares could pull himself away from making himself grizzled and scary for ten minutes, we'd be begging her to shut up already."

"He's in his room, writing a letter for his son on his computer. I can hear him. He thinks aloud." The Sentry's eyes had become golden and distant, focused on something far away. "Should I get him?"

Osborn appeared to consider it.

"No," Victoria said quickly. Ares was fiercely private. The last thing she wanted to be dealing with now was for the two most powerful Avengers to be going head-to-head aboard the Helicarrier. There could only be one outcome, but it would be enough of a fight to ensure that the rest of them would not be flying away from it unless it was downwards. "We've only had her in custody for a few hours, sir. Let Lester do his work."

Osborn grumbled, but the notion had already passed him by and the Sentry, trusting that the director had his best interests at heart, didn't press it.

Victoria breathed a quiet sigh of relief.

"I'll have someone send for you the minute she says something, sir. But since you're awake, you should go back to your quarters and call Washington. They have been calling for you every half an hour since we mobilized from Al Anad base."

"One of these days I'm going to run for president myself," Osborn said, in a stage mutter for an audience of one. "It doesn't seem so hard. I've already paid for half the legislature, and I'm still taking orders from that imbecile just because seventy million people decided he looked slightly less moronic on TV than the other guy? I'm a genius, you know. I'm a billionaire. I'm a bone fide American *hero*. The people would take me in a second. Did you know that the Iron Patriot is the second highest selling action figure in forty-nine states? Spider-Man remains bizarrely popular in New York even though he eats people now. Nationally, I'm second only to Ms Marvel, but thirty-four percent of the market is teenage boys and there's no accounting for their tastes, is there, Ms Hand? And I doubt any of them would want her for president." He paused just long enough to breathe.

"The man who just happens to have that information to hand is a man who's not only popular but on top of his details. The people demand that. No, they deserve it. And when I'm elected to the White House you've my solemn promise, Ms Hand, that as director of H.A.M.M.E.R. you'll never have to sit up by the phone in case the president has a nightmare and couldn't get hold of his mommy. And if you're a super-powered interest group that wants your own island? Fine. Have your own island. Take one of those bits off California. No, really. I'll invite a couple of friends over to the White House lawn for a beer while the Sentry throws the whole lot of you into the sun. How is my Ms Marvel?"

The sudden shift in gear caught Victoria, who had been following the tirade with increasingly dumb horror, flat-footed.

"Sir?"

"Do the doctors expect her face to heal?"

"I didn't ask, sir. It didn't seem the most important question at the time."

"Well, you thought incorrectly, Ms Hand. You know that she's partly on the team for her looks."

"Sir!"

Osborn gave her a pitying grin, as though his face was as malleable as clay and could adopt any shape, express any emotion, to any degree. This was condescension, dialed to its highest setting. "I know. It's not fair. Ares looks like the love-child of Man-Ape and the Thing that someone has gone and beaten around the head with a bus, and nobody cares. Put that chump on a cereal box." He snorted at her expression. "Don't give me the how-could-you eyes, Ms Hand. The world is messed up and upside down. We both know that. That's why you took this job."

"Sir," said Victoria, firmly. She had never seen the director like this before and it was starting to frighten her. "With the Patriot List and the other stolen documents back in our hands, you can finally take the night off. Let me walk you back to your room and we can work through some of the exercises that I know you've been putting off."

"No, Ms Hand." Osborn shook his head violently, shrugging off Victoria's hand as she reached out to calm him. "Not yet. Arabian Knight got away again. Lightbright is nothing more than a high-powered lackey. The mastermind behind the plot against me is still at large, and the original footage they passed on to the

Bulletin is still out there. And there is still one page of the Patriot List missing."

"The retrieval team picked the documents up from the rubble of the villa, sir. It's only one missing page. It was probably burned up in the attack, or blown into the sea."

"Then I want the sea bottom combed. I want the ashes raked over. I want it *all* back, Ms Hand." He rounded on the TV screen, his face a rictus of barely human fury. His finger trembled as he pointed up. "And I want my turn on the mutant woman. I'll get her to talk. She'll tell me who's behind this attack on me."

"Perhaps, sir," said Victoria, as gently as she could, her hands raised so as to appear unthreatening, "with Moonstone out, Ares taking himself AWOL for the night, and Daken still in surgery, the Avengers are spread a little thin. Perhaps it's time to bring Venom back off the bench."

"Spider-Man is finished," Osborn snarled. "Is that understood, Ms Hand? Finished! And in my first official act as president of the United States of America, research into radioactive spiders of any kind is to be outlawed, retroactively and immediately. Write that down, Ms Hand."

"Never mind all that, sir. Let me call your therapist. It's only the middle of the evening, East Coast Time. I'm sure he'll still be in the office."

"Fine. Call him. You can put him on speakerphone and hold the handset for me while I beat that mutant to death with my bare hands. Because that, people, is what happens when you mess with President Norman V. Osborn." He threw his head back and laughed.

Victoria realized her mouth was hanging open.

The Sentry cleared his throat in his usual, slightly reflective, fashion, as though all of this were perfectly routine, and Victoria was the only one here whose grip on sanity was in question. His head turned questioningly towards them both, his hand rising to point at the screen.

"What is it?" said Victoria, glad of the interruption.

"Is it morning already?"

"Technically," said Norman.

Victoria shot him a concerned look. "Why?" she asked.

"It's just you said that Ares was going to take over in the morning." The Sentry turned back to the TV. "And someone's just pulled Lester out."

CHAPTER TWENTY-SEVEN
Good Cop

The interrogator slid stiffly into the chair.

The mutant, Lightbright, stared listlessly at him for a second or two while he settled in, her gaze then drifting steadily back towards the camera installed in the ceiling. He winced as he leant forward. His chest hurt. His sides hurt. He felt as though he had been dissected by a team of well-meaning but clueless amateur anatomists.

He was, in point of fact, having a very bad day.

The mutant pulled her gaze from the camera.

She was perfectly lucid, he knew. It was only the effect of the chemotherapy on her mutant phenotype, dulling the brilliance of her eyes, that made her appear groggy.

"Are you here to be good cop?" she said.

"We really don't do that around here."

His smile widened, because however horrifically he hurt, he could still smile. It was what elevated him above a cold-blooded, street-level psychopath like Bullseye.

"So, what makes you think that I will talk to you?"

"Because you want to."

"Really?"

He nodded.

The woman opened her bloodied mouth to retort something, but hesitated. He sensed the barely perceptible softening of her body language. She retreated a little into her seat, relaxed her hands, turned her head fully towards his, and as he leant conspiratorially across the tabletop, she unconsciously mirrored his posture as closely as her restraints allowed.

He stared into her eyes, as close as two lovers across the gear lever of a car.

"I am not what you would call a team player, and you made a mistake when you decided to fill my chest with enough bullets to make me care." His bone claws thunked into the metal tabletop. "This attraction that you are feeling towards me now," he murmured, too intimately for the camera to pick up. "I'm afraid it's my little secret. So, although you're going to tell me everything I want to know quite willingly..." Daken brandished the other set of claws between them, and gestured towards the camera overhead. "I'm afraid I'm going to have to make this look convincing."

Norman Osborn's eyes twitched as he watched the interrogation. He was impressed. Given his abysmally low opinion of his staff, the meagre achievement of simply surpassing expectations should have been no surprise, but it was welcome nevertheless.

After only a few minutes of inane questioning, Lightbright had already defiantly screamed that she was working for a splinter S.H.I.E.L.D. faction independent of Fury and Dugan, that she was part of a reformed pan-national Desert Sword opposed to all forms of American-led interventionism in the Middle East and

East Africa. She had even gone as far, with almost no prodding at all, as confirming that her group had been behind the recent rioting and anti-H.A.M.M.E.R. protests in that part of the world. The ensuing violence and looting had been a cover, she went on to explain, for the acquisition of security codes and equipment necessary for the Avengers Tower raid.

He laughed.

It felt good, freeing.

Daken wasn't entirely terrible at this.

One of the burdens that came with being the man whose job it was to know everything was that the little things lost their capacity to surprise. He would be sure to add this moment to the gratitude diary that his therapist had been insisting he keep. Just as soon as he could be bothered enough to get Victoria to buy him a blank book and start it for him.

"Ask her about Lindy," the Sentry murmured to himself, as though shy of uttering it aloud. He gripped the table edge. The soft alloy warped around his fingers, the metal bubbling and hissing as it trickled along the finger-channels towards the floor.

Victoria held her hand up for patience. "She's just talking now. Daken isn't even asking her questions anymore. Let her talk. If she knows anything, it'll come out soon."

The Sentry sat back in his chair, leaving a semi-molten handprint in the table, brushed his long hair back from his face, and bit on his bottom lip. Norman turned back to the TV, just as Lester entered the briefing room.

He flung the door open, causing it to bang loudly against the bulkhead, saw Norman and Victoria in the room already, and scowled. He walked in like a tantrum with legs, brandishing a crumpled sheet of paper that he held rolled up in one hand like a baseball swatter. Norman had pumpkin-bombed men for less.

"You were gonna replace me with Fred Myers? Boomerang? This is some bull–"

"Ms Hand." Norman held up a finger, causing Bullseye to stop mid-rant and fume. "You can call off the divers. It looks as though we've found our missing page."

"Myers?" Lester went on, bloodshot eyes glaring. "That Australian clown? He can't do half of what I do for you." He held the rolled paper an inch from Norman's nose. "You think having a half-decent aim is all it takes to be Bullseye?"

"You still don't get it, do you, Lester?" Norman pushed the paper out of his face on the edge of a finger. "You're not Bullseye. You're *Hawkeye.* Ninety percent of your job is *looking* the part. The other ten percent is giving me exactly what I want, doing as you're damn well told, and knowing when it's time to shut up before your whining causes my migraine to explode." He brought his wagging finger up to banish the sneer from Bullseye's face. "Do that with some vague degree of competency and whoever I've got in line to replace you won't matter, will it? You want to stay on the team? You want to keep drawing a government check and have the idiots on the NYPD filing the bodies they keep on finding whenever I let you out as suicides? Well, good. Perhaps, from now on, it'll help you to remember that your breathing right now is a privilege, not a right."

"Yeah. Well." Lester backed away, and Norman laughed to see him subside. He kicked a chair leg, knocking it out from under the table. "This is still messed up." He slumped down into the chair. "I'm still better than Myers."

"One more thing, Lester."

Bullseye looked up, his expression surly. "What?"

Norman slapped him on the back. Victoria looked at him as though he'd just put his arm down the toilet. "You *are* better than

Myers. You did good work today. You got in and you kept your head. You got my files and you got out. And you got to shoot a lot of guys while doing it. Think of it as my way of saying thank you. That's why you're an Avenger while Myers is kicking his heels in the little leagues."

"Damn right." Bullseye looked down at the table, as though unsure what was happening to him. He crossed his legs, and then muttered uncomfortably, "Sir."

And this, ladies and gentlemen, is what people management looks like. It's how I've been such a success in business, politics and, indeed, in life.

While Lester turned to watch the TV, looking anywhere but at Norman's benevolent smile, Victoria spirited in and took the last missing piece of the Patriot List from his hand. Good Victoria. Wonderful Victoria. The daughter he'd never had and who wouldn't disappear off to France. Still staring at him as though he was doing cartwheels in Iron Man pants, but still. Victoria. The one person he could always rely on to not screw up.

At a buzzing in his trouser pocket, Norman looked down.

He pulled out his phone.

There was an unknown number on the caller ID. That was unusual enough to immediately pique his interest. He was Norman Osborn, director of H.A.M.M.E.R., king of the world, not the pizza delivery guy. He wasn't on any old customer plan. A call to his number got routed through Oscorp's own secure network of masts, subjected to ever more rigorous levels of security and data-mining, pulling out any and all information on the dialing device before connecting it.

"If this is the president, then I swear to God..."

He swiped the ACCEPT CALL icon and held the handset to

the side of his face, following Lightbright's full confession with half an eye.

"Director Osborn," he said.

"Norman," came the voice at the other end of the line. It was female, and accented. Italian, he thought, though it was faint. His own voice was similar in that regard. He had been coached to sound more authentically American on TV, but his natural accent was that of a person who had never been rooted in one part of the world for long. "I was not sure that you would pick up, but I had to take the chance. Some people just cannot resist a ringing telephone, even when they know that they really should."

Victoria was looking a question across the table at him.

He turned his back and bowed his head to the wall.

"Who is this?"

"Of course. I have seen so much of you on the television this past year that I sometimes forget that we have never actually met. My name is Contessa Valentina Allegra de Fontaine. You have one of my people. And I believe you have just bombed my house."

"Give me twelve hours and I'll do a whole lot more than just bomb your house."

"Sir, who are you talking to?" said Victoria.

Norman ignored her. "The agent of yours that Ares captured is talking. Any minute now we'll get her to shut up long enough to ask her where you're hiding and then this little game you've been playing is over. I've won. There won't be enough of you to detect in a particle accelerator by the time I pull the Sentry off you. Taking his wife, by the way? Bad idea. I mean, seriously. You've got the captain of the Titanic, you've got King Priam taking in that ridiculous horse, you've got Hitler invading Russia, and *then* you've got this. Now me, I never got all that attached to the mothers of my children. I'd forget their names if I didn't have Victoria to write them all down for me. But that's why I get to wear the grown-up pants while the Golden Guardian of Good gets to watch his friends beating up a mutant while giving me doe eyes."

"I could listen to you rant all day, Norman. Really, I could. It is a forgotten art. But you should probably know that I am recording this call."

He snarled down the phone. "You think anybody cares? I've said worse. I've done worse. So long as I keep them safe, I could pull mutant babies out of their mothers' arms and toss them in the Atlantic for a reality TV show and nobody would care."

"I called partly as a courtesy, Norman, and partly, I confess, out of morbid fascination. I know you have Obax, and I know she is talking. I know that because I have a magician on my team and you do not." Norman ground his teeth as she tutted. "An oversight there, Norman. You left New York in too much haste. When I was Nicholas' deputy, he always made certain that his transportation was fully warded against psychic and arcane intrusion before travelling anywhere."

"I heard you were a lot more than Fury's deputy."

The voice sounded amused. "An insult to my virtue, Norman? Please. We're both better than that."

Norman swung around.

He looked up and caught Victoria's eye.

"Can I assume then, Ms Fontaine, that we have you to thank for the bullets we pulled out of Hawkeye's stomach? And for the unfortunate reaction that Spider-Man had to his last round of chemotherapy?"

Victoria fumbled for the tablet computer that she carried with her everywhere.

"Tell her I've kept the bullet, just for her," Lester growled.

"He's fine, by the way," Norman went on. "Raring to go, in fact. The guys that got in Spider-Man's way, though? They're doing less well. So, get whatever threats you want to make out of your system now while Ms Hand here traces your call, and I can set them both on you."

"I didn't call you to make threats, Norman. On the contrary, I want to tell you everything. So, call off your Wolverine, hand Obax over to the Yemeni authorities that I know you've been liaising with, and let us talk."

Norman paused, surprised.

He looked around the briefing room.

Bullseye was staring at him intently, as though looks could remotely send daggers through the telephone. Victoria had her tablet open on the table, busily pulling up files on the Contessa. She need not have bothered. There were a handful of individuals in the world who were, or had once been, important enough to warrant the honor of having their S.H.I.E.L.D. files personally memorized by Norman Osborn and Valentina Allegra de Fontaine was one.

Daughter of anti-communist terrorists. Minor European royalty. Several years as an international dilettante with a suspicious array of intelligence connections and some impressive close combat skills. Recruited into S.H.I.E.L.D. by Timothy Dugan. Rose to become deputy director before a reassignment as S.H.I.E.L.D. special liaison to the British government and MI-13.

And then after that…

After the dismantling of S.H.I.E.L.D., the Contessa had fallen off the map.

If she hadn't, then Norman would have gone after her as hard as he had gone after Fury, Hill, and Stark.

In contrast to Bullseye and Victoria, the eyes of the Sentry were drilling straight into him. Gone was the self-pitying wetness that he had been carrying with him these past few days and, in its place, a burning intensity that would have melted a hole through a Vibranium wall.

It was a look that knew exactly what it was for.

Of course.

Super-hearing.

Norman giggled, feeling the threat of nuclear annihilation bring a strange balance to his thoughts. He might suggest that to his therapist the next time he was in New York.

"Of course, Contessa. Whatever you say." He walked around the briefing table to the TV. There was a control panel bolted to the wall beside it. On it was an intercom switch. With the phone held to the side of his face so that the Contessa would be able to hear, he activated the intercom. "Wolverine. This is Director Osborn. That's enough."

On the TV screen, Daken turned to face the camera.

Lightbright continued to rant in the background, raging now about how Arabian Knight had been passed the Avengers Tower security footage from an old S.H.I.E.L.D. comrade, then handed it to a former Middle East correspondent now working at the *Bulletin*, but it was pushed to the background by Daken's snarl. "We haven't even got to the real information yet."

"I said that's enough. Don't make me come down there. Give her to the guards and get up here. Oh, and wipe your claws. I don't want you spotting blood all over my Helicarrier."

Cursing in what sounded like colorful Japanese, Wolverine got stiffly out of his chair and left the shot. The camera picked up the stomping of feet, a door banging.

Norman shook his head. He commanded the Earth's greatest team of surly teenagers.

With his eyes on the screen, he turned his face towards the handset. "It's done. Victoria will arrange for the transfer to the Yemeni navy now." He nodded to Victoria that he wasn't simply putting on a show for the Contessa's ears, and that she should actually do just that. With her tablet already open, she got to it. "But I reserve the right to renege on this agreement at any point and blast the Yemenis out of the water if I suspect you're holding out on me."

"I am sure you do, Norman."

"So talk. Where are you?"

"All in just a moment. Since you are standing by the television, switch it over to BBC World News."

Norman hesitated with his hand over the set, wondering if this could just be another ruse, a trick to get the Contessa and her associates into the Helicarrier's systems somehow.

He had confidently established that he had only idiots working for him.

"Humor me, Norman. I promise I'm not trying to trick you. There is something I need you to see before I tell you what you want to know, and given that it is a live broadcast, it is somewhat time critical."

"Fine."

With a grunt, he switched the TV to receive satellite input and then found the Contessa's channel. He stepped back from the TV as the live report played.

First he felt cold.

Then he felt hot.

A thousand voices screamed at the same time inside his head, and they were all his own.

On the TV screen, a reporter in a sober suit and a cut-glass British accent was speaking over video footage that seemed to originate from one of the closed-circuit cameras in the Avengers Tower cafeteria floor. It was a medium-security zone, and so footage from its cameras was not routinely destroyed within twelve hours. The color was in 4K high definition. The sound quality was superb.

There was absolutely no denying that the subject was Norman Osborn.

He was screaming in the face of a hotdog attendant while a crowd of terrified H.A.M.M.E.R. employees looked on: a full, spitting, puce-faced tirade against the president of the United States, his vice-president, the joint chiefs, the DOD, House Oversight Committee, the Treasury, the entire charade of democratic checks and balances in general, and all in the most personally offensive and expletive-laden terms that the man whose job it was to know everybody's dirty secrets could come up with off the cuff. Norman remembered it. He'd been reliving it since Victoria had come to his suite with the call from Miss Greene of the Bulletin. He'd just come out of a meeting with his procurement officer to learn that the White House had effectively killed off the long overdue merger of the extraterrestrial defense organization, S.W.O.R.D., into H.A.M.M.E.R. It had cost Norman billions of dollars of contracts and months of wasted paperwork. Any perfectly sane human doormat in his position would have lost their temper.

The news anchor continued talking.

The time stamp on the video ticked beyond ten minutes, while its Norman Osborn continued spraying insults at the government of the United States, even as the manager of the hotdog stall attempted to restrain him.

Yes, he was describing the man at whose pleasure he served in terms usually reserved for the new lovers of ex-wives, but that wasn't the worst part.

The worst part was that he was looking like a crazy person while he did it.

Close your eyes and you could be looking at the Goblin.

Close your eyes.

He closed his eyes.

Ha-ha-ha-ha!

"Is this it?" came Lester's voice. Norman opened his eyes. Bullseye was leaning across the table, gesticulating towards the TV. "Is this *it*? This is what you had us running around New York, getting our asses kicked over? Because you called the president a bad word and beat up the hotdog girl?"

"Sir..."

"Seriously, who cares?"

Victoria looked up from her tablet. "Sir."

Norman looked up.

The news report had segued into a video cutaway showing Hawkeye entering the *New York Bulletin*, caught on the dashboard camera of a passing vehicle, and followed by later shots of the building on fire and aerial scenes of a devastated East Midtown apartment.

Bullseye gave a low whistle.

"OK, sure. It looks bad when they cut it together like that."

Norman gripped his phone so tightly that he had cut the circulation to his fingers.

"I know that you will tolerate almost anything, Norman," said Valentina. "Anything but an attack on your image. And maybe people will still love you after this. Maybe you will find a good enough excuse for rampaging through New York in pursuit of a fugitive. But ultimately you do not answer to them, do you? You answer to the man who has just watched you eviscerate him for the world. I'm not Fury. I'm not Dugan. I don't want to take the world back to what it was. I'm like you, Norman. I'm going to make the world better, and the world will accept me as it never, ever, truly took to you. I'm coming for your job, Norman, and if you want to stop me then you are going to have to do it before somebody wakes up the president and you lose yours."

The fires of a burning New York shone in Norman's eyes, curt banner text and painstakingly neutral BBC commentary condemning him to every TV in every country in the world. He wanted to scream and rage, but all that came out of him was a laugh that grew wilder even as his chest started to hurt and his vision blur. It was just so *funny*. How did the world expect to get by without Norman Osborn to check under its bed for monsters every half an hour and pat it on the head? The only thing more absurd was that he was the only one here laughing.

He wiped a tear from his eye. "Sure. Why not? I could do with a day off."

"We will see, Norman. You can find me and the rest of Desert Sword at Fury Secret Base Iceberg in Kuwait City. I have Lindy here w–"

Before the Contessa could finish what she had been about to say, Norman felt an implosion in the seat behind him. He spun around, grunting as the flash-flare from the Sentry's sudden departure faded from his eyes. When it did, he saw that the super hero was gone, a smoldering hole punched into the bulkhead behind his chair and through every other bulkhead from there to the outer hull.

Air whistled out of it.

Norman looked at the hole, laughter bubbling back up from inside him as though his head was carbonated.

"Sir?" Victoria screamed, her dyed hair whipping towards the breached hull. "Sir, where has the Sentry just gone?"

"I'm waiting for you, Norman. The world is watching." The Contessa hung up.

"Sir!"

Norman stared down at the blank phone. "Get this ship to Kuwait."

"What about the Sentry, sir?"

"That's where he's going, and I don't want to miss the show."

"Even with Moonstone fit and able, we'd never get someone there ahead of him."

Norman swiped a finger across his phone screen, and punched in a number. He put it to the side of his head and grinned as he listened to it ring. "Watch the Go– I mean, *a genius* at work, Ms Hand."

PART THREE

KUWAIT

CHAPTER TWENTY-EIGHT

Not Insane

The city was serenely beautiful: a bright, twinkling neon jewel, hemmed in from all sides by the absolute darkness of desert and sea. It was a bauble of glass, steel, and concrete, a trinket that a careless god might crush with a careless gesture or an intimate word. Skyscrapers ached for the dark clouds, the gleaming fingers of mortals grasping for the fluttering blue cloak of their savior, and their destroyer, like Babel of old, humbled in the familiar despair of failure. The city mumbled in its sleep. Its roads. Its malls. Its airport. Its docks. A single voice, hushed in desperate prayer. To the east, the horizon suffered the first gash of dawn. Early sunlight turned the Persian Gulf the color of pewter. It caught the steel poles of the bridges that bent off to north and west, turned them into gory spikes, and transformed the enameled spheres of the Kuwait Towers into Earths in miniature, the dawn casting hemispheres across their globes.

This was the world as it appeared to the Sentry: an orb that he could destroy at any time, and which every day, and every second of every day, he made the conscious decision to leave be.

Because he was good.

In frustrated omnipotence he hung over Kuwait City, a fallen angel returned to his errant kingdom. The arid wind blustered through his cape. He barely felt it.

Every one of the million vehicles on the roads beneath him had a voice that was recognizable and distinct to his ears. Every drowsy utterance from a husband to a wife or vice versa as families roused themselves for the day was as clear as a bell. He could hear, and place, every opening door, every shoe scuffing the sidewalk, every grain of sand hitting a windshield. He could hear the other Avengers, Osborn and Bullseye and Hand, fifteen hundred miles away, arguing with each other over how best to stop him. He could hear CLOC, sixty-five hundred miles away, as he puttered quietly through the self-repairing corridors of the Watchtower.

But for all his perspicacity, for all his might, he could not hear Lindy.

He clutched his head in his hands, fingers tangling in wind-blown hair, as his face twisted into a silent scream. He did not know what else to try.

Robert had once given up the powers of the Sentry to save the world from the Void. He could still remember the man he had become when the powers were gone, because deep down inside he knew that he would always be that man. If it had not been for Lindy, then he would probably have succumbed to addiction years before he had been given the chance to see his memories and strength restored. And she forgave him. She forgave everything. Now it was his turn to be there for her, and with all his power he could not even do that. His blunted fingernails dug into his scalp. It hurt as only he, in truth, was physically capable of hurting himself. If he had been half the hero that Lindy deserved then he would have gone to Reed, rather than Norman Osborn, the moment he had heard the Void's voice again in his head.

But he was scared.

He was the most powerful man in the universe and he was scared of becoming that guy again. That disappointment. But look past the power, past the golden costume and the cape, and that sad, lazy addict was still the man underneath it all. No one else saw it.

No one else saw because there was just so much power, and it was blinding.

Sometimes, even the Sentry forgot.

He was confronted by it now, and could not look away. With his head in his hands, he surveyed the city that woke blithely beneath him in its innocence.

The Contessa and her Desert Sword had to be holding Lindy underground somewhere. A hotel parking lot or a basement. Or a bunker. Soundproofed. Hidden from sight. Yes, he silently congratulated himself. This was thinking. This was what his friend, Reed, would do. Now all he needed to do was put himself into Colonel Fury's shoes, imagine that he wanted to build a secret military base under one of the most populous cities in the Gulf.

Where would he put it?

Where?

Looking across a hundred square miles of ultra-modern, high-rise urban sprawl, raising five million souls out of the desert, he felt the golden rays of hope trickling away into the darkness of the sand.

With the self-control of an addict, he rushed back to the comfort of his powers, knowing they would bring him no good even as strained his ears until they bled. With a too-easy expression of impulse to thought to action, he scoured the city with his senses, combing it for the slightest trace of her aura. She was his wife. He knew her spirit better than he did his own. If she had passed through the city at all then he should have felt it: the brush of her hand against a stranger's coat, the press of her finger on the button of a traffic crossing, her breath on the mild morning air. But there was nothing. He sensed nothing. He played pin the tail on the donkey from a thousand feet away and with no pin. And worse, every time he felt that he did have a sense of something, of Lindy walking down a corridor with an elegant woman in a blue S.H.I.E.L.D. jumpsuit, he felt his mind being turned around. It was as though some other force was leading him willfully astray, amused by his persistent failure.

He could almost feel the cold, dead touch of hands on his shoulders.

He whirled, laughter rasping in his ears and fading onto the breeze.

Nothing there.

"LINDY!"

The golden aura that enveloped him guttered.

Though he was not observant to it, the sunrise for a moment ceased its climb and sank back towards the eastern horizon, dark clouds like tentacles smoking up from the hidden abyss from whence the majesty of the Void always arose, just beyond the next curve of the Earth.

In spite of all the power he wielded, the fury of it exploding inside him, the dread he felt was the exact same fear that he'd used to cry himself to sleep over on Lindy's couch.

That he was going to lose her.

"You will have to tear the city down to find her," the Void whispered in his ear. "It's the only way."

The Sentry shook his head violently. “No. I won’t do that.”

“You can hear Osborn and the others as well as I can. It’s what they expect you to do, and they’re your friends. They know you as well as I do.”

The Sentry looked despairingly over the city, spread out beneath him.

His friends. Those monsters were his friends.

What did that make him?

“No. The others … the others will find her. We’re a team. That’s what teams do.”

“And you’re just going to wait and hope? Can you imagine what Desert Sword is doing to your wife right now? Because I can.”

The Sentry closed his eyes, made a fist of his hand, and screamed as he beat his head against it. “Norman will help me. He promised. He’s smart.”

“Not as smart as Richards. Or Strange. They were your friends, too, and they kicked you into the gutter and forgot about you. He’s not even as smart as you used to be. I wouldn’t put my faith in Osborn. Not when we could pull this city apart block by block until they come out to defend their city, or burn up in their bunker like cowards.”

“No. That’s not how a hero should act.”

The Void sneered.

He hovered in the air in front of the Sentry, swathed in a shadowy coat and with a night-black fedora dipped forward over his features.

“Listen to yourself. You talk like Captain America in those comic book adventures you used to love. But you’re no Captain America. Anyone, literally anyone, could have been the Sentry. You’re just the lucky loser who broke into his chemistry professor’s lab looking to get high, found a mysterious vial, and was dumb enough to drink it. You tell yourself that you're ill, but there are plenty of guys with schizophrenia out there who manage to function just fine without trying to end the universe. You made yourself the way you are, just like Osborn did. You tell yourself that you're a hero even though you know that for every life you pull out from a fire, I push another under a bus. You save a pregnant woman in Dallas from an armed robber? I make sure a kid in Bangkok dies of cancer. You save the world…" He left the loose ends of his threat dangling. "That's how this arrangement between us works."

"Shut up!" The Sentry pulled on his hair. "You're not real. Norman promised me that you're not real."

"Then you're talking to yourself right now, and you know what that makes you."

"I AM NOT INSANE!"

The Void was no longer in front of him. He was him. Black infinitendrils snaked around his forearms, strangling off his golden light. Two perfectly balanced powers went to war over the single body they shared, with poor Robert Reynolds caught helplessly in between. A mile below their feet, their struggle was played out in misfiring car alarms and earthquake early warning systems triggering throughout Kuwait City.

The Sentry felt a buzzing in his ear.

He bared his teeth, the taste of blood in his mouth, as he fought to rip the Void's infinitendrils from his chest.

The buzzing grew more insistent.

Of course. It was the communicator he used to carry so that CLOC would always be able to contact him and direct him towards the most urgent emergency. He was not sure why he still wore it, except, perhaps, that it made him feel like a real hero, waiting for the cry for help that was never coming.

He tapped his right ear.

The Void tapped his left.

"CLOC?" they both said.

"Sorry, no." A little laugh scratched along the line. It was Norman's voice, but strained by a kind of forced levity that neither the Sentry nor the Void had heard in it before. "CLOC allowed Moonstone to have this number, in case of psychiatric emergencies. And she, on account of being congenitally untrustworthy, gave it to me."

The Sentry bit down on the Void's response. "I think… I think I would like to speak with Karla now."

"I'm sorry, Bob, I'm afraid I can't allow that. But that's all right, Bob. How about we talk this out between the two of us right here and now?"

The Sentry and the Void vied for control of the communicator. Way below, pedestrians stumbled on the sidewalks. They held their heads in their hands, blood streaming from their ears under the sudden pressure, dust from slowly splintering skyscrapers drizzling over their bent heads.

"Are you… are you all right, Norman?"

"Me? Never better. And I want to help *you* now, Bob. You're hurting. You're angry. These guys took something from you, and you want to make them pay. Even more than you want Lindy back, you want to make them pay, because they made you feel weak. Am I right?"

"No. Y- yes. But–"

"Part of you almost wants to let the Void out. Because he'll do that for you, Bob. He'll make the people who hurt you pay, and you won't even have to feel bad about it afterwards. Because it wasn't you. Believe me, Bob, I understand. I understand better than anyone else ever could."

A tear crept down one cheek.

The relief.

Reed had never really understood.

"What do I do, Norman? Tell me what to do. The Void is going to destroy the city."

"Then maybe it's the Void I need on my team right now."

"Wh- what?" The Sentry shook his head. This wasn't right. Norman had promised to help. "No."

"Do you remember how you told me that for every person the Sentry saves, the Void balances the scales by killing another? I guess what I'm saying is, try looking at it from the other side for a change."

The Sentry felt himself choking. The Void's infinitendrils were around his throat. The hands he used to pull on them were dark.

Everything was turning dark.

He heard what sounded like an argument from the other end of the line, but he was too distracted to listen, finishing with Norman's muffled voice saying, "Shut up, Ms Hand. Can't you see I'm making an important call here?"

"What… what do you mean?" said the Sentry.

"Think about it, Bob. You let the Void slaughter all of those poor, helpless, innocent little people down there. You let him have that. Just this once. Just for today. And what do you think happens next, Bob?"

His voice was a croak. "What happens next?"

"What happens next is that you own him. You *own* the Void. That's four-point-five million people that you could save without owing him a cent. You'd be free, Bob. Free to be the hero. Isn't that what you really want?"

The Sentry hesitated.

He was drowning. But that *was* what he wanted.

"But... Lindy."

Norman sighed. The static of his weary disappointment crackled in the Sentry's ear. "I get it, Bob. I do. I know what it's like to hurt people. People I hate, people I might have loved if I'd ever really wanted to. Random strangers. Accidentally, and oh-so-very much on purpose. I know, and I– Bob? Bob?" The Sentry was gasping hard, groping at the shadow noosed around his neck as the darkness closed fully over his head. "Sentry. Are you still there?"

The arid wind blustered through the Void's heavy coat.

He barely felt it.

"No, Norman. He isn't."

"Good. Because what I think I'm trying to say is: you can get over it."

CHAPTER TWENTY-NINE
Cryptic and Weird

Karla Sofen woke from a place of screams and fire, returning again to the welcoming pains of her own body. She groaned, curling over onto her side and holding the sides of her head in her hands. The massive rumbling of the Helicarrier's engines vibrated through the bunk and through her, but with the breaks, bruises, and fractures that Lightbright had given her it felt more iron maiden than massage chair. Working her sleep-gummed eyes open, she reached across the mix of sleeping tablets and painkillers scattered over her nightstand, picking up the half-empty bottle of wine to reveal the entirely empty one behind it. She set it down and flopped back into the bed.

What did it take to get a full night's sleep without dreaming?

Eyes closed again, but wholly awake now, she tried to conjure the dream again in her mind. She remembered gunfire, screaming, smoke. It had to be her fight with Lightbright in the Desert Sword compound. It had made an impression on her body, it stood to reason that it would have made one on her subconscious mind as well. Dreams, in her opinion, didn't mean nearly as much as Dr Freud used to think they did, but now she thought about it she wasn't sure that the recollections from her dream represented her fight in the villa after all. She shivered as something passed through her, an echo of something half-remembered, a sympathetic vibration in the pit of her stomach as her moonstone responded.

Her lips twitched as she brought her awareness inwards.

The gravity stone was responding to an awesome release of energy, somewhere close.

She knew only one person that powerful.

Knocking the bottles off the nightstand and onto the carpeted metal floor, she pushed the intercom button on the wall.

Victoria answered.

Awake now, but still under the residual influence of too many prescription drugs and a lot of alcohol, Karla wondered why she wasn't talking to Norman.

"Ms Marvel, are you up?"

"I think I just felt the Sentry powering up. What's going on? Are we under attack?"

"The Helicarrier is heading into Kuwaiti airspace in pursuit of him right now. Are you strong enough to fly?"

Karla experimentally sat up in bed and grimaced. "I'm strong enough to fall."

Victoria's voice dropped. "Then I won't tell you to get suited up and prepped right now."

"It's not even dawn yet and you're being cryptic and weird."

"I wouldn't tell you to do that because Director Osborn has ordered the Avengers to remain aboard the Helicarrier. I certainly wouldn't tell you that he's set the Sentry to destroy the city below us and that you're the only other person still aboard that Robert might listen to. Is there anything else you need me to not tell you?"

Karla's head swam. It was too early in the day for her to be dealing with Victoria Hand. "No, I… I think I got it."

She took her finger off the button.

Groaning from a hundred and one points of stiffness and complaint, she eased her legs out of the bed, drawing the bedsheets up around herself and inadvertently eliciting a corresponding mumble of sleepy protest from the other side of her bed.

She turned and frowned down at what appeared to be a naked H.A.M.M.E.R. trooper in her bed. She had no memory of his arrival, or of the interim, but she could only assume that whatever had transpired therein it hadn't quietened her dreams either.

"Wake up," she muttered, swinging a leg back up to poke him in the ribs with a toe.

His eyes fluttered drowsily open. He gave her the most toe-curlingly infatuated smile.

"Morn–"

"Look, I have no idea who you are. I have to leave in, like, ten seconds, and I'm not leaving you alone in my room."

"But–"

"Ten seconds. You've got three before I throw you out. Seriously. I'm not even going to open the window."

"Wait a–"

"One."

The guy fell out of the bed, scooped up a pair of combat pants and tried to hop into the leg.

"Two."

He bundled up the rest of his scattered clothes, wearing one leg of his pants, and hurried for the door.

"I'll send you some flowers or something," Karla called after him. The guard standing outside the door just looked amused as the trooper stumbled away at speed. "Just as soon as I find out who you are."

The door closed behind him.

With a heavy sigh, she got out of bed.

The bedsheet fell away, revealing the immaculate black and red of Ms Marvel. Brushing tangled hair from her face, she consciously drew the black mask of her alter-ego across her eyes. Looking through the armored glass of her cabin's porthole window into the night-dark clouds beyond, she studied her reflection. Lightbright had done more than teach her how badly she needed to learn how to fight. She had forced her to reassess a few of her priorities. She had come to realize that pretending to be Ms Marvel wasn't enough for her anymore.

She wanted to *be* Ms Marvel.

And God, how she hated it.

"Time to look like a hero, Dr Sofen," she muttered to herself, and turned towards the door.

The guard in the corridor was not for her protection. She was an Avenger, but she was *Norman's* Avenger, and as long as that remained the case, she would never be free.

With a shimmer of intangibility, she stepped back into the window and through it, exiting the Helicarrier on her own terms to be the hero, or the villain, that she chose to be.

The Helicarrier drew into position, settling into a stable hover five thousand feet above the southern outskirts of Kuwait City where suburbs broke up into open desert, Kuwait International Airport and Abdullah al-Mubarak airbase drawing geometrically perfect lines across the faltering conurbation and blowing sand.

With a rattling of armor panels and iron chains, the Helicarrier rolled out its guns. Primary and secondary flight decks hurled F-22 fighter screens and helicopter gunships into its immediate airspace like chaff. H.A.M.M.E.R. marines in clattering field armor rushed to the gunwales to defend against hypothetical boarders. Corridors were locked down. Bulkheads were sealed. They would not be needed. The Sentry was taking care of even hypothetical foes.

And on the bridge, when the heavy doors unlocked to admit Victoria Hand and her escort, the sound that emerged would not have been out of place in a football stadium.

Operatives bound to their desks by their headphones screamed over the top of one another with updates on buildings destroyed, military assets mobilized, units wiped out. Spotters on the lookout deck equipped with high-powered binoculars and specially adapted equipment called out the last known coordinates of the Sentry, the information out of date almost as soon as it left their mouths to be cast to the din.

She displaced a junior officer, shaking her head at the ridiculously avoidable crisis they all found themselves dealing with and sat down at the central workstation, accessing a computer and immediately authorizing the prompt to transfer data from her smart glasses to the larger console.

There had been rumors of a secret base program circulating around S.H.I.E.L.D. even when she had still been working in the New York station as an accountant. After her searches, with full access to all of Fury's files, had turned up nothing she had filed it away as just another myth of the kind that all clandestine organizations inevitably generate over time. Like the Roswell grays, Area 51, and Montezuma's treasure.

Suffice to say, neither Norman Osborn nor the Sentry had

any clue where Iceberg was. But now that she had proof that it existed, Victoria Hand intended to find it. She was a S.H.I.E.L.D. accountant, after all. Ordinarily that was leveled against her as an insult or a joke.

Well, today it was going to save a city.

And possibly her job.

She looked up as one of the radar crew reported another building destroyed. They were lucky that the Sentry had started in downtown. The buildings there were taller, and more densely packed, but at that time of the morning they were unlikely to be fully occupied. If the Sentry had attacked just two hours later when everyone was at work then Victoria would have been looking down on a massacre. "We should send in Ares and Hawkeye," she yelled over the din. She suspected it was hopeless, but she had to try. "With a full H.A.M.M.E.R. division and the Helicarrier brought in to provide close support."

"Do you really expect any of that to do the slightest good against the Sentry, Ms Hand?"

Norman Osborn strutted the main deck with his hands in his pockets and a smile on his face, like a second term president at the peak of his powers, all his enemies vanquished, and owning the party conference stage.

"We did this, sir. We have to do *something*!"

"What does it look like I'm doing, Ms Hand?" He waved grandiloquently towards the lookout window. "We're letting the Sentry take out the trash for us. And once he's worn himself out a little bit, then we'll let Ares off the leash and bring him in. We'll tell everyone that the Sentry went mad and turned against us. Everyone will buy it. I mean, it's not as if Stark never lost control of Scarlet Witch and left the world to wake up to Eric Lehnsherr as their king, is it?" His laughter set Victoria's teeth on edge. The bridge staff, in the midst of that much chaos, made a point of pretending they could not hear. "Can you imagine, Ms Hand? Putting a power-mad fanatic like *that* in charge of anything? Setting the Sentry loose on the Middle East is nothing compared to what the people of the world are going to be unconsciously braced for. We could even blame it on the Contessa and Desert Sword. We'll say it was Raazer, corrupting the Sentry with some kind of magical influence. Book us a black magic expert to say something to that effect on the evening news tonight, Ms Hand. Who do we know?"

"Sir," said Victoria, trying one more time to break through. "There's more at stake right now than the evening news."

"I'm going to pretend I didn't hear that, Ms Hand."

"And if the Void isn't satisfied with destroying Kuwait City? If Ares can't stop him?"

Norman gave that doomsday scenario a half-second's thought. "You worry too much, Ms Hand. I suppose that's why I hired you."

It was, indeed, precisely why the director had hired her.

Pushing her glasses back up to the bridge of her nose, mentally resigned to the fact that the director was lost to her for the moment, she dialed out the distractions of the bridge and turned her attention to her computer.

On it, various spreadsheets that she had uploaded from her glasses' display showed her S.H.I.E.L.D. shipping manifests, invoices, requisition orders. The construction of a string of secret bases could be disguised through shell companies and contractors, if you had the know-how and the resources, but it couldn't be completely hidden. Given a restricted geographical search area and a finite number of possible locations within it, locating Iceberg, in the end, was not even going to be all that hard. She blinked methodically as she sifted the data, the small movements of her eyelids coupled with the position of her irises controlling the columns on the screen.

“What are you up to over there, Ms Hand?” The director crossed the busy deck towards her, officers scurrying to clear his path. “The look on your face says it’s important.”

“Iceberg, sir. If I can find it. If I can find Lindy, then–”

“It’s a *secret* base, Ms Hand. You’ll probably find it under the emir’s swimming pool.”

A callsign blinked up on Victoria’s glasses’ overlay. “It’s Washington for you again, sir.”

Osborn sighed. “Do I have one of those numbers that are easy to pocket-dial? Look into it for me, would you, Ms Hand.”

“Sir. They probably just want to know why you’ve deployed a Helicarrier to an allied capital, and what’s attacking the city.” She waited for an answer, silently pleading. “Sir?”

The director whirled away from her, arms spread wide towards the lookout deck windows. The smoky pall of urban destruction was just beginning to darken the thin skies of cruising altitude. “Let the answering machine pick it up, Ms Hand. We still have one of those, right? Obviously, I could tell the president exactly what this is, but I think the message will be that much clearer if he’s allowed to at least try to figure it out on his own. This is what happens, Ms Hand. Cross me, do it in public, try to bring *me* down, then this is what happens.”

Victoria didn’t know what frightened her more: that her boss was wildly insane or that he meant every word that he said. Or that she just couldn’t tell.

She checked the information in front of her one last time before shutting the screen down. There were a few facts that she needed to confirm on the ground, which was going to require backup, but it was becoming clear to her that she couldn't rely on Director Osborn's support in this. If he did really want to see the city burn in order to spite his prosecutors then there was as good a chance of him shutting her down before she could stop it as there was of him helping her. She couldn't afford to take the risk. Moonstone was on her way to the city now, but there was no guarantee that she would be successful. Recovering Lindy was still their best chance. The responsibility was Victoria's, but she couldn't do this alone. She needed help.

What she needed was the Avengers.

A thought occurred to her.

There *might* just be someone that the director wouldn't miss.

She rose from her desk. "Permission to leave the bridge, sir."

The director looked back over his shoulder and gave her a jagged jack-o'-lantern smile. "Granted. Just be sure to be back in time for the press conference. I've scheduled it for eleven." He turned back to the lookout deck and didn't wait to see her leave.

CHAPTER THIRTY
Desert Sword Assemble

Valentina Allegra de Fontaine held the rifle to her chest and sprinted down the main corridor from Perimeter C to Habitation Zone A. Iceberg was the most well-defended S.H.I.E.L.D. facility in the Middle East. The main bunker was buried deep under the desert. Its tough outer skin was of reinforced concrete, coating a skeleton of hardened steel. Vibranium trusses further strengthened its critical infrastructure while emergency force fields hummed patiently in reserve. It had been built to withstand a hydrogen bomb from a hostile state, or a laser strike from a Kree battleship in orbit. The entire secret base program, of which Iceberg was but one, had been Fury's contingency against doomsday. It had been built to be the last thing standing after the rest of South Asia had been turned into a cloud of radioactive ash.

That was what had always charmed her about Nicholas.

He was so wonderfully prepared.

Iceberg would have withstood a hydrogen bomb. It would

have taken a laser strike from a Kree battleship in orbit. Valentina was not sure it was going to survive the Sentry.

Lightbulbs flickered in their ceiling fixtures as they swayed, sending the shadows of staggering S.H.I.E.L.D. troopers racing wildly across the walls and floor. The trunk cabling and exposed pipework that ran through the ceiling conveyed the groans of the exterior shell to every corridor.

It was one thing to pick up a classified dossier and understand that the Sentry was powerful. To feel that power as it was turned upon you in full was an entirely new exercise in perspective. Valentina was not sure that she had quite believed the conclusions in that S.H.I.E.L.D. report, that the Sentry was essentially undefeatable, until now. In fact, she had the feeling that the report's authors had not entirely believed it either.

If anything, she felt that they had understated his power.

"Allah, he is attacking the city."

Navid Hashim ran alongside her, looking to the trembling ceiling whilst easily matching her pace. Young and robust as he was, he looked little the worse for his ordeals on the Gulf of Aden. Much of the credit for his survival lay with the indestructible uniform of the Arabian Knight. While his face and arms showed a scrape or two, his outfit's luster of emeralds, turquoises, and golds was undiminished by its beating at the hands of Wolverine. Valentina found herself idly wondering what the outfit might sell for at auction, and smiled to herself as she decided it had probably been worth more as a carpet.

"I do not know how you can be so calm." He regarded her angrily from underneath his thick eyebrows. Valentina disapproved of that look. He had been angry since his return from Africa and she suspected it was directed at her as much as it was at Norman Osborn. No sooner had it crossed his face, however, than it was gone again, yielding to the greater demands of his anxiety by a fierce shake of the head. "You all think me naïve for hoping that Ares might be won over to our cause. I know. But of all Norman Osborn's heroes I had believed that the Sentry, at least, was the one who would forsake his evil in the end. It was Iron Man who first made him an Avenger. He saved the world alongside Captain America and Luke Cage, did he not? Or is even he now a villain hiding behind a hero's mask?"

Valentina stared straight ahead. "Not even Norman could find a villain powerful enough to masquerade as the Sentry."

At the door to Habitation Zone A, she pushed her way inside. At the same moment, the ceiling above the lintel collapsed, showering Hashim in chalky white dust. With the Arabian Knight coughing and pawing at his hair, they went inside.

Habitation Zone A was gray and mostly bare: a utilitarian living space that nobody had ever actually lived in.

Envisaged as one of a network of fallback positions in the event of a global calamity or the complete disintegration of S.H.I.E.L.D. as a functioning peacekeeping force, Iceberg contained barracks for several hundred soldiers and quarters for the entire regional command structure. To ensure maximum secrecy, its pre-activation garrison amounted to six Live Model Decoys, all still in cryogenic suspension, while Valentina had brought barely a quarter of the force that the base could comfortably hold.

The Black Raazer had Habitation Zone A all to himself.

The sorcerer was an ominous, muttering cloud-form of a man, floating cross-legged above a cleared space in the middle of the room. Metal chairs and bunks had been shunted to the bare concrete walls to make room for a Zoroastrian faravahar that had been drawn on the floor with black chalk, and that now crackled with arcane static. The sorcerer's features were masked by a thousand glamours, each one darker than the last, but so deep was his concentration that Valentina could almost feel the drying out of her skin as it succumbed to the effects of mummification. There had been mattresses on the beds. Cushions on the chairs. Paper notices pinned to the walls.

All of it had withered to nothing or become dust.

There was one other person in the room, and she had retreated as far into the corner as she could get. One of Valentina's mercenaries had found her a jumpsuit that nearly fit, hanging baggily over her like a set of blue pajamas with a S.H.I.E.L.D. patch sewn into the breast pocket. She sat on a desiccated mattress at the back end of the room with her knees drawn protectively up to her chin, watching the Black Raazer with a mix of fascination and dread. Valentina sympathized. She would not want to share a room with Raazer either, but with the sorcerer's spells currently all that was obscuring them from the Sentry, it was the safest place in the world for Lindy Lee-Reynolds to be.

Still battling the dust in his hair, Hashim started towards Raazer. His toes scuffed the chalk outline of the mystic faravahar sign before Valentina halted him with a tap on the shoulder and a disapproving shake of the head. The Arabian Knight relented, barely, and jabbed a finger across the barrier at the levitating sorcerer.

"You were supposed to be stopping him!"

The sorcerer looked up.

He continued to mutter his incantations.

His red eyes were blisters of pain.

From the corner of the room, Lindy unfolded her legs and moved to the edge of the bed. "I didn't want this. When I asked you to take me with you, I… I wasn't expecting the whole world to have to suffer for it." She shook her head and wiped tears from her eyes on the back of her hand. "Please. Just send me back, before more people get hurt. Once he finds me, he'll leave you alone. I know he will." She sniffed. "If anybody can send the Void away for a time and bring Robert back, it's me."

Valentina shook her head. That simply wasn't going to happen.

But with the sound of old teeth rattling in yellowed skulls, Raazer stirred and paused his chant. "Yes. We should hand her back to her husband."

"It is not the tenth century, Raazer," said Hashim, backing off reluctantly, under Valentina's gentle pressure, from the sorcerer's mystic wards. "We cannot simply give her to him."

"To end this before it truly begins and save the lives of millions?" Raazer replied. "Including all of us and the woman herself?"

Hashim's look became pained.

"It's my choice to make," said Lindy, glaring at them both. "I want to go."

"I am sorry, Lindy," said Valentina. "But we cannot let you do that."

The woman shuffled back along the mattress, pulled her knees up again and, her courage used up, softly began to cry.

Valentina would have sacrificed her to the Void if she had to. If it served her purpose to do so, and there was absolutely no other way, then she would have shot the woman herself. But right now it served all their interests better to keep Lindy close by. So long as the Sentry remained unaware of the bunker half a kilometer beneath the city's suburbs, then she was confident that Iceberg could ride it out.

"If the magic of the Black Raazer can no longer stop the Sentry from attacking the city then we have no choice," said Hashim. "We must return to the surface and face him."

"You can't win," Valentina pointed out, with the patience of all the saints. "Not against the Sentry."

Hashim let out a breath. "That does not matter."

True belief, Valentina had always thought, whether it be in a god or in a cause, was an admirable quality in a foot soldier and very much a required trait in a revolutionary. It was considerably less desirable in a person with whom one was forced to share a bunker. "The Sentry is showing his, and Norman's, true face to the world now," she explained. "People are going to have no choice but to look their heroes in the eye and see them for the monsters they are."

Valentina had learned to choose her facial expressions the way she did her weapons, to pick her favorite and keep it, and compared to her practiced composure Hashim was laughably open.

His expression morphed from defiance to horror.

"You planned this. Didn't you? Right from the beginning, just like you planned for what happened in New York. Is that the real reason you sent me to Somalia in your place? Did you always intend for the Avengers to follow me there?"

"No," Valentina replied, firmly. "No."

She had never wanted the director's job. Not even when it had been there for the taking as Nicholas' deputy. It had always seemed like so much responsibility for so little recompense. But with Nicholas out of the frame, and Norman insisting on making such a pig's ear of the whole endeavor, Valentina had grown quite bored of watching other people fail. It was time for her to step in, and step up. Norman had not been entirely off target with some of his ideas, extending olive branches to the more amenable tendrils of Hydra and the like, but he did not have the contacts or the panache that Valentina had: she had been exposed as a double- or triple-agent for more organizations than poor Norman even knew existed.

Someone had to make the hard decisions.

Since everyone else who had tried it had failed, that someone might as well be her.

"The plan was always to sell the files on, to bleed H.A.M.M.E.R. from a thousand small wounds while we waited, watching with the rest of the world as Norman flailed and his organization weakened. But it was always going to end this way, Hashim. Norman was never going to just fade from the scene. There was *always* going to be the moment when his back was pushed to the wall, and he decided to push back hard. Yes, there are five million people up there, but there are seven billion who are counting on us to make their deaths count for something. Being able to think those thoughts is what it takes to be the Man on the Wall."

She held Hashim's gaze.

It was clear that all he wanted to do was look away.

"The only question you need to ask yourself then is this, Hashim – do you believe that the world would be better off with me, or with Norman Osborn?"

"I… Forgive me, I do not even know anymore."

Valentina nodded. She was neither disappointed nor surprised. "Majid would have understood. If she were here."

That comment seemed to settle something for Hashim.

He drew his sword.

It was an impressively heroic gesture, with half a kilometer of rock separating them from their omnipotent foe.

"Every fight she took on was for her people and her home. The people up there." He looked up. "They are mine. If it had been the Sentry in Somalia instead of Ms Marvel, then I believe she would have fought him anyway. I am going to take the Perimeter C elevator to the surface, and I am going to fight."

He held out a hand to Raazer.

The sorcerer shook his head, the movement as faint as that of a dark shawl blowing in the sand on an empty line. "After two thousand years of un-life, I have no desire now to die."

"Can you even die?"

"I fear that the Sentry will show us, one way or the other."

"Please, Raazer." Leaving Valentina's side, Hashim took another step towards the faravahar. "You joined us to rid your old king's empire of the Americans once before. The odds were against you then, and you fought. Fight with us again now. This is your land, Raazer. We may find that the Black Sword of Baghdad can cut him. With all of Desert Sword assembled, maybe we can even beat him."

Valentina noted the subtle appeal to the ancient one's pride. Hashim may have had more rough edges than the desert, but she had chosen well when she had recruited him as her second in command.

Raazer was silent for so long, Valentina wondered if the last residue of life had finally left him and been returned to its prison in the Black Sword.

"I cannot believe that you would even consider this," said Valentina. "This is not the Raazer I found hiding in the mountains, preying on Kurdish shepherds while the world fell apart around him."

"I was a hero once," said Raazer, his voice the breathless caw of the never-dead. "I wore the splendor of Ahuru Mazda. I shone with the majesty of kings." Without his appearing to move at all, his sword was suddenly held flat across his mummified hands. "Before I sought the strength and long life of this accursed sword." His voice dropped to less than a whisper. "I yearn to retake the glory that was once mine, as it hungers for a taste of the Sentry's golden soul."

Valentina felt the electric tension that had been a constant throb in her gums and beneath her skin recede. She felt no better for its abeyance.

It was the feeling of her protection from the Sentry evaporating in the ether.

Hashim stepped across the faravahar.

There was a ghost of movement and Raazer became upright. He lay a hand on Hashim's shoulder, and neither the living man nor the dead one recoiled from their brief recognition of brotherhood. His eyes shone starkly red against the black within his hood. "I will carry you more swiftly to your grave, at least. I promise no more."

"Raazer!" Valentina screamed, but before the word was out the two men were already gone, both of them reduced to tricks of the swaying lightbulbs and the uncertain vagaries of memory.

She cursed, once again resorting to her favored language to do it.

Norman had been right about that as well.

Heroes always disappointed you in the end.

From the back of the suddenly empty room, Lindy sniffed. "If he's gone..."

"Then he's no longer shielding us from your husband," Valentina finished for her. Looking up as another earth-shaking blow rocked down through Iceberg's protesting bones, she made another hard decision.

She did not believe for a moment that Desert Sword could defeat the Sentry.

But maybe they could distract him for long enough.

"I hope you were not getting too attached to the place," she said, turning back to Lindy. "Because we're leaving."

CHAPTER THIRTY-ONE
Professional Courtesy

Victoria Hand brought the hover bike down over an area of industrial brownfield to the far northwest of Kuwait City, on the edge of the town of Al Jahra. From the information that Victoria had been able to put together, it had been the site of an exploratory oil well, drilled by a company with no record of ever producing oil called Sans Petro that had duly abandoned the site and declared bankruptcy shortly afterwards. Rusty chain-link barriers and intimidating junkyard walls still enclosed the site. Regular signage in both Arabic and English warned of chemical hazards, and the hefty legal penalties for trespassers.

The guard on the gate was reassurance that she had come to the right place. He was outfitted in nondescript black leathers over basic combat armor, Kevlar panels sheathing his forearms and chest. Victoria stunned him. He fell back against the gate with electricity from the tranquilizer bolt writhing through him. A second ran to intercept her descent angle, pulled out a handgun as he hurdled through the no man's land of exploratory craters and rusted machinery. Victoria stunned him, too. He stumbled on another yard before his nervous system packed in and his legs gave out.

A blast of engine thrust from the hover bike sent sand flying in all directions as she brought the vehicle in to land. When she was a foot above the ground, she flipped the anti-grav control lever by the throttle and the brute machine *thunked* to the ground, its massive inventory of weapons clattering in their stowage compartments. Stiff from the flight down and numb from the landing, Victoria swung out of the padded seat and dismounted the bike.

Dawn was coming, the sky lit up by the onslaught of the Sentry just a few miles to the east, but it was dark enough around the abandoned well that she turned on the lamp pack fixed to her rifle.

Her hand lingered over the ammunition selector on the hard plastic of the receiver. The slider was still on stun.

She was a cop, not a soldier. The people working for the Contessa were the same people that she used to work with, not so very long ago. They might not have worked in the same building, or in the same state, but they had been doing it for the same reasons. Global security. World peace. No one disagreed that these were laudable things to strive for. Ninety percent of the world's problems stemmed from disagreements over how hard the various parties were prepared to push to get them. For refusing to accept that Norman Osborn had won that argument, Victoria would ensure that her former colleagues got a fair trial and went away forever, but she wouldn't kill them. Not unless she had to.

Following the beam of her torch, she looked around the site.

Derelict mining equipment and old trucks sullenly absorbed the torchlight, sitting and rusting wherever they had been abandoned. A string of dilapidated shacks ran along the western edge of the site, their white plastic walls just visible under the sheets of corrugated metal and rotten pallet boards stacked up against their sides. Dominating the site, the hulking brown-steel shell of a drilling rig stood to a height of about thirty feet, its feet straddling a sun-bleached site office with boarded windows.

It might have passed for any abandoned site, if not for the guards.

Arab men in plain armor, armed with store-bought pistols, they could easily have passed as local security as was surely the intention, if not for the fact that the Sentry was pulling up skyscrapers a few miles away, breaking the sky with his thunder, and they were still here.

No one was that committed for the sake of a paycheck.

Satisfied that she had all the confirmation she needed, she drew up her rifle and deactivated the lamp pack, turning on the built-in radio in the hover bike's steering block to call in her backup. Before she could say a word, the rusted steel doors to the site office between the drilling rig's legs flew open and a squad of S.H.I.E.L.D. troopers clattered out.

They might have been alerted to the failure of their plain clothes comrades to make some pre-arranged check-in. It was also possible that another component of the secret base program had been tracking sensors that Victoria was unaware of, and that the stealth suite of her bike was unable to compensate for. They could have registered the engine emissions or the applied pressure of her landing, detected the pulse of her gunfire, or perhaps her presence had nothing to do with their appearance at all. It was possible that the Contessa and her subordinates were simply foolish, and thought that they could defend their secret hideout from the Sentry.

Whatever the reason, it didn't matter.

Five soldiers in bulky S.H.I.E.L.D. tactical armor and carting heavy assault rifles of a similar gauge and model to Victoria's emerged through the office doors and immediately noted the H.A.M.M.E.R.-purple attack bike parked in the middle of their site. Dropping to their knees and into the copious amounts of cover afforded by the abandoned machinery and tilled ground, they unanimously opened fire.

Victoria threw herself behind the hardest cover available, which was the bike itself. Built to ferry H.A.M.M.E.R. troops into combat zones in support of superhuman agents, it was a tank that had been stripped down into a passably agile single-pilot profile. Gunfire drummed against its side armor, her counterparts not according her with nearly the same professional courtesy that she had shown to their comrades.

She agonized again over the ammunition slider. Outnumbered five to one, if ever there was a time for the improved rate of fire and the shorter reload cycle then it was now. She pushed her hand along the receiver to the handguard and took a firm grip there. That wasn't a decision that she ever intended to take in the heat of the moment.

Without waiting for good sense to catch up with her, she rose from cover, fired off two short *blats* of electrical discharge, and then dropped back. She sat with her back hard up to the shuddering bike, her breath coming in short and fast, her heartbeat seriously stress-testing her breastplate. She didn't think that she'd hit anything. There hadn't been enough time to find targets before being forced to pull her head down. She had, however, glimpsed two soldiers out of the five advancing to flank her. With the extra guns to pin her down and ample cover between them and her, they could afford to take the risk.

Rolling to the rear fender, she swung her muzzle around the back of the bike. She squeezed the trigger, ready to gun down the trooper advancing on her right, only to see the soldier stagger before the pressure had registered as a shot. He stumbled, falling instinctively into the cover of some discarded drill heads, bringing his hand to claw at his face where something black and tarry had smeared across his helmet visor.

Victoria eased her finger off the trigger, drew her rifle in, and looked up.

She had never been so pleased to see anyone.

Venom was perched on the drill floor of the derrick. He couldn't fly and Victoria had brought him part of the way on her bike, only dropping him off once they were at rooftop height so he could launch a surprise attack if needed. She'd brought him along to Kuwait just in case, and now she was pleased she had.

He was suited entirely in black, as though he had treated himself in oil, but for the white spider emblem on his chest and the empty glaze of his masked eyes. A yank on the rope-like strand of symbiote webbing stuck to the soldier's faceplate pulled the man screaming into the air. Another shot of webbing left the trooper dangling twenty feet off the ground and upside down, and then Venom sprang off the drill floor.

He landed amongst the three soldiers in front of the site office.

One swung the butt of their rifle. The second attempted to throw their arms around Venom's chest and grapple him to the ground. The third drew a knife. Two seconds of weaving symbiote suit and blurring limbs later, and three S.H.I.E.L.D. troopers with horribly disjointed limbs, one with a knife stuck through their hand, littered the ground around him. The fifth and final trooper, who had been moving to flank Victoria's bike on the left before the abrupt reversal in who outnumbered who, swung around and fired. He got off one barking shot of an automatic burst before Victoria sent a hundred thousand volts of pulsed direct current wracking through his peripheral nervous system.

Venom looked around, his tar-slick mask splitting in half around a sickly, jagged smile.

"I thought you had a spider sense," Victoria called out over the gunfire echoes, the temporary euphoria of not being dead making her breathless and giddy.

"I do. I sensed you were gonna shoot him."

Easing herself up from cover, her knee armor crunching spent shell casings, Victoria ran her hand across her totaled bike's cowling. She wasn't going to be evacuating Lindy to the Helicarrier this way. There was no going back now, though, even if she had been minded to give up and go home. Lingering only to open up the bike's stowage racks and stock up on spare magazines and grenades, she left the vehicle to the machine graveyard where it had fallen and walked to join Venom.

The hunger in him was barely restrained, every molecule in his symbiote suit straining to break free of its enforced humanoid shape and devour the soldiers it had beaten. But it *was* restrained. Victoria knew it wouldn't last. The symbiote always adapted, but for a short while at least it appeared as though Dr Fiennes had finally refined a treatment plan that worked as it was supposed to.

She pointed her gun towards the site office. The silent drill looming over it moaned with the warm, ash-scented wind that the Sentry sent blowing through its metal bones. "According to my information, a subsidiary of a subsidiary of Worthington Industries imported several million tons of concrete to construct an underground chemical waste storage facility."

"A good place for a secret base."

"Ready to be the hero?"

A look of strange and unsettling longing passed across Venom's fluid features. He sighed, and said simply, "*Yes.*"

CHAPTER THIRTY-TWO

Anything But Heroic

Navid Hashim had fought in cities before. Many times. Some might have said too many, but not Hashim. He would take all that Allah gave and then some. He had once held a road barricaded with burning tires against an armored brigade of Iranian Karrar tanks. He had faced down wave after wave of US cruise missiles with naught at his side but an indestructible suit and a magic sword. His work for the House of Saud had put him on the opposite side of the line just as often. He knew what it was to fight street by street, house by house, room by room. He had led men in charges across minefields that had been buried in children's playgrounds. He had lived in fear of the sniper's bullet and the improvised bomb. He knew the peculiar insanity of urban war.

But he could recall no battle as bizarre in its horrors as the battle for Kuwait City.

He had never been called to defend a city against an army of one.

Black Raazer deposited him in the Hawalli district, just south of downtown Kuwait, in the relative quiet of Kuwait University's sports field. The modernist architecture of Jabriya campus was hemmed in on all sides by jagged, cliff-high walls of glass and concrete, their gleaming spires emblazoned with the Arabic names of international tech conglomerates and banks. The imposing skyline was already a toxic blur of smoke and ash, the strobing red and blue lights of emergency service vehicles coming apart through the dust into a million broken pieces of light. Sirens wailed. A city screamed, and its voice was flesh and steel and stone and every note on the spectrum of electronic pain.

It was the screams, more than the enemy, that made this battle surreal. An atrocity relived through a nightmare.

When conventional forces invaded a city there was warning. In the months beforehand there would be rumors and rhetoric, the build-up of forces across some real or imagined border. There would be leaflet drops urging civilians to flee, progressing to air raids and shelling that could go on for days, weeks, or even months. Fresh food and clean water would run out and more people would flee, so that by the time the dust cloud of the enemy's tanks blotted the horizon all but a handful of the most battle-stubborn or defiant were long gone. The coup de grâce, when it came, was to a ghost city that did not scream.

Kuwait had been given no warning.

It had been given the Sentry.

Raazer made a complicated gesture and dipped his cowled head, his red eyes baleful as he faded back into the darkness, leaving Hashim alone in the middle of the soccer pitch, in the heart of a screaming city.

Hashim could only trust that the sorcerer intended to return.

Taking his sword in a reassuring two-handed grip, he scanned the sky, expecting to spot some glimmer of the Sentry's golden light, but finding only darkness layered upon more darkness. Guided only by the thickness of the smoke and the intensity of the flashing lights, Hashim picked a direction almost at random and started running.

He was halfway across the field when the destruction stopped being abstract.

One by one, the high-rises looming over Jabaliya campus began to die.

Fulminating beams of black energy carved through the skyscrapers like a factory laser running wild through plaster models, filling the air with shards of glass and volcanic plumes of vaporized concrete.

The first of them fell.

It did not fall in the choreographed manner of a demolition, but rather as a crudely felled tree went down, five hundred feet high and smashing violently through the building beside it, sending hundreds of thousands of tons of rubble raining down over the crowded east-west highway of Shari' Bayrout.

Hashim had never seen destruction like it.

He prayed never to again, but as if in direct repudiation of his prayers the Sentry did not stop. Another building fell. Then another.

And another.

Hashim gave thanks that the hour was still early and that the thousands who might otherwise have been doomed with those skyscrapers were still at home. When the world died, he decided then, it would be to the sound of glass falling from the heavens.

A slow rumble built through the re-drawn sky and Hashim looked up, blinking dust from his eyes, as several squadrons of Kuwaiti F/A-18s arrowed through the smoking ruins of Hawalli. They converged on the Sentry as he watched, sidewinder missiles whistling from underwing pods, Gatling cannons grinding up twenty millimeter ammunition like coffee from a mill and spraying bullets into the air. The Kuwaiti air force was minuscule compared to that of the US or even its Gulf neighbors, but it was supported by the Americans and provided with only the best. It boasted a fleet of twenty-eight top of the line F/A-18 Super Hornets of the same type flown by H.A.M.M.E.R.

It did not have them anymore.

Twenty-eight flaming wrecks dropped out of the sky, falling over the Hawalli business district like debris from an incompletely destroyed asteroid. If anything, however, the destruction they caused came as something of a reprieve as the Sentry, just for a moment, turned his powers and attention towards annihilating something else. Hashim could have pitied those pilots their sacrifice, but instead he felt only pride. They had bought their city seconds, and those were seconds in which hundreds more citizens might flee the destruction of downtown Kuwait and escape into the safer suburbs. From somewhere amidst Hawalli's smoldering bones a stinger missile, launched by a Kuwaiti soldier or perhaps one of the Contessa's mercenaries, shot towards the Sentry. Faster than twice the speed of sound, it climbed, but still not fast enough to hit its target. The missile exploded amongst the chaff that the destruction of the Kuwaiti air force had left in the sky. The Sentry took a moment to flatten the block it had come from.

In so doing, he gave Hashim something to aim at.

And even the Sentry was not going to be fast enough to dodge this.

He aimed his sword up, feeling the familiar kick across his shoulder muscles and chest as mystic light blasted from the golden blade. Dawn came again, and at last, to that small green square of Kuwait City as the light ripped through the pall and lanced upwards. The Sentry was a writhing blackness in the heart of the beam, and Hashim exulted in seeing him struck.

He never saw the return blow coming.

One second the Sentry was several thousand feet above him and a mile away, the next he was hammering his fist into Hashim's gut. If he had targeted his head or a limb then Hashim would have lost it, but the Sentry went straight for the center of his mass and the costume just about took it. Even so, it was a million times harder than any Arabian Knight had ever been hit before. The air exploded from Hashim's lungs and he flew backwards, so blindingly fast that he was not even aware of what he was crashing through until he came to, coughing up blood and dragging himself upright, looking back through a corridor of modernist rubble to a patch of fuzzy, burning green.

The Sentry descended, dark boots crunching into the pebble-strewn campus foyer.

Wincing with the pain of what felt like several broken ribs and torn muscles, Hashim brought his sword en garde. Given that he could not begin to match the Sentry's speed and power, it was a superficial gesture, but he made it gladly. Never mind his dreams of a more compassionate S.H.I.E.L.D., of being the Captain America of the Contessa's World Avengers, the full extent of his ambition now was to buy the city one more minute. If he could defy the Sentry for just that long, then he would consider his sacrifice to have been worthwhile.

The Sentry walked towards him, a demon determined to take its time, and now that the golden hero was close enough to *feel*,

Hashim found himself in the improbable position of wondering whether the Contessa had been mistaken and there really was an imposter in the Sentry's place. If this was another of Osborn's stand-ins, however, he was poorly chosen and putting in no effort at all to look the part. Absent entirely was the golden uniform and the sky-blue cape, in their place a heavy coat that negated all light and a hat that, though narrow-brimmed, cast his features wholly into shadow. If Hashim were to stare long and hard into the darkness, though, then he had to admit that it *was* the face of the Sentry looking back.

"Sentry?" he whispered, from behind his wavering sword.

The darkness smiled at him.

Even his teeth were black.

Hashim felt a chill go through him. His stance wavered.

Lindy had warned them about the Void.

The Sentry, *the Void,* raised a fist as though to blast him then and there, only to issue a frustrated snarl, seemingly unable to move his arm from its upright position.

Shackles of dense Medean cuneiform snaked around the Void's forearm, spitting out red embers of magical energies as it countered the villain's struggles. Hashim became aware of a pickled scent and a rasping chant at his left side. He turned to see the Black Raazer with one shadow-shrouded claw upraised to the Sentry, every dry syllable uttered a link in the ever-renewing chain that bound the Sentry's arm in place. With every furious attempt to tear his wrist free of Raazer's chains, the Void became less a defined form than an outline of a once-certain shape, anchored by the Medean brand at its center but too vast a power to be fully bound by it. His human form deliquesced with every pull against the bound arm, his upper body streaming off before Hashim's eyes into a viperous clutch of tentacles.

"You think you can stop me, sorcerer?" said the Void, in a voice that came from a hundred sources, all of them dying at the exact same moment in time. "I am the Void. I am the end of all life."

"I am not alive," Raazer returned, during a pause in his chant.

A chuckle. "You are alive enough."

Raazer hissed as the Void roared, and the Medean chains blazed as red as the fires of Jahannam. The ground beneath them trembled. The last free-standing walls of the campus foyer slowly crumbled under the devolution of the monstrous thing within their grounds. The wind picked up, screaming as it raced through the ruins. Hashim's first assumption was that it was the power pouring out of the Void. Or perhaps the sound of the world dying, a hole punched through the skin of the atmosphere resulting in all of their air whistling out into space. Hashim felt it tug at his uniform. It explored every bruise, prodded every scrape; it gusted through his long hair, through Raazer's ethereal body, and whipped itself like clay on a potter's wheel into the funnel of a whirlwind that touched down at Hashim's right.

It deposited a sand-scarred older man with a goatee beard, scuffed armor, and a Bedouin shemagh headscarf around his face.

Bent with the effort of summoning a mighty enough gale to batter the Sentry, the newcomer blasted the spreading tentacles, weathering the Void back into his limited, magically restrained human form.

Hashim knew him as Sirocco. The Bedouin had never shared his real name, but in Arabic it meant East Wind. Discounting the unliving Raazer, he was the last original member of Desert Sword. Hashim wished he could be more pleased to see him.

"It is good to stand united again," Sirocco spoke through gritted teeth and sand-coated lips. "It has been too long."

"We are blessed," said Raazer, with equally pronounced effort and heavy irony.

"A pity that Ahminedi, Veil, and Qamal could not live to be here. We will say a prayer for our fallen brothers and sisters when this is done."

"You were always a pathetic optimist, Sirocco."

"It is what keeps me looking young."

With a sound like a burning airplane being flown against a wind tunnel, the Void forced a step towards them, the Black Raazer's brand sputtering red around his arm as he dragged it with him.

"I cannot hold him," Raazer hissed.

"Nor I," said Sirocco.

Hashim firmed his grip on his shamshir.

There were worse ways to mark the coming end of one's life, he decided. He could have died alone and unremarked, but instead he had been given the chance to fall alongside his team. They had already bought the city more than the minute he had been hoping for. He could think of no worthier end to his career as the Arabian Knight.

The Void forced a second step towards them, just as a flurry of searing yellow beams from above drove him to raise his unshackled arm to shield himself and pushed him one step back.

Too occupied with holding the Void at bay, neither Sirocco nor Raazer could spare the attention, but Hashim looked up, an unexpected surge of hope bringing buoyancy to his heart.

Lightbright!

The fourth member of their team must have escaped her Yemeni captors and made her own way to Kuwait.

He shaded his eyes against the woman's terrific radiance, resisting the urge to perform a double-take as the super hero descended through the shattered roof, red cape fluttering, and set down alongside Sirocco. He gaped at her, heart thumping, as the villain who was definitely not Obax Majid brushed blonde hair back from her face, alien energy coruscating halos around her fists. The sneer that Ms Marvel bestowed on Hashim before turning her attention back towards the Void was anything but heroic.

"You seem to have suffered something of a relapse since our last session, Bob," she yelled, sternly. "Do you want to talk about it?"

"You'd dare to strike at me, doctor," the Void raged, his voice obscured by the fast-spinning fury of Sirocco's hurricane. "After last time?"

"I beat you last time. Remember? You spent three days in bed, crying, while I took the boys on holiday."

The Void thrashed his head, the muscles of his neck bulging as he strained to push again through Sirocco's wind and break Raazer's sorcery.

Ms Marvel raised her energized hand.

"That's enough, Bob. Really, you can stop now. Look around you. Just stop for a moment and look." She glanced dismissively over Sirocco, Hashim, and Raazer. "Desert Sword are all here. The people who took your wife. You've forced them all out to face you. So, you can stop now. The Void can stop, and then we can go and save Lindy together. How does that sound, Bob? Does that sound good to you?"

"No, doctor."

Ms Marvel looked taken aback. "What?"

"I said no. Lindy makes all three of us weak. The Sentry worries, Robert pines, and neither of them will let me do what needs to be done about it. We'd all be better off if she were gone." The shape of a grin appeared through the chopping wind. "Norman was true to his promise, doctor, he really did help us: he convinced Robert to let me do this for him. He'll cry, tell himself that it wasn't his fault, that he's sick, but secretly he'll thank me, and we'll all thank Norman." He chuckled as tentacles beat his unshackled fist against the wind. "Believe me, doctor, no one will be more surprised by that particular debt of gratitude than me. I always thought of him as a hollow suit."

"Is Bob even listening to me right now?"

"He's trying hard not to, doctor."

"I know he's still in there."

The Void laughed.

Hashim tightened his grip on his sword. "It's not working!"

"You are wasting your efforts," Raazer hissed from the corner of his desiccated lips.

"Please." Ms Marvel employed the use of her haughty disdain. "I think I know what I'm doing."

"He was of two conflicting minds," Raazer continued. "That is how my spells against him were effective. Now he is of one. The Sentry is no longer here. It is the Void alone that we deal with now."

The Void grinned from behind the wall of Sirocco's wind.

Hashim turned to Ms Marvel. He was hoping for some inspiring words from the world-famous hero, something defiant to buoy their hearts and carry them into their last battle in spite of the odds against them. It was surely what any hero would do, at their bitterest moment. What Ms Marvel did instead was to lower her glowing hand. The mask of supreme indifference that she had been wearing slipped from her, and what Hashim saw underneath was the face not of a defiant hero, but of a woman wondering what on earth she had been thinking.

"Oh, crap," she said.

And with that stirring cry ringing in his ears, the Arabian Knight swept up his golden shamshir and charged towards his doom.

CHAPTER THIRTY-THREE
An Accountant with a Grudge

Gunfire from a dozen heavy assault rifles lashed the corridor. Victoria Hand sheltered behind a light steel door that opened onto the hall space. All she could hear was the *bang-bang-bang* drumming of bullets hitting metal. The S.H.I.E.L.D. mercenaries at the other end of the corridor appeared to have no interest in advancing which, given their colossally superior firepower, they could have done easily, nor of forcing her out of cover with grenades. This told Victoria that they were probably in radio contact with a second squad, and were simply pinning her down until they could get in behind her.

This was why she had determined that she would need help. Some jobs were not worth taking on without the proper superhuman backup.

"You're up."

Holding her OS-11 rifle at arm's length, she poked the muzzle around the mauled door stub and blazed away. Its bronco kick almost dislocated her arm, and probably would have if not for the shock-absorbent padding of H.A.M.M.E.R. body armor. She wasn't even sure when she'd made the switch from tranquilizer bolts to solid rounds. Probably when she'd stopped expecting to live long enough to worry about guilt.

"*Give me a second?*" Venom growled, already scrambling along the exposed ceiling pipework. "*Maybe make it two.*"

"Just clear the way!" she yelled after him, unable even to watch as the weight of incoming fire drove her back behind her protesting door. "We grab Lindy, and then we get out."

His answer, assuming of course that he'd heard her at all, was the sound of a fist crunching through ceramic body armor, a scream, and a sudden cessation of the bullets hammering against Victoria's shelter.

Hauling herself out of cover, she dragged her rifle after her and charged towards the sounds of close combat. Venom was tough, she knew, but he couldn't take an entire S.H.I.E.L.D. base on his own.

By the time she caught up, Venom was surrounded by an indeterminate number of bodies. The odd juxtaposition of parts made an exact count challenging, particularly when Venom continued to add more. She was numbed past caring.

He blocked the swing of a rifle butt against his wrist, locked the soldier's arm around his, torqued it until the mercenary was bent double and screaming. Mocking the merely double-jointed with a display of boneless dexterity, he launched a roundhouse kick around the conveniently placed human fulcrum, crushing a second agent's helmet, slamming them hard into the concrete wall and dropping them cold. Positioned now on the opposite side of the still-screaming mercenary, he twisted her arm again, forcing her to arch upright and receive the punch to the face that shattered her visor. The last soldier ran.

Almost as an afterthought, Venom turned, webbed the back

of the soldier's head, and yanked. The man's legs flew out from under him.

Victoria heard the *snap* of his neck from twenty feet away.

"My God."

She looked over the heaped bodies.

Was it strange that Venom outright terrified her when the Sentry, who could kill a thousand times as many with a fraction of the effort, did not? Was it because Venom was near enough to her level, whereas harboring a proper dread of the Sentry required a degree of understanding that nobody on Earth was qualified to hold?

"I'm going to kiss Judith Fiennes when this is over. Right on the lips."

Venom didn't answer. He looked away and growled.

"Where's Lindy?"

"Not far. They were heading straight towards us, before turning around at the shootout."

"You're sure?"

Venom turned and gave her a smile: the kind a spider might give to a fly if it had teeth as long as fingers, a face that could stretch into whatever horrible shape it chose, and no sense of humor at all. *"My sense of smell might not be as good as Daken's, but it's good enough."*

"Wolverine's."

She pointed to the ceiling. A small CCTV camera was trained on them, the red light on its box side blinking. That was the Contessa's game plan, as it had been at every step: to bring out Norman Osborn's darkest side and then let the world see it, as though anyone should be judged solely on the demons they fought. She swore that once this was all just another crisis behind them, when the Contessa was modelling an orange jumpsuit in the ultra-secure wing of the Raft and the Sentry was under the care of the best psychologists in the world, that Norman Osborn would get the same help. She'd strap him into his therapist's chair herself if she had to.

"I need you on your best behavior."

"*Two of my middle names.*"

"Then say it."

"*My sense of smell might not be as good as Wolverine's,*" Venom growled, "*but they're heading that way.*" He pointed at the wall.

"Further west. Out of the city. Another exit, do you think?"

Venom shrugged. "*I just work here.*"

"How many with her?"

"*Just one.*"

Valentina Allegra de Fontaine held the door while Lindy Lee-Reynolds dashed past and into the cage room. Finding amusement in the thought of the regal Contessa de Fontaine holding a door for anyone, let alone some low-class "*Americana*", she covered the corridor with her rifle.

The passage was arrow straight and empty, but the sporadic bursts of screams, gunfire, and the snarls of something bestial rang closer with every echo.

Once Lindy was inside, she backed through and kicked the door shut.

With her rifle in one hand, she drew a base ID and ran the magnetic strip against the reader beside the door. The panel trilled. The door clunked as the heavy locks engaged and the indicator light on the panel clicked from green to red.

She kissed the headshot of Nicholas Fury printed on the card's front and slid it back into her breast pocket.

The elevator cage rested within a bare steel frame on a concrete platform, the limited space in a circle around it crowded with the large machinery involved in its operation. A single vertical shaft rose to the surface. Ropes of highly engineered steel disappeared into the darkness, twanging like the low E-string of a guitar in the fresh breeze from the surface and in fraught syncopation with the Sentry's punishment of the city above. The effects of his rampage on the main base had been severely curtailed since the decision of Desert Sword to engage him, to the extent that Valentina could barely feel them at all. She had not expected Hashim and the others to hold off the Sentry as well as they had. She had certainly not expected them to occupy him this long.

Brushing off guilt as she would the attentions of an unwelcome admirer, she strode towards the waiting cage.

While Lindy struggled to drag the two sets of doors closed, Valentina went to the controls. They were not complicated. There was not a great deal that an elevator needed to do. A small green button made it go, while a larger, back-lit red one made it stop. Lindy gave the doors a solid rattle to be sure they were shut fast and Valentina pushed down the green button.

With a clattering of old, infrequently tended machinery, the cage lurched into a climb.

Exhausted from her efforts, Lindy slumped to the wire floor of the cage with her back to the bars. Valentina put one hand on the control board for balance, and looked up, hoping for an early glimpse of daylight. Iceberg was half a kilometer down. At the elevator's current rate of ascent, it would take the cage several minutes to reach the surface. The slow-moving elevators were a feature of Iceberg's security, rather than a bug. They ensured that no hostile force could storm the surface beach heads and expect to find the main garrison unprepared.

How H.A.M.M.E.R. agents had managed to crack the oilfield's access above Perimeter C and gain the cage room without alerting security, was something she looked forward to puzzling over once she was on the Iraqi side of Highway 80 and halfway towards her Basra safehouse.

The cage shuddered in its climb, and Valentina tensed. It shuddered again, clunking over the guide rails bolted at intervals to the shaft wall.

She forced herself to relax.

For appearances' sake, if nothing else.

Lindy brushed her hair from her face as she looked up, the sleeve of her too-large S.H.I.E.L.D. jumpsuit sliding down her arm. Her face looked drained of all interest in her own fate. "What happens now?"

"There has only been the one breach that we know of. The Perimeter J exit should have a full complement of S.H.I.E.L.D. guards. After that, a large air-conditioned truck and a hundred-mile drive to a palace in southern Basra that Sheikh Abbas doesn't mind me frequenting from time to time. We will be safe there."

"From the Void?"

Valentina paused. Its length spoke more candidly than she might have deliberately intended. "The Void won't be able to hurt you after today, Lindy. Even if Desert Sword fail in their attempt to defeat him, and Norman is unable to rein him in, then he will be stopped. The Fantastic Four will stop him. Or Nicholas will stop him. The world will come back together to stop him. Whatever happens once we reach Basra, you will be free. That I promise."

The woman looked reluctant for a moment, then nodded.

Valentina eased her own relief into a reassuring smile.

The safest place for anyone in Kuwait City right then was in the six-foot radius around Lindy Lee-Reynolds. With the Patriot List back in Norman's hands and the *Bulletin* video loose in the world, Lindy was the last thing left to ensure Valentina's safe passage. If Norman's agents or even the Void himself were to intercept her convoy, then Lindy could come in useful as either a bargaining chip or as a hostage, depending on how the other side wanted to play it. Valentina could not, after all, remake H.A.M.M.E.R. if she were to be incarcerated in some Middle Eastern black site or slain.

Valentina was a masterful liar.

The trick to it was to never believe your own, and to always ensure that every lie contained an honest thread.

She *did* mean to bring Lindy with her to Basra. She *did* fully intend to repatriate her back to the US, once the confirmation hearings for her directorship of H.A.M.M.E.R. were underway. She simply afforded herself some flexibility over whether or not she delivered.

"Robert wasn't always like this, you know," said Lindy, quietly, as the elevator cage rattled on past the halfway marker. "He was so sweet when I first met him, before he took the Golden Serum, and so excruciatingly shy. It took him the whole of our first semester at college to work up the courage to ask me out, and even after we were married, he never really accepted that he was good enough. I miss that about him." Her smile came from a place of happiness, but colored by so much grief since that it was hardly recognizable as such. "I miss my husband's insecurities. How terrible a person does that make me?"

"You're not a terrible person," said Valentina. "I have known terrible people."

"There wasn't a bone of ambition in Robert's body. If he hadn't felt like he needed to become something more… But I liked being the wife of an Avenger. I *liked* living down the hall from Captain America."

"He's an addict with a personality disorder who fell under the control of a manipulative man. You didn't make him take the serum. Did you?"

Lindy shook her head.

"Or support Osborn?"

"No."

"Then this is not your fault."

Lindy sniffed, about to say something more when the elevator cage gave a violent lurch that threw her to the floor and knocked Valentina into the bars.

Their rate of ascent ground to a drunken crawl, the cable groaning as the mass pulling on it more than doubled, sparks weeping through the sides of the cage as the bars were dragged against the shaft.

Lindy looked down and gave an ear-splitting shriek.

A masked head, human in shape but grossly disproportioned with teeth, leered up at her through the crossbars. Long claws and hook-like tendrils grapnelled the wire bottom, inky musculature bulging in the darkness of the under-shaft as the monster heaved against the mechanical strength of the pulley just a quarter of a kilometer above their heads.

"Venom!" Lindy shrieked.

The creature's mouth became a gash of pirate's silver. "*I wasn't sure you'd remember me.*"

"Out of the way," Valentina cried.

Aiming her assault rifle down, she fired straight through the wire floor of the cage.

Venom seemed to react before the first flare had even lit the muzzle of her gun. Bullets tore through the floor and rattled away down the shaft. Venom scrambled across the underside of the flooring, slamming the cage into the wall of the shaft and sending Lindy rolling towards the control board. Firming her footing, Valentina sprayed fire everywhere it was safe to point a gun, not indiscriminately in panic but with complete certainty in what she was doing. When one fought a superhuman, it was best to get another superhuman to do it for you. When that was impossible, total and ruthlessly applied force was the only path to take.

Lindy pulled herself up by the lip of the control board and hammered her fist down on the emergency stop button.

The cage gave an arthritic shudder and then stalled. It had already been rising so slowly that Valentina was able to adjust to it with a short backpedal.

"What did you do that for?"

"I know him better than you. He was going to pull against the cable until it broke."

"Get behind me!" Valentina snapped, as Venom wrenched aside a pair of side bars and forced his shoulder inside. His weight on the stalled elevator canted the entire floor, sending Lindy stumbling into his arms before Valentina could catch her. "Lindy!" she screamed. Venom looked up from spinning a web out of his boneless arm, sticking the screaming woman to his back, to launch a tarry gobbet of black spit at Valentina. It knocked the rifle from her hands, webbing it securely across the bars behind her, and kicked her to the floor.

"Cute."

"Get Lindy to the surface," said the woman that Valentina had not even noticed arriving alongside Venom. She wore bulky H.A.M.M.E.R. body armor, her dark hair powdered gray with dust, turning the colored stripe through the fringe pink. Her glasses flickered with the ghost of a tactical display playing out on the inside of the lenses. A heavy automatic rifle with a purple plastic casing was aimed at Valentina's chest. A S.H.I.E.L.D. jumpsuit offered superlative protection for its weight, able to turn a low-caliber bullet or a knife, but against a military-grade assault rifle at point blank range she might as well have been wearing a T-shirt. "Do whatever you have to do to finish this. I'll deal with the Contessa."

With a snuffle of acknowledgment, Venom dragged Lindy out of the elevator cage and sprang onto the roof, making it squeal, then web-zipped his way to the summit.

Valentina masked her grimace beneath an indifferent sigh.

There went one part of her plan. They were both probably on the surface already.

"So that was how you infiltrated the base without activating the elevator and alerting the garrison. I should have known, but I thought Venom had already been taken out of the game. Bravo, Ms Hand."

She came a step closer. "That's *Deputy* Hand."

Valentina smiled. "Not that it matters now, of course. Even if you get Lindy back and take me prisoner, it's over. I won't spend a week in jail before you're working for me."

Deputy Hand fought to keep her expression neutral. "You took advantage of a man's mental illness and used him to destroy a city to advance your career. Believe it or not, you're not the good guy here."

"Touché, but what I did I did for S.H.I.E.L.D."

"Please. I heard you were spying for the Russians even before you were brought into S.H.I.E.L.D."

"Darling, everyone who is *anyone* in S.H.I.E.L.D. used to spy for the Russians."

"We'll see what the court martial makes of it." Covering

Valentina with the rifle in one hand, Victoria Hand walked to the control board. "You're still technically a serving agent, which means we can try you for treason." She pushed the green button.

It was the opening Valentina had been waiting for.

The elevator shrieked as the pulley once again began to pull, snapping the cable taut and dragging the cage free of the wall. The canted floor suddenly tipped the other way, throwing Victoria Hand off balance and giving Valentina the half-second distraction she needed to draw the Beretta from its sidearm holster. She got off two shots, all there was time for before the swinging cage hit the other wall and pitched Victoria back towards her. The bullets cracked the ceramic plates of a H.A.M.M.E.R. breastplate instead of punching holes in her skull, as the woman tripped over Valentina's feet and sprawled across her. Their guns clattered along the see-sawing floor.

The two women grappled for a moment.

Victoria was a decent fighter, but Valentina was superb.

Wrapping her legs around the deputy's waist, buying herself extra leverage with a hand around the woman's throat, Valentina threw her to the floor and rolled on top of her. Victoria reached for the Beretta. Valentina punched her in the face, splintering one lens of her glasses and bending the frame, cracking the back of her head against the floor. The woman continued to will an extra half-inch of growth into her wriggling fingers.

"Give it up," said Valentina, knocking the gun away on the outside of her hand and then punching Victoria in the mouth. "You're not a deputy director. You are an accountant with a grudge."

Victoria worked her bloody mouth. "What I did… I did… for America."

"You are Norman Osborn's useful idiot. I was born in Europe

after the war. I have seen what people like you will do to the country you claim to love."

She hit Victoria once more, hard, knocking her out cold against the metal floor, then crawled across the gradually steadying cage to pick up the loose Beretta. She knew better than to try to retrieve the rifle. Getting up and smoothing her posture, she collected herself just as the pulley dragged the cage in with a *clang* that sounded almost as relieved as Valentina felt inside. Ignoring the doors, as Venom had left a gap in the bars more than large enough for her to pass through, she stepped out of the cage.

Exit J was a windowless shed filled with winches and pulleys, almost the mirror of the those at the other end of the shaft. A pair of unlocked doors led to an industrial park on the northern outskirts of Al Jahra where a dozen S.H.I.E.L.D. agents and a convoy of armored trucks would be waiting to speed her across the Iraqi border.

Hauling open the doors, she stumbled into a gunship roar of wind and noise, blinking into a sodium-bright flood of lights.

<<*Contessa Valentina Allegra de Fontaine,*>> came the helmet-distorted voice from the glare. With one hand shielding her eyes, the other white knuckle-tight around the grip of her Beretta, she caught a flash of red, white, and blue. There was a purr of armor. <<*You are under arrest.*>>

Squinting against the glare, she fired.

The first few bullets burned off against her target's force fields. The next dozen or so banged harmlessly off hard nickel-titanium armor, her adversary clearly deciding to show off at the last by powering down his shields and letting her shoot.

She clicked to the end of the clip.

<<*Are you done?*>>

The Iron Patriot stood across from her in the middle of the vast truck park with his hands on his hips, lit from behind and from above by a thousand sources of light. Behind him stood Ares. The God of War waited as patiently as a bull, clad in a dark bronze cuirass and a hoplite helm, his axe resting on his pig-stubbled shoulder. Wolverine leant insouciantly against one of Valentina's trucks. Hawkeye leered at her down the shaft of a nocked arrow, eyes dead behind his hero's mask, waiting on the verbalization of the intent in his leader's mind to loose. Behind *them*, an entire platoon of H.A.M.M.E.R. special forces had been deployed to secure the industrial park. Her disarmed squad knelt in front of one of her trucks with guns pointed to the backs of their heads. The impossible roar that was blocking out even the battle for downtown Kuwait was the sound made by a Helicarrier in a low hover, a few hundred feet above their heads.

Such awesome power at his command, and instead of marshalling it to defend the city from the Void he had chosen to take down Valentina Allegra de Fontaine.

That was Norman Osborn.

<<*I had a tracker placed on Ms Hand before she left my bridge,*>> said the Iron Patriot. <<*She is very good at what she does. So good, in fact, that she sometimes forgets I'm better.*>>

"You've already lost, Norman." Unlike the Iron Patriot, aided by the powerful speakers in his suit, she had to scream to be heard. "You're not Steve Rogers. You can't fly around the Middle East wearing stars and stripes and expect nobody to care."

<<*We'll see. Now are you going to come quietly, Contessa?*>> The Iron Patriot raised his hand, the hellish burn of the repulsor emitter turning the reflective metal orange. <<*Or am I going to have to act in legitimate self-defense?*>>

Valentina looked away, for some reason seeking out Ares, one of Tony's Mighty Avengers, though she was not sure what help she expected to find there. He looked back at her, and no god ever cared less.

Such a waste.

Throwing away her useless pistol, she raised her hands as though being fitted for a new dress, and brought them behind her head.

CHAPTER THIRTY-FOUR

What It Feels Like

The shortest route to the south of the city would've been to cut across downtown, but the Void had left so little of it standing, smokestacks rising in the dawn gloom like the ghosts of dead skyscrapers. Mac Gargan went around, web-swinging between gutted low-rises and the scuffed gold domes of blast-crippled mosques. Dust and grit and whole bits of metal struck his suit, like jumping across the Hudson in mosquito season with your mouth open, but he barely felt it. The symbiote skin gave a peristaltic gurgle as it absorbed and digested the city's debris.

"It's always the quiet ones," he muttered to himself as he swung low to pass under a particularly dense thicket of smoke.

A column of burnt-out tanks and armored vehicles gouted pollution from the right-hand lane. Heading the same way Mac was going. He didn't know what the Kuwaiti flag was, but presumably it was the scorched tricolor painted on their turrets.

Men, women, and children streamed between the wrecks in the opposite direction. The wretched sounds of their panic threatened to trigger the nerveless rump of something he'd forgotten the name of in his thoughts.

He tried to focus on what the feeling was, but it was difficult for him to exercise those lobes of his brain. The symbiote had been eating away at his personality for too long. Thinking about anything other than sating its alien hunger, or killing the people that it loathed, left him confused, and even more suggestible to the monster's will. But he was still a human being underneath the nightmare.

He was more than just Osborn's scary cannibal.

He could be more.

Kill Norman Osborn, the symbiote mumbled in its batrachotoxin torpor.

Ignoring it, Mac glanced over his shoulder, his neck twisting further than any human neck ought to safely twist. Lindy stared a silent scream into his masked face. Her wide eyes alone were still visible above the web of symbiote matter smothering her mouth. He gave her a reassuring smile. For some reason that only made her squirm against the webbing bonding her to his back and try even harder to scream. He looked away, a fluttery sense of what could only have been pride puffing his misbegotten chest.

Time to be the hero.

At the top of his swing, he yanked on his web, slurping it back into his second skin as he free-fell a dozen or so feet and landed in a spreadeagled splat on the ceramic-white slope of a rooftop. The apartment building trembled, earthquake running into earthquake and gaining a decimal point on the Richter scale each time, the solid debris absorbed by Mac's suit grinding against his bones as they vibrated. Clinging to the eaves and keeping to all-fours, he looked out over southern Kuwait City.

The apartment building was part of the last intact line of houses overlooking an urban warfare theme park of half-broken buildings, burning cars, and buried roads. He experienced that same sticky feeling in his prefrontal cortex that he'd felt watching the fleeing civilians, and remembered what it was.

New York.

He was looking at New York after the Skrull invasion: the last time he'd done something genuinely selfless and good.

The Void was up to his knees in the destruction, literally, but the scale of it was deceptive. Mac's supposed friend had grown to mammoth proportions, transformed into a raging, ink-black Medusa of endlessly sprouting tentacles, emerging from a bottomless central body that was almost as large as the white-brick ruin it appeared to have broken through as it grew.

Badass, the symbiote murmured dreamily.

The fight, such as it was, wasn't going too well.

The wreckage of Kuwaiti gunships and troop carriers filled the roadsides alongside those of buses and cars, and displayed every imaginable method of destruction, from flipped over, crushed, or hurled through buildings by tentacles, to being immolated by solar energy.

Moonstone and some guy with a golden sword fought side by side at the Void's "feet", fighting to protect an old man in bloody white robes who smelled pretty dead already.

Several pitch-black tentacles were wrapped around Moonstone's limbs and body, but she had one arm free and was using it to send yellow beams slicing through the Void's tentacles to the black shape at his core. The sword guy hacked at the tentacles that were encircling Moonstone, working himself into a lather of exhaustion just to keep his apparent ally's one hand free of the Void's clutches. Mac looked up. Way up. Above the tooth-decay horror show of Kuwait City's redrawn skyline, a second battle was underway. Mac recognized the fighter from their own encounter in the *New York Bulletin,* and winced with sympathetic pain each time his Black Sword clove through one of the Void's tentacles.

Mac wondered if it would have made any difference to the outcome if Norman, Vicky, Bullseye, Daken, Ares even, and all the might of H.A.M.M.E.R., were here where they ought to be rather than in a parking lot halfway across the city.

Probably not, he decided, watching with some satisfaction as the Black Raazer, enveloped by heaving tentacles, disappeared in a gasp of ether and a shriek that went through the psionic connections binding his mind to Venom's and almost roused the beast from its torpor.

Mac fought it back down.

They were all depending on him now. Vicki was counting on him.

Lindy tried again to say something, wriggling in her web-sac as he launched himself from the rooftop fascia, webbed the lantern of a leaning lamppost, and swung towards the fight.

An urgent, alien sense of discomfort burrowed its way up from his gut. He experienced a short, vivid premonition of being burned alive, and immediately threw out another web, pulling himself sideways as a blast of dolorous light seared across him and demolished the apartment building he had been using as a perch. With another web-shoot, he corrected course, swinging low enough to the ground to whip up a train of dust.

The Void was fast. But how fast did you need to get to hit something that could react to your attack before you made it?

Swinging around, under, and through a succession of searing energy blasts and groping tentacles, he landed in a crouch on a patch of ground paved with rubble, a hundred feet from where Moonstone and Sword Guy struggled on. Neither of them noticed his arrival, or acknowledged it if they did, just another droplet of liquid black in a world corrupted by black.

The Void, though, extended a head that had become skeletal and crocodilian on a long, long neck, and gave a roar that shed the skyline of another handful of blast-wrecked buildings.

"YOU CANNOT FIGHT ME, BUG. ACTUAL GODS COULD NOT FIGHT ME."

Mac staggered back from the sonic onslaught of the Void's voice, less exquisitely tuned to the symbiote's particular frequency of weakness than Dr Fiennes' torture device but about a million times more powerful. He felt Lindy struggling to break free as the symbiote shriveled from the attack and the webbing sticking her in place weakened. He sacrificed several layers from his own symbiote suit, leaving ropy patches of bare skin on his forearms and thighs to keep her secure. He had to get her to the Void. No one had ever outright *told* him what the deal was between the Sentry and the Void. He was too dumb an animal to get it, or so they thought, but he'd been in the room when Osborn and Moonstone and Vicki had talked about it, and neither Mac Gargan nor Venom were as stupid as everyone seemed to think they were.

He knew, for instance, that his own life wasn't going to be worth much if he couldn't get the Sentry to re-emerge and banish the Void again.

With Lindy tightly held at the expense of his own protection, Mac lowered his head as if into a shrieking gale and pushed on.

A mass of tentacles burst through the air towards them.

Venom's ESP saw them coming from a mile off. He saw that he didn't have a prayer of avoiding half of them, but tried anyway, because that was what heroes did, still howling in protest as tendrils squirmed around his ankles, wrists, waist, throat, and hoisted him off the ground like a piece of leather on a tanning rack. His bones creaked, the symbiote suit rippling and flexing as it combatted the Void's terrible, infinite strength with its own. Under the most awesome of pressures, the symbiote regurgitated Lindy.

She landed with a wet slap on the broken ground, and smeared black symbiote goo from her mouth on an almost equally soiled sleeve. She gasped for breath, and then yelled, "I said, let me talk to him!"

Mac groaned in pain as tension passed through the mass of tendrils holding him in place, a monstrous head appearing through the squalid mass like clouds parting to reveal not the sun, but the face of Galactus, Devourer of Worlds, with his mouth opening wide.

"L-LINDY?" it said.

"IT DOESN'T MATTER," said the same head in a crueler voice. "DESTROY THEM ALL. DESTROY EVERYTHING."

"LINDY."

"OSBORN PROMISED TO HELP US."

"LINDY!"

Mac felt the holds on him loosen, tendrils sliding around his arms and legs as several tentacles reached tentatively, almost shyly, towards Lindy. Venom could smell the terror on her, see the look of it stricken into her face as she forced herself to stand her ground and meet the gargantuan, inhuman gaze of her husband all the same.

"I CAME TO SAVE YOU!"

"I didn't need saving. I came here to get away from you. From *him*."

"KILL HER!" the second voice roared, but it sounded weaker now, on the losing side of the argument.

A tremor passed through the gelatinous heave of the transformed Void's inky musculature. Fresh tentacles ceased to squirm free of the gelid black core with the same regularity, while those already at large whipped and flailed without direction, or even doubled back to throttle one another as whatever minds sought to guide them vied for control. From the corner of Mac's eye, the sword guy found a second wind to winnow back the wavering tendrils, bringing a triumphant, vengeful shout from Moonstone as she found herself free.

"COME BACK TO NEW YORK WITH ME."

Lindy leant back to avoid the brushing tentacles, but held her nerve. Mac found himself wishing he'd met a woman like that. "No," she said.

The Sentry and the Void cried out together in their anguish. The remaining tentacles began to retreat, but rather than swell with the accretion of mass, the great monster shrank and shrank: he shrank like a collapsing star, the first rays of new, golden light pulsing through the Void until the symbiote was forced to film Mac's eyes over to protect its host from blindness.

"Be nice to him!" Mac yelled.

"No," Lindy shouted back, from somewhere in the blackness beyond Venom's impenetrable eyelids. "I'm done being afraid. I want my husband back." And then to the Void, "We'll go back to New York, but not together. You'll go back to the Watchtower and to being the hero you used to be. Or you'll retire altogether. It's up you. You'll start talking to Reed and Sue again and stop listening to Norman. You'll beat the Void forever. I'll be going back to our old place in Queens until you do. If you ever want me to come back then that's how it's going to happen."

Even through the black scabs over his eyes, Mac saw the human figure that walked out of the glare. He carried the glare out with him, the symbiote web still sticking to her evaporating like black ice before a flamethrower.

"I'm sorry," he whispered, coming for her with arms outstretched. "I'm so, so sorry." Lindy pushed him off her, a mortal pitting her strength against the mightiest force in the known universe and leaving it sobbing uncontrollably at her feet.

Mac looked away, feeling unaccountably discomforted by the omnipotent hero's humbling. The ruination of downtown Kuwait City was grossly accentuated by its return to stillness in the aftermath of the Sentry's return to dominance over the Void, and by the godlike hero wailing his heartbreak into it on his hands and knees. Moonstone and Sword Guy were both looking at Mac, confused but too exhausted to ask what was going on, which came as a strange relief because Mac really didn't have a clue.

I don't understand, the symbiote mumbled. *Why doesn't he just eat her*?

Mac shook his head numbly as Lindy left her husband in his crumpled-up heap and came to put her hand on his shoulder. He felt unexpectedly uplifted that she would touch him without worrying that he would bite her hand off. Even Vicki was scared of him. He wondered if this was what it felt like to be the good guy: to do good things and have people like you.

He could get used to it.

If the symbiote would let him.

If Norman would let him.

Kill Norman Osborn…

"Take me home," said Lindy.

EPILOGUE

The guy on the giant composite TV screen looked as though he'd been to the top of the world and was enjoying the view.

"...with considerable pleasure that I can report that the criminal terrorist, Valentina Allegra de la Fontaine, a known associate of the wanted fugitive Nick Fury, was apprehended today after a lengthy battle in Kuwait City at approximately nine am local time. There was, regrettably, some material damage and loss of life, but I can assure you that, had it not been for a little luck and the fearless intervention of my Avengers, you would all be reporting on a far greater tragedy this morning."

The guy smiled: honest, understanding, and open, as he took questions from the floor.

"I'm glad you asked me that, Jennifer, as it allows me to correct a few falsehoods I've already seen circulating around the region's early morning shows. It is, of course, preposterous to hold the Sentry in any way responsible for the destruction of downtown Kuwait City. As the limited footage that survived the incident clearly shows, our very own Ms Marvel and

New York's favorite hero, my friend Spider-Man, can be seen battling a shadowy behemoth that, I think you'll agree, bears no resemblance whatsoever to the Golden Guardian of Good we all know and love. I have preliminary information from H.A.M.M.E.R.'s paranormal investigators that positively identifies the villain in question as the Black Raazer, a long-time anti-American agitator and senior subordinate of Ms Allegra. Raazer is believed to have been responsible for the attack on New York a week ago, as well as the mental injuries suffered by Spider-Man and the resulting incident in Avengers Tower that some of you will have heard about already. Raazer is, I'm afraid to say, still at large. However, I am very hopeful that the Contessa and another of her associates now in H.A.M.M.E.R. custody, Navid Hashim, AKA the Arabian Knight, will prove cooperative under questioning to prevent similar attacks on our way of life in the future."

His tanned skin gleamed under the relentless camera-flash of the world's media.

"We're also looking into possible collusion within the US government, military, and in other world governments in a plot, instigated by Ms Allegra, to depose me from my democratically mandated role as director of H.A.M.M.E.R.: a coup d'etat that would not only be illegitimate and immoral, but un-American."

He grasped the wings of the lectern and looked straight into the camera, awfully, painfully sincere.

"Now, as everyone watching this will know, because I have never made any secret of my condition, I have suffered with mental illness for most of my life. It is something for which I have sought help and for which I continue to be treated and I think, as I'm sure most decent people out there will think, that it is shameful for a publicly funded state broadcaster to exploit stolen footage of a private breakdown for commercial or political gain."

He nodded, as though worn down by his confession, as further questions were called.

"All possible sanctions against the British government and the BBC are being considered at this time. As I'm sure you know, Brandon, H.A.M.M.E.R.'s authority, and therefore my authority, extends into every national jurisdiction on this planet…"

Norman Osborn picked up the remote off his desk and pointed it at the giant bank of screens. He hit pause, wound it back, and played again.

"…every national jurisdiction on this planet…"

Grinning, he scraped the half-dozen differently colored tablets that Karla and Victoria had insisted he start taking in concert with an aggressive period of talking therapy into his hand. He swallowed them with five hundred dollars' worth of Macallan whiskey from a chipped mug, then set the mug down on the desk alongside the TV remote. The goblinoid face painted across the mug's side leered up at him from beneath the childishly drawn characters "WORLDS GRATEST DAD". The message made him smile, although he had no idea which of his children it had come from, or how it had got into his office, even as something in his green-faced cartoon likeness made him cringe away and turn instead towards his transcendent avatar on the world's screens.

There, he was the hero. There, he was whoever he said he was.

"…so, unless you're completely sick of hearing my voice, I'll take a few more questions…"

The guy laughed, and the world laughed with him.

"Great to be that guy," he told the face on the mug.

But the Goblin didn't answer.

He just laughed.

ABOUT THE AUTHOR

DAVID GUYMER is a scientist and writer from England. His work includes many novels in the *New York Times*-bestselling *Warhammer* and *Warhammer 40,000* universes, notably *Headtaker* and *Gotrek & Felix: Slayer*, and the bestselling audio drama *Realmslayer*. He has also contributed to fantastical worlds in video games, tabletop RPGs, and board games.

bobinwood.wixsite.com/thirteenthbell
twitter.com/warlordguymer

WORLD EXPANDING FICTION

Do you have them all?

MARVEL CRISIS PROTOCOL

- ☐ *Target: Kree* by Stuart Moore

MARVEL HEROINES

- ☐ *Domino: Strays* by Tristan Palmgren
- ☐ *Rogue: Untouched* by Alisa Kwitney
- ☐ *Elsa Bloodstone: Bequest* by Cath Lauria
- ☐ *Outlaw: Relentless* by Tristan Palmgren

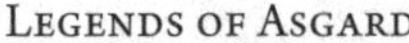

LEGENDS OF ASGARD

- ☐ *The Head of Mimir* by Richard Lee Byers
- ☐ *The Sword of Surtur* by C L Werner
- ☐ *The Serpent and the Dead* by Anna Stephens
- ☐ *The Rebels of Vanaheim* by Richard Lee Byers *(coming soon)*

MARVEL UNTOLD

- ☐ *The Harrowing of Doom* by David Annandale
- ☑ *Dark Avengers: The Patriot List* by David Guymer
- ☐ *Witches Unleashed* by Carrie Harris *(coming soon)*

XAVIER'S INSTITUTE

- ☐ *Liberty & Justice for All* by Carrie Harris
- ☐ *First Team* by Robbie MacNiven
- ☐ *Triptych* by Jaleigh Johnson
- ☐ *School of X* edited by Gwendolyn Nix *(coming soon)*

EXPLORE OUR WORLD EXPANDING FICTION

ACONYTEBOOKS.COM
@ACONYTEBOOKS
ACONYTEBOOKS.COM/NEWSLETTER